R. E

MW01673918

Stray Leaves from the Diary of an Indian Officer

SALZWASSER VERLAG

R. B. Cumberland

Stray Leaves from the Diary of an Indian Officer

Reprint of the original, first published in 1865.

1st Edition 2022 | ISBN: 978-3-75258-966-5

Verlag (Publisher): Salzwasser Verlag GmbH, Zeilweg 44, 60439 Frankfurt, Deutschland
Vertretungsberechtigt (Authorized to represent): E. Roepke, Zeilweg 44, 60439 Frankfurt, Deutschland
Druck (Print): Books on Demand GmbH, In de Tarpen 42, 22848 Norderstedt, Deutschland

STRAY LEAVES

FROM THE

DIARY OF AN INDIAN OFFICER.

STRAY LEAVES

FROM THE

DIARY OF AN INDIAN OFFICER,

Account of the Famous Temple of Juggernáth

ITS DAILY CEREMONIES AND ANNUAL FESTIVALS.

AND

A RESIDENCE IN AUSTRALIA.

London:

1865.

CONTENTS.

CHAPTER I.

CHAPTER II.

CHAPTER III.

CHAPTER IV.

CHAPTER X.

CHAPTER XI.

CHAPTER XII.

CHAPTER XIII.

CHAPTER XXVII.

CHAPTER XXVIII.

CHAPTER XXIX.

CHAPTER XXX.

CHAPTER XXXI.

CHAPTER XXXII.

CHAPTER XXXIII.

STRAY LEAVES FROM THE DIARY OF AN INDIAN OFFICER.

CHAPTER I.

Introductory.

WISHING to preserve an incognito, the writer of these pages originally prepared them for the press without a single personal reference; but friends have advised that he should give some account of himself; and Addison, in the first number of the Spectator, says, "I have observed that a reader seldom peruses a book with pleasure, until he knows whether the writer of it be a black or a fair man, of a mild or choleric disposition, married or a bachelor; with other particulars of the like nature, that conduce very much to the right understanding of an author. To gratify this curiosity, which is so natural to a reader," &c., I will describe as much as I think necessary concerning myself. Well, then, I am not a black man, but more of the Jacob type, standing five feet ten inches in height, rather fat than lean, and of a mild or choleric disposition according to circumstances. When everything goes well, a child might play with me; but if a man were to call me a liar, my choler would fire my tongue and make it as explosive as gun-cotton. I am not a bachelor, but a happy benedict with six children, a retired officer of Her Majesty's Bengal army, in which I had the honour to serve rather more than a quarter of a century.

For a period of nine years I was stationed at Juggurnath Pooree, and may reasonably claim to know as much about the famous Temple at that place as any of my contemporaries, seeing that I made it my business to inquire there anent, and had access to the records of the Temple, as well as to public documents in the Government offices.

From the foregoing data, my identity can readily be discovered by any one who thinks it worth while to ascertain "Who's who" in this instance. Ah, my "Pooree Caloro," and C——, and H——, and M——, and R——, &c., my friends and brothers!—for as such ye were to me in a strange land—how many sad and joyous scenes your names recall to mind! Should your eyes ever rest on these pages, ye will at once recognize the writer.

In addition to Addison's observation, I have remarked that a reader peruses a book with more pleasure if every person introduced to his notice has a name, and not simply an initial letter, followed by a dash ——. I shall therefore generally give a name, though, to avoid wounding the sensibility of others, it will in no case be the true one. Thus I beg to introduce myself as Mr. Carlisle.

CHAPTER II.

Embark for Calcutta—Return to Port—Sail again—Arrive in Calcutta—Ordered to Cawnpore—Theatricals—Move to Mynpoorie, and thence to Sangor in Malwah—Amateur Theatricals—Lieutenant Phillips in the part of Mother Brulgruddery—The General—My First Wig—Mrs. Gregson speaks to Nick about it—Quit Sangor—Ordered to England—Arrive at the Cape—Sail, and touch at St. Helena—Napoleon's Tomb—Departure—Pirates suspected—Preparations for Defence—The Discovery—A Man overboard—Rescue.

In 1828, I embarked for Calcutta, and on the evening of the third day was so incontestably at sea, that there was, with exception of myself, a pretty general casting-up of accounts with Neptune and the passengers; in the midst of which a heavy squall carried away our topmasts, and we were compelled to return to port to refit. In the course of a week we sailed again, and, after an uneventful voyage of five months, landed at Calcutta in September. In December, I was ordered to Cawnpore, where I remained some months, doing duty with H. M.'s 44th regiment. Balls and theatricals were all the rage. At the Cawnpore theatre I saw the parts of Minna and Brenda Troil performed by two troopers of the 14th Dragoons; and truly, with exception of rather a military strut, their acting was fair, exciting much laughter and merriment. How little did we dream in those days, while dancing in the assembly-rooms of Cawnpore, of the dreadful atrocities to be committed there by the dark and vile treachery of Nana Sahib in 1857! My next move was to Mynpoorie; thence to Sangor in Malwah, where I remained nearly a year, doing duty with the 71st Native Infantry, at that time commanded by Colonel Nott, who subsequently distinguished himself in his defence of Candahar and advance to Cabul.

Amateur theatricals were all "the go" in Saugor, where we had some excellent performers amongst the officers of the several regiments. On one occasion a most laughable scene occurred. A very stout officer, Lieutenant Phillips, took the part of Mother Brulgruddery. He happened to be looking through a slit in the curtain, when it was suddenly drawn up, and his dress, becoming entangled in it, was pulled above his knees before the accident was discovered. It is impossible to describe the shouts of laughter that filled the room, in which genial fun the old General joined most heartily. Poor Phillips's consternation may be imagined. I can see him now, with his fat arms below his short-sleeved dress. Alas! poor Phil! he has long since performed his last part.

The General commanding at Saugor was a fine old gentleman, but a strict martinet, insisting upon the officers appearing in full dress at the theatre. I was not aware of this on joining the regiment, and being only a griff, was attired simply in a red jacket. On meeting the General at a dinner-party previous to proceeding to the theatre, he drew me aside, and asked, "Are you going to the theatre this evening, Mr. C.?" I answered in the affirmative. "Then you must put on your dress-coat, Sir." "I have not got one," I replied. "Then you ought to have one, and you *must* have one," said the General, turning round and leaving me. This being my first *wig*, I thought it rather a bad fit; for I was not posted to any regiment, and liable to be ordered off at any time, when a change of uniform might again be required.

I mentioned to Mrs. Gregson, our hostess, what the General had been saying, and added that I could not accompany them to the theatre. "Oh, never-mind," said she; "I will speak to Nick (the aide-de-camp) to explain matters;" and the result was that I went to the theatre that evening, but next day a stringent order was issued that in future all officers must appear in full dress at all places of public amusement, which I *now* think was perfectly right.

In 1830, I quitted Sangor on medical certificate, having orders to proceed to Calcutta, and eventually to England. Nothing occurred to break the monotony of the homeward voyage until we arrived at the Cape of Good Hope, where we remained several days, amusing ourselves by excursions into the country, and an attempt to ascend the Table Mountain, with an equally vain attempt to like the Cape wine, which in those days was not so palatable as it is now. We took on board some passengers for England, and resumed our voyage. We next touched at St. Helena for a few hours, and in the interim paid a visit to Napoleon's tomb and Longwood House. The sergeant in charge of the tomb took out one of the iron palisades surrounding it to enable us to go inside, but I could not bring myself to tread on the grave of him before whom almost the whole world once stood in awe. I contented myself by cutting a slip off the willow which hung over the grave, and carried it safely to England, where it flourished and became the parent of many other slips. As soon as we arrived on board we made sail, and when off the South-American coast, which was at that time said to be infested by pirates, we were surprised in the morning at seeing a low, rakish-looking craft right ahead, and standing towards us. We made all haste to defend ourselves. Our ship belonged to a

Quaker firm, so we had only two old carronades on board, and a few pounds of powder for signals. There were no muskets, swords or boarding-pikes; as a substitute for the latter, sundry carving-knives were fastened to the ends of long pieces of bamboo. Some of the crew armed themselves with handspikes, while the passengers mustered a few pistols and guns. Our only lady passenger was placed below, with her three children and female attendant. Our red jackets were donned, to make us look as warlike as possible. The supposed enemy approached, and passed astern. We were speculating on what she was, and thinking we were well rid of her, when lo! she suddenly fired a gun, and, hoisting a signal of distress, made sail after us. We did not like this at all; she sailed much faster than our lumbering ship, and would certainly overhaul us in the course of a couple of hours. So we quietly held on our course. Our two carronades were run out again, one on each side; besides these, we had some half-dozen "Quaker guns" (wood, shaped and painted so as to resemble guns), three on each side; so we *looked* rather formidable, albeit we were in a very sorry plight for a hostile reception. However, the crew were summoned aft, harangued by the captain, grog served out, three cheers given, and all swore to defend the ship to the utmost. Having completed all our preparations, such as they were, I had leisure to picture to myself how I should feel in "walking the plank," a feat which there seemed every probability of our being called upon to perform. It is done in this way: a plank is thrust half-way over the ship's side, and the prisoners with their arms pinioned, invited at the point of a cutlass to walk thereon, or rather there*off*, into the sea. Sooth to say, I did not like the prospect "at all, at all," as an Irishman would say; so no wonder we determined to defend ourselves to the utmost. After some time the supposed pirate came up to windward, when our skipper roared out through his speaking-trumpet, "You are very suspicious-looking; if you don't keep off, I'll fire upon you!" whereupon, to our great relief, she fell astern, and came up to leeward. Our windward gun was immediately run over to the opposite side, amidst the screams of the lady passenger and her children, who thought from the uproar that the pirates were upon us. They hailed us to send a boat on board with a doctor, alleging that their chief officer had wounded his hand by the bursting of a musket, which he fired off after passing us a few hours previously. We thought that this might be a ruse to weaken our crew, so positively refused compliance, telling them to send their own boat with the wounded man. This they ultimately did, when we found the statement correct; the man's hand was very much shattered, and we arranged to take him to England. He proved to be an honest, inoffensive Yankee. And so ended our alarm about pirates. One of the passengers (a lawyer), whom we took on board at the Cape, made his will, enclosed it in a bottle, which he threw overboard.

Amongst our crew was a man named Cornwallis, who had been in the East-India Company's marine service, had taken his discharge, and was working his passage to England. He was a bit of a genius, and could do almost anything, in a way. He got up a sort of band on board, made a big drum, and played upon it too. In short, C. was a general favourite with all on board. One day I was sitting in the cuddy, chatting with a fine young Irish officer whom we took on board at the Cape, when suddenly a cry was heard, "A man overboard!" With a thrill of horror we sprang up and rushed on deck. Lieut. H., with great presence of mind, carrying with him the chair on which he had been sitting, ran to the side of the vessel and threw the chair overboard, while I assisted some one else in heaving a hen-coop over the stern, whence we could see poor Cornwallis for some time swimming towards the ship. However, we soon lost sight of him ; a boat was lowered as speedily as possible, with no lack of volunteers to man it. Away they went, but as a rather heavy sea was running, we soon lost sight of them. The most gloomy forebodings began to be whispered amongst us, fearing that the boat's crew was lost as well as poor Cornwallis. At length a seaman aloft sang out that he saw the boat returning. I can never forget the state of horrible suspense we were in for a considerable time, to learn whether the man was saved or lost. As the boat approached, some thought they saw him, others said the contrary ; and, in fact, until the boat was nearly alongside, no one knew that they had really saved the man. No sooner was this ascertained, than a general cheering took place. Lieut. H. ran into the cabin, laid his head on the table and burst into tears. I honoured him for it. Poor Cornwallis had been above three quarters of an hour in the water before he was picked up. He was an excellent swimmer, and had contrived to pull off his boots and pantaloons, so as to enable him to strike out better. The next day I asked him what he thought of when in such jeopardy. He replied that he thought of his sins, and that he should never see his poor old mother again. The last time I saw the honest fellow was about a year after we arrived in England, when I met him with a white apron on, standing at the door of a pastry-cook's shop in the Strand. I had some conversation with him about his present prospects, and was glad to find that he had tumbled into a better trough than Neptune's.

CHAPTER III.

Embark for Calcutta—A Man lost overboard—Arrive in Calcutta—Ordered to Balasore—My Moonshee—Narrow Escape of shooting Grantham—Game about Balasore—Wild Hog—Anecdote of Mac—— and a Wild Hog—Ordered to join the 47th Regiment N.I. at Cuttack—Two Regiments in Cuttack—An Officer seized by a Tiger—Singular and fatal Accident to a Sepoy—Anecdotes—Military Funeral—Party at Billiard-room—Visit Pooree—Two late for Muster—House struck by Lightning—Old Fort—Treasure-seekers.

AFTER a residence of nearly two years in England and France, I once more embarked for India, the only striking incident of the voyage being the fall of a fine young man from the foretopmast-yard into the sea. He held up his hand towards us as he floated astern, and that was the last we saw of him. A heavy gale was blowing, and we were under double-reefed topsails. The first impulse of the captain was to order a boat to be lowered; but an old naval officer said, "You will lose your boat, Sir." So we bore away, without an effort to save the man. What a horrible feeling of despair must have been his when he saw us leaving him to his fate, as he doubtless must have done, when floating on the top of a wave, for he was a good swimmer. Poor fellow! his sad fate haunted us for many days.

Shortly after our arrival in Calcutta, I was directed to proceed to Balasore. During my sojourn here, I resided with my friend Grantley, and employed my spare time, of which I had more than enough, chiefly in shooting and studying the Hindoostanee language with a Moonshee. The old fellow had such a musty smell of pawn and stale hubble-bubble, that I was always glad to get rid of him, and away to the billiard-room to knock the balls about until tiffin-time, after which we usually went out shooting. On one occasion we were joined for a time by Grantham and another gentleman, and afterwards parted company, each pursuing his own line, with a few beaters. I unexpectedly came across Grantham. After some time a quail was sprung, and I fired, when to my horror Grantham immediately stepped from behind a bush in the line of fire within thirty yards of me. I shuddered at the thought of having shot my friend, and felt that peculiar sensation of what is called "the blood running cold." Happily the bush was so thick, that only a few pellets of No. 7 shot passed through and struck G. in his padded shooting-coat, without doing any further damage.

There was plenty of jungle about Balasore, and quantities of game, such as snipe, quail, partridges and hares. In the more remote jungles there were wild buffaloes, leopards and tigers.

It is generally supposed that the snipe is a particularly clean-feeding bird, and the entrails, commonly called "the trail," are considered a delicacy. My friend Grantley and I did as most others do, that is, ate the snipe and its trail as a matter of course, until we had ocular demonstration that it was in reality the dirtiest of feeding birds. We declared that we would never eat a snipe again, much less the trail.

The quail is belied in being called a dirty-feeding bird. We always found it in clean places, and, to my mind, a plump quail is one of the nicest game birds that we could place on the table, though the Israelites soon got tired of it; but theirs was a case of "toujours perdrix." What a hurry-scurry the quail makes in its flight! Bang! There is not much time to lose; one rarely gets a right-

and-left shot at such birds in close jungle, as they fly but a short distance, and then take to their scrapers. Once when beating a low jungle, with bushes here and there, we started a wild hog. On galloping off, Dickson foolishly peppered his hind quarters with a charge of small shot. At this insult, piggy instantly halted, and faced about. We fancied that he was coming to the charge, but he thought better of it, and after grinding his tusks at us, scampered off again. He might easily have ripped us up, as we had nothing but small shot for defence.

In India, to shoot a wild hog is considered almost as unsportsmanlike as to shoot a fox in England. Nevertheless, I did once shoot one, and an old friend of mine, J. Mac——, a stalwart Highlander, well known in Dacca and Monghyr as a noted pig-sticker, once attacked and killed a wild hog with a single blow of a kodalee (a native hoe); but I would not advise any one who has a regard for his life or limbs, to try a similar experiment. By the way, a sty-fed jungle pig, when caught very young, is, I think, the best of all flesh meat. It is necessary to take the animal when only a few days old, otherwise they are quite untameable, and their repeated struggles to escape prevent all means of fattening them.

The *dolce-far-nienti* life at Balasore was too good to last long, and at the expiration of four months I was directed to proceed to Cuttack and join the 47th regiment Native Infantry, ordered "on service" for no other purpose than to capture a refractory old Ranee, who had been misbehaving herself, and refused to submit. I forget the particulars. There was, however, no fight; for before I arrived at Cuttack on the 8th May, 1833, the regiment had returned with the old woman as a prisoner.

There were two regiments in Cuttack at this time. One of the officers was lame, from having been seized by a tiger when shooting. The beast was walking off with him, as a cat may be seen to carry a kitten, when Capt. F. drew a pistol from his belt and shot him dead.

Shortly after my arrival, a very singular and fatal accident occurred to a fine strapping young sepoy of my regiment. The man was fishing in a tank near the cantonments, and having caught a small fish, popped it into his mouth while adjusting his bait. The fish in its struggles got into the windpipe, and the man was suffocated before assistance arrived. I saw him lying on the green turf where he fell, with the bright sun shining down upon him, and could scarcely believe that he was dead; but he never answered to the roll-call again.

While in Cuttack, I resided with my friends, J. K. Edwards and his brother, Captain John E. The latter and myself were frequent antagonists at chess, and occasionally, if he were beaten, had an ugly trick of upsetting the board, until I declined playing with him. Nevertheless, we were always very good friends; I esteemed him highly; indeed, we three were like brothers. We frequently dined at the 33rd mess, and a more gentlemanly set of fellows I never met with. On Christmas-day, when a large plum-pudding was placed on the table, it quite warmed one's heart to witness the hearty cheers with which the youngsters greeted it. The Major joined in the fun as merrily as any of them. After dinner, one of the "boys," who had taken wine enough to make him sleepy, without being exactly tipsy, lay down to take a nap; but there was no rest for him amidst the quips and cranks of the wide-awake ones. At last the poor lad, with his eyes shut, drawled out, "Leave me alone; I'm in a happy state of indifference." This ludicrous appeal was irresistible.

I was very intimate with one of the officers, who died,

poor fellow! some years later, and was buried in his tent. The ground was afterwards levelled before the tent was struck, to prevent the place of his sepulture being discovered by the enemy on the advance of the army towards Cabul.

Amongst the visitors at Cuttack was a member of the M—— Board. He had come from Calcutta for change of air, and had been some time at Pooree with little benefit. In short, the poor old man was worn out, and died in Cuttack. This was the first military funeral I ever attended, and I was much struck with the ceremony, for of all others I think a military funeral the most impressive, particularly that of a mounted officer, when the dead man's charger is led along, with the empty boots reversed and dangling in the stirrups, while the sword and helmet, &c., are placed on the top of the coffin. The wild strains of the Dead March in Saul, the troops leaning on their muskets, with the muzzles resting on the ground—all form a sufficiently mournful pageant. I dislike the firing over the grave, and particularly the jaunty airs played by the band when returning from the funeral, as if to erase as soon as possible every salutary impression such a scene is calculated to inspire. I could wish the ceremony to terminate with the sublime Service, commencing, "I am the Resurrection and the Life." This is all very well, the reader may say; but the man's dead, and there an end; and so many of those thought who had been at poor old B——'s funeral. Few of them had ever seen him alive, and thought it a great bore to be obliged to turn out in the afternoon in full dress for the occasion. There was a large party at the billiard-room that night; and so the little world of Cuttack went on, as if poor old B—— had never existed. *Tel est vie.*

I had not been long in Cuttack before I obtained

leave to visit Pooree between musters, i.e. from the 1st of May to the 1st of June. The change from the heat of the former place to the cool sea-breezes of Pooree was most delightful. The magistrate and collector, Mr. Wilkins, to whom I had an introduction, kept open house; and there were, I think, eight or ten of us who availed ourselves of his hospitality at one time. There were not rooms enough for us all, and I, being the last comer, slept in my palanquin in the veranda, which arrangement I liked quite as well as having a sleeping apartment to myself. We were a very jolly party, half civil and half military officers; and very sorry I was to leave on the last day of the month to attend muster parade in Cuttack on the following morning at sunrise. The distance from Pooree to Cuttack is about fifty miles. I travelled all night, and, putting on my uniform in the Palkee, went straight to the parade-ground, where I arrived just in time to be too late for muster. The consequence might have been the loss of a month's pay, besides being presented with a nice well-fitting wig in the shape of a reprimand, and being returned as absent without leave. I was about stepping into my buggy, which Edwards had kindly sent to take me home, when Colonel Waterfield came up and said, "So you are too late for muster." I apologized. "You'll lose your pay." "I hope not, Colonel." After taking a further *rise* out of me, the kind-hearted old gentleman, who was Acting-Brigadier, said, "Well, drive me to the 33rd parade, and I'll muster you there." I was but too happy to do so, and thus get out of the scrape.

After this visit to Pooree, I always had an eye to a vacancy occurring there, and determined to fill it if possible, which event actually did occur some three or four years later, as will be seen by and by.

One Sunday morning, the two friends with whom I was living and myself had returned from church. Captain Edwards sat down to write, while his brother and I had chairs placed in the veranda on the upper story of the house. The sky was overcast, but no appearance of a storm, when suddenly a loud report was heard. I thought that a gun had been discharged at us. If we had not been sitting down at the time, we should have fallen to the ground. My pet dog, fancying (I suppose) that it had been struck, started up, and commenced barking furiously. When James E. and I had somewhat recovered from the shock, we heard a tremendous hubbub down-stairs; we knew not what to make of it, so confused were we with the blow. Captain Edwards, who was sitting on one side of the room, could not imagine what was the matter with us; for in his situation he had not felt the shock, whereas James E. and I had been sitting in a line between the window and door which was struck by the bolt. On approaching the stairs to ascertain the cause of the row below, we found that the Venetian doors at the head of the stairs had been shattered to pieces, and there was a strong smell of brimstone. We then knew that the house had been struck by lightning. Finding the stairs intact, we descended; and saw a man rolling on the ground, and crying out lustily that he was killed, but he was more frightened than hurt. There happened to be a large iron perambulator standing under the stairs; the electric fluid played round the wheel, and left a circular mark on the wall, and also a hole therein, into which I could thrust my fist for some distance. This was the extent of the damage done, save that we felt rather headachy for a day or two.

A short distance from the cantonments there was an old fort, surrounded by a wet ditch swarming with alligators. This fort, called "Barrabuttee," was the last stronghold of the Mahrattas in Cuttack, whence they were driven by the British in 1803. Reports were rife of vast treasures being buried within the walls; and a gentleman, long resident in the station, frequently seen poking about, found that in one place the ground when struck returned a hollow sound. Here, no doubt, was the long-looked-for treasure, and he obtained permission to dig for it; the Government stipulating for a certain portion of whatever might be found. A gang of coolies, under the superintendence of Mr. B., was set to work; and after a long search, three pice or cowries, I forget which, were found; neither do I recollect what portion of the treasure-trove was carried to the credit of Government. Frustrated in his hopes, it was said that the treasure must have been thrown into the wet ditch when the Mahrattas retreated. Some few years later, another treasure-seeker, who was in command of the station, ordered the ditch to be drained. The alligators made their escape into the adjoining river, but no treasure was found. In fact, the Mahrattas were far too clever at looting (plundering) to leave anything behind, and generally made a very clean sweep. The natives used to say that these Mahrattas always slept with one eye open.

CHAPTER IV.

Posted to the 34th Regiment N.I. at Midnapore—Amateur Theatricals—Sad Fate of one of our Performers—Old Soobahdar, Orderly of the Great Duke—Little Jemadar, been in Egypt—Shocking bad Hats—Breach of Discipline—The Regiment leaves Midnapore—Captain Crofton goes to the assistance of the Colonel—Brown Bess—Beware of marrying a Native—Coffee-houses—Epitaph on Ensign Tompkins's Dogs—Attempted Murder of Martel's Bearer—Alarming Attack of a Deer.

In October, 183—, I was posted to the 34th regiment Native Infantry, then stationed at Midnapore. I had met this regiment at Sangor, and was consequently well known to most of the officers, amongst whom the greatest unanimity in general prevailed. Five of us lived together in the mess-house, or rather the house belonged to us, and we allowed the mess, for the sake of economy, to be held in the largest room of the house. In a detached bungalow near by, we had occasionally amateur theatricals. The scenes were painted chiefly by Captain A—— and the present Lady D——. Sooth to say, they would not have disgraced the first London theatres. The acting was in general by no means despicable, albeit the female characters were performed by men. The rehearsals were capital fun; and after a performance we adjourned in our respective costumes to the mess for supper. My friend Martel made a good-looking, buxom girl. I had to act the part of a lover towards her when she appeared at a second-story window. "Dear Laura!" I exclaimed; "you bid me approach; should I fail, I were unworthy of love and thee." I rushed to the door, where I found that Laura had jumped off the ladder and had a pipe in her mouth. "What fools we are!" said Laura, laughing. "Never mind, give me a light." So I lit my cigar at Laura's pipe. I have one of our play-bills still. Few of these performers are now in existence. The sad fate of one of them I will here relate. A trooper under his command, who had been punished by extra drill for some misconduct, determined to revenge himself on his officer, and proceeded early in the morning to B——'s quarters, where he found his victim asleep. It is supposed that he awoke B—— to a full sense of his situation by a puncture in the neck, and that then B—— sprang up to grapple with the trooper, who, armed with a sword, proceeded to cut down his officer, whose arms, hands and head, were found fearfully gashed. B—— shouted for assistance, and one of the sergeants hurried towards the bungalow, whence he saw the murderer issue with a bloody sword in his hand. He was called upon to stand, but fled past the main guard. The sergeant ordered the guard to fire, when he was shot dead before his victim had ceased to breathe. On the sergeant's proceeding to the bungalow, poor B—— was found alive, but insensible, and shortly after expired.

In the 34th regiment was an old Soobahdar Major, who had been an orderly to the great Duke when in India, and prided himself highly in the thought. He was one of the finest men I ever saw, and attracted the notice of the Commander-in-Chief—himself a very fine man—who drew himself up opposite the old native officer as if to measure heights, but the Soobahdar overtopped him.

Amongst the other native officers was a little Jemadar, who used to tell stories about his march with Sir David Baird's force across the desert into Egypt, where they

VERY COMFORTABLE AFTER TIFFIN.

arrived in time to be too late to cross bayonets with the French, and so marched back again. The old warrior liked to take a cup of coffee with the officers occasionally.

It is the custom amongst bachelors in India to sit with their legs on the table after meals. This attitude may appear very absurd, but, if not elegant, it is exceedingly comfortable, particularly after a day's sport, whether at cricket or shooting. On the opposite page is a sketch of two "of us," very comfortable after tiffin.

We all wore "shocking bad hats," but none the less comfortable. Every man pleased himself. Some wore a "wide-awake;" others a sort of pudding shape, quilted with cotton; others a helmet; and others, again, a sort of turban twisted round a common hat. I adopted every variety of the chapeau. Our shooting-coats, too, were of divers kinds. We cared little for appearance, for we studied comfort. Our commanding officer was much too easy with us. I have known a young ensign to smoke a cigar when the regiment was drawn up in line on the parade-ground and the officers in their respective places. On this great breach of discipline being pointed out, the commanding officer merely remarked, "Poor fellow! it is a very cold morning;" and this was all the notice taken of it. Can it be wondered at, that this regiment was one of the first to mutiny?

The medical officer of the regiment was once requested to visit the Colonel's father-in-law, and on going to the house was conducted by the Colonel to a mud hut in the compound, where the "father-in-law" was seated on a common charpoy.

When the regiment left Midnapore, Martel and myself (who had obtained another appointment) accompanied its first march, or rather we drove out with some of the officers two or three hours after the regiment had started.

It was dreary work in camp. Things had not settled down. No one seemed to know what to do with himself. I wandered about from tent to tent, and tried the hardness of every officer's bed, which in the day-time served for a couch as well. After dinner we took leave of our friends, and returned home in company with Captain Crofton, who had obtained leave to England. We found the Colonel's tents still standing. Captain C. approached to offer some assistance to the poor old gentleman, and he *was* a *gentleman*, although married to a regular native wife, not a half or quarter caste even. We used to call her "Brown Bess." Captain Crofton found the Colonel in a quandary, his wife refusing to assist in packing up some of her traps. "Parck, what for I parck? you parck yourself," said the spit-fire. The old gentleman has been dead many years, or I would not mention it. The moral of it is, let all English gentlemen beware of marrying a native wife.

For if you do,
I'm sure you'll rue,
As long as life remains,
That e'er you let the syren's chains
Ensnare your foolish heart.

Rather "shut yourself up in your room," young man, "and take pyson," as old Weller said to Samivel, when cautioning him against marrying a widow.

After morning parade some of the officers occasionally met at one of the coffee-houses. The coffee-house of a station is where two or three officers, residing together or near neighbours, have chairs placed outside the house, where they sit, smoke, drink tea or coffee, with friendly converse. Frequently visitors join the circle, or go from one house to another until the sun becomes too hot for them to remain outside with comfort. At one of these meetings a young ensign was lamenting the fate of one of his dogs. Tomkins had two dogs: one, an especial favourite, he called "Wretch;" the other, a good-for-nothing beast, he called "Blunder." The latter he shot purposely; the other from misadventure. Tomkins was returning home in the dusk of the evening with a gun in his hand, when suddenly his favourite dog, "Wretch," sprang through the garden-hedge to meet him. Tomkins, thinking that it was a jackal, hastily raised his gun and shot poor "Wretch" dead. T. expressed his intention of erecting a monument over his dogs. "Then," said H——, "I will give you an epitaph for them:

"Here lies 'Wretch' killed by a blunder;
Here lies 'Blunder' killed by a wretch."

This very neat impromptu *jeu d'esprit* was loudly applauded.

One evening, while at mess, intelligence was brought that Martel's sirdar-bearer was nearly killed by another man. Some of us hastened with M. to his house, where we found the bearer with a very severe wound across his neck. It seems that he was asleep in the veranda, when the would-be murderer attempted to cut off his head with a sword, but, owing to his agitation, the dimness of the light, or some other cause, the force of the blow was broken in great measure by the sword striking the collar-bone: this in all probability saved the man's life. The fellow who wounded him made his escape. Not long after this, Martel, Richards and myself, dined at the Park, nearly a mile from cantonments. I drove Richards home in my buggy, and M. followed some short time after in his palanquin. The night was so dark, that one of the bearers carried a lantern. Richards and myself were sitting in the veranda, waiting Martel's arrival, when suddenly a tremendous hubbub arose at the entrance of the compound. Our first thought and Richards's exclamation were, that M. was being murdered. R. caught down a sword that hung against the wall, and I, a stout cudgel, and rushed towards the place whence the row proceeded. At first we could not distinguish one object from another; M.'s palanquin was down, and the bearers appeared to be all heaped together, shouting in their lingo with all their might, "Murder!" At last we made out M. stooping down and grappling with a large deer. R. was going to pass his sword through the animal, but M. begged him not to do so, as he could hold the beast until properly secured. It appeared that one of M.'s deer, of which he had several in a large enclosure, seeing the light from the lantern approaching in front of the palanquin, sprang over the fence, and charged the leading man. Down went the Palkee, and out sprang Martel, who seized the brute by the horns ere he could do further mischief. And so all's well that ends well; but the circumstance was sufficiently alarming at the time, occuring as it did just after we had heard of the assassination of an officer in the upper provinces, and the attempted murder of Martel's bearer.

CHAPTER V.

Shooting from a Mechaun—Left behind on a Hunting Morning—Martel's Wrestle with a Bear—Snakes and Scorpions.

A MECHAUN is a rude sort of platform erected in the jungle with boughs of trees, and sometimes, if convenient, in a tree, with a leafy screen to conceal the hunters stationed on the platform. It was in one of these latter that Martel and myself, with two other friends, one morning took our places. The sun was shining brightly and the wind blowing almost a gale, so that our tree rocked to and fro in a way that made us rather apprehensive as to the stability of our platform.

We had been led to expect tigers, so agreed amongst ourselves not to shoot at any smaller game, such as deer, pea-fowl, partridges, jungle-fowl, &c. Anon, distant shouts were heard proceeding from a semicircle of many hundreds of natives, employed to beat the jungle a mile or two off, so as to drive the frightened animals towards the mechaun. Gradually the natives closed as they drew nearer, and their shouts and yells, mingled with the beating of tom-toms (native drums), &c., formed a most unearthly din. The sport became intensely exciting, as we stood, with guns ready, and eyes scanning every opening in the jungle whence we expected to see our game issue. Occasionally a dear bounded past, but we had no shot for him. Birds innumerable flew over us unregarded. At last our beaters came forth, but no tiger. We had drawn a blank; nevertheless, I never enjoyed a day's sport more, such as it was. We rocking away on our tree, with a spanking breeze,—the beautiful jungle and glades illumined by a glorious (cold-weather) sun,—the wild shouts of the natives,—and our excitement,—had enjoyment enough for me.

Intelligence was one day brought into the station that a tiger had been seen in the neighbourhood. A party was formed to beat up his quarters early the next morning. I had been out so often in vain pursuit of tigers, that I declined going. One of my friends, on this or some other occasion, presented me with a sketch of a lazy fellow left behind on a hunting morning.

I regretted much that I did not accompany them, although they did not meet with the tiger they went in pursuit of: but, amongst other game, a bear was by the numerous beaters driven towards the mechaun on which the shooting party were standing; they fired at the beast, which then turned round and re-entered the jungle. Martel, watching the direction of his retreat, immediately jumped down and followed, armed only with a small native axe. The others prudently stopped to re-load their guns. Meantime, Martel spied the bear sitting disconsolately at the foot of a tree. M. walked up and gave him a crack on the head with his axe, whereupon the animal sprang up, and instantly threw M. down. Then commenced one of the most singular struggles for dear life. M. thrust his hand down the bear's throat, thus literally keeping him at arms' length, while the beast was striving to give him a hug with his paws. Luckily for M., one of the shots fired from the mechaun had broken the bear's lower jaw, thus preventing his closing it effectually on Martel's arm. A native attendant, who had followed M. into the jungle, saw this fearful struggle going on, and hastened back to the other sports-

A LAZY FELLOW LEFT BEHIND ON A HUNTING MORNING.

men, but was so terrified that all he could say was, "Bal, bal!" Bear, bear! So they told him to shew the way, which he did; and they found M. on the ground covered with blood, and the bear on the top of him. Of course they thought that it was all up with poor M. However, Morney stepped up and sent a ball through Master Bruin's head, which caused him to stagger forward a few paces and fall down dead. M. (my Laura in the play) now sprang up, and asked for a cigar, remarking that it was hard work wrestling with a bear. Beyond a few scratches, he was not injured, the blood he was covered with being from the bear's wounded head and jaw.

Martel was certainly one of the pluckiest fellows I ever met with. A scion of one of the oldest families in England, he was the soul of honour, gentle as a woman and courageous as a lion. At the same time he was a practical Christian. During the many years we were thrown together, I never heard an oath or obscene expression issue from his lips; in short, he was a perfect gentleman. It would afford me great pleasure to give his real name; but I refrain, knowing it would cause him pain. Those who have been favoured with his companionship will recognize this portrait.

Various tales have been rife about snakes and scorpions. Having often heard that the mungoos *(viverra ichneumon)*, a little animal somewhat like a weasel in shape and size, would seek for and kill the venomous cobra de capello, we determined to try the experiment. Accordingly, some snake-charmers were directed to procure a lot of cobras and mungooses, or *mungeese*, as one of our friends would insist was the proper plural of mungoos, which, however, is frequently pronounced mungoose. To prevent these nimble little animals running away, they were attached by a long string to stakes driven into the ground. The snakes were turned out loose, and, as they attempted to escape, men were stationed with long sticks, to throw them back again. The mungooses had hardly fair play, as the string round their necks must have interfered somewhat with their freedom of action. However, after many attempts to escape, the trial commenced. We had some four or five snakes and mungooses loose at the same time. The sight was most interesting and exciting. The snakes were evidently afraid of the mungooses, which crouched down ready for a spring. After vain attempts to escape, and being poked nearer to the enemy, a snake would raise his head, at the same time expanding the hood, and with a swaying motion face the mungoos, which carefully watched his motions. This went on for two or three minutes, when, presto ! as quick as lightning, both appeared to dart at each other, and roll over and over on the ground. We could not tell whether the snake had hold of the mungoos, or the mungoos of the snake, until after a minute or two, when the motion of the snake gradually ceased, and it was found that the mungoos had seized both the upper and lower jaws of the snake, and, thus pressing both together, effectually prevented any injury to itself, while its teeth were fixed in the brain of its foe. Several snakes were killed in this manner, but one poor little mungoos was bitten, and appeared to be dying. It has been said that the mungoos finds a plant in the jungle which cures the bite of a snake. So we placed the wounded animal on the edge of the jungle, while we went to tiffin, expecting on our return to find it dead ; but it was gone. Whether it found the plant, or crawled into the jungle to die, I know not ; but we saw no more of it. We thought that the snake-charmers might have played us a trick by extracting the fangs of some of the snakes ; so after death we examined the jaws, and found all intact; and the death or injury of one mungoos proved that there was no trickery of the kind.

Some years later, when on sick-leave in Australia, I had a favourite bull-terrier dog (a descendant of the famous "Billy"). This dog was in the habit of attacking and killing the most venomous snakes, even the dreaded "black snake" of the bushmen. However, he tried it once too often, being found dead in the bush, a short distance from my house, with unmistakeable signs of having been bitten by a snake. I have seen a cat which was a famous snake-killer, though I never witnessed her performance.

It is a popular fallacy that a scorpion will sting itself to death if it cannot escape. We tested this two or three times by surrounding a scorpion with a fire of live charcoal. The scorpion ran round the enclosure with his tail erect. Gradually we diminished the fiery circle, but the scorpion rather preferred roasting to stinging himself to death; so we concluded that he did not possess the power of committing suicide.

CHAPTER VI.

On Baldness—Orthography—Expression of the Eye—Embarrassing Scene at a Country-house—Banyan-tree and Tomb—Amusements—Bear-shooting—A Native shot—Raine's First Ride on an Elephant—Antipathy of an Elephant to a Horse—Child killed by an Elephant—My Elephant—Woman killed by an Elephant—Bear Hams.

At one of our pleasant parties the conversation turned on baldness, when one gentleman said that men with large whiskers and beards had usually bald heads. This assertion set us all thinking of our friends, and we unanimously acknowledged the corrrectness of E.'s opinion. "But what about the ladies?" asked one. "Well," replied E., "who ever saw a bald-headed woman?" I never did. E.'s theory was, that nature bestowed only a certain quantity of hair on each person, and if a man had it not on his head he had it in whiskers or beard. I myself am an instance of the truth of E.'s theory, seeing that I have lots of hair on my head, but with little beard or whisker. There are exceptions to the rule perhaps, but I do not know of any; do you, my bearded or non-bearded reader? Another member of the party said that he would give us a brief sentence of little more than a dozen words, and challenge us to write it correctly. It was this: "A pedlar's pony ate some potatoes and a plum-pudding out of a saddler's bay window." The words were simple enough, but out of some twenty or more in the party, not one but made some mistake in the orthography of at least one word.

After this, he gave us the story of that venerable old

woman, whom we all know, who bought 180 apples at 3 for a-penny, and 180 at 2 for a-penny, and sold them at 5 for twopence. Query, Did she lose or gain by the transaction? We at once declared that she neither gained nor lost, but on working the sum we found that she had lost sixpence,—a fact which the old woman could not comprehend. All this occasioned an abundance of mirth. Then we had a discussion respecting the expression of the eye. Forthwith, a curtain, with a small slit in it, was suspended in a doorway between two rooms, and one after another of the party peeped through the hole. It was truly ridiculous to witness the wide guesses we made as to the possessor of the eyes presented to us. There was one lady in the party who had very fine eyes, and I pronounced our worthy but rather blear-eyed Major's visual organs to be those of Mrs. ——. After this I was obliged to give up my faith in the expression of the eye.

I once formed one of a large party at a country-house —no matter where—when I was placed in a very embarrassing situation. A gentleman and lady whom I knew very well were expected. Since I last saw them the gentleman had become a widower and the lady a widow. I had seen her little more than a year before, when she was in attendance on her sick husband, who died not very long after, in the first year of their union, and now I was to meet her for the first time as the wife of another. Sharp work certainly. I said to the friend who accompanied me to the party, and who was acquainted with the circumstances, "I wonder what Mrs. Dalby will think when she sees me!" Well, some thirty or forty guests had arrived before Mr. and Mrs. Dalby made their appearance with some others. I watched them with some curiosity as they entered the room, laughing and chatting with one and another of the friendly circle, until they approached the spot where I was standing. The instant she caught sight of me, she shrieked and fainted away, and was carried to another room. Here was a pretty fix for a modest and retiring gentleman like myself to be placed in! The lady's husband did not come forward, but stood still, looking as foolish as such a clever man could do. Some forty pairs of eyes were fixed upon us, and we formed altogether rather a striking *tableau vivant.* At last I faced about, and with affected coolness commenced an examination of the pictures on the wall. I did not envy Mr. —— his thoughts. I only know from his subsequent conduct that they wronged me; for as sure as there is a sun in heaven I was innocent of any impropriety in thought, word or deed. The truth is, I suppose, that the lady was very young—not out of her teens, I believe—and time had not healed the wound occasioned by the loss of her first husband before she was married a second time, and the unexpected sight of me instantly recalled to mind her previous situation, and she fainted as I have said. In the course of an hour or less, she re-entered the room, walked deliberately up to me, shook hands, and asked why I had not been to see her. All this, in the coolest way imaginable, as if what had so recently passed was but a dream. Truly, I could not help wondering at her sang froid, and thinking, as Jemmy Jumps used to say, "it's a funny world!"

In the collector's compound at Midnapore, there was a magnificent banyan-tree, under which was the tomb of some Mahometan saint. The natives said that tigers came at night and swept the earth round about the tomb with their tails! We had many pleasant archery parties beneath this tree.

Pic-nics and shooting were amongst our other amusements. Bears were numerous in the jungles near the parade-ground and other places. Frequently people were brought into the station terribly wounded by these animals. On one occasion a poor woman was shockingly mangled. A party was formed to avenge her. The bear's den was well known to the villagers, and word was sent that we should be out early in the morning. After an early breakfast, some six or seven of us proceeded to the ground, about five miles off. I was on an elephant with Morney, and a buggy was ordered to be brought as far as the road would admit, to meet us on our return. When we arrived at the scene of action we dismounted, and found a great many natives assembled, several of whom were armed with matchlocks and other weapons. Some scouts, mounted on trees, were keeping watch on the bear's den, into which they had seen the animal enter, so that they were certain she was there. We advanced cautiously on foot along the bank of a shallow stream, until we came opposite to a hole in the precipitous bank on the other side. This was the den. I had with me a native lad, whom I called "Jacob Faithful," from an excellent habit he had of sticking close to me with a spare gun for my use after discharging the first. We were within a dozen yards of the bear, but she would not come forth. Some shots were fired into the hole without effect. At length a few squibs were manufactured and thrown in, when out rushed Bruin with a "huh, huh!" Bang went some half-dozen guns. The bear then turned tail, and scrambled up the bank into the jungle. My friend Martel dashed across the stream, and crawled into the den, whence he soon issued with a couple of cubs a few weeks old. It was certain that the dam would not go far, so we proceeded to cross the stream and follow her into the jungle. Before I was well over, a brisk firing commenced above. In our haste, poor old Mac——, who never greeted me afterwards without an imitation of the bear's "huh, huh!" was scrambling up the bank, and had just reached the top, when a branch which he had laid hold of gave way, and down he came upon me, driving my hat over my eyes. I in turn fell upon "Jacob Faithful," who rolled into the stream. I certainly thought that the bear was upon us. We quickly picked ourselves up, looked to our arms, and again clambered up the bank. On advancing a short distance, I saw the thick jungle grass moving within a dozen paces of me, as if some large animal were passing swiftly through it. I could not see what it was, but fired into the waving jungle: had I waited to see the game, she would have been upon me. No further move was made in my direction; but the bear was found dead. Of course every one laid claim to the honour of having killed the bear. I modestly thought that it was I who had done the deed; but the truth is, the jungle was so thick, that we could not well see what we were about. What a scene it was! the natives shouting and blazing away at random with their matchlocks, —the wonder was that some of our party were not killed, as well as the bear. One of the natives was shot through the foot; but all declared that they did not do *that*, whatever they did to the bear. However, we made a purse for the wounded man, whom we sent to be cured at the station hospital, from which he issued in a few weeks as well as ever in person, but much richer in purse, than he could ever have hoped to be in his wildest dreams. This was perhaps wrong, as people said that the man would in future throw himself in the way of being shot in hopes of reaping an ample reward.

Well, the cubs and their dead mother—of whom more

anon—were directed to be sent in to the station, and we, mounting our several conveyances, proceeded towards home. When within about three miles, we fell in with my buggy; so I and Morney slipped off the elephant and got in. But before we drove off, up came Raine, a fine young griff, who had lately joined the regiment to do duty pro tem. He had never mounted an elephant, and requested that he might make use of ours. No sooner said than done, Jacob Faithful remaining in the back part of the howdah with my guns. The mahout (driver) had got down for some purpose, and when preparing to mount again, the elephant turned tail and walked off into the jungle. Morney and I could not possibly do anything, but called out to Raine, "Get down by the tail!—get down by the tail!" We watched the elephant for some time driving about the jungle, and thinking that the mahout would surely manage to catch and pacify the brute, we drove off, as we had our respective duties to attend at the station. Well, tiffin-time came, but no Raine. Time passed, and dinner came, but still no R. or any tidings of him. We became really alarmed; but not long after Raine made his appearance in sorry plight. For many hours the elephant had been careering about the jungle, under the trees, and through the villages. Jacob Faithful managed to escape (with my guns) by springing on to the roof of a house. Thus poor Raine was left to himself, and had many narrow escapes of having his brains knocked out by the branches of trees under which the elephant ran. At length the beast walked into a pool of water to refresh, and Raine, calling to mind what we had shouted before we drove off, slipped down by the elephant's tail into the water, and reached home in safety. Raine has risen to distinction in the Seikh wars, but I venture to think that he will never forget his first ride on an elephant, or the many pleasant hours we passed together, albeit many years have elapsed since we parted.

The antipathy which an elephant bears towards a horse is very singular. I was once riding through a narrow lane in Pooree, when I met an elephant. There was just room for us to pass without touching; but my horse did not like the elephant, and still less did the latter like the horse; so the mahout turned his animal round; when the brute, not liking an enemy in the rear, set off at a swinging trot, and, suddenly turning a corner, killed a little child who was playing in the street, by placing a foot on its head. A minute after the accident, I was on the spot, and saw the distressed mother with the dead child in her arms. The poor little creature must have been killed instantaneously, as its head was crushed into a shapeless mass.

Many people form a strong affection for their elephants. I possessed one for several years, but never could feel quite *at home* with him, although he was tractable enough, and would do anything he was ordered. If, when on his back, I happened to drop any article, such as a cigar-case or ramrod, he would pick it up with his trunk and present it to the mahout. But I never could fathom the expression of the brute's piggish little eyes. And then his trunk was so handy if at any time I unintentionally offended him, so that when I gave him a piece of bread, or ventured to pat his trunk, I fancied that I ran a risk even in performing these friendly acts.

My distrust of these animals originated in hearing, shortly after my arrival in India, of a poor woman being struck dead by one. The elephant had been teazed by a little dog, and the woman snatched up her pet to preserve it from his fury, when the brute immediately killed her by a single blow of his trunk.

I will now give the final history of the bear. She was skinned, and eleven balls were found to have penetrated her body. Having read somewhere that bears' hams were good eating, Martel and I determined to have them cured, which was done in due season, and fine plump-looking hams they were. Some of the ladies having expressed a wish to taste a bear's ham, we decided on giving a ladies' party on the occasion. The guests having taken their seats, the cover was raised from the ham, which was placed opposite to me, and was the object of curiosity to our visitors, for whom I commenced to carve; but soon a horrible odour pervaded the room. The ladies looked at one another, and hoisted signals of distress by raising handkerchiefs to their faces. I ordered the ham to be removed; but Martel declared that he would have some first, so I sent him a slice. He raised a piece to his mouth, but could venture no further. We all arose from the table, opened the doors, and sprinkled vinegar and lavender-water about the room before we could resume our seats. The ham was well cured, but it was the peculiar rank smell of the beast which overpowered us. Martel and I procured from the carcase several bottles of grease, which the ladies found very acceptable. I have since been informed by others that they have tasted bears' ham in India and found it very good; but we found it most unpalatable, which may have arisen from the animal's being a nursing mother when slain. *Au reste,* she was a common black bear.

CHAPTER VII.

Leave Midnapore and arrive at Pooree—Sea-shore—Paddling in the Sea—Topographical Account of the Country—History—Names and Titles.

I LEFT Midnapore on the 27th December, 1836, and the last day of the year found myself cast on the sea-shore of Juggurnath Pooree,—hungry, certainly, but neither naked nor miserable; for instead of being shipwrecked, I turned out of my palanquin after a few days' travel, and considered myself rather a prosperous gentleman, seeing that it was in compliance with my own request that Government had thought proper to appoint me to this much-coveted station.

My house was situated on the sands of the sea-shore, about 300 yards distant from the sea, where not a blade of grass could be seen within a quarter of a mile or more. A broad path of mud plastered over with lime led from the house to the sea-side. If I stepped off the path, it was to be over shoes in sand,—not a pleasant situation certainly; but then there was the glorious and ever-changing sea, over which a spanking breeze blows from the S. W. throughout the hot season, i.e. from the end of March to the middle or latter part of October; so that we did not often require the use of a punkah. There is usually very little beach at Pooree, save in the cold weather, when there is, on the receding of the tide, a fine hard space for a gallop. Until my visit to Pooree, I had not been on the sea-shore since my childhood, when

I once spent a day in dabbling in the water near Cromer, in Norfolk. Retaining a pleasant reminiscence of this, I took off my boots and stockings, and, tucking up my trousers, paddled about in the sea, picking up shells, for some hours, quite as much a boy as ever, albeit I was on the shady side of thirty. I paid, however, for my freak in an unexpected manner, which quite cured me of my childish propensities in that way. From exposure to the sun and sea-water, my legs became so extremely painful and swollen, that it was some days before I could walk without suffering.

The usual residents of the station—three in number and all bachelors—were in the moofussil (district) on duty. When somewhat recovered from my "sea sorrow," I proceeded to join one of them at Khoordah. As I shall have frequent occasion to mention the southern division of Cuttack, I will call it, for the sake of simplicity, the Pooree district, which in truth it is.

I shall now give a short description of the country, &c., which I consider interesting; but it may be thought by some very dry reading. If so, the remedy is easy—skip it.

Having, in compliance with a requisition of the Bengal Government, written a topographical and statistical account of the Pooree district, commonly called the southern division of Cuttack, which was forwarded to the Hon. Court of Directors by the Government of the day, I shall make such extracts therefrom as may prove interesting to the general reader. I shall also quote freely from Mr. Stirling's account of Orissa Proper, printed only amongst the Asiatic Society's Transactions, and therefore not likely to fall under the observation of the public in general, though I have read extracts from it word for word, without acknowledgment, by more than one writer on Juggurnath.

In pursuance of my topographical and statistical inquiries, I traversed the district in question in various directions as occasion served, and collected specimens of the rocks and soil for analysis, &c. The natives of Khoordah, seeing me pick up pieces of rock and soil, wrap them carefully in paper and write thereon, could not possibly understand the motive, and reported to my friend Colville, the magistrate, that I was "paugul ho guya,"—literally, "gone foolish" or mad.

The Khoordah division of the Pooree district consists of hills and jungles, with numerous streams and fertile valleys intersecting them. None of the hills attain a greater altitude than twelve or fourteen hundred feet. "The rocks," as Mr. Stirling says in his account of Orissa, "are chiefly of granite formation, remarkable for its resemblance to sandstone, and for its containing vast quantities of imperfectly formed garnets, disseminated throughout with veins of steatite, considerably indurated. The prevailing colour of the principal rock is red."

"The rock most abounding in this district, next to granite," says Mr. Stirling, "is that singular substance called iron-clay by Jamieson, and laterite by Dr. Buchanan. It lies in beds of considerable depth on the feet of the granite hills, often advancing out for a distance of ten or fifteen miles into the plains, where it forms gentle swelling rocky elevations, but never rises into hills. Sometimes it is disposed in the manner of flat terraces of considerable dimensions, which look as if they had been constructed with much labour and skill. The composition and aspect of the Cuttack iron-clay are very remarkable, from the innumerable pores and amygdaloid cavities which it contains, filled with white and yellow lithomarge, and from the quantities of iron-ore pebbles and fragments of quartz embedded in it. By far the most interesting circumstance, however, connected with it is, its complete and intimate mixture with the granite, which has been traced in several instances, and specimens of which are in my possession, exhibiting the one rock entirely investing the other, though it is not easy to pronounce which is the enclosing substance. We have here an instance of a rock of the Wernerian newest Floetz trap formation, resting upon the oldest primitive rock and actually in conjunction with it. The granite, at the place where the specimens were principally collected, appears to burst through an immense bed of laterite, rising abruptly at a considerable angle. Numerous broken fragments are strewed all around the line of junction, and in some specimens the rocks are so mixed together as to form a sort of coarse breccia or rather conglomerate."

The foregoing is a very good description of the laterite rock in Khoordah. Instances of the commingling of granite and laterite may be found in various parts of the district, particularly in the pass between the hills at the base of which the road leads from Khoordah towards Pooree. Gneiss and veins of quartz are also found in this direction. A description of the manner in which these rocks are here met with may be interesting; so I give it as related in my account of the district. On the gentle ascent from the fort of the Khoordah hill, and proceeding towards Pooree, we meet with laterite, which may be traced for several hundred yards; then more compact iron-stone and veins of quartz, in some places having a stratified appearance, in others mixed together. After crossing this bed of iron-stone and quartz, which is about six feet in width, laterite is again found, at first mixed with pieces of quartz and iron-stone; afterwards the laterite is continued a few hundred yards further, when another bed or vein of quartz is found; then again laterite; and proceeding onwards through the pass, granite is found in large masses strewed about the surface, and also embedded in the laterite. The road is here continued over the bare rock, and being worn smooth by the passage of hackeries, &c., presents for a short distance somewhat the appearance of an irregular tesselated pavement, from the strange manner in which the rocks are here intermingled. It seems as if a stream of melted laterite had poured down the hill, bearing in its course masses of granite of various size and shape. In some places, however, the granite appears to be the enveloping substance. Proceeding down the pass, gneiss is next found, then conglomerate, and lastly laterite, shortly terminating in the plains. A specimen of laterite submitted to analysis was found to contain 8 per cent of per oxide of iron.

The granite and laterite rocks are cut into convenient sizes for building, and transported across the Chilka lake to Pooree.

The history attached to this country is equally curious with its formation. Mr. Stirling has given the history of the ancient sovereigns of Orissa; I will therefore content myself with giving a short account of its ancient administration and more modern history, chiefly compiled from official documents.

The Pooree district formed a part of the once-powerful kingdom of Orissa before its dismemberment by the Moguls in the first instance, and in later years by the Mahrattas. That part of the district which was in possession of the former is known by the name of Mogulbundee, and comprised, with the exception of four Pergunnahs, which were afterwards taken by the Mahrattas, nearly the whole of the plain and fertile portion of the country belonging to the Maha Rajahs of Orissa in the

Pooree district. On the expulsion of the Moguls by the Mahrattas, the confines of the Rajah's territories were still further curtailed, and he himself reduced to the rank of a tributary, holding his remaining estate of Khoordah by the payment of a peshkush or tribute of ten thousand rupees annually. Notwithstanding the comparative insignificance of their power, the Rajahs of Khoordah, as they are henceforth called, were still formidable to many of the neighbouring Khandaits* or independent chiefs, most of whom were descendants of ancient officers and even of the Rajahs themselves, who, in consideration of the performance of certain services of a feudal nature, had assigned the Khandaits those portions of country over which their descendants ruled as independent chiefs. These estates now became of importance in the eyes of the Khoordah Rajah. Many of them were seized, and, to prevent future disputes respecting the proprietorship, the entire families of the Khandaits were put to death. Thus the three Khandaits of Pulla (as related by Mr. Forrester), together with their families, numbering from forty to fifty individuals, were put to death in one day, and their estates seized by the Rajah. Many others are stated to have suffered in the same way.

Respecting the origin of the Khandaits, Mr. Stirling says that "it is probable they first received estates in the twelfth century. Rajah Anang Bhim Deo, having created sixteen sawants or great lords, who were posted all round and along the frontiers of the Raj, with the view of defending it from the irruption of neighbouring powers or the incursions and devastations of the savage inhabitants of the wild region in the interior, such as

* Khandait, an Orissa name signifying persons entitled to wear the Khanda, or national sword of Orissa.

the Khunds and Coles, who to this day give serious annoyance in many parts of the hill estates; and if the belief of their origin and ancient situation be well founded, were doubtless in former ages far more numerous and formidable than at present. In this point of view, their situations and duties resembled much that of the Lords of the Marches in Europe. Nor is the above the only striking feature of analogy between the feudal lords of India and the western hemisphere. The estates or jurisdiction of that class in Orissa were always called by the Hindus, Gerhs; and by the Mussulmans, Killahs, or Castles. A certain part of the lands under the head officer were parcelled out amongst several military retainers and dependents called Naicks, Dulaes, Dulbehras, and sometimes Khandaits, who held of their superior on much the same principle as he did of the supreme Rajah, though, generally speaking, by a more limited and imperfect tenure. Under these, again, a portion of the lands of each subordinate Gerh was assigned as service-land to the feudal militia of the country, called Paiks, who, following equally the occupations of soldier and cultivator, were obliged at any time, when called on by their leader, to take up arms and accompany him to the field. In times of war, the Khandaits or nobility of Orissa, at the head of their respective contingents of this landed militia, ranged themselves under the standard of their sovereign, and formed the main part of his military array. Thus we frequently read of the Gajapati assembling the chiefs to attend on a warlike expedition, and find that the sunnuds granted by the Mogul Government (in cases where they exercised the right of investiture) always contained a condition that the Khandait should be ready to attend with his contingent when summoned by the military officer of his division. Besides the general obligation of military service, the Indian feudatories were bound to do homage, and to perform certain nominal duties or offices resulting from their tenures, when in actual attendance on their liege lords, called by the expressive word Sewa, seva or service (in Persian, Khidmut), a consideration of which, to compare small things with great, reminds one strongly of some of the ancient forms of the Germanic Constitution. Thus it was the business of one to bear the sword of state, another held the shield, a third carried the umbrella or royal standard, a fourth presented the Rajah's slippers, a fifth fanned him with the regal chowrie, &c. The above services are to this day performed in the presence of the Khoordah Rajahs by several of the hill zemindars as often as they visit Pooree, though the distinctive character of the office appropriated to each has become a good deal merged in the simple duty of holding the chowrie and punkah in the presence of the representative of their ancient Lords Paramount."

Four of these chiefs, or Rajahs as they now style themselves, whose territories are situated on the northern and western frontiers of Khoordah, now pay tribute into the Pooree treasury.

The last of the native rulers of Khoordah was Maha Rajah Mukund Deo, who by the following act of treachery drew upon himself the vengeance of the British Government. Previous to the march of the Madras troops, under Colonel Harcourt, towards Cuttack in 1803, for the purpose of attacking the Mahrattas, who held the fort of Burrabuttee, the Khoordah Rajah entered into engagements with the British Government to afford every assistance in his power to the troops on the march through his territories. In consideration of such service, the Rajah was to receive a large sum of money, one half of which was paid before the troops marched, and on completion of the service the other half was to be forthcoming. In the mean time, the storming of Fort Burrabuttee at Cuttack by the troops under Colonel Harcourt took place on the 14th of October, and such of the Mahrattas who escaped retreated through Khoordah. The Rajah, contrary to the advice of his Bukshee, was persuaded to join his forces to theirs, and proceeded immediately to cut to pieces all the small detachments which had been left for the purpose of keeping open the communication with Ganjam, at that time the head-quarters of the northern division of the Madras army. For this perfidious conduct the Rajah paid dearly. He was at once attacked, driven from his fort at Khoordah, taken prisoner, and confined in the fort at Midnapore. On the expiration of three or four years he was released, and permitted to reside at Pooree, receiving a pension of two thousand rupees a month from the British Government, in lieu of mali khana (territorial revenue), for his support, —a measure which in the present day appears to have been demanded neither by justice nor policy. After the death of Rajah Mukund Deo, his son, Ramchunder Deo, was awarded a like pension, which he still enjoys, or at least did so when I left Pooree, and was greatly dissatisfied at its being so small.

The natives of Khoordah still look up to the Rajah as their chief. Most of them present him with a nuzzer on the occasion of a marriage, birth or festival-day. The Rajah even bestows titles upon petty chiefs and inhabitants of the Rajwarra, sometimes for a sum of money; and such is their veneration for this descendant of their chiefs, that the titles so procured are highly prized. The privilege of having a torass (a sort of standard, in shape resembling a shield) borne before them, is also sought by the hill chiefs.

On the accession of a Rajah to either of the hill estates of Runpore, Duspulla, Bankee, Dompara, and ten others adjoining, it is customary for the new chief to visit Juggurnath, where, by order of the Khoordah Rajah, he is invested with a saree cloth which has been worn by the idol. He then presents a nuzzer to the Khoordah Rajah, as his feudal lord and representative of the ancient sovereigns of Orissa, from whom, as before mentioned, the hill chiefs derived their respective estates. The new chief is finally presented by the Khoordah Rajah with a dress of honour and two horses.

The following are some of the Paik and other titles or names of distinction conferred by the Rajah, the signification of which was obligingly furnished by the late Mr. Wilkinson:

Surjun Sing—Surjun, performing; Sing, a lion—one who can do anything that a lion can.

Indurjeet—Indur, god of the clouds; Jeet, conquering—one who can even conquer the god of the clouds.

Mutguj Sing—Mut, performance; Guj, an elephant; Sing, a lion—both an elephant and a lion in performing anything.

Oodey Bhanoo—Oodey, rising; Bhanoo, sun—a person who can throw as much light on a subject as the rising sun.

Oodundra—Oodund, afraid of no one; Ra, superior—a person who cares for nobody.

Nisunkh—Ni, without; Sunkh, fear—fearless.

Runbeer—Run, fight; Beer, strong—strong in fight.

Runjhamp—Run, fight; Jhamp, to be ready—always ready for fight.

Runchunchan—Run, fight; Chunchan, an eagle—an eagle for destroying in fight.

Bharee Mul—Mul, strong man; Bharee, superior—first of strong men.

Khandaetra—Khanda, a sword; Aet, power; Ra, superior—skilled in the use of the sword.

Dhunoorjye Sing—Dhunoo, an arrow; Jye, conquering—best of bowmen.

Havra Sing—Havra, attacking; Sing, a lion—a lion in attacking.

Byree Kump—Byree, enemy; Kump, shake—a person who always frightens his enemy.

Putla Sing—Putla, thin; Sing, a lion—though thin, yet a lion in courage.

Patjoosee—Pat, royal assembly; Joosee, praised—the most praised in the royal court.

Putnaick—Put, writing; Naick, fit—best of writers.

Oogul Sing—Oogul, stop; Sing, a lion—a person who can even stop a lion.

Runhundol—Run, fight; Hundol, expert—expert in fight.

Runbijlee—Run, fight; Bijlee, lightning—quick as lightning in fight.

Mungraj—Mung, body; Raj, superior—beautiful in form.

Sawuntra—Sawunt, a great man; Ra, superior—first of great men.

Paikra—Paik, a soldier; Ra, superior—first of soldiers.

Dhuradhur Dhamut Sing—Dhuradhur, a hill; Dhamut, make powder of; Sing, a lion—a person who is so strong as even to beat the hills to powder.

Run Behar—Run, fight; Behar, a hill—firm as a hill in fight.

Chumputtee Ra—Chum, army; Puttee, leader; Ra, superior—superior to a leader of an army.

Rawutra—Rawut, a horse-soldier; Ra, superior—first of horsemen.

Sooboodhee Ra—Soo, good; Boodhee, sense; Ra, superior—first of the most learned.

Jutroosal—Jutroo, enemy; Sal, enemy—the enemy of your enemy.

Run Munthun—Run, fight; Munthun, destroying—a person who is destructive in fight.

Jugdeb—Jug, world; Deb, great—greatest in the world.

Sungram Sing—Sungram, fight; Sing, a lion—a lion in fight.

Nurindur—Nur, man; Indur, god of the clouds—superior amongst men.

Bahoobulindur—Bahoo, arms; Bul, strength; Indur, god of the clouds—a person whose strength of arm is great as the god of the clouds.

Maha Ruthee—Maha, great; Ruthee, a person who fights—the first of fighters.

Bidyadhur—Bidya, science; Dhur, seizing—very learned.

Byreegunjun Sing—Byree, enemy; Gunjun, destroyer; Sing, a lion—a lion in destroying enemies.

Runjeet—Run, fight; Jeet, victorious—victorious in fight.

Kuhul Sing—Kuhul, anger; Sing, a lion—fierce as a lion.

Chooal Sing—Chooal, offspring; Sing, a lion—son of a lion.

Chotra—Chot, less; Ra, king—only less than a king.

I have many more of these fierce names, but the reader may probably exclaim, "Hold, enough!" and I think so too.

CHAPTER VIII.

How the British Government became connected with Juggurnath—Temple of Juggurnath—Idols—Soodursun—Servants of the Temple—Mahapursad a Holy Food—Grasping Priests of Juggurnath—The British Government not Immaculate—Offerings made to Juggurnath—Dhujjas—Usual Offerings of poor People—Number of Pilgrims—Self-sacrifice—Accidental Passage of the Car over the Bodies of Eleven Men—Abstract Statement of Pilgrims and Pilgrim Tax—Pilgrim Tax as a source of Revenue—Pilgrim Hunters—Account of their Proceedings—Cuttack Missionaries—Distribution of Tracts to Pilgrims—Means of spreading Christianity.

In order to shew how the British Government became connected with Juggurnath, I will give a brief history of the temple since it passed out of the hands of the independent sovereigns of Orissa.

In 1558, the province was, according to Stirling, invaded by the Affghan Mahometans under Kala Pahar, the General of Soliman Gurzani, king of Bengal, who, after defeating and killing the Rajah, carried off and finally burnt the idol of Juggurnath on the banks of the Ganges, and also broke to pieces every idol in the country.

Feristeh relates that Khan Jehan, the General of Akbar, wrested the province of Orissa from the Affghans, and annexed it to the roll of the empire in 1578.

"The severity with which the Moguls treated the priests and worshipers of Juggurnath, is to this day spoken of with horror by the natives of the province. These acts of severity," says Mr. Stirling, "were the source of frequent conflicts, until this religious warfare was at last set at rest by the institution of the tax on pilgrims, which, if one may credit the author of the work translated by Gladwin under the title of 'History of Bengal,' yielded to the Mogul Government a revenue of nine lacs of rupees. No portion of this sum, it may with reason be assumed, was ever given by these bigoted iconoclasts to the priests of Juggurnath to defray the expenses of the temple; but any deficiency in the receipts, with regard to the disbursements, are by local tradition said to have been made by the Rajahs of Khoordah."

The Mahrattas made their first appearance in the province in 1743, but did not remain as its undisputed rulers until 1755. They continued the pilgrim tax. The amount levied from each class of pilgrims was as follows: A pilgrim travelling in a palanquin paid 50 rupees; on horseback or in an ekha, 25 rupees; the three next classes, from 20 to 5 rupees; poor people, from 1 to 4 rupees, according to what, after a rigid search, was found on their persons.

"The practice of bestowing a money donation to defray the expenses of the temple is said to have originated with the Mahrattas. The first payment was probably made about 1759 or 1760, when the pergunnahs containing the principal land endowments of the temple, together with other fertile portions of the Rajah's territories, were surrendered to the Mahrattas. The Rajah, being deprived of so considerable a part of his estate, was probably ill able, if at all, to defray the deficiency in the sums required for the due support of the temple. Hence motives of self-interest as well as religion may have induced the Mahratta Government to establish a money donation about this time."

The amount of the donation was not fixed, but varied

every year according to the actual expenses incurred. The land endowments of the temple continued to be managed by the officers thereof, but the Mahrattas took the superintendence of the temple affairs into their own hands, and, according to Mr. Groeme's Report, paid every attention to the due appropriation of its assets. The average amount of the annual donation paid by the Mahrattas during the last twelve years of their rule, was upwards of 21,000 rupees. The amount of the two last years' donation, viz. 1801-2 and 1802-3, were respectively 24,283 and 21,807 sicca rupees.

On the 18th of September, 1803, possession was taken of Pooree by part of the Madras army, under Colonel Harcourt; previous to which event, however, letters had been obtained by the Governor-General from the most eminent pundits in Bengal, and addressed to the principal Brahmins at Juggurnath, exhorting and encouraging them to place themselves and the temple under British protection. Colonel Harcourt was instructed by the Governor-General in Council to "employ every possible precaution to preserve the respect due to the temple and the religious prejudices of the Brahmins and pilgrims." He was also desired "not to disturb the actual system of collections at the pagoda." "And at the same time was interdicted from contracting any engagements which would limit the power of the British Government to make such arrangements with respect to the pagoda, or to introduce such a reform of existing abuses and vexations as might hereafter be deemed advisable." He was also desired to assure the Brahmins that "they would not be required to pay any other revenue or tribute than that which they had been in the habit of paying, and that they would be protected in the exercise of their religious duties."

The pilgrim tax was temporarily abolished "because the Mahratta Government had exercised great oppression in levying the collections, and it was deemed expedient to postpone the collections arising from these sources until a system of collection void of oppression and inconvenience could be arranged; at the same time, authority was given the collector to incur the expenses necessary for the support of the temple, on the scale on which it was maintained under the Mahratta Government."

The Governor-General, in a despatch addressed to the Secret Committee, dated 12th of April, 1804, stated that it was deemed advisable no immediate changes should be introduced in the existing establishment at the temple of Juggurnath. On the recommendation of the Commissioners, the Governor-General in Council confirmed in his situation the principal officer of the Mahratta Government at Juggurnath. The Commissioners were directed to furnish a detailed statement of the system which heretofore prevailed in the temple of Juggurnath, in order to enable the Governor-General in Council to form a final arrangement for the regulation of the affairs of the temple.

On the 11th of March, 1805, the Commissioners directed the collector (Mr. C. Groeme) to proceed to Juggurnath for the "purpose of obtaining information in regard to the establishment and customs thereof, in order that suitable arrangements might be adopted for the permanent regulation and support of the important religious institution of the temple of Juggurnath." The Commissioners further observe that "the establishment of a moderate rate of collecting the duties on the pilgrims proceeding to Juggurnath, is in every point of view highly desirable and proper, as well from the circumstance of its affording the Brahmins, and other persons desirous of performing the pilgrimage, confidence and security in the idea that the expenses of the pagoda will be regularly and permanently defrayed by Government, and that its attention will always be directed to the protection of the pilgrims resorting to it; as the heavy expense attendant on the repairs of the pagoda, and the maintenance of the establishment attached to it, which has always been defrayed by the Government of the province, render it necessary, from considerations connected with the public resources, that funds should be provided for defraying the expenses."

Mr. Groeme's Report to the Commissioners conveying the information required, is dated 10th of June, 1805; and on the 5th of September following was passed the famous Regulation XII. of 1805, the 30th Section of which has of late years been the theme of so much discussion. The Section in question declares "that nothing herein contained shall be construed to authorize the resumption of the established donation for the support of the temple of Juggurnath, the charitable donation to the officers of certain Hindoo temples, called unnoochuttree,* and the allowance granted for the support of the Hindoo temple at Cuttack, called Seetaram Thakoor Baree."

By a Regulation of 1806, the pilgrim tax was re-established, and the 6th Section declares that "the fees of the officers of the temple should be paid out of the funds which have been or may be assigned for the support of the temple."

* The unnoochuttree is a place where food is bestowed in charity, and frequently attached to a temple. Besides the temple mentioned in Section 30 of Regulation XII., an allowance is granted to seventeen small temples attached to the unnoochuttree, and pensions are paid to the officers of certain other Hindoo temples for religious purposes; these pensions are declared to be hereditary.

The amount of tax leviable on each pilgrim was in most cases less than one-half of what it had been under the Mahratta Government.

On the 14th of June, 1807, the Governor-General in Council, "in consequence of the unsatisfactory accounts rendered by the collector of the receipts and disbursements, and the very imperfect information obtained at the expiration of so long a period of the resources of the temple," vested the superintendence of the collection of tax and of the temple in the collector of Cuttack, and directed that officer (Mr. Webb) to bring up the account of the disbursements of the temple, and to make a full inquiry respecting the lands assigned for its support. This information was supplied in Mr. Webb's Report, dated the 19th of November, 1807. The average expenses of every kind for six years, namely, the two last years of the Mahratta and four first years of the British rule (which were somewhat clumsily taken together), were stated at 65,999 sicca rupees; the average receipts of the temple, at 30,884 rupees; and the cash advanced by the ruling power, at 29,355. Taking the last two years of the Mahratta rule apart, it will be found that in the four years which had elapsed since the occupation of Pooree by the British, the disbursements claimed from Government to defray the increased expenses (real or alleged) of the temple, were, for want of proper surveillance, nearly double what they were under the Mahrattas. In consequence of this jugglery, Mr. Webb disallowed various charges. The Sataees Hazaree Mehal and the Khunjahs attaching to it, were taken under the management of Government officers; and, including the revenue therefrom, the money to be disbursed by Government was for the future limited to 56,342 rupees (exclusive of broadcloth for the cars). The average receipts of the temple of every kind being only 30,884 rupees, left a deficit of 25,458 rupees to be paid by Government.

In a letter, dated 5th of February, 1808, the Governor-General in Council approved of the "proposition for limiting the expenses of the temple in future to a sum not exceeding 56,342 rupees; and with respect to the accounts of the disbursements during the four first years of the British rule—viz. 1211, 1212, 1213 and 1214 amli —the Governor-General in Council was of opinion that the sanction given by the Commissioners to expenses actually incurred and inserted in the public accounts for the year 1211, would naturally be construed by the officers of the temple into an authority for incurring similar expenses in the subsequent years. On a reference, however, to the accounts submitted by the collector (Appendix 11 and 12), you will observe that the collector divides the charges into two distinct heads,—1st, Charges for which no authority can be shewn, and which were never incurred; and, 2ndly, Charges for which no authority can be shewn, and which are therefore deemed inadmissible."

"On the grounds above stated, the Governor-General is of opinion that the last-mentioned charges," amounting to 15,739 rupees, "should be allowed. It does not, however, appear to Government that any reason whatever exists for the admission of charges which it is stated were never incurred, even in the year 1211, as the insertion of them in the accounts can only be deemed an attempt at fraud. His Lordship in Council is accordingly of opinion that these fictitious charges," amounting to 28,424 rupees, "should be rejected." And, subject to these deductions, the accounts were ultimately passed.

The following is a remarkable instance of the impudent tricks resorted to by the priests of Juggurnath to swell the expenditure of the temple. In 1804, the purchas presented a petition to the collector, requiring a variety of articles as presents for the priests and servants attached to the temple, in order to avert the famine and mortality which they affected to apprehend from the circumstance of an adjutant bird having alighted on the spire of the goddess Bimola's temple, when the image of the goddess perspired so profusely as to saturate her saree or dress (an omen of the direst import). This petition was transmitted by the collector to the Board of Commissioners, who considered it as a direct attempt to impose upon and extort money from Government, but nevertheless acquiesced in its prayer on account of the alarm which had been created in the minds of the people, who believed that the measures proposed by the priests were the only means by which the dreaded calamities could be averted. The Commissioners, however, warned the priests against such practices in future.

By Regulation IV. of 1809, "the superintendence of the temple of Juggurnath and its interior economy, the conduct and management of its affairs, and the control over the priests, officers and servants attached to it, are vested in the Rajah of Khoordah."

In 1840, the pilgrim tax was abolished.

In 1843, management of the land endowments of the temple were made over to the Khoordah Rajah, still leaving a money donation to be paid by the British Government. During the administration of Lord Canning, to the best of my knowledge, it was disposed of, but in what way I must refer my readers to the Appendix.

The temple of Juggurnath is situated about a mile from the sea, and forms a conspicuous landmark for vessels approaching the coast.

"The building in its form and distribution," says Mr.

Stirling, "resembles closely the great pagoda at Bhovaneswar, nor do the dimensions of the two edifices greatly differ. Altogether its appearance is certainly imposing from its loftiness and the mass of masonry which it comprises, but the execution is extremely rude and inelegant." "The present edifice was completed A.D. 1198, at a cost of from forty to fifty lacs of rupees (£500,000 sterling). The material used for the construction of the temple is chiefly the coarse granite resembling sandstone, found in the southern division of Cuttack."

The outer wall which encloses the temple is nearly a square, being 675 feet long by 655 in breadth. This wall is about 30 feet high. Within that, again, is a second lofty wall, about 70 feet from the first. The space between these two walls corresponds to the outer court of the Gentiles in the temple of Jerusalem, as no low-caste people are admitted to the inner enclosure. However, for their consolation I suppose, in this outer court are fifteen small temples, dedicated to Mahadeo, Hanuman, &c. Juggurnath's kitchen is also in this enclosure, and the prepared food is conveyed from the cook-rooms to the temple under a covered way, in order that there may be no chance of defilement by a passing bird.

In the inner enclosure stands the great temple, besides which there are eighty or more smaller temples. One of them is dedicated to Gunness, the elephant god; one to Sarasuttee, the goddess of knowledge; one to Luckshmi, the goddess of fortune; and one to Soorya, the sun. The others are mostly dedicated to Mahadeo and Krishna. There are four large gateways, one in each face of the wall. That on the east side is the principal, called the Sing Dwara, or Gate of Lions, from the circumstance of there being a large and uncouth figure of one of these animals on each side of the gateway. In front stands a very beautiful polygonal column formed of a single shaft of black basalt, 33 feet in length. This column was about a century ago brought from the famous Black Pagoda, "where," says Mr. Stirling, "it supported the appropriate emblem of Aruna, the charioteer of the sun, but which has now given place to a figure of the monkey god, Hanuman." This figure of Hanuman was blown off in a gale of wind while I was at Pooree, and had not been replaced when I left. The people did not seem to care much about it, or even the twisting of the chuckra at the top of the temple in the same gale.

The land for ten miles around the temple is holy ground, but the "holy of holies" is the site of the great tower, containing the idols of Juggurnath, Bulbhudra and Soobudhra (Juggurnath's brother and sister). The throne or platform on which the idols are placed is said to be built on 100,000 salagrams, which are round stones about the size of an orange, with numerous perforations throughout, and are considered peculiarly holy as emblems of Vishnu. They are brought from the Nepal hills and elsewhere. I was fool enough to give a gold mohur (16 rupees) for one.

New idols are made about once in twelve years, or whenever there are two new moons in the month of Assar (June and July). They are made out of a neem-tree *(melia azadirachta)*, which has been set apart for that purpose some years previously, when the priests say that it becomes converted into sandal-wood. The story is, that the selected tree is henceforth guarded by a winged serpent, which deters any birds from alighting upon it, and also prevents the approach of any other animal. A small guard is also stationed at some distance to watch the sacred tree.

When the time approaches for making the new idols, the superindendent of the temple is warned by Juggurnath in a dream to send the chattah and torass of the idol, together with the bearers, drummers, carpenters and others, to cut down the tree. They first hang a garland of flowers, which has been worn by Juggurnath, on one of the branches, when the winged serpent disappears. The whole posse of drummers, carpenters, &c., sleep under and around the tree at night, and next day cut it into the required pieces, conveying them to the temple, where the idols are fashioned by Viswakarma and his assistants.

When the idol of Juggurnath is completed, the mysterious deposit, which the priests say no one has ever seen, is taken out of a cavity in the old idol, and placed in the new one. The person who performs this act, it is said, seldom survives more than a year. This mysterious substance is by some supposed to be a bone of Krishna, or a piece of the original idol, which has been transferred from one idol to another since the worship of Juggurnath was established; by others it is said to be a bag of quicksilver or a salagram. The latter is most probable.

The idols of Juggurnath, Bulbhudra and Soobudhra, are placed on the same throne, and near the first, Soodursun reclines against the back of the throne. The image of Soodursun is a mere log or pillar of wood, being one of the four parts into which the divine timber splits of itself in forming the four-fold image or Chatur Murti, viz. Juggurnath, Bulbhudra, Soobudhra and Soodursun. The three former are distinct individuals, but all unite in Soodursun,—an evident attempt to embody a trinity in unity, and also an allusion to Brumh, the uncreated Spirit, from whom proceeded Brahma, Vishnu and Siva, who are here represented by Juggurnath, Bulbhudra and

Soobudhra. Soodursun, the priests say, is shapeless and is never seen,—in allusion, doubtless, to "Him whose glory is so great, there is no image which illumines all, delights all, whence all proceeded, that by which we live when born, and that to which all must return." Vedas, vide Moor's Hindoo Pantheon, p. 4.

Soodursun is brought out of the temple four times in each year, and is sometimes, though rarely, carried about the town of Pooree, in hopes of staying the ravages of peculiarly fatal epidemics. During the absence of Soodursun no ceremonies can be performed in the temple, the power of Juggurnath being in abeyance.

There are about 4000 priests and servants of all denominations attached to the temple. Upwards of 600 of them are in daily attendance.

Nearly all the offices are hereditary, and even divisible to a certain extent. For instance, a pundah or priest, whose privilege it was when living to officiate in the temple two days in each year, leaves four sons. In this case the days are not divided into twelve hours for each man, but the two eldest officiate one day each the first year after their father's death, and the two youngest on the following one. After which it is again the turn of the eldest, and so on. Some families of pundahs and others whose numbers have not much increased, are said to be very wealthy, while others who have been more prolific are very poor. The emoluments of the pundahs and others are chiefly derived from a share of the offerings made to the idols by pilgrims, and also from the sale of mahapursad, the value of which is, on the authority of one of the principal officers of the temple, stated at upwards of three lacs of rupees, £30,000 annually.

The pundahs are the proper priests of Juggurnath. Their duty consists in the performance of the various religious ceremonies, making offerings to the idols, and reciting muntras or prayers, &c. They also visit distant countries to beat up for pilgrims, and employ others to do so. When officiating in the temple, their dress must be of a pure white. In other respects it is similar to that commonly worn. At the same time they must not wear any ornaments, save a gold or silver ring on the fore-finger of the right hand. A ring of this kind is indispensable in the temple offices; on other occasions a ring of kusa grass is frequently substituted.

There are about six hundred families of Juggurnath's cooks. The office is no sinecure, as offerings of food must be presented to the idols at least six times a day. On the occasion of a great influx of pilgrims there is an increased demand for mahapursad, or holy food, and offerings are presented to the idols eight or nine times a day. Five hundred cooks are in daily attendance. The cook-room is 288 feet in length by 22 in breadth, and contains 300 fire-places. Each fire-place has a surface that will contain five vessels placed thus $\overset{o}{\underset{o}{o\,o\,o}}$. On the top of the first layer of pots a second is placed, and another over that to the height of five or six. The cooks tell the people as a miracle that the contents of the upper vessel are cooked first; the fact being that they change the top ones to the bottom during the process of cooking, so that all are ready at the same time. Pilgrims while at Pooree must not wear shoes to defile the holy ground, and their diet must consist solely of mahapursad, or food (chiefly rice) which has been consecrated by having been offered to Juggurnath. All classes may partake of this holy food together without losing caste. It is generally supposed that different classes of people while at Pooree may partake together of other kinds of food without losing caste, but this is a mistake; it is only the holiness of the mahapursad which sanctifies the act of various castes eating together. "So great is its virtue," says Mr. Stirling, "that it cannot be polluted by the touch of the lowest caste, and the leavings even of a dog are to be carefully taken up and made use of. The Khetr Máhátmya says that Maha Luckshmi herself prepares and tastes it. He who eats it is absolved from the four cardinal sins of the Hindoo faith, viz. killing a cow, killing a Brahmin, drinking spirits, and committing adultery with the female of a gooree or spiritual teacher. The most tremendous and inexpiable of all crimes is to handle and eat the mahapursad without the proper feeling of reverence." If a pilgrim offers a rupee for mahapursad for immediate use, he only receives nine annas' worth, other four annas going to the pundah and three annas to the cooks.

No sum, however contemptible, is beneath the notice of the grasping priests of Juggurnath. From a pice to a lac of rupees, all is welcome. Even the clothes are taken off a pilgrim's back if he has no money, and an agreement is drawn out, with the names of Juggurnath, Bulbhudra and Soobudhra as witnesses, that if the pilgrim should at any time become possessed of property, he will bestow a certain portion of it on the priest who officiated at his introduction to Juggurnath. These engagements are faithfully performed, and it is said that some of the priests of Juggurnath have thereby acquired considerable wealth. When the pundah has fleeced his credulous dupe of all the property he possesses about his person, he will then, if the pilgrim has property in his own country, offer him a loan—say of one hundred rupees—to defray his expenses on the way home. For this loan the pundah receives a bond, bearing enormous interest of course. Finally, when the pilgrim takes leave of Juggurnath, some forty or fifty rupees out of the loan are extorted by the pundah on one pretence or another, such as offering of bhoge (food), &c., to Juggurnath. The creditor or his servant accompanies the debtor to his home to receive the amount of the bond with interest, and generally contrives to obtain both. The pundah or his servant then beat up for more pilgrims in the same neighbourhood or elsewhere.

All the world knows that even now we are not immaculate, and were no better fifty years ago. It was not the custom in my time for Government to commend the European collector of pilgrim tax, or to wig him, whether the collection was large or small; but I have seen instances of both in old official documents. Happily, the pilgrim tax has been entirely abolished by the British Government, and the management of the temple and its land endowments made over to the Khoordah Rajah.

No offerings can be made to Juggurnath without an accompaniment of money. The amount of the gift varies according to the wealth and zeal of the donor. Two pice will be accepted from a poor man presenting a flower. Gifts of horses or elephants must be accompanied with a sufficient sum for their future maintenance, otherwise they are immediately sold, and the proceeds carried to the account of the superintendent of the temple.

To hang a dhujja, a sort of pennant or streamer, on the top of the temple, is esteemed a peculiarly meritorious act, and to be paid for accordingly. The dhujjas are of four kinds. The first is a piece of cloth, one end of which is fastened to the chuckha (an emblem of Vishnu) on the top of the temple, and the other extended to the sea (about a mile distant), where the devotee who presents the dhujja holds the end in his hand while bathing and praying, his eyes being fixed on the other extremity of the cloth, or the top of the temple. This is a very expensive ceremony, and is rarely performed. The second dhujja is a cloth, one end of which is fastened to the chuckha on the top of the temple, while the other is extended to the Chur Numut Khoond, a small cistern within the enclosure of the temple, into which the water flows after washing the floor of the temple. In this reservoir the pilgrim bathes while holding one end of the dhujja in his hand, the attendant pundah at the same time reciting certain muntras (prayers) over him. This ceremony is performed by wealthy pilgrims three or four times a year. The third and fourth dhujjas are of various sizes, from twenty to one hundred feet or more in length. The value of the smallest piece must not be less than one rupee, and the offering accompanying it not less than two rupees. From two hundred to one thousand rupees are not unfrequently given with one of the second and third kinds. The top of the temple may daily be seen decorated with streamers of various length. The larger pieces, after flying for a day or two, are taken down and placed in the store-room of the temple to be otherwise disposed of. The smaller are allowed to fly until nearly or altogether blown away.

The usual offerings of the poor people of the Pooree district, if above the lowest castes, are a few flowers, especially the toolsee *(ocymum sanctum)*; occasionally they must give a few annas to a priest, who in return supplies them with a handful of nirmalo or rice, which after being offered to the idol is again dried in the sun. This rice is carried home by the poor man, and a grain of it eaten daily after the performance of the customary ablutions.

Juggurnath's old clothes are turned to good account.

Every rag bears a price. The sree kupra (most excellent cloth), a sort of necklace made of these rags, is eagerly purchased and worn by pilgrims.

The number of pilgrims to the shrine of Juggurnath has been greatly exaggerated, as also has the mortality occurring amongst them. During the last ten years of the existence of the pilgrim tax, when note was taken of every person entering the gates of Pooree, the average annual number of pilgrims amounted to 116,400. The average annual mortality amongst them while at Pooree certainly did not exceed 500. The greatest mortality known by the medical officer during a residence of seven years was in the year 1843, when the deaths amounted to between six and seven hundred. The season in question was unusually sickly, and cholera prevailed to a great extent.

The number of pilgrims dying on the road to and from Pooree is also greatly exaggerated. The greatest mortality no doubt occurs when such vast numbers of people are crowded together in the confined streets of a filthy town at the festival of the Ruth Jattra. When travelling in ordinary seasons, there is little, if any, reason why the mortality should greatly exceed that of other classes, notwithstanding the privations some of the poorer pilgrims are said to undergo. More pilgrims probably die on the road between Pooree and Cuttack (a distance of fifty miles) after the Ruth Jattra festival, than on any other part of the way, as many of them leave the town when barely recovered from sickness, and others take the seeds of disease with them. The medical officer of Pooree was accustomed at this season to ride many miles beyond the gates of the town, and was astonished to find how greatly the number of pilgrims said to be dying on the road had been exaggerated. One author, quoted by

Hamilton, says "that the concourse of pilgrims to Juggurnath is so immense, that at fifty miles distance its approach may be known by the quantity of human bones strewed by the way." If the traveller had no other clue to depend upon in finding his way to Juggurnath, he would speedily wander from the path. Many writers about the temple of Juggurnath appear to have vied with each other in magnifying its attendant horrors. Hence the cars are supposed by some people in England to be constantly travelling, and never to move save over the bodies of prostrate pilgrims. Nothing can be further from the truth. Only one instance of self-sacrifice occurred during my residence at Pooree, a period of nearly nine years. It is true that in 1840 the wheels of the car passed over the bodies of eleven men, who were thrown down by a rush of the crowd when the cars were moving unusually fast, but no one pretended that the people voluntarily sacrificed themselves. Three of the victims were conveyed to the pilgrim hospital, and two of them ultimately recovered. Many of the so-called sacrifices have doubtless been occasioned by accident; and considering that the ponderous and unwieldy vehicles sometimes move at the rate of four miles an hour amongst a dense crowd of people, one can scarcely help wondering that accidents do not occur more frequently. It is, however, to be remarked that sacrifices are said to have occurred oftener prior to the British rule. Many accidents occur to people being thrown down and trampled on in the rush of the crowd to enter the temple when the gates are opened on the morning of the Ruth Jattra. In 1813, thirty-four pilgrims were crushed to death on the opening of the tax-office gates; and five others were killed in the same manner in the narrow street leading to the Seetagunga tank, so great was the rush made by the pilgrims to bathe in the sacred waters.

Abstract Statement of Pilgrims of every description resorting to Juggurnath from the year 1829 *to* 1839, *shewing also the amount collected by the Pilgrim Tax, and the excess remaining in the Public Treasury after defraying all charges.*

Years.	Total number of Pilgrims.	Total amount collected by Pilgrim Tax.	Total remaining to Government after defraying all charges.
		RUPEES.	RUPEES.
1829-30	140,716	93,555	53,736
1830-31	167,077	184,637	136,391
1831-32	75,462	47,880	5,023
1832-33	69,888	65,372	23,711
1833-34	100,836	72,676	29,812
1834-35	114,361	89,091	46,486
1835-36	158,251	93,141	48,659
1836-37	93,743	60,880	8,805
1837-38	92,793	68,606	28,019
1838-39	150,905	150,612	108,209
Grand Total	1,164,032	926,450	488,851

As a source of revenue, it will appear from the foregoing table that the amount carried to the credit of Government, after defraying all charges, was £48,885, or, in round numbers, an average of £4888 annually,—a small sum in comparison with that levied by the Moguls, which, as mentioned elsewhere, amounted to £90,000 per annum.

The principle of levying a tax on pilgrims is in the abstract utterly indefensible, but it cannot be said that it was levied in an oppressive manner by the British Government, as was the case with the Moguls.

The pilgrim hunters are pundahs and purheearees (guards who keep watch over the temple gates), who, as well as going themselves, employ agents, called churee burdhar, to beat up for pilgrims from the most remote parts of India. These agents sometimes receive monthly wages, but more frequently have a share of the spoil, or, in other words, as much as they can squeeze out of their credulous dupes. The following graphic description of the pilgrim hunters' proceedings is taken from a narrative of the Orissa Mission, published by Rev. A. Sutton, stating that it was written by a Brahmin who is now a Christian:

"At this present time, in consequence of the power of the English extending through numerous countries, many causes of alarm are suppressed. On this account, the pundahs spread themselves through the different parts for the purpose of collecting pilgrims. Having arrived at their respective stations, they repair to people's houses and compel them to eat mahapursad, and by much flattery induce them to receive various kinds of cakes. Having furnished themselves with strips of cloth which have touched the sacred limbs of Juggurnath, they suspend them round their necks, saying, 'See, you are highly favoured; sitting in your houses you have obtained these precious relics.' Then they say, 'Come, accompany me to my country. There God is revealed. There the goddesses Luckshmi, Sarasuttee, Bimola, and 10,000 others, constantly serve him; moreover, the gods of heaven, earth and hell, all the three hundred and thirty-six millions of gods, worship him. His glory is immense. All castes before him eat out of one vessel. In the month of Assar is the Goondicha Jattra. He himself comes out of the temple and sits on his car. He himself causes the car to move. In one day he eats seventy poatu (about a thousand pounds' weight), but all that he eats of different kinds, who can tell? Listen, however, to a truly wonderful fact. In the cook-house they place seven cooking-pots one above the other over one fire. The bottom pots are not cooked, but the top one is!' In this manner they tell a number of tales, and persuade the people to come. Having arrived, they direct them to different houses, saying, 'This is the holy land; here the fruit of pious actions is enjoyed. Come, I will obtain for you an interview with Juggurnath; and cause you bathe in the five holy places, namely Indradumun tank, Lokenath tank, Seetagunga tank, Markund tank and the sea; that you will obtain salvation for seven generations of your ancestors: but bear in mind how you will propitiate me!' In this way they lead them to the temple, and give them a sight of Juggurnath. At that time many priests surround them, and, stroking their heads, exclaim, Behold the visible god glorified! present him with an offering of twenty-five rupees; come quickly, no delay. Give us a present of ten rupees. In this way, by much talking, they wheedle them out of their money, and take all they can get. Others come begging to their lodgings. If they have no more money, these pundahs coax them out of a promissory note, and make them engage to pay when they reach home. They also make a number of cakes, and bring them for the pilgrims to eat. For that which is worth four annas, they exact twelve; for one annas' worth, they take six annas. If they refuse to have them, they abuse them with filthy curses and speeches (which I omit), and say, 'You—where will you get such food as this!' Thus saying, they cram it by main force into their mouths. Thus the pundahs exceedingly oppress the people, and by a variety of cheating tricks get from them their wealth. Sometimes, when the pilgrims enter the enclosure of the temple, they steal the ornaments from their noses and ears, and take away their clothes and money. If they resist, the pundahs assemble and beat them, till they make off, crying out, 'O father, O mother, I die, I die!' and thus they escape from the temple. Or if the pundahs see a beautiful young woman, they allure her into the temple, and having seduced her, let her go, telling her, 'This is a holy place; I am a holy man. By having surrendered your person to me, it is purified; the sins of a million of births are destroyed; know that god and his worshiper are inseparable.' On other occasions, giving the pilgrims some portion to eat, they render them insensible and rob them of their wealth."

In speaking of the foregoing extract, Mr. Sutton says "that no one can tell what Hindoos will do so well as a Hindoo, and especially a Hindoo Brahmin; while as to what is transacted within Juggurnath's temple, they alone can give us information."

Since the abolition of the pilgrim tax, the number of pilgrims is said to have increased considerably, but there are now no certain means of ascertaining this, by reason of the gates being thrown open to all, and any information derived from the priests of Juggurnath must be viewed with suspicion.

The annual donation by Government for the support of the temple was always, and justly so, a sore subject with the Cuttack missionaries, on account of the sanction (as the priests alleged) that Government offered to the worship of Juggurnath, which hindered the conversion of the natives. This may be true to some extent, but far the greatest obstacle is to be found in the dominant Brahmin priesthood. All obstructions, except the last, have, to the best of my belief, been removed; and it remains to be seen with what success the missionaries will encounter the wiles of the priests. I heartily wish them God-speed!

It is not too much to say that the mantle of the venerable and apostolic Swartz has not fallen on any of the missionaries of modern times in India. There have been many good and zealous men, but none have met with such success in converting the natives as that truly great and pious man. The Memoirs of his Life and Correspondence, by Hugh Pearson, D.D., &c., is one of the most interesting works I ever read.

I wish to speak with all respect of the Cuttack missionaries, particularly of Dr. S——, with whom I was more intimately acquainted. In common with many other gentlemen, I can bear testimony to the good which he and his estimable wife have done in the Orissa Mission School at Cuttack, on the premises of which they resided, so that the pupils were under constant supervision, a most important consideration in India.

Dr. S—— is a most zealous missionary, but I cannot help thinking—perhaps erroneously—that he is wanting in discretion in his efforts to convert the natives. I have repeatedly seen him, at the Ruth Jattra festival, take up a position near the car, and preach to the people when the idol of Juggurnath was brought from the temple. The natives at that time are worked up to the highest pitch of enthusiasm. Surely this was not the proper season to attack the faith of the pilgrims; the wonder is that the good man was not torn to pieces on the spot.

Dr. S—— informed me that he was not very sanguine about the stability of most of his professed adult converts, and was of opinion that more good was to be done by educating orphan children, of whom they generally had (when I was at Pooree) upwards of a hundred of both sexes in the Mission School at Cuttack, where they were clothed, boarded, educated, and taught some trade. Many of the pupils from the school had intermarried, and resided in a part of the town called Christianpore. Here, undoubtedly, is the seed of great good; and if the missionaries have done nothing more, they are deserving of all support. These native Christians attend divine service in the Mission chapel, and are of course visited occasionally by the missionaries.

I distrust the reports sent home by the missionaries, not that I believe they wilfully mislead their supporters, but, as might be expected from their devotion to one object, they are apt to take too sanguine a view of the progress they are making in the conversion of the natives, who may be seen surrounding a missionary while he is preaching in the streets, and apparently listening attentively to his discourse; but it is, I believe, a mere matter of curiosity to see a sahib preaching, that induces them to remain. There may be exceptions, but such I am sure is the rule.

When the pilgrims leave Pooree after the Ruth Jattra festival, persons employed by the missionaries are seated at the gates of the town, with large piles of tracts beside them. These tracts are offered to every pilgrim passing through the gates. Now a native will take anything if there is nothing to pay, so, as the missionaries truly say, they gladly receive the tracts; but, alas! it is to be hoped that the missionaries are ignorant of what I have seen, namely, the road for a couple of miles from Pooree strewn here and there with torn tracts. I saw this for the first time when travelling in my palanquin on the Cuttack road, and was puzzled to know the meaning of the numerous pieces of clean printed paper flying about. The mystery, however, was explained when I entered the gates of Pooree, and witnessed the distribution of tracts by natives employed for that purpose. Of course, I cannot venture to assert that every man receiving a tract tore it to pieces, yet it is reasonable to infer that few or none would prize a paper which attacked the religion they had shewn their devotion to by having just completed a weary pilgrimage in hopes of meriting eternal rewards in a future state.

If the good missionaries should ever read what I have felt bound in the interest of truth to relate, I hope they will not feel mortified or discouraged. God forbid that I should do anything to weaken their hands! My opinion may not be worth much, but as it coincides with that of the Rev. Dr. S——, I give it. *Early* education affords by far the best means of spreading a knowledge of Christianity amongst the Hindoos. I would humbly advise that, above all other means, especial attention should be paid to the Mission School in Cuttack, to which in my time I have sent several orphan children.

CHAPTER IX.

Byraghees and other Mendicants—Dundees, Bhyrobs and Bhyrobees—Freemasons amongst the Priests of Juggurnath—Snan Jattra, or Bathing Festival—Ruth Jattra, or Car Festival—Bahora, or Returning Festival—Gumma Poonimah Festival—Kaleea Dobun Festival—Maha Joist Festival—Worship of the Goddess of Snakes—Festival in honour of Sarasuttee, the Goddess of Knowledge—Dosohara Festival.

NUMEROUS byraghees and other mendicants may be observed at the festivals of Juggurnath, lying extended on their backs in the streets or in a puddle of water, some with eyes closed and a straw in their mouths, others with a quantity of earth heaped up on their faces, so that it is difficult to imagine how they can breathe. A stranger to their tricks would suppose them to be dead, as they remain perfectly still; even the heaving of the chest in inspiration is imperceptible. Some amongst them have an earthen vessel containing fire placed on the stomach. Extended by the side of these people are some dirty cloths, on which may be seen a few grains of rice or a few cowrie shells, bestowed in charity by the passengers. These byraghees (religious mendicants) are the "blood-suckers" of the country, and swarm about the Sing Dwara of the temple, under the garb of sanctity practising every species of debauchery. Their bodies are usually naked, save a narrow piece of cloth, scarcely sufficient for decency, passed between the legs and fastened before and behind to a string tied round the waist. They wear their hair long, and to increase its bulk twist and plait other hair with it. This, from constant exposure, becomes of a rusty colour, and is matted with filth. Their bodies are smeared with the ashes of cow-dung, giving them a most unearthly guise; their eyes are generally inflamed and watery from filth and debauchery. Anything more disgusting than the appearance of these wretches can scarcely be imagined. Many byraghees have assumed the disguise, to escape the punishment of crimes committed in other districts. Surely some legislative enactment would suffice to abate the nuisance. All religious mendicants might be compelled to produce a sort of passport, specifying the country whence they came and other particulars, the truth of which might be ascertained by the police authorities, so that in the event of any criminal assuming the disguise he would be readily detected.

Amongst the devotees at Pooree are ten learned Brahmins called "Dundees," who are pure deists, as indeed are nearly all learned Brahmins. Idols, they say, are merely personifications of God. Thus they look upon the idols of Juggurnath, Bulbhudra and Soobudhra, as emblems of Brumh, or the Spirit.

The first step for the aspirant of a dund is to become "Bano Prosto"—signifying, to come out from—by leaving his family, and taking up his abode under a tree in some solitary place, where he passes his time in meditation and studying the Shasters. He also visits different holy places. After seven years thus spent, the Bano Prosto becomes a Sunyassee. He then shaves his head, performs a shrada for his ancestors, and then for himself. After thus performing his own funeral obsequies, he throws away his poita (Brahminical thread) and receives from another Brahmin a "dund." The dund is a slender bamboo about six feet long, with a piece of orange or buff-coloured cloth tied at one end, the precise meaning of which I have not been able to ascertain. The devotee is now hailed as "Narain," or pure, and is henceforth called a Dundee. The dund is an emblem of Brumh, and as such the Dundee places it before him and contemplates it while engaged in prayer. Dundees are never seen without their dunds, and are esteemed above all other castes. They wear a sort of buff or orange-coloured dress, and are generally very much respected by the people, though, singular enough, they are considered impure, and a person inadvertently touching them must afterwards bathe. In fact, they are looked upon in the same light as a corpse, seeing that they have renounced the world and even performed their own funeral obsequies. The Dundees must not possess any property, and are chiefly supported by lands set apart for their maintenance. There are five classes of Dundees, differing chiefly in the decoration of their dunds. Some of them tie a poita on the staff. The duties of Dundees are chastity, teaching, meditation and reading the Shasters. At Pooree, they are also consulted on the occurrence of any bad omens, accidental impurities, and other affairs relating to the temple.

Few of the Dundees act strictly up to what they profess ; for instance, one of the Dundees has two of his sons at Pooree, and another lately had a Bhyrobee for his mistress. After a lapse of twelve years from the time of leaving his family, the Dundee can, if he chooses (though few avail themselves of the privilege), become a Purumhungso. He then buries his dund, strips off all his clothes, and partakes of any kind of food except beef. He will even eat human flesh; so pure has he become by his acts of piety and penance, that the holiness of the individual sanctifies even this act. After a further period of twelve years, the Purumhungso may become Ubdhoot. He then renounces the use of speech, even to ask for food, and sits under a tree wrapt in meditation. Twelve years thus spent and he becomes Ga'anee. He has then obtained *perfection*, and may speak if he chooses, but seldom does so, being wholly devoted to meditation. In fact, he may be considered as insane. Some of the Dundees at Pooree, from twelve years' austerities alone, are subject to aberration of intellect. A few years ago, there was a Purumhungso at Pooree who went about perfectly naked, and was very properly expelled from the town by the magistrate.

There is another class of devotees called Bhyrobs. They will partake of any kind of food save beef. There are females of this sect called Bhyrobees, the wives or mistresses of the Bhyrobs, who are taught to read some of the Shasters. Both Bhyrobs and Bhyrobees worship Kali and Mahadev. They wear a sort of buff or orange-coloured dress like the Dundees, but are by no means so much respected as the bearers of the dund.

There are also a few fanatics called Agoorees, who delight in committing all sorts of abomination. My friend Captain R——, who is a freemason of high mark, assured me that there were freemasons amongst the priests of Juggurnath.

The power and sanctity of Juggurnath do not prevent his being plundered. In 1828, silver articles to the value of five thousand rupees were stolen; and in 1837, the diamonds of his head-dress, valued at three lacs of rupees (£30,000), were purloined.

Runjeet Sing, a short time before his death, sent funds to defray the expense of re-building the western gate of the temple, and also jewels to a considerable amount—amongst them, the famous Koh-i-noor—to be presented to Juggurnath; but the agent (who favoured me with a visit), hearing of his master's death, took the jewels away with him. The Koh-i-noor is now amongst the Crown jewels of England, this splendid diamond having become a prize to the British army on the conquest of the Punjab.

Daily Ceremonies of the Temple.

Mungul Arotee. *Mungul* signifies excellent, and *Arotee*, light. Two hours before dawn the Beeturcho on duty inspects the seals which had been placed on the Jowah Bejowah, or outer door of the temple, the previous evening, and after ascertaining that they remain intact, proceeds to open the door. Some lamps are lighted, the seals of the Samoo, or door of the idols' chamber, are inspected; after which the door is opened and three arotees of camphor in gold cups are held before Juggurnath, Bulbhudra and Soobudhra. A silver lamp containing twenty-one branches is then lighted and held before the idols. Three small silver racups, or saucers, in which are placed lamps made of rice-flour and water, with a lighted wick dipped in ghee, in each, are in like manner held up. The beds are now taken away and sandal-wood water sprinkled about the floor.

Prooshootum Uppokoss. The Posoopalloky, who may be called Juggurnath's valets, ascend the Singhasun and remove the flowers, clothes, &c., with which the idols had been adorned the previous evening. Bathing dresses are then placed on them, the implements of the toilet are brought forth, such as gold tongue-scrapers, sticks or brushes for the teeth, towels, and three mirrors about three feet high, composed of silver and bell-metal highly polished. The mirrors are placed in three shallow brass vessels standing on the floor in front of the idols. The tongue-scrapers, &c., are held before the idols, after which the ceremony of bathing is performed by pouring over the reflected images in the mirrors a mixture of ghee, curdled milk and water, so that the bathing of the idols is merely imaginary. After this, the morning dresses are adjusted and the floor washed. The tara, a sort of curtain, is fastened across the doorway, not so as to obstruct the view of devotees, but to prevent any person entering until the toilet is completed.

GOPAL BULLUB. An offering of sweet cakes on gold plates to the idols about two hours after sunrise. While the gods are supposed to be eating, a priest recites certain muntras, after which he claps his hands, and, ringing a bell, signifies that Juggurnath has finished his meal. The plates are then removed and the floor washed.

SOKHUL DHOOP. The doorway is again secured by the tara, while the idols are undressed, and more splendid clothes put on them. The second meal of the day is then acted, and concluded with an offering of pan beera (betel-nut, &c.). Musicians and dancing-girls perform during the latter part of this ceremony, after which the floor is washed.

JUGGURNATH BULLUB UPPOKOSS. The dresses are again changed; another meal is offered and the floor washed. This ceremony concludes about noon.

MUDUNO DHOOP. The same ceremonies as in the foregoing, but with different kinds of food, terminating about two o'clock.

PROOSOOTUM BULLUB UPPOKOSS. The dresses are changed previous to the siesta.

SHYAN, or POHROO AROTEE. Three beds are brought from the store-room and placed near the Singhasun. Camphor lights are then burnt, and the idols invited to descend and repose. The doors are then closed.

TARAPITAH UPPOKOSS. At four o'clock the doors are opened, the beds removed and the dresses changed.

SHUNDIAH AROTEE. Camphor lights are offered to the idols, and the floor washed.

SHUNDIAH DHOOP. Musicians and dancing-girls perform while the fifth meal of the day is acted. Pan beera is offered to the idols, and the room washed six hours after sunset.

BURRA SINGHAR UPPOKOSS. The dresses are changed for more splendid ones.

CHUNDUN LAJY. A mixture of camphor, spices and sandal-wood water, is rubbed on the bodies of the idols, and sandal-wood water is sprinkled about the floors of the temple, while some Brahmins sing parts of the "Geet Govind Jye Deb," a poem relating to the loves of Krishna and Radha.

BURRA SINGHAR BESS. The most splendid dresses are put on, garlands of flowers are suspended from the ears and hung around the necks of the idols; after which the floor is washed.

BURRA SINGHAR BHOGE. About eleven o'clock the last meal of the day is performed, but with different ingredients. Pan beera is offered, and the floor washed.

BULLUB BHOGE. Sweetmeats are offered to the idols, and the floor washed.

PAHOORA AROTEE. Camphor lights are burnt before the idols. Three beds are brought from the store-room. A small idol of Krishna, called Adonarain, is placed for a few minutes on each of the beds, after which it is carried to the door, and seated on a dumboor (a sort of morah); cocoa-nuts, pan beera and sweet cakes are there offered, while musicians and songsters perform before it.

POOSPANJEELY. Musicians and dancing-girls perform while flowers are strewn over the idol of Adonorain, which is then taken before Juggurnath for a few minutes, and afterwards conveyed to the store-room.

SHYAN. Cocoa-nuts and pan beera are placed under the beds. Three cloths are extended from the latter to the Singhasun. All persons are turned out of the temple (except the officiating priests), and the lamps extinguished. A Brahmin calls aloud, "O Mooneemah, Lord of all worlds, descend from thy throne, and repose on the bed prepared for thee!" after which the doors are closed and sealed for the night.

Several annual festivals are held at Juggurnath. I will give a short description of a few of them.

MOKUR, or MAUG. A name of the Sun, also of the Zodiacal sign, Capricorn. The month of Maug is sacred to Vishnu, who in the Purans declares that "amongst the months I am 'Mokur' or 'Maug.'" This festival is held in January and February. Vishnu personifies the sun. He is also worshiped as Krishna and Juggurnath, &c. The fifth day of the moon in Mokur is the Bosunt Bess festival, when the winter dresses of the idols are exchanged for cooler ones. During the whole month of Mokur, offerings of mooah, a sort of sweetmeat to which Krishna was partial in his childhood, are daily offered to Juggurnath. On the last day of the month the ceremony of "Mokur Barah" is performed, by the priests and worshipers walking several times round the temple, preceded by an image of Mudun Mohun (Vishnu), some of them singing the praises of Juggurnath.

DOLO, DOLE JUTTRA, or Swinging festival, is held on the full moon in Falgoon or Chyte, in honour of Krishna. Two images of Krishna (avatars of Vishnu), under the names of Govind and Mudun Mohun, and one of Radha (Luckshmi, or Luckee, as she is called at Pooree), are carried with some state to the Dole Munch, an elevated stone platform, with a beautiful arch of black chlorite in the centre. The arch is about sixteen feet in height; a sort of swing or tray is suspended from iron rings fixed in the pillars of the arch. On this tray the images are placed, and swung to and fro by the attendants, the people making offerings of sweetmeats, flowers, &c. While this is going on at the swing, the image of Juggurnath is clothed with great splendour in the temple, and placed in state to receive the offerings of his votaries. The images are besmeared with "aubeer," the red powder so well known at the Hooli festival in other parts of India.

RAMNOMEE. Rama's birthday festival takes place on the ninth day of the moon in Chyte (March or April), and sometimes in Bysack. Rama, an avatar of Vishnu, destroyed the ten-headed and twenty-handed giant Ravana, which event is commemorated at this festival by carrying about the streets images made of sola, with ten heads and twenty hands, in each of which is a bludgeon. Rama is personified by a man armed with a bow and arrows, who encounters and destroys the image of Ravana. Idols of Rama, his wife Sita, and of Lukun his brother, are carried to Juggurnath Bullub, where the scene of Rama's encounter with Ravana is performed before them; after which, offerings are made, and the idols re-conveyed to the temple.

CHUNDUNA—Sandal-wood festival. Sandal-wood is esteemed particularly pure. This festival commences on the third day of the moon in Bysack (April or May), and sometimes in Joiste continues twenty-one days. Idols of Mudun Mohun (Vishnu), Bala Ram (Krishna), Luckee (Radha), Sarasuttee (Saraswati), and five other inferior deities, are carried every afternoon to the little temple situated in the Chundun Tank, where they are immersed in baths in which sandal-wood has been infused. Vishnu, Radha and Sarasuttee are together in one bath, Krishna and Bala Ram in another, and the rest in a third. While the idols are in their baths, hundreds of people climb up the walls of the temple, and casting themselves headlong into the tank, swim and splash about with great glee, the waters during this time being esteemed peculiarly holy and pure. Alligators are numerous in this tank, but accidents rarely happen on these occasions, owing probably to the noise kept up. In the evening the idols are taken out of the baths and decked by the shevocks (attendant Brahmins) with various sorts of clothes, ornaments and sweet-scented flowers. They are then placed in three boats, in the same order as in the baths, and rowed or pushed with long poles round the tank, after which they are carried to the great temple, preceded by music and dancing-girls, the people making offerings of sandal-wood, flowers and sweetmeats, &c.

Dona Hurran, or Dona Chooree—Stealing the Dona plant *(Artimisia Indica).* The legend attached to this festival is, that Domanuck, one of the asuras—good angels, who are nevertheless engaged in continual warfare—was killed by Juggurnath. When expiring, Domanuck entreated that he might be transformed into the sweet-smelling dona plant. His prayer being granted, he was secretly conveyed by his victor from the midst of the asura's army, and in estimation of his great virtues placed in the head-dress of Juggurnath. In commemoration of this event, this festival is held on the thirteenth day of the moon in Chyte or Bysack (March and April). An idol of Mudun Mohun is carried to Juggurnath Bullub, where the dona plant is preserved. A sprig is secretly broken off, and the next day placed in Juggurnath's head-dress.

JOOLUN JATO. This festival commences on the ninth day of the moon in Shrabun or Bhadur (July and August). Idols of Mudun Gopal (Krishna) and Luckee (Radha) are carried in the evening to a place called Mooktee Mundub, within the enclosure of the temple, where they are swung to and fro until midnight, Moharees dancing and singing before them. The story attached to this festival is that Krishna, when young, and in the character of a herdsman, as a signal to Radha to join him in the fields, commenced playing on the bunsee, a sort of pipe, the divine harmony of which attracted the neighbouring herds around him. The shepherds and shepherdesses commenced dancing and singing, while Krishna and Radha diverted themselves by swinging each other in a swing attached to a tree.

SHYANA, or SOHUN EKADOOSEE. The Lying-down or Sleeping festival continues four months, i.e. from the eleventh day of the moon in Assar (June and July) to the eleventh day of the moon in Kartick (October and November). On the second day of the moon in Assar, the Ruth Jattra commences, and on the ninth day after the idols ought, according to the ceremonial observances of the temple, to have returned from their excursion; but this is rarely the case, as they frequently remain at the Goondicha Noor more than a week. The Sohun Ekadoosee is, notwithstanding, proceeded with in the great temple at the appointed time, by placing small images of Soobudhra (as Brahma), Vishnu (as Juggurnath), and Bulbhudra (as Siva), on a bed in the temple. On the eleventh day of the moon in Bhadra (August and September), the priests turn the idols over on their sides, and again on the eleventh day of the moon in Kartick, when the gods awake, "evidently," says Moor, "alluding to the sun at the solstices." The Sohun Ekadoosee appears to be in some degree a season of humiliation, and by Vaishnobs, i.e. sectaries of Vishnu, is observed by fasting two days and nights in each month, abstaining from particular kinds of food, such as oosnah, or twice-boiled rice, and subsisting chiefly on fruits and arooah rice.

KOJINGARA, or KOONAR POONABEE. The Waking festival is held on the night of the full moon in Aussin, and sometimes in Kartick. Luckshmi is invoked, and the night is passed in playing at games of chance and merriment. The people carefully abstain from sleep, by which means they hope to obtain certain benefits, wealth being the chief. On the same night, though not connected with the festival, Soodursun is carried about on a beebano (a sort of palanquin) by the shevocks, from one quarter to another, thereby conferring a blessing on the neighbourhood.

URANA—GHOR NAGEE—the Warming festival. On the sixth day of the moon in Aughrun (November and December) the idols are dressed in their winter costumes. Twenty-one pieces of cloth are shewn to them, and when approved are consecrated by various ceremonies. They are then put on the idols, and changed several times a day until the fifth day of the moon in Maug, when they assume their spring clothing.

SNAN JATTRA—Bathing festival. This festival takes place on the full moon in Joist (May and June), and sometimes in Assar (June and July). Idols of Juggurnath, Bulbhudra and Soobudhra are carried by the dytahs (bearers of the idols), preceded by music and the sacred canopy called chandoona, to the Snan Moondub, an elevated terrace overlooking the walls of the temple. Here they are exposed to view during the day. Holy water is poured over them in the morning, and their attendants are busily employed in fanning them, and waving chowries to keep off the flies and mosquitoes. After bathing, the idol of Juggurnath is made to assume the form of Gunness, by placing on it the figure of an elephant's head. The reason of this transformation probably arose from the desire of the priests to entice all classes and sectaries to the shrine of Juggurnath. The legend here runs that many pilgrims who visit Juggurnath expressed their disappointment at not seeing their favourite Gunness, exclaiming that this was not their god. Juggurnath then desired them to look upon him again, when, lo! he had assumed the form of the elephant-headed god, Gunness. In the evening the head is taken off, and the idols are conveyed to a room called "Unsur," where they are reported to be ill for several days. During this time no persons except the dytahs and pullee mahapatturs are allowed to see them. The true reason of the seclusion of the idols is, that the dytahs and pullee mahapatturs are busily engaged in re-painting and adorning them, preparatory to the approaching festival of the Ruth Jattra.

The Ruth Jattra, or Car festival, commences on the second day of the new moon in Assar (June and July), and sometimes in Shrabun (July and August). This is the great festival to which pilgrims flock from the remotest parts of India. Three new cars or "Ruths" are built for the idols every year. Juggurnath's Ruth is 46½ feet in height. It has sixteen wheels, 6½ feet in diameter. The two other Ruths are a little smaller, and have respectively fourteen and twelve wheels, 6½ feet in diameter. All the cars are covered with coarse broadcloth, in strips of green, blue, red and yellow, decorated with tinsel in the most tawdry manner. They are seldom completed until late in the day on which they are required. They are all drawn up in line near to the gate of lions. The tops of the neighbouring houses and the walls of the temple are crowded with spectators. Extending half-way down the street is a sea of waving heads. Here and there amongst the crowd are seen the elephants attached to the temple, covered with scarlet trappings, and mounted by men bearing long streamers or standards. At a time varying from three to six o'clock p.m., after certain ceremonies have been performed in the temple, the idols are brought forth, amidst astounding shouts of "Jye Juggurnath, swamy ke jye!"—Victory to Juggurnath our Lord—as a glimpse is caught of the unwieldy logs pitching and tossing amongst the crowd. A rope is tied round the neck of Juggurnath, and by this he is pulled up the inclined plane leading to the platform of the car, numbers of people pushing and shoving behind, some even beating the wooden god to make him exert himself, being so very heavy. The idols are mere clumsy logs, about five feet in height, with a rude and hideous representation of a face painted on the upper part, the lower part being swathed in clothes. Juggurnath's face is painted black, with a large red mouth, and white circles for the eyes. The face of Bulbhudra is painted white, and that of Soobudhra yellow; but little notice is taken of the latter, Juggurnath being the principal attraction. After the idols have been placed on their respective cars, the golden arms and feet are carried up, but are not fastened on until the next day. A scarlet-coloured silk scarf is wound round the body of Juggurnath, and a tawdry sort of head-dress is put on. Crowds of people rush up the inclined plane to touch the idol; many of them are pushed down by the attendant priests, and the rattan is by no means sparingly used to keep off the crowd. However, the poor creatures, many of whom have travelled a thousand or more miles to see Juggurnath, are not likely to mind a few blows, if they can obtain the object of their dearest wishes by touching the great idol. The platforms of the cars are swept, and sandal-wood water sprinkled on them by the Khoordah Rajah, who receives as a distinguishing reward the head-dresses of Juggurnath and Bulbhudra, and a garland of flowers from Soobudhra. The wooden horses are then attached to the cars, and in due time, when, as the priests allege, it is the pleasure of Juggurnath to move, the coolies, called kalabetias, who are allowed certain immunities for the performance of the duty, seize the immense cables attached to the cars, and at a given signal advance a few yards, amidst the acclamations of the crowd; the charioteers of the gods flogging the wooden horses, shouting and performing a number of obscene gestures, to the great entertainment of the people. Respectable females, closely muffled up, may be seen to place a hand on the car behind, in hopes of meriting the approbation of the god by thus accelerating his journey. The progress made towards the Goondicha Noor (commonly called Juggurnath's country-house) varies each day according to the state of the road, number and zeal of the pilgrims and coolies, or, as the priests say, according to the pleasure of the god. However, the time occupied in progress to the Goondicha Noor (a distance of a mile and a half) is generally three or four days. On the fifth day, an image of Luckee (Luckshmi), Juggurnath's wife, is carried from the temple to the car, around which she strews mustard-seed, at least the priests do it for her, and ends by breaking off a piece of the car, hoping by these charms to expedite the god's return. She is then carried back to the temple. The other idols remain at the Goondicha Noor five or six days, receiving the worship and offerings of devotees. On the ninth day from the commencement of the festival, the idols are replaced on the cars; but this is a distinct festival, called Bahorah, or Returning festival. Archdeacon Currie, describing this festival in 1823, says that "on the occasion of a partial insurrection about two years since, the priests gave out that Juggurnath would no longer suffer the English to remain in India, and would not return to his temple (on quitting it at the annual festival) till they were expelled, and mentioned a certain day for their overthrow. This was justly considered by the General commanding the district as an attempt to aid the insurgents against the Government; and he sent a private order to the officer in charge here" (Pooree), "that if the idol were not carried back as usual on the stated day, he should replace it by force, and take military possession of the temple. The natives about the General no doubt gave notice to the priests, and Juggurnath returned before his time." Well done, General Thomas! for that was his name.

Bahorah, or Returning festival, is sometimes called the "Ooltah Ruth." On the ninth day from the commencement of the Ruth Jattra, the images, after various ceremonies, are replaced on their respective cars, and commence their return to the temple. Many more days are occupied in returning from than in going to the Goondicha Noor. Almost all the pilgrims and many of the coolies have left the town, so that it is sometimes with great difficulty the cars are dragged back again. At the returning festival in 1842, the cars were entirely deserted by the kalabetias, who had all returned to their homes. The Khoordah Rajah in person, assisted by the inhabitants of Pooree, dragged the cars to the temple. Such an event had never before occurred. On the arrival of the cars at the Sing Dwara, the temple gates are found closed, Luckshmi being angry at her lord's long absence. Juggurnath, by means of his attendant priests, knocks at the door. "Who are you?" inquires a female voice from within (a Nautch girl representing Juggurnath's wife). "I am Juggurnath!" is the response. "Then you shall not come in," says the wife. "You have been enjoying yourself, and gallivanting in such a place." The god assures her that it is a scandalous report. "But I have proof of what I say;" and adds that she had broken off a piece of his car to convict him on his return, &c. After a little more of this silly conversation, the priests of Juggurnath on one side of the gate, and the attendant Nautch girls on the other, abusing each other in the most opprobrious terms, a peace-offering, in the shape of a tray of jewels, is sent in to the wife, who then consents to admit Juggurnath, and so ends the festival. Many of the other ceremonies, if such they can be called, are equally puerile and absurd. It is said that they are modern inventions.

Gumma Poonimah, or Rakee Poonimah. "Gumma" relates to the worship of cows; "Poonimah," the full moon; "Rakee," is a sort of consecrated thread tied on the arms of worshipers by the Brahmins. This festival is held on the full moon in Shrabun (July and August), or the following month. At the end of each moon, and at full moon, it is considered meritorious to give alms to Brahmins. On some occasions, however, it is thought more especially meritorious, as at this festival, when the Brahmins, reciting certain muntras (prayers), tie a rakee round the arms or wrists of devotees, exhorting them at the same time to be as charitable as Rajah Bullee or Maha Beli, who, as the story says, when possessed of the universe, gave heaven and earth to a Brahmin dwarf (Vishnu, in his avatar of Vamana, the dwarf). The

Brahmins only bestow their blessings and threads on those who can pay for them; a few pice, however, are sufficient if the man has no more. The owners of a bull or cow worship them on this day. The bull represents Mahadev, and the cow, Luckshmi. The animals are bathed, or their feet only are washed. Sandal-wood water is sprinkled over their heads, wreaths of flowers hung round their necks and on their horns, and some sweetmeats given them to eat. Offerings of gumma mundah (cakes composed of cocoa-nut, flour and kullae) are made to Juggurnath, Bulbhudra and Soobudhra. At night, Soodursun, entirely covered with silk clothes, is carried to the Jonee Mundeea, a raised terrace in one of the streets of the town, where various ceremonies are performed, offerings made and blessings entreated; after which, Soodursun (all this time invisible) is re-conveyed to the temple.

KALEEA DOBUN—Killing the Snake Kaleea. This festival is held on the eleventh day of the moon in Bhadra (August and September), and sometimes in the preceding month, in celebration of the death of Krishna by the snake Kaleea, his restoration to life, and subsequent victory over the reptile. An idol of Mudun Gopal (Krishna) is carried from the temple to the Markund tank, where it is placed in the small temple overlooking the water. Previous to this, a long and narrow boat is covered with red cloth to represent the body of the snake, and at the prow a piece of sola (the pith of a water-plant) four feet in diameter and painted chequerwise, represents its head. On a platform, erected in the tank for the occasion, lies extended one of the priests, who is supposed to be sleeping, personifying Krishna. His body is covered with a wet cloth, which, from time to time, the pretended sleeper moistens with water by means of a bunch of leaves, which he dips into the tank and sprinkles over his body. The boat is pushed round the tank several times by two men at the stern, each time approaching nearer to the platform; while another man, stationed behind the head of the snake, nods it backwards and forwards, in the manner of a snake about to spring on its prey; the boat at the same time advancing and retreating, until at last it is suddenly pushed up to the platform amidst the shouts of the people. A sort of wild-fire or fuse is lighted, and the sparks fall on the body of the sleeper (which, however, is protected by the wet cloth). This is intended to represent the bite of the snake, and the man feigns death. After some time, a figure dressed up with wings and a yellow mask with a huge beaked nose, to represent Garuda (the vahan of Vishnu), is conveyed in a boat to the platform, and restores the pretended Krishna to life, which he evinces by cutting a summersault off the platform, and swimming ashore. The idol is then carried back to the temple, where the very remarkable ceremony of the destruction of the snake by Krishna is performed. The idol of Juggurnath, representing Krishna, is dressed out with an artificial snake twined round the body; the head of the snake being crushed beneath the foot of the idol—a singular coincidence (to say the least) to the latter part of the 15th verse in the 3rd chapter of Genesis.

MAHA JOIST—the great month of Joist. This festival occurs only once in two centuries, on some particular conjunction of the sun, moon and nakshatras (mansions of the moon). The Snan, or Bathing festival, occurs, on this occasion, at the same time; and the idol of Juggurnath is bathed with sea-water instead of fresh, as at other seasons. The water is not actually poured over the idol, but over the reflected image in a large mirror, composed of silver and bell-metal highly polished, and placed opposite the idol.

A pilgrimage to the shrine of Juggurnath at the Maha Joist festival, is called Jaeg Aswamedh (sacrifice of a horse). No mortal, it is said, can really perform Jaeg Aswamedh. Brahma performed Dus Aswamedh, or sacrifice of ten horses near Cuttack, on which occasion all the gods assisted. The merits derivable from Brahma's work, are supposed to be conferred on pilgrims to the shrine of Juggurnath at this season. The merit is in proportion to the difficulties they have encountered by the way. Thus one day's journey is equal to one aswamedh; ten days' journey to ten aswamedh; and so on. The expected benefits are entirely in a future state. A man performing 108 aswamedh becomes after death equal to Indra, and is absorbed in the Deity. Colebrook, writing on the Vedas, says that the aswamedha "is not really a sacrifice of horses. In the white yajush (Yajur Veda) the ceremony is directed to be performed in this manner." "Six hundred and nine animals of various kinds, domestic and wild, including birds, fish and reptiles, are made fast; the tame ones to twenty-one posts, and the wild ones in the intervals between the pillars; and after certain prayers have been recited, the victims are let loose without injury." The story here is, that Indra, the lord of the heavens, or, according to others, Brahma, loosed a fleet horse to run round the world, and forbade any one to stop him. On the return of the horse, all the gods were invited to assist at his sacrifice; after which, he was again restored to life, and pursued his course round the world,—an evident allusion to the completion of one cycle and commencement of another. The horse in this instance may be considered to represent the sun.

I was a witness to this festival in 1840, when it was computed that 250,000 pilgrims were present,—a far greater number than usually visit Juggurnath at any other time.

On the sixth day of the moon in Bhadra (August and September), certain castes, such as Sonars, Kyeths, Kunsaries, and some Brahmins, &c., worship Munsa, the goddess of snakes, and entreat her protection from these reptiles. The usual cooking place of the family is purified and plastered with cow-dung. The figures of eight snakes are painted thereon, with a whitewash composed of powdered rice and water. A branch of the munsa sij *(euphorbia ligularia)*, the leaves of which are marked with seendurs (spots of vermilion colour), and sprinkled with sandal-wood water, is stuck up in the fire-place. Offerings and prayers are then made through the officiating Brahmin to Munsa, "who, while Vishnu and all the gods were sleeping, sat in the shape of a serpent on a branch of the munsa sig, to preserve mankind from the venom of snakes." The Khoordah Rajah, and some others, instead of performing the above ceremony, worship a living cobra di capello in the month of Kartick.

In the small temple of Lokenath, a short distance from Pooree, a festival called the SIBOO RATTREE, is annually held at midnight in honour of Siva. A lingam and golden serpent are also worshiped in this temple.

At midnight, on the seventh, eighth and ninth day of the moon in Aussin (September and October), and sometimes in Kartick, sheep are, with pretended secrecy, sacrificed to Bimola (a form of Kalee) in the little temple dedicated to that goddess within the outer enclosure of the temple of Juggurnath.

Once a year, a festival is held in honour of SARASUTTEE,

the goddess of knowledge. The Naeks, who are also astrologers and schoolmasters, prepare cocoa-nuts, on which are painted pictures of Juggurnath, Gunness (the god of wisdom) and Sarasuttee. The latter is represented with four arms. In one hand is a style or pen, in another a book, in the third a sitar—for she is also the goddess of music—the fourth hand is expanded, to signify that the blessings of knowledge are open to all. Near her is a centipede, which is said to be her vahan or vehicle. When the image is prepared, a priest is sometimes called in to consecrate it, or the schoolmaster himself recites appropriate muntras, and afterwards conveys it to the temple of Gunness, when a priest approaches, who touches the head of Gunness with the newly-painted image of Sarasuttee, from which act the latter is supposed to derive a portion of the god's wisdom. The Naek then returns to the school with his image, when flowers are strewn over it by the boys, who, breaking a cocoa-nut, each pours the water on the ground as a libation to Sarasuttee, and entreats that she will be propitious towards them. When all is prepared, the boys, accompanied by the schoolmaster, each with a painted cocoa-nut placed on an artificial white lotus, as an emblem of Sarasuttee, in his hand, and one of them bearing the image itself, proceed in a body to the houses of their respective friends, where they sing some verses from the Bandoee Neetee and Bandoee Hurree Purans, in praise of Sarasuttee; in return for which, it is customary for the friends of the lads to bestow presents on the schoolmaster. This festival lasts fifteen days; and when concluded, the painted cocoa-nuts are thrown into a river or tank. Apart from the superstition attending them, these processions of children have a very pleasing effect. The boys are crowned with flowers, and decked out with all their finery—some with yellow, crimson, white, or other bright-coloured dresses, with wreaths of flowers and golden ornaments round their necks, and each bearing in his hand a gaily painted, gilded cocoa-nut, on a large white lotus flower formed of sola, the whole surmounted with a string of flowers, a bird or other device. Groups of ten or twelve little fellows thus attired, and with happy, smiling faces, may daily be seen traversing the streets of Pooree during the festival.

On the tenth day of the moon in Aussin (September and October), is held a festival called DOSOHARA, when the people, with the assistance of a Brahmin, perform certain ceremonies and worship the instruments of their labour. Thus the carpenter worships his hammer, the mason his trowel, and the Maentee, or writer caste, worships a pen, a book, and an inkstand. Offerings are made to Kalee, Doorga, and other deities. Blacksmiths, carpenters, and some other artificers, make offerings to Viswakarma (the architect of the gods). These ceremonies appear to be an offering of gratitude to the gods, through the instruments by which the people have obtained a livelihood during the past year, and also beseeching a blessing on their labours during the ensuing one.

There are seventy-nine other annual festivals, but the most important of all are the Snan and Ruth Jattra. It is on these occasions only that the idol of Juggurnath is exhibited to the numerous class called "Neechee Jato," or low-caste people, who are never admitted into the temple, but must content themselves at other seasons by bathing in the five holy waters, viz. the Chundun, Markund, Indradumun and Seetagunga tanks, and Soomsdur (the sea), and by making offerings through the priests. A sight of Juggurnath is of course eagerly desired by these people, as whatever crimes a man may have committed, even to the killing of a cow or a Brahmin, all are expiated by a sight of Juggurnath, and the soul after death is absorbed in the Deity.

CHAPTER X.

Encamped under a Magnificent Banyan-tree—Walk by Torch-light—Up and down the Sand-hills to the Chundul—Festival in honour of the Sun—Singular Scene—My Tents pitched near the Black Pagoda—Departure of the Pilgrims—Return Home—Legend attached to the Festival—Stirling's Description of the Black Pagoda—State of the Black Pagoda at my last Visit.

ON the 30th of January, 1836, I was encamped under a magnificent banyan-tree at Karkutpore, a few miles from the famous Black Pagoda. The extended branches of this tree, supported by numerous down shoots, covered a space of ground one hundred and eighty measured yards in circumference. I have read of much larger trees of the kind. There is one on an island in the Nerbudda, twelve miles from Broach. Ten thousand cavalry, it is said, might find shelter under its branches. In comparison with this, the Karkutpore tree is but a butcha (young one); nevertheless, it is a noble tree, and the largest I have seen in Orissa. Next day, I visited the salt aurungs* about the Davee river; and on the 1st of February, at 4 a.m., set off by torch-light to walk to the Chundul, where the annual festival in honour of the sun takes place. Our proper course was south-west, but we went due west for some distance, then took a turn north, and another east, until we were brought up by a thick hedge. Having a pocket-compass, I noted the various turnings we had made, and approaching a hedge,

* Places where salt is manufactured.

saw that the guide was at fault. I said nothing, however; and off he started again, taking us trotting about for an hour, and evidently going back to the place whence we came, yet he would not confess that he knew nothing of our whereabouts. At last I lost patience, and, dismissing the guide, undertook, with the aid of my pocket-compass and the stars, to steer for the road myself. Away we went, up and down sand-hills, at a swinging pace, for fear of being too late to witness the sun's rising, of which there was considerable doubt, owing to the time we had lost. After pursuing our course for a couple of miles, we stumbled on the road, such as it was, still up and down across the sands, which were marked in every direction by the hoofs of antelopes, but we saw none of them, as they had been frightened away by the people flocking to the sacred water. After a most harassing tramp, with shoes full of sand, for about six miles, we heard the shouting of thousands of people, and on ascending a sand-hill just before sunrise, the whole spectacle was before us. Imagine a piece of fresh water, several hundred yards in length and about fifty in breadth, surrounded by sand-hills and separated from the sea by a sand-bank, some thirty or forty yards wide. One mile and a half to the north-west was seen the Black Pagoda towering through the mist of the early morning. The sand-banks surrounding the sacred water were crowded with men, women and children, tattoos, palkees, &c.,—some people praying in the shallow sea on the rising of the sun, others praying in the fresh water when his beams overtopped the banks,—tom-toms (native drums) beating and horns blowing,—some people dressed in red, some in yellow, some in white, and some in nature's russet brown, with the exception of a cloth round the loins. On one hand was the Khoordah Rajah, with his gilded chattah and torass (a sort of standard) borne aloft; on the other, a parcel of lazy byraghees, all squalidness and filth;—imagine all these jumbled together, and you may form some idea of the scene. No habitation was visible, excepting the temporary straw mats of the pilgrims slung across a pole,—all around a perfect desert,—and in this spot were collected from twelve to fifteen thousand people. After performing their ablutions and prayers, the tide of people turned towards the Black Pagoda, and away they went in a long, straggling column, singing and shouting with all their might. When they arrived at the temple, they appeared to amuse themselves more by scrambling about the ruins than by praying.

By this time my tents had arrived, and were pitched a short distance from the temple. I amused myself for some time watching the crowds of people. Gradually they went away, and by noon not one of the numerous and noisy crowd remained, but all had departed, leaving the ruins again in solitude. The silence of the place, contrasted with the recently animated scene, was then almost oppressive. Occasionally the booming of the sea might be heard, or a bird seen to flit across the jungle; but other moving object there was none, out of my own camp and a little temple near by. At sunset, after taking a sketch of the ruins, I struck my tents and marched to Pooree, where I arrived about nine o'clock p.m., and never enjoyed a bottle of cool claret more in my life, for the day had been a most fatiguing one.

The legend attached to the foregoing ceremony, called the Chunda Vagah, is, that Rama Chundra (a descendant of Surya, or the Sun), in his pursuit of Ravanna, stopped to bathe and perform the "turpun" (offering of water to the manes of ancestors, or to the gods) in this place. Hence the waters, on the anniversary of his visit, are considered so pure and holy, that one day's bathing therein at this season is deemed equal to twelve years' daily ablution in the Ganges. The auspicious moment is when the people, standing in the water and holding some in the palms of their hands, first catch a glimpse of the rising sun, when the air resounds with their acclamations. I have since visited the ruins of the Black Pagoda many times, and will here transcribe what the accurate Mr. Stirling says about them, in preference to any description of my own.

"The Jagmohan, or ante-chamber, is the only part of the building which exists in tolerably good preservation. The great tower has been shattered and thrown down by some extraordinary force, either of an earthquake or lightning, and in its fall seems to have injured that side of the adjoining edifice which looks towards it. A small section, however, still remains standing, about one hundred and twenty feet in height, which, viewed from a distance, gives to the ruin a singular appearance, something resembling that of a ship under sail. The whole of the outer enclosures of the temple have long since disappeared, and nothing is left of the edifice called the Bhog Mandap, but a heap of ruin completely buried under a sand-hill.

"The Black Pagoda, even in its present imperfect and dilapidated condition, presents a highly curious and beautiful specimen of the ancient Hindu temple architecture; and as it has long been completely deserted, we may here study at leisure and without interruption some of the most striking peculiarities of the style. The deity of the place is called by the vulgar, Sooruj Deo (Surga), and at full length, Chunder Sooruj Birinji Náráyan. The origin of the worship of a divinity so little honoured in India, generally speaking, is ascribed to Sámba, the son of Krishna, who, having been afflicted with leprosy and banished from his father's court at Dwarka, as a punishment for accidentally looking in upon the nymphs of the palace whilst sporting naked in the water, was cured at this spot by the sun, to whose service he in gratitude raised a temple.

"The present edifice was built by Raja Langora Narsinh Deo, A.D. 1241, under the superintendence of his minister Shibai Suntra. . . . . The natives of the neighbourhood have a strange fable to account for its desertion. They relate that a kumbha pathar, or loadstone of immense size, was formerly lodged on the summit of the great tower, which had the effect of drawing ashore all vessels near the coast. The inconvenience of this was so much felt, that about two centuries since, in the Mogul time, the crew of a ship landed at a distance, and stealing down the coast, attacked the tower and carried off the loadstone. The priests, alarmed at this violation of the sanctity of the place, removed the image of the god, with all his paraphernalia, to Púri, where they have ever since remained. . . . .

"The wall which formed the outer enclosure may have measured 250 yards on a side; within this was a second enclosure, having three entrances, called the Aswa or Horse, the Hasti or Elephant, and the Sinha or Lion gate, from the colossal figures of those animals which surmounted the several side-posts. The horses and elephants, in the north and south, have long since been precipitated from their bases; but the lions, or rather griffins, still retain the attitude and position assigned to them by Abulfazl, except that they are standing, instead of sitting, on the bodies of elephants, and have one paw lifted in the act of striking. . . . .

"From the eastern gate of the inner enclosure, a flight of ruined steps leads to the only tolerably perfect part of the building now remaining, called the Jagmohan, or Ante-chamber of the Sanctuary. No one, certainly, can behold the massive beams of iron, and the prodigious blocks of stone used in constructing this edifice, without being struck with amazement. The ground plan is a square, measuring sixty feet on a side, or if we take in the four projecting doorways, it should rather be called a cross. The walls rise to a height of sixty feet, and have in some parts the unusual thickness of twenty feet. They support a noble and curiously constructed pyramidal roof, the stones composing which overhang each other, in the manner of inverted stairs, until they approach near enough towards the summit to support iron beams laid across, on which rests a prodigious mass of solid masonry, forming the head-piece or crowning ornament. The slope measures about seventy-two feet, and perpendicular height, sixty-three or sixty-four. The total altitude of the building, from the floor to the summit, is about one hundred feet, or a little more. The outside of the roof is divided into three tiers of steps, formed by slabs projecting curiously from the body of the building, which are all bordered with a very fine pattern of elephants, birds, and various figures, executed with considerable skill and spirit. Each of the terraces between the tiers is decorated with statues of nymphs and heavenly choristers, dancing and playing upon sundry instruments, but with countenances expressing very little passion or feeling of any kind. The third story has the usual mythological animals, more nearly resembling lions than anything else, which support on their shoulders the outer rim of the huge turban-shaped ornament on the top; besides these, there is a four-headed statue over each of the doorways, the crowns and sceptres of which mark them as intended to represent the majesty of Brahma.

"Each face of the Jagmohan has a fine rectangular doorway, with a porch projecting considerably beyond, and lined with superb slabs of the grey indurated chlorite, many of which measure fifteen feet high by a breadth of six or eight feet. The architrave of the doorway, as well as the roof of the passage leading to the interior, and an enormous mass of masonry resting upon it, are supported by nine iron beams, nearly a foot square by twelve or eighteen long, which are laid across the side-ways in the most rude and inartificial manner. The whole fabric is held together by clamps of the same metal, and there is no appearance of any cement having been made use of. . . .

"One cannot but wonder at the ease with which the architects seem to have wielded and managed the cumbersome masses of iron and stone used for the work, in an age when so little aid was to be derived from any mechanical inventions;

and it must be allowed that there is an air of elegance, combined with massiveness, in the whole structure, which entitles it to no small share of admiration. There is much, however, about this remarkable building which it is difficult to describe or comprehend. The interior is filled, to a height of several feet, with large blocks of stone, which seem to have fallen from above. Amongst the heap are to be seen two iron beams, measuring twenty-one feet in length by about eight inches square, absolutely crushed beneath a superincumbent mass of stone, many of the blocks composing which measure fifteen and sixteen feet in length, by about six feet of depth and two or three of thickness. . . .

"The exterior of the side walls, as of the roof, is loaded with a profusion of the richest sculptured ornaments. A remarkably handsome cornice or border occupies the upper part all round, for a depth of several feet. Below this, the surface is divided by another fine cornice into two tiers of compartments, parted off into niches by clusters of pilasters, in each of which are placed figures of men and animals, resting on pedestals, with a sort of canopy overhead. The human figures are generally male and female, in the most lewd and obscene attitudes. Amongst the animals, the commonest representation is that of a lion rampant treading on an elephant or a prostrate human figure. Generally speaking, the style and execution of the larger figures are rude and coarse, whilst the smaller ones display often much beauty and grace; but it should be observed that the whole have suffered materially from the corrosion or decomposition of the stone of which the building is chiefly composed, viz. the coarse red granite of the province, which is singularly liable to decay from exposure to the weather.

"The skill and labour of the best artists seem to have been reserved for the finely polished slabs of chlorite, which line and decorate the outer faces of the doorways. The whole of the sculpture on these figures, comprising men and animals, foliage and arabesque patterns, is executed with a degree of taste, propriety and freedom, which would stand a comparison with some of our best specimens of Gothic architectural ornament.

The workmanship remains, too, as perfect as if it had just come from under the chisel of the sculptor, owing to the extreme hardness and durability of the stone. A triangular niche, over each doorway, was once filled with a figure cut in alto relievo, emblematic of the deity of the place, being that of a youth in a sitting posture holding in each hand a stalk of the true lotus, or *nelumbium speciosum*, the expanded flowers of which are turned towards him. Each architrave has, as usual, the nava graha, or nine Brahminical planets, very finely sculptured in alto relievo. Five of them are well proportioned figures of men, with mild and pleasing countenances, crowned with high pointed caps, and seated cross-legged on the padma (*nelumbium speciosum*), engaged in religious meditation; one hand bears a vessel of water, and the fingers of the other are counting over the beads of a rosary which hangs suspended. The form of the planet which presides over Thursday (Vrihaspati, or Jupiter), is distinguished from the others by a flowing majestic beard. Friday, or Venus, is a youthful female, with a plump, well-rounded figure. Ketu, the descending node, is a triton, whose body ends in the tail of a fish or dragon; and Rahu, or the ascending node, a monster all head and shoulders, with a grinning, grotesque countenance, frizzly hair dressed like a full-blown wig, and one immense canine tooth projecting from the upper jaw; in one hand he holds a hatchet, and in the other a fragment of the moon. These are, doubtless, the 'sun and stars' mentioned by the author of the Ayin Acberi. Why they occupy, so uniformly, a position over the doorway of every temple in Orissa, sacred to whatever deity, I have never been able to learn.

"The walls of the interior are, as usual with Hindu temples, entirely plain and devoid of ornament, but each of the projecting steps in the square pyramidal roof has been curiously rounded, and formed into a sort of cornice, which gives a slight finish to that part of the building. From the fragments remaining of the great tower, it would seem to have been covered with rich and varied sculptured ornaments, in the style of the Bhovaneswar temple. Like all edifices of the kind, too, it had evidently an inner false roof, of pyramidal shape, formed of inverted stairs, used by the old architects of the province as a substitute for the arch."

Since Mr. Stirling wrote the foregoing account of the Black Pagoda, corresponding pretty closely with the state in which I found it in 1836, the building has become still more dilapidated, partly by the operation of time, but more so by the removal of stones by the natives.

On the occasion of my last visit to the temple in 1845, I found that only one of the lions retained its altitude. Two of the porches or doorways had been almost entirely destroyed for the sake of the slabs of grey chlorite with which they were lined. A considerable number of the finely sculptured figures and arabesques still remained about the principal doorway, but even they were undergoing rapid demolition by the Khoordah Rajah, who was desirous of taking them to Pooree, until a stop was put to the work of destruction by order of Government (as the ruin was a well-known landmark for seamen), but not before the Rajah had caused to be pulled down the Nava Graha mentioned by Stirling. They are sculptured on a single block of grey chlorite, measuring nearly twenty feet in length, and averaging, the sides being unequal, about four feet square. Such difficulty was experienced in getting this immense mass down, that some of the figures were damaged, and one of the workmen (pity 'twasn't the Rajah!) killed by the fall of the scaffolding. This stone lies prostrate on the other ruins. The iron beams still remain. One of them measures twenty-two feet nine inches in length, and ten inches square.

Bears and porcupines frequent the ruins of the Temple of the Sun, and the interior of the Jagmohan is occupied by bats and pigeons. I only saw the excrements of bears, but picked up some quills of the "fretful porcupine." A small and insignificant temple, dedicated to Surya (the sun), stands about a hundred yards distant, contrasting strongly with the magnificent ruins of the other. No houses or habitations of any kind (save the little temple just mentioned), are visible from the Black Pagoda, although the village of Kunnaruck is only a mile off, but the ruined temple stands alone in its desolation, surrounded by sand-hills and jungle.

CHAPTER XI.

Excursion to Bhovaneswar—Stirling's Description of the City and Temples of Bhovaneswar—Ruins of Palaces—Superb Tank—Caves in the Sand-stone Hills—Temple of Parasnath and Jain Remains—Palace of Lala Indra Kesari—Ancient Inscriptions in the Sand-stone Rock—Remarkable Statue—Similarity of the Hindoo and Egyptian Mythology—Worship of the Serpent—Hieroglyphics of Egypt—Table of Abydos—Attempts to Spiritualize the Egyptian Mythology—Hindoos stooping to kiss the Feet of the Brahmins—Egyptian Priests—Hindoo Chronology—Institutes of Menu—Sudras.

My next excursion into the district was to the celebrated temples at Bhobaneser or Bhovaneswar, forty miles due north of Pooree. I had heard a great deal about these temples, and was not disappointed when I saw them. Bhovaneswar is indeed the most extraordinary place I have ever seen. There are scores upon scores of deserted temples buried in the jungle, and only an insignificant village in the neighbourhood. The natives say that there were 999 temples; and truly, after what I saw, I am inclined to admit that they have some reason for the assertion. While standing on the ruins of one temple, I could count upwards of fifty others; and on proceeding further into the jungle, I was astonished at the numbers which one after another opened to the view as we passed along. Enormous monkeys, leaping from branch to branch of the overhanging trees, advanced, grinning, within a few feet of us, and shaking the boughs, seemed inclined to dispute our progress. We saw no other living animals, though leopards and bears are not uncommon in the more remote jungle.

Some of the temples are in good preservation, and not more than thirty or forty feet in height; but many are considerably more than that. The temple of Vasadeo and some others are one hundred and fifty feet high; and that of the Ling Raj is, from the ground to the top of the tower, two hundred feet in height, and richly ornamented in arabesque and curious devices to its very summit. This tower is, indeed, a noble structure; that of Juggurnath in Pooree, though of nearly the same size, appears a paltry affair in comparison; the one is a highly artistic building, while the other is quite the reverse, and seems such as any ordinary stonemason might construct.

Of the ancient city of Bhovaneswar but few traces remain, nearly the whole being overgrown with jungle. On a subsequent visit I spent several days amongst the ruined and deserted temples, making sketches of the most noteworthy, at least of those I saw, for there are many in the dense jungle which I did not see. Only three or four of the temples are in use at this day for religious purposes, but some miserable beggars have taken up their residence in the ruins of others. Pitying these poor creatures, shivering in the cold morning air, with scarcely a rag to cover them, I offered some of them employment in my gardens at Pooree; but, no! they preferred their wretchedness and rags; so I left them.

Opposite one of the temples I found a beautiful arch, which I sketched while sitting in the entrance of the temple. Arches are frequently seen near the temples of Orissa, but I have never seen any so elegant as this. These arches are used to support a swinging tray, on which the idols are placed at the Dole Jattra, or Swinging festival.

While standing amongst these deserted temples, imagination re-peopled them with teeming crowds, and white-robed priests ascending to worship. I indeed saw some women strewing flowers on the lingam (phallus) in front of one of the temples. The present priests are a squalid set of fellows.

It seemed strange to think that these temples were erected at a period when England was, as compared with the present time, in a semi-barbarous state, and by people whom we in our days are accustomed to consider as little better than barbarians; however, such as they are now, they have been for more than two thousand years. Strange, too, it seems at first sight, that, having made such progress in the arts of civilization, they should have advanced no further; but the accursed system of caste has bound them in unchangeable fetters.

One cannot but be struck with the grossly sensual character of the religion of the Oorias; as witness these temples of Bhovaneswar, where the yoni and lingam are to be found in front of them all. The more intelligent Brahmins say that they worship Mahadeo in the form of a lingam, but the more ignorant and vast majority of the people only see the impure object presented to their view, and it is this that they worship. One of the devotees of Juggurnath, who occasionally paid me a visit, explained that he did not worship the idols, which were only wood or stone, but the great God who was everywhere. I shewed him the frontispiece of Moor's Hindoo Pantheon, where the mysterious and sacred syllable *Aum* is found, and asked him what it was, and how to pronounce it. He tried to evade the subject, but on my pressing him, he said that it was the name of God, and after looking cautiously round to ascertain if we were quite alone, he whispered the dread word, and seemed somewhat afraid at what he had done.

I will now quote Mr. Stirling's interesting description of Bhovaneswar and the temples, feeling assured that I could not do such justice to the subject myself.

"Bhobanéser was the site of a capital city founded by Raja Lala Indra Kesari, the third of the princes bearing that surname, who reigned from A.D. 617 to A.D. 660. If we are to judge of its extent and populousness, during the period that it formed the seat of government of the Rajas of the Kesari Vansa, from the countless multitude of temples which are crowded within the sacred limits of the Panj Kosi, we might pronounce it to have been, in the days of its splendour, one of the greatest cities which India ever saw. Standing near the chief pagoda, one cannot turn the eye, in any direction, without taking into view upwards of forty or fifty of these stone towers. The natives say that there were originally more than seven thousand places of worship consecrated to Mahádeo, within and around the city of Bhobanéser, containing no less than a crore (million) of lingams, and the vestiges that remain fully warrant a belief that the place may have comprised some *hundreds* of buildings of this description, when in its most flourishing state. . . . .

"Nor is the astonishing number of the Bhobanéser temples the only remarkable feature of the place. The style, size and decoration of these singular buildings add greatly to the wonder and interest of the scene. They are all constructed, either of reddish granite resembling sand-stone or else of the free-stone yielded plentifully by the neighbouring hills, in the form of towers rounded towards the summit, with other edifices attached rising from a square enclosure, the wall encompassing which is now generally in ruins. Their height is never less than fifty or sixty feet" [I saw some much less than that], "and the loftier towers reach to an elevation of from one hundred and fifty to one hundred and eighty feet. Not a wooden beam, it may be observed, has been used throughout. The stones are held together with iron clamps. Iron beams and pillars are used where such aids could not be dispensed with, but in general the architects have resorted, in the construction of their roofs, to the method of laying horizontal layers of stone projecting one beyond the other like inverted steps, until the sides approach sufficiently near at the summit to admit of other blocks being placed across. The exterior surface of the buildings is in general adorned with the richest and most elaborate sculptured ornament, and the ruined courts which surround them are strewed with a vast variety of curious relics, as bulls, lingams and other symbols appropriate to the worship of Mahádeo, representations of Ganésá, Hanumán, and various forms of Siva and Parvatí, Durga, or Kali, Carticeya, the god of war, with his peacock, the female or energy of the same, called Caumárí, and the Narsinha and Báman Avatars. The more finished temples have frequently large well-polished slabs of the grey chlorite slate or pot-stone, let into three of their sides, on which are sculptured, in alto relievo, nearly as large as life, some of the above personages, executed with no mean degree of skill and symmetry. Carved in the coarser stone of which the walls are constructed, one observes figures of Apsarasas, or dancing nymphs, in groups or solitary; forms of Maháдeo and Parvatí sitting or standing together, generally in the most obscene attitudes; representations of warriors, horses and elephants, engaged in combat or arranged in state processions; monsters resembling lions, with grim grotesque countenances, in various attitudes; and groups of a peaceful character exhibiting a muni, or philosopher, imparting instruction to his pupils. The architrave of the doorway of every temple in Orissa is ornamented with the nine figures in a sitting posture, called the Nava Graha, or nine planets, of which seven represent the divinities presiding over the days of the week, and the other two the Brahminical ascending and descending nodes, Ráhu and Ketu.

"The forms and character of all the principal temples at Bhobanéser, and indeed throughout the province, being exactly similar, a more particular account of the plan and distribution of the great pagoda will answer the purpose of a general description. The edifices which compose it stand within a square area, enclosed by a substantial wall of stone, measuring six hundred feet on a side, which has its principal gateway guarded by two monstrous griffins or winged lions, in a sitting posture, on the eastern face. About the centre, the great tower, Bara Dewal, or sanctuary, in which the images are always lodged, rises majestically to a height of one hundred and eighty feet. It is composed of a cluster of stone ribs, alternately flat and semicircular, eight principal and eight inferior ones, springing from a square ground plan, which towards the summit curve inwards, without, however, meeting. They bear, as it were on their shoulders, a cylindrical neck, and this, with the aid of brackets in the form of eight immense griffins or lions, supports the crest or head-piece, shaped somewhat like a turban, which forms so distinguishing a feature in the temple architecture of Orissa. It consists of a huge solid circular slab, called the Amla Sila, from some fancied resemblance to the fruit of the amlica *(phyllanthus emblica)*, on which rests another circular ornament, in the form of a large inverted earthen dish, thence called the 'Dihi Bandhi.' Sometimes the two ornaments are repeated. On the summit stands either an urn or the chakra of Vishnu, according to circumstances, surmounted by an iron spike, to which pendants are attached on occasions of ceremony. The best illustration that can be given of the shape and appearance of the generality of these towers, is to compare them to a medicine phial or comfit bottle with the stopper inserted, though the comparison does not do justice to the picturesque effect of the grand and massive building which I am now describing. From each face of the sanctuary, at different degrees of elevation, a huge monster projects to a distance of several feet, which has the body of a lion, but a most grotesque and unnatural countenance, resembling nothing in the catalogue of terrestrial animals. The figure on the eastern face is by far the largest, and has between its feet an elephant of comparatively diminutive size, on which it is trampling. This, it may be observed, is the common mode of representing the lion of Hindu mythology, one of the epithets of which is, Gaja Machula, or the destroyer of the elephant. The entrance to the tower lies through a large square vestibule or ante-chamber, crowned with a pyramidal roof, and surmounted by the crest or series of ornaments above described, which joins on to the eastern face of the sanctuary, and rises to about three-fourths of its height. It is called the Jagamohana, or that which delights the world, because it is thence that the idol is generally seen and worshiped by pilgrims. These two buildings form the essential and most sacred part of the temples of Orissa. Further in advance of the Jagamohana, and connected with it by a sort of colonnade, is another square edifice of precisely the same form but smaller dimensions, which is called the Bhag Mandap, or apartment in which the idol's food is served up, and afterwards distributed amongst the officiating priests, &c. The court of the Ling Raj contains many other towers and temples apart from those already enumerated, in which a variety of the inferior deities, or less esteemed forms of the greater ones, are worshiped, and which add, by their style and number, to the general grandeur of its appearance, but do not need a separate description. The whole are adorned by a profusion of sculptured work, consisting of elaborately wrought cornices, beadings, arabesque and reticulated ornaments, and clusters of pilasters, with figures of men, animals, serpents and flowers, intervening, arranged in such an infinite variety of devices, that the eye is absolutely bewildered in endeavouring to trace out any particular pattern or design. Amongst the ornaments on the great flat central ribs of the Bara Dewal, there is one peculiarly remarkable from its resemblance to some armorial bearing or heraldic device. Mr. Erskine, I observe, has given the figure of a strikingly similar ornament in his account of the cave temples of Elephanta. . . . . The Brahmins explain it to be a compound of the Gadá, Padma, Sankh and Chakra, or Mace, lotus, conch-shell and discus of Vishnu; and it would, therefore, seem rather out of place, in the conspicuous position which it occupies on the walls of the Ling Raj; but it may be observed generally of these edifices, that the sculptors have by no means confined themselves, in their choice of ornaments, to emblems peculiar to the deity of the place."

On examining through a telescope this resemblance to an "armorial bearing," from the top of a double-storied house overlooking the outer wall of the temple, I found it to be a yoni or female emblem, surrounded by the symbols mentioned by Mr. Stirling, and therefore quite in place on a temple dedicated to the worship of the Ling Raj, or Lord of the Lingam,—the phallus of the ancients.

"The temple of the Ling Raj," says Mr. Stirling, "at Bhobanéser, is both the finest monument of antiquity which the province contains, and likewise indisputably the most ancient. It took forty-three years to build, and local tradition, as well as the histories of the country, concur in fixing the date of its completion as A.D. 657.

"We have no particular accounts of the period and causes of the decline of the city of Bhobanéser and the worship of Mahádeo. Nearly all but the great temple have been long since completely deserted; and the establishment kept up there is on a very small and inadequate scale, under the patronage of the Khoorda Rajas, whose ancestors granted all the lands and endowments by which the Brahmins attached to it now subsist. It is occasionally visited by the Bengalee pilgrims on their way to Juggurnath; and every year, at the Sheo Ratri, considerable numbers of Desi, or country pilgrims, are gathered together under its walls to hold a mela or fair.

"The ruins of two extensive palaces, belonging to the Rajas of the Kesari line, are shewn at or near Bhobanéser. There is likewise a very superb tank, lying north of the temple, called the Bindu Ságar. It is 1426 yards in circumference, which forms a conspicuous object in the scenery of the place, and another, faced with stone, on the east, remarkable for its being bordered all round with rows of small antique-looking temples, about thirty on a side, just large enough to contain the human figure in a sitting posture, in which sixty female ascetics, who had devoted themselves to the worship of Devi, are said to have lived and died many ages back.

"About five miles west of Bhobanéser, near the village of Jagmara, a group of small hills occur, four in number, from one hundred and fifty to two hundred feet in height, which present many objects of interest and curiosity. . . . They are composed of a silicious sand-stone of various colour and texture, and are all curiously perforated with small caves, disposed in two or three irregular stories. Each of the caves is large enough to contain from one to two human beings in a sitting posture. Some of them appear to be natural cavities, slightly improved by the hand of man; others have obviously been excavated altogether artificially; and the whole are grotesquely carved and embellished. In one part, a projecting mass of rock has been cut into the form of a tiger's head, with the jaws widely distended, through which a passage leads into a small hole at the back, secured by a wooden door,—the residence of a pious ascetic of the Vishnavite sect. The ridiculous legend which the natives relate to explain the origin of these isolated hills, is, that they formerly constituted a part of the Himalaya, at which time they were inhabited by numerous Rishis, who dug the caves found in them. They were taken up bodily, ascetics and all, by Mahábír Hanumán, with other masses of rock, to build the bridge of Rama, but by some accident were allowed to drop in their passage through the air, when they alighted in their present position. I am almost tempted to add, as a curious coincidence, that they are the only real sand-stone hills found in this part of the country; but the geology of the district has not been sufficiently explored to warrant my advancing such an assertion positively.

"The summit of the highest rock is crowned by a neat stone temple of modern construction, sacred to the worship of Párasnáth, all around and in the neighbourhood of which are strewed a quantity of images of the Nirvánas, or naked figures worshiped by the Jain sect, executed chiefly in the grey chlorite slate rock. At the back of these temples, a highly remarkable terrace is shewn, called the Deo Sabhá, or assembly of the gods, which is covered with numberless antique-looking stone pillars or temples in miniature, some standing, others lying on the ground, about two or three feet long, having on each of the four sides a figure of the naked Jain deity rudely sculptured. The place is still frequented by the Jain or Parwár merchants of Cuttack, who assemble here in numbers, once every year, to hold a festival of their religion.

"A short way up the Udaya Giri hill, the nour or palace of the famous Lalat Indra Kesari is pointed out. It consists of a sort of open court formed by a perpendicular face of sand-stone rock, about forty feet in height, with shoulders of the same on either side. Rows of small chambers have been excavated in each face, arranged in two stories, and divided by a projecting terrace. Both the exterior surface and the inner walls of the chambers are decorated with cornices, pilasters, figures and various devices, very rudely sculptured, and the whole exhibits a faint and humble resemblance, in miniature, to the celebrated cavern temples in the south-west of India. The rude and miserable apartments of the *palace* are now occupied by byraghees and mendicants of different sects, who state that the place had its origin in the time of Buddha, and that it was last inhabited by the Rani of the famous Raja Lalat Indra Kesari, a favourer of the Buddhist religion. Many odd fables are related of the scrapes into which she was led by her heretical notions, and of the way in which her conversion to the orthodox system of worship was at last effected.

"Farther up the same hill, on the overhanging brow of a large cavern, one meets with an ancient inscription cut out of the sand-stone rock, in the very identical character which occurs on the pillars at Delhi, and which as yet has been only partially deciphered. . . There are, I think, two eminently remarkable circumstances connected with the character used in the above inscription. The first is the close resemblance of some of the letters to those of the Greek alphabet, and the second, the occurrence of it on sundry ancient monuments situated in widely distant quarters of India. In support of the first assertion, I need only point the attention of the reader to those of the characters which are exactly similar to the Greek ou, sigma, lambda, chi, delta, epsilon, and a something closely resembling the figure of the digamma. With regard to the second, any person who will take the trouble of comparing this inscription with that on Firoz Shah's Lat at Delhi, on the column at Allahabad, on the Lat of Bhím Sen, in Sarun, a part of the Elephanta, and a part of the Ellora inscriptions, will find that the characters are identically the same. . . . The natives of the district can give no explanation whatever on the subject. The Brahmins refer the inscription with shuddering and disgust to the Budh Ka Amel, or time when the Buddhist doctrines prevailed, and are even reluctant to speak on the subject."

Besides the inscription noted by Mr. Stirling, there are several others at Kundigiri (the general name of the place). They are all in the same character, and equally illegible to the people of the district. Some portions of them have been deciphered by later visitors. Captain Kittoe informed me that he had discovered the name of Antiochus the Great, in some of the inscriptions.

At the entrance to one of the caverns I found a very remarkable figure sculptured in relievo in the sand-stone rock. The face is entirely destroyed, probably by the iconoclast General of the Affghans, Kala Pahar, "who invaded the province in 1558 A.D., and at the sound of whose kettle-drums the noses and ears of all images for many miles round fell off." Be that as it may, the figure is now about five feet in height, and is habited in a sort of tunic and buskins; a scarf is wound loosely round the waist, and a short, straight sword hangs by the left side; the right hand rests on the hip, and that of the left, or rather what remains of it, is placed on the breast. The figure is evidently very ancient, and probably coeval with the inscriptions. No dress of that kind is worn by the people of Orissa, or, as far as I know, any other natives of India. It is said to be the dress of a people from the west. There is another figure near to, and somewhat different from, the above, but more defaced. Is it possible that any of the followers of Antiochus the Great could ever have penetrated as far as Orissa? History makes no mention of such an event. The dress of this figure certainly bears more resemblance to that of the Greeks than that of the Hindoos. Then, again, Mr. Stirling traced several letters of the Greek alphabet in the inscription. The coincidence is singular, and forms a nice little nut for some future Dr. Dryasdust to crack.

In taking a final leave of these Indian temples and antiquities, amongst which I had spent many days, I cannot avoid noticing, as others have previously done, the remarkable similarity which exists between some of the mythological characters of the Egyptians and Hindoos, inferring, as Mr. Murray says in his work on "The Truth of Revelation," "that both must have had a common origin."

Mr. Murray further remarks that the Sepoys who formed part of the army sent with Sir David Baird into Egypt, "soon recognized counterparts of the objects of their idolatry in India," such as Siva in Osiris, Parvati in Isis, Hanuman in Cynocephalus, &c. Again, both Egyptians and Hindoos worshiped the serpent. I have cursorily remarked elsewhere that the Khoordah Rajah and others in Pooree worship a living snake at certain seasons. Whence did these nations derive their worship of the serpent? Can it be from the fall of man, as related by Moses in the book of Genesis, for even the devil, that "old serpent," has his worshippers amongst the Yezedees at this day? Or can it be from the elevation of the brazen serpent in the wilderness by Moses, as related in the 21st chapter of Numbers, and which our Saviour, in the

3rd chapter of St. John, vers. 14, 15, declares to be a type of himself?

Of the ancient history of Egypt, we absolutely know nothing more than what is related in the Bible in the first place, and in the second by Hecatæus of Miletus, Herodotus and Manetho, and some later writers of less importance; the two last being the authorities chiefly relied on. Query, Is not Moses as good an authority as any of them? Herodotus wrote 408 B.C., Manetho at a later period, and Moses more than a thousand years before either of these old pagans was born. Manetho pretended to trace back the Egyptian history some thirty thousand years before the Christian era. The Hindoos, with equal reason, lay claim to a much greater antiquity; but is it credible? Without other corroborative evidence, the hieroglyphics on the temples and monuments of Egypt should be received with some degree of suspicion, and not with the unlimited faith of some authors, seeing that they were the production of the priests, those arch-deceivers and monopolizers of all power and knowledge.

A remarkable instance of the caution necessary to be observed in examining the records of Egyptian chronology, is afforded by the discovery of the famous Table of Abydos, by Mr. William Banks, in 1818. Up to this period, Manetho's dynasties of the Egyptian kings had been received by the learned as authentic. Mr. Murray, in his remarks on the Table of Abydos, says, "It is quite evident that this curious and interesting fragment of the antique, whether considered as a phonetic or symbolic, that is, ideographic, document, must be deciphered from the top to the bottom, and not horizontally, for in the latter case the *same word* would be repeated twenty-six times in succession. Now the difficulty has been to reconcile the canon of Manetho's dynasties with the chronology of Scripture; and this Table of Abydos had been supposed to corroborate Manetho's statement, while in the same ratio it impugned the sacred chronology. We are, therefore, deeply indebted to Dr. Lamb, who has, with considerable sagacity, sifted the evidence afforded by this fragment of antiquity."

Dr. Lamb (as quoted by Mr. Murray) says that the Table of Abydos yields us evidence of only "twenty-five sovereigns, predecessors of *Rameses-Sesostris,* and allowing to each of these the average of twenty-five years, we shall have five hundred years from the first king, probably *Menes.* Now if the great monarch to whose honour this tablet was engraven, died about fifteen hundred years before the Christian era, a short time before the Exodus, we bring the reign of *Menes* to about three hundred and fifty years after the deluge, a period when the descendants of Misraim, the son of Ham, would have become sufficiently powerful to form a great nation; and so far is this monument from confirming the statements made by Herodotus and Manetho, that, so far as it goes, it is a witness against them, and confirmatory of the chronology derived from sacred history."

Attempts have been made by admirers of the ancient Egyptians to spiritualize their mythology. Admitting that the priests retained some vague ideas of the unity of God and a divine government, yet they withheld this knowledge from the people, who were purposely kept in the grossest ignorance, and simply worshiped the idols presented to them by the crafty priests. In short, the whole system, reared with so much art for the selfish ends of a dominant and exclusive caste, was utterly vile and corrupt, and, instead of apologies, merits our utmost abhorrence. Often, when riding in the streets of Pooree, have I felt my blood böil on seeing a poor Hindoo stoop to embrace and kiss the dusty feet of a "twice-born" Brahmin, who received the homage as a matter of course. And such were the Egyptian priests, who made themselves like unto gods, to the people. They had some knowledge of the light, but their grovelling craving for power led them to withhold it from the people, "lest their eyes should be opened and they should see." "For the people," as one of their apologists says, "they made laws which they enforced without rendering any reason, holding that the people had 'nothing to do with the laws but to obey them.' They explored many regions of natural science, giving the people the results in the form of divination and magic." In fact, they treated them very much like children, as do the "twice-born" priests of India treat their dupes at the present day.

With regard to the Hindoo chronology, that distinguished eastern scholar, the late Colonel Mark Wilks, said, that "neither their literature, science nor arts, had any just pretensions to a high antiquity."

"The Hindoos, like the Egyptians," says Mr. Murray, "have a train of fabulous *gods* and *demi-gods* figuring away in the legends of their mythology prior to the deluge.... The gigantic excavations in the granitic mountains of Elora, forming the temples of Indra and Visvacarma, and other temples and dwellings, with those of Karli, Elephanta and Salsette, seem in their majestic grandeur to dispute with the pyramids a title to overpowering effect, without the slightest pretension to any useful purpose whatever. *Effect* seems to have been the design kept in view, in order to overawe the devotee by the unearthly majesty of giant forms.....

"The astronomical tables of the Hindoos, according to M. Bailly's calculations and reasonings, made the *observations* on which the Hindoo chronology was formed, 30,000 years before the Christian era; but M. Delambre discovered a gross error existing in the divisor, which neutralized the entire conclusions. . . . .

"La Place, in his *Systeme du Monde*, in reference to these tables of Indian chronology, says that they are *not* of high antiquity, and, moreover, that one of the epochas is necessarily *fictitious*, and the other *not grounded on observation.* The illustrious Cuvier (who by the way had the grandest head I ever saw) remarks [I quote from Mr. Murray], the whole system of the Indian tables, so elaborately conceived, falls to pieces of itself, now that it has been proved that the epocha was adopted from calculations *retrospectively* made, the result of which is false. Mr. Bentley has discovered that the tables of Tirvalour, on which the assertions of Bailly were principally founded, must have been computed towards the year 1281; and that the Sourya Siddhanta, which the Brahmins esteem their most ancient scientific treatise on astronomy, pretending that it was given by inspiration twenty millions of years ago, could have been composed only seven hundred and sixty-seven years before our own period. . . . We have also the authority of Mr. Davis, who has diligently examined the Hindoo astronomical writings, and who confirms the conclusion that they are founded on a retrograde calculation, exactly as our Julian period has been."

One of the most remarkable, as well as most ancient, of all the Hindoo writings, is that of the Institutes of Menu, containing the Vedas and Puranas, and which is admitted by the Brahmins to contain their purest code. This famous code was, says Mr. Elphinstone in his History of India, drawn up about 900 B.C., and is still the basis of Hindoo jurisprudence, and the principal features remain unaltered to the present day. The following extract from Mr. Buckle's History of Civilization in England, will shew what a precious specimen of Eastern wisdom is contained in this celebrated code:

"To the great body of the Indian people the name of Sudra is given (the Sudras are estimated by Ward at three-fourths of the Hindoos), and the native laws respecting them contain some minute and curious particulars. If a member of this despised class presumed to occupy the same seat as his superiors, he was either to be exiled or suffer a painful and ignominious punishment. If he spoke of them with contempt, his mouth was to be burned; if he actually insulted them, his tongue was to be slit; if he molested a Brahmin, he was to be put to death; if he sat on the same carpet with a Brahmin, he was to be maimed for life; if, moved by the desire of instruction, he even listened to the reading of the sacred books, burning oil was to be poured into his ears; if, however, he committed them to memory, he was to be killed; if he were guilty of a crime, the punishment for it was greater than that inflicted on his superiors; but if he himself were murdered, the penalty was the same as for killing a dog, a cat or a cow. Should he marry his daughter to a Brahmin, no retribution that could be exacted in this world was sufficient; it was therefore announced that the Brahmin must go to hell, for having suffered contamination from a woman immeasurably his inferior. Indeed, it was ordered that the mere name of a labourer should be expressive of contempt, so that his proper standing should be immediately known. And lest this should not be enough to maintain the subordination of society, a law was actually made forbidding any labourer to accumulate wealth; while another clause declared that even though his master should give him freedom, he would in reality still be a slave; 'for,' says the lawgiver,—'for of a state which is natural to him, by whom can he be divested?'"

These old Indian legislators had no more conception than the Egyptians of Bentham's grand principle of "the greatest happiness of the greatest number."

I have done for the present with the antiquities and temples of Egypt and India, and the reflections to which they have given rise, but may resume the subject in a future work.

CHAPTER XII.

Romantic Charm of Eastern Scenes and Life—Lady Hester Stanhope—The Pagan East never produced a Philanthropist or a Noble-minded Woman—Travellers confine their Observations on the East—Bishop Heber on the Cruel Treatment of Draft Oxen by the Hindoos—The gentle Hindoo twisting a Bullock's Tail—Recommendation to visit the *far* East of Ind.

THERE is a romantic charm about Eastern scenes and Eastern life, as portrayed by some modern writers, which is apt to lead astray the imagination of those who have never visited or resided in the East; but they may rest assured that, in this case as in others, 'tis distance lends enchantment to the view. I should like to ask the admirers of Eastern life, in sober earnestness, whether they would rather live in civilized Europe or in their charming East? Lady Hester Stanhope tried it, and from all accounts her life must have been most wearisome, until even her reason seemed to give way; for no sane person would, in these days, have cherished an Arab-horse for our Saviour to ride upon on his entry into Jerusalem, as Lamartine says that Lady Hester did. At first sight, the contrast of the dolce-far-niente, slip-shod life of the East, to the bustling and exciting pursuits of the West, appears sufficiently enchanting. But what is there ennobling or dignifying to human nature in the East? The pagan East never produced a Howard, a Man of Ross, or a Wilberforce, or ever a noble-minded woman like Mrs. Fry, Mrs. Somerville, or Florence Nightingale, and others whom you and I know. Of conquerors and oppressors of their kind, there have been more than enough, but never a philanthropist; and the less that is said about their women, the better. Notwithstanding all this, I cannot help thinking "the East," as I know it, is a very interesting country; and I do not see why travellers who write about "the East" par excellence, should confine their observations to Egypt, Syria, and perchance part of Persia or Turkey, as if there were no other East. To be sure, those countries have been called the "cradle of the human race." What then? Who, in these days of steam, electric telegrams and photography, retains a sentimental affection for the cradle and pap-boat of his childhood? Man has long since attained his majority, and taken possession of his heritage, the world; the extent of which is now pretty well known. Pity none of its "dirty acres" belong to me! I was once the lord of four hundred acres, but somehow or other they slipped away! The far-east of Ind contains a country and people quite as worthy of observation as any other on the face of the globe. There are to be found the grandest scenes of nature, the most stupendous mountains, the largest rivers of the old world, beside deserts and the richest vegetation, together with almost every variety of animal life known to the naturalist. Then there are the caves of Elephanta, the temples of Ellora and Orissa, the Taj Mehal, and innumerable other works of man. Moreover, it is, as Bishop Heber said, "the land of the gentle Hindoo and fierce Mussulman." By the way, the good Bishop, when he used these words, had never seen the gentle Hindoo twist a bullock's tail. After he had been some time in India, he writes, "They treat their draft oxen with a degree of severity which would turn an English hackney-coachman sick." Seated on a hackery (native cart), close behind his bullocks, the gentle Hindoo, instead of using a whip to accelerate their pace, generally gives a twist of the tail, which has the desired effect; and one rarely sees an old bullock without several dislocations of the joints of the tail, giving it a knotted appearance. In these days of steam-boats and railways, the journey to India is by no means the formidable undertaking it was "when George the Third was king," or even twenty years ago; and to any one blasé with the European world and the beaten track of tourists, I would recommend a visit to the *far* East, and if he did not find much to interest him, I am greatly mistaken. I know one English gentleman who spent two years in travelling about India very much to his satisfaction. He was particularly struck with the ruins of the Black Pagoda, to which I accompanied him.

CHAPTER XIII.

March to Kontillo and Burmool—Burmool Pass infested with Tigers—Wild-looking Guards—Footprints of Tigers—Description of Camp—Astonishing the Natives—Party of Twenty Men in charge of Bullocks laden with Cotton come down the Pass—Boats at Burmool—Mahanuddy River—Singular Scenery—Shallows and Rapids—Arrival of Bearers with one of their Companions in a state of Hydrophobia—Night of Horrors—Start for Boad—Alarm of Tigers near Boad—Travellers stopped—Advance and Arrival at Boad—A Tiger in the Town at Night—Cross the Mahanuddy River—Start for Sumbhulpore—Road leading through Jungle strewn with Quartz Rock—Arrive at Sumbhulpore—Situation of the Town—Errors in the Maps—Gold and Diamonds found in the Eeb River—Singular Appearance of the Mahanuddy River at Sumbhulpore—Course of the River—Evening Drive—Three Human Heads on a Pole by the Road-side—Cocoa-nuts and Vegetables at Sumbhulpore.

AFTER marching through the northern parts of the district, I left my tents at Kontillo, on the right bank of the Mahanuddy river, and proceeded on foot, accompanied by two servants and a palanquin with a dozen bearers, to the Burmool Pass, where twenty other bearers were to meet me, on the 20th of December, for the purpose of conveying me to Sumbhulpore, a distance of about one hundred and thirty miles. The Burmool Pass had been so much infested with tigers some years previously, that the village near by had been abandoned. I was credibly informed that these man-eating tigers even tore down the bamboo mats in the doorways of the villagers' huts for the purpose of getting at their victims. This is so contrary to the usual habit of this animal in seizing its prey, which is by a sudden spring, that I found it difficult to believe the account. However, "I tell the tale as 'twas told to me."

On our arrival at the Pass no bearers were in attendance, but the Rajah of the country sent his dewan (minister) to offer any assistance I might require in the way of procuring supplies, &c. He also sent a guard of ten or a dozen wild-looking men, armed with bows and arrows, and wherever I went, two of these men stalked after me. In the evening I got into a boat to proceed up the river, when in stepped two of the guard. When I disembarked in pursuit of some game, they did so too; and, sooth to say, I felt rather glad of their presence when I saw numerous footprints of tigers on the soft bank of the river. I started with surprise, as much as Robinson Crusoe did on seeing the footprint of a man on his island. The sun had set unnoticed by me in the excitement of pursuing some pea-fowl, but the sight of these footprints brought me up "all standing," as the sailors say. I immediately slipped a couple of balls over the charges of shot in my gun, and commenced a cautious retreat, feeling that if I had eyes all round my head I could make use of them. The guards held their bows and arrows all ready for a flight, but, luckily for us, we did not encounter any tigers; had we done so, one or other of us would in all probability have remained behind to supper, or to be supped upon, as from the nature of the ground we could not have seen the tiger until he had sprung like a flash of lightning upon us; one blow of his paw on the head of his victim giving a quietus, and away with his prey into the jungle, as quick as thought. That is something like the way of it, as I have heard described by one who actually saw such a scene. However, we were happy enough to gain our camp in safety. Fires were lit round the camp at night, for the sake of warmth as well as to keep out the wild animals. My camp consisted simply of my palanquin, in which I ate, smoked and slept; for I had no tent. The bearers, wrapped in a blanket, slept on the ground near the fires, while some of my wild-looking guards kept watch throughout the night. Before retiring to rest I boiled some water for tea in a little "Etna" (my constant travelling companion). When the people saw me strike a light with a lucifer-match, they could not imagine how I procured fire in such a simple and instantaneous way; but when the spirit lamp of the Etna threw out two long jets of flame with a roaring noise, great was their amazement; and when, in three minutes, the water boiled and I proceeded to drink my tea, I feel convinced that they thought me some wonderful magician,—an idea which, in my then position, I did not care to disturb.

The next day a party of twenty men, in charge of four hundred large up-country bullocks laden with cotton, came down the Pass. Each bullock carried two large packages slung across his back. Each package weighed about one hundred and twenty pounds. The men said that they had been seven months in coming from Jubbulpore, and were going to Kontillo, where they expected to get forty rupees for each bullock-load of cotton, which is at the rate of a fraction more than fourpence a pound. Their return cargo would consist solely of cocoa-nuts, procured from Sutbady, near Pooree. It is curious to trace the course of traffic. Here were people who came from Jubbulpore, a distance of several hundred miles inland, with the produce of their country, and in return take cocoa-nuts, which grow plentifully within the range of the sea-breeze, but not much beyond that. From Kontillo, the cotton is sent, viâ Cuttack, to Calcutta, and thence to England; whence it is possibly, if not probably, returned in a manufactured state, again to find its way to Jubbulpore.

At Burmool we found two large flat-bottomed boats from Cuttack waiting for cargoes of wood, which is procured from the forest in the neighbourhood. These boats left Cuttack three months ago. Toon *(cedrela toona)* and sal *(shorea robusta)* are the principal woods they procure. The wood is not put into the boat, but across the boat; and projecting over each side about eight feet are laid the trunks of young saplings, five or six inches in diameter, at intervals of four or five feet apart; and to these cross-beams the trunks of the trees, cut into convenient lengths of six or eight feet, are suspended in rows fore and aft and resting in the water, and are thus, when the water rises in the rains, floated down to Cuttack.

In the absence of the expected bearers, I amused myself by a row, or rather a *push*, up the Mahanuddy river; for in soundings the boatmen used very long bamboo poles to push the boat along. The river scenery at Burmool is very singular and beautiful; for several miles the waters flow between two ranges of hills, springing by precipitous slopes from the very margin of the stream. These hills are, as near as I could judge, about a quarter of a mile apart, and from one thousand to twelve hundred or more feet in height, and partially clothed with forest and jungle to their summits, huge masses of granitic rocks jutting out here and there amidst the foliage. At this season (December) the current of the river was scarcely perceptible, but it flowed gently in a very deep and clear stream. Proceeding onwards, the view continually changed with the winding of the river, and presented the appearance of a succession of lakes; and when the sun declined behind the hills, the gloom cast upon the waters was, together with the solemn silence and solitude of the scene, most impressive. No other moving object than my boat was to be seen on land or water. When returning down the stream and emerging from the hills, on looking backwards I saw the river gradually lost in dim obscurity, until in the far distance it was, as I find recorded in my journal, "dark as a wolf's mouth," while at the same time, in striking contrast, the open country was illumined by the last rays of the setting sun.

When the Mahanuddy emerges from the hills at Burmool, it suddenly spreads out over a sandy bed, with rocks interspersed here and there. In the rains the stream must at this place be from two to three miles wide and very deep; but at this season (December) it would not admit the passage of boats drawing more than six inches of water, owing to the numerous shallows. In these places it forms rapids, and runs with great velocity. On getting over one of these shallow places it suddenly deepens again, insomuch that the boatmen cannot fathom the bottom with the long bamboo poles used in propelling their boats; and so it goes on, in alternate shallows, rocks and deep pools, as far as Kontillo. The river could never be made navigable for vessels of large burthen in all seasons, on account of these shallows, which are continually shifting their site. The flat-bottomed boats of the natives are well adapted for its navigation above Cuttack.

On returning from my trip up the river, I found that the long-expected bearers had arrived, bringing with them one of their companions in a state of hydrophobia. The man had been bitten by a mad jackal some weeks before, and was seized with the complaint the day before he arrived at Burmool. His cries were dreadful, and continued throughout the night. Fires were lit around the camp, as on previous occasions. We sometimes heard the howlings of wild animals mingling with the cries of the madman, and every now and then, when tired out I had perhaps just dropped asleep, my wild guards would raise a most unearthly shout close to my palanquin. Up I started, and, with pistol in hand, thrust my head out to ascertain the cause of the row. Thus the night wore away, and such a night of horrors I devoutly trust I may never pass again. At sunrise the wild animals retreated into the jungle, and there was peace in the camp. I concluded that the madman was dead, and my first inquiry was respecting him. "There he is, Sir," said my khidmutgar, directing my attention to a man wrapped in a blanket, and seated on the ground. He was quite sensible, and answered my questions rationally enough. I felt his feeble, fluttering pulse, but could do nothing for him; and as I was obliged to be at Sumbhulpore by a certain day, I left two men to take care of the poor fellow as long as life remained, and started on my journey through a country rarely traversed by Europeans, as it was beyond the bounds of the East-India Company's territories, and subject to tributary chiefs.

The road through the Burmool Pass was a very bad one, and quite impassable for wheeled carriages. On either side was a forest of toon and sal trees, with masses of granite and gneiss rocks jutting out into the path, here and there, for some miles. We rested for three hours in the middle of the day, and reached Kolepore at 9 p.m. The road or track was chiefly through forests and hills, and the distance travelled about thirty-two miles. We remained all night at Kolepore, and next day started for Boad. About seven miles from Kolepore, we emerged from the hills and forests into an extensive plain, in which is situated the village or town of Ramghur. About one tenth of the land was under cultivation, the principal crops being cotton, castor-oil plants, and a little rice, besides the usual vegetables required by the natives. The whole plain, as far as I could judge, might be easily cultivated were there a sufficient population. A few miles beyond Ramghur, we again met with forest and jungle, which, with short intervals, extended as far as Boad, five miles from which place we found a party of some twenty or thirty natives, who informed us that three men had been killed by tigers the previous evening, a hundred yards or so in advance of the spot where we then were. My servants inquired what was to be done. "Why, go on, to be sure; we can't stay here all day." Then, thinking that they might say to themselves, "It is all very well for you to talk about facing tigers when you are shut up in a palanquin, while we poor devils have to meet them on foot," I got out, to take my chance with the rest of them. My khidmutgar dismounted from his tattoo (pony) and drove the poor animal before him, thinking that the tiger might take a fancy to it first. It was amusing to see the unconscious beast trotting along, and the man giving it a fillip now and then to hasten its pace. The travellers seeing us determined to proceed, followed in our wake. On the left, a short distance from the road, a lot of vultures and kites were perched on a tree, and there, doubtless, were the remains of the men carried off the evening before. However, we saw nothing of the tigers, and arrived safely at Boad, where we remained all night. Boad is a fortified town—or rather has been—for the mud wall which protected it is in some places in a tumble-down state. A tiger walked through one of the breaches in the middle of the night, and carried off a cow, which excited a great hubbub. The shouting and yells of the natives, mingled with the beating of tom-toms, was enough to awake the seven sleepers. Becoming accustomed to these night alarms, I took little notice of the tumult, and went to sleep again.

On the following morning we crossed the Mahanuddy river at sunrise, and started for Sumbhulpore. The road for many miles ran through jungles, with lumps of quartz rock strewn about. I have since thought that it was a very auriferous-looking place. Approaching Sumbhulpore, we passed through a fine upland country, clear of jungle, but with noble groves of mango, tamarind, banyan and palm trees, forming a scene like an English park. After travelling all night, we arrived at Sumbhulpore on the morning of the 25th December. The town is situated on the left bank of the Mahanuddy river, which "derives its source amongst the mountains of Gondwaneh." It pursues an extremely winding and devious course, which has never been accurately surveyed; even in the parts which are better known there are many errors. In Arrowsmith's map, the towns of Sooree, Narrain, Kurkurdah, and Chunderpore, to the northward of Sumbhulpore, are all placed from twenty to thirty miles distant from the left bank of the river; whereas I was informed by Mr. Babbington, who had resided several years at Sumbhulpore, and was well acquainted with the country, that they are all situated immediately on that bank. Ten miles above Sumbhulpore, the Eeb river, which takes its rise near Jushpoor, joins the Mahanuddy at Buggra. This river is noted for the gold and diamonds found in its bed. A short distance below Buggra there is a rapid in the Mahanuddy, and it is at this place that the diamonds are chiefly procured. In 1836, a large one of fine water was found. It is of a somewhat pyramidal shape, and about the size of a large walnut. It is, or was, in the possession of the Rajah of Sumbhulpore. In fact, all the diamonds found in the rapid are his property. Below Sumbhulpore there are numerous other rapids, but it is from the Eeb river that the diamonds and gold are derived, as they are not met with at any of the rapids below the one near Buggra. Small particles of gold are indeed occasionally found in the sandy bed of the Mahanuddy at Cuttack, but they may probably have been washed down from the upper parts of the river.

At Sumbhulpore, the Mahanuddy is about a mile and a half wide in the rains. In the cold season, the bed of the river for several miles, both up and down the stream, presents a very singular appearance, being thickly strewn with masses of granitic rocks from six to ten feet high, and around these the water winds. In some places pools have formed, and in others low brushwood is found growing on the sands, thus giving to the river the appearance of a large lake studded with innumerable little islets. From Sumbhulpore, the Mahanuddy flows nearly due south to Sohnpore, a distance of about fifty-five miles. It then suddenly bends east by north, and after pursuing a tolerably straight course, terminates in the Bay of Bengal, due east from Sohnpore. In this course it receives numerous tributary streams, and gives off several branches, the "largest of which is the Kajoori, and it is in the bifurcation formed here that the town of Cuttack is situated." I may here mention, *en passant,* that the Kajoori river in the rains is about two miles wide at Cuttack, and in 1834 the waters rose twenty-six feet in one night. This may appear incredible, but it is nevertheless a fact, correct measurements having been made of the rise of the river.

To return to Sumbhulpore. My host was the postmaster, as well as a merchant, and with his wife and an assistant were the only Europeans within a hundred miles of the place. The house was situated on the elevated left bank of the river, and overlooked the singular scene I have described. I also observed two ranges of hills running north and south. The hills on the western side were about a mile from the river, and those on the east about four miles distant.

In the evening, I drove out with my host, and by the road-side, within sight of his house, we passed three human heads, quite fresh, and stuck upon a pole one above the other. One head was that of a grey-bearded, savage-looking old man; the other two were those of young men, about twenty or twenty-five years of age. It was with a feeling of horror I looked upon this barbarous sight, but my host spoke in the coolest manner imaginable about it, and informed me that they were the heads of three dacoits (robbers), forming part of a formidable band which had infested the country for a considerable time. The Rajahs of Boad, Sumbhulpore, and another neighbouring chief, with their united forces, surrounded the hill on which it was known that these desperadoes had fixed their residence, and, simultaneously advancing, captured the three men whose heads I saw elevated by the road-side. Many others of the gang escaped. After hearing this account I felt much more reconciled to the event, seeing that I had advanced, and should be obliged to return, through the very district infested by these robbers; albeit these gentry rarely venture to attack Europeans, but they might make a mistake. Three days after my arrival at Sumbhulpore, the two men whom I had left at the Burmool Pass to look after the madman returned, and reported his death a few hours after my departure.

In my host's garden I found a few cocoa-nuts growing, which surprised me, as it is far beyond the influence of the sea-breeze. There, indeed, they were, and flourishing very well. Vegetables in general thrive remarkably well. I measured a brinjal *(solanum melongena)* fourteen and a half inches in circumference; a casuarina tree, planted four years ago, measured sixteen inches round the trunk, one yard from the ground.

CHAPTER XIV.

Leave Sumbhulpore—Splash of Blood by the Road-side—Passing through the Burmool Pass—Recent Footprints of a Tiger—Site of a Catastrophe—Arrive at Burmool and procure Boats—Join my Camp at Kontillo—Depart from Khoordah—Afternoon's Shooting Excursion—Lost in the Jungle—Safe Return—Drummoyne's Shikaree-wallah kills a Tiger in the Jungle—Captain Drummoyne—Malabar Hornbill—Feeds on Seeds of Strychnos Nux Vomica.

EARLY on the morning of the 3rd of January I left Sumbhulpore, and arrived at Boad on the 5th. No fresh bearers were to be had for love or money ; so, with a promise of ample buckshish, I induced those whom I had brought from Sumbhulpore to proceed to Burmool. Accordingly we left on the morning of the 6th, and when walking a-head of my palkee, as was my custom for ten or twelve miles, I saw a large splash of blood by the road-side, and the tall grass beaten down, as if the body of some large animal had been dragged through it. I had no time to stop, but pushed on, speculating on the tragedy that had evidently been recently performed there. On the morning of the 8th, in passing through the Burmool Pass, and walking as usual a-head of my palkee, I perceived the fresh footprints of a large animal proceeding onwards. I took no notice, for fear of alarming my people, but kept a sharp look-out right and left. After proceeding this way for a hundred yards or so, my servant who was behind me exclaimed, "Sahib, Sahib, bhag hy!"—"Sir, Sir, a tiger!"—and pointed to the footprints.

I desired him not to say anything; but to give him confidence, I sent him to my palkee for a pair of pistols, one of which I gave to him, and advanced myself, sometimes treading in the footprints of the tiger. The impressions which they made in the sandy path, wet with the morning dew, were nearly, if not quite, as large as a moderate-sized cheese plate. This may appear exaggeration, but it is not so; and any one who has seen the footprints of a large tiger would corroborate this statement. Our pistols would have been of little use in an encounter, for if the tiger had been lurking on either hand, we could not possibly have seen him, by reason of the jungle and rocks, until he had sprung upon us. By and by, all the people saw the dreaded footmarks, and stopped. I persuaded them, however, to go on, and to keep close together, I, of course, leading the way; and so we went on for perhaps a quarter of a mile further, when we came upon the site of a catastrophe. In the middle of the path lay a couple of small baskets, such as the natives carry on their heads, and a few cowrie shells were strewn about—this was all. We saw no more footprints; the bearer of the baskets and cowries had evidently been swept from the path. A short distance further on we found some natives sitting on the ground and lamenting one of their companions, who, they said, had just been carried off by a tiger, in the place where we found the baskets. I must confess that we breathed more freely after hearing this, as there was less chance of the tiger wanting any of us to break his fast on. The deed was done, and we could not help it, so pushed on, and soon arrived at Burmool, where I procured a boat, and, after rewarding my bearers, embarked with my two servants, and dropped down the Mahanuddy to Kontillo, where I found my tents; and I never felt so heartily glad in all my life as I did then, in feeling that I was, as it were, at home again, and once more within reach of civilized society.

From Kontillo I marched through the Bankee Rajah's territories to Khoordah, and paid a visit to my friend Captain Drummoyne, who, as if I had not had enough of tiger alarms, unintentionally led me into a situation of perhaps greater risk than I had hitherto been in. The way of it was this. We went out for an afternoon's shooting, accompanied by Captain Drummoyne's shikaree-wallah (huntsman), and gradually drew near to a jungle which was well known to be the haunt of tigers. However, as it was a short cut homewards, my friend proposed to pass through it, as there would not be much danger in doing so before sunset; but wandering about in pursuit of game, the sun went down, and left us in the jungle—where, exactly, we knew not, neither did the shikaree-wallah, which was worse still, for we thought that he of course knew every inch of jungle about Khoordah. Here was a pretty fix! It was now dusk, and had there been a decent-sized tree, I think I should have climbed into it for a night's lodging; but there was nothing of the kind. To stay where we were would be to invite the tigers to a good supper; so we blundered along, sometimes thinking that we had got on the track, and then losing it again. A few hazy-looking stars began to wink at us above, and at last darkness fell like a pall upon us, so that we hardly knew in what direction we were going: every now and then as we pushed through the brushwood, a branch which had been bent aside by the preceding man would come with a thwack against one's leg, giving one a momentary idea of the snap of a tiger's jaws. How I did grumble and growl at my friend D.! "Pretty sport this, you have brought me to see; if we get out of this jungle alive, I'll be shot if you ever catch me here again," &c. Drummoyne answered not a word, and so we went on, *ventre a terre*, that is to say, with finger on trigger, in the almost forlorn hope that in the event of an encounter we might by a lucky hit in the dark from our *shot* guns, disable the tiger before he could make mincemeat of us. The night had been dark as Erebus for at least an hour before we emerged from the jungle into the open space near Drummoyne's house. He then spoke for the first time, saying, "Thank God, we are well out of it, old fellow!" I had no doubt about it myself.

And never, never more,
Did I that jungle's depths explore! Wah! Wah!

In the morning my friend said to his shikaree-wallah, "You are always talking about tigers being in that jungle; I don't believe anything about it; had there being any, we should surely have met with some last night." This put the man's monkey up, and away he went, day after day, alone to the jungle, armed only with a long match-lock gun; and at last, in broad daylight, he met a tiger face to face in the path, about thirty or forty yards off. The man, keeping his eyes (as he told us afterwards) steadily fixed on the tiger, moved cautiously to one side, so as to get a good shot at his enemy; for if he failed in killing or disabling the brute with the first shot, it would have been all up with the shikaree-wallah. He, however, succeeded in his aim. The ball must have passed through the heart, judging from the position of the holes in the skin, which D. gave to me. Great was the triumph of the poor shikaree-wallah in shewing his master this proof of his truth and courage. Captain D. said that he would never taunt the man again, for if he had been slain on this occasion he should have felt that he had been the cause of it. I sent the skin of this tiger to

England. It measured, as far as I recollect, nearly eleven feet from the snout to the end of the tail.

My friend Captain Drummoyne was a great sportsman, and the only European resident in Khoordah, the nearest white face to him being thirty miles off. He was Commandant of the Khoordah Paik Companies, mustering some two hundred men, who were dressed and armed like the troops of the line. Captain D. accepted this appointment solely from his love of sport; at the same time he had a regard for his military duties and independent command. We had a scramble over the ruins of the old fort and the neighbouring jungles in pursuit of large game, but were unsuccessful. In one of our shooting excursions I procured a fine specimen of the Malabar hornbill *(buceros malabaricus)*, and also a smaller species of a greyish colour, about the size of a crow. The first is called by the natives kuchila khae *(kuchila-eater)*, from the circumstance of its feeding on the seeds of the kuchila *(strychnos nux vomica)*, about which trees this bird is frequently to be found. I was sceptical as to its feeding on these seeds, which, to other animals, are a deadly poison; but on opening the stomach of the one I shot, I certainly found parts of the husk of the seed. Another singular thing is, that the natives eat the flesh of the bird to cure rheumatism.

CHAPTER XV.

Return to Pooree—Description of my Sitting-room—Arrival of the Ship "Robarts"—Passengers at the Red Lion—Wild Animals on the Sea-shore—My Bheestie chased by a Wild Boar—Captain Severn—We make a Plum-pudding—Our Interview with the Wild Hog—Fatal Result to the Pig—Reflections on shooting a Pig.

I WAS glad to reach my home at Pooree after my wanderings, which, however, produced some addition to a curiously furnished room in my house. This room was fifty-seven feet in length by sixteen in breadth, and the walls were decorated with bookcases, heads of antelopes, bison and stags' horns of various kinds, native swords, battle-axes, spears, bows and arrows, &c., interspersed with framed engravings of some of Wilkie's pictures. The floor was strewn with the skins of bears, leopards, tigers, deer and antelopes. This was my usual sitting apartment. Looking through a billiard-room, I could see the blue sea three hundred yards off. On the other side of the house was a garden, which I had made on the sands; and beyond I could see the tower of the temple of Juggurnath. Ships sometimes passed so close to the shore that we could distinguish the figures of persons on board. On two or three occasions some passengers were landed. Thus the ship "Robarts," Captain Elder, arrived one morning for the purpose of landing a Madras officer with his family, who were proceeding to Cuttack. Some six or eight of the other passengers, and amongst them a lady, availed themselves of the opportunity to pay a visit to the famous temple of Juggurnath. Of course all came to the "Red Lion," as my house was often called, and I procured elephants, or conveyances of one kind or other, for them. I had two friends from Cuttack staying with me at the time; so at dinner we formed quite a large party for Pooree. One and all, from the novelty of the situation, seemed to enjoy themselves very much, and threw off all reserve, so that we seemed to have been acquainted for years, instead of a few hours only. In the evening, Captain Elder and his passengers re-embarked, and my two friends started for Cuttack. I was now alone in the house, where there had so lately been such unusual sounds of merriment. It was like the awaking from a very busy dream.

During a season of drought many wild animals found their way to the sea-shore. One morning my bheestie (water-carrier), who had been down to the shore for water, returned without it, and reported that he had been chased by a wild boar. We did not believe him, but the intelligence was soon confirmed by another person; whereupon my friend Captain Severn——(By the way, my dear S., if your eyes should rest on these pages, please tell the publisher where you are to be found, for I should like to grasp your hand once more. Do you remember our undertaking to teach my cook how to make "my plum-pudding" from Dr. Kitchener's receipt, and the botch we made of it?) But the pig is waiting. Captain Severn proposed that we should go and have a look at the wild beast, so, taking a couple of guns, we sallied forth to have an interview with the pig. On reaching the bank and looking over, sure enough there he was, a regular jungle wallah, enjoying a bath in the salt water; but no sooner did he espy us than up he came full gallop. We both fired, without checking his charge. My chuprassy, who had armed himself with a long Mahratta spear, drew up alongside me, and planting the butt-end of his weapon firmly in the sand, stood ready to receive the beast. Seeing us stand fast, piggy halted for an instant, grinding his tusks at us, and then scampered down the bank into the sea. By this time we had re-loaded, and took another shot at him. He came no more to the charge, but was washed ashore by the waves quite dead. We had some of his chops for dinner. This is the only wild hog I plead guilty to having shot, and under the circumstances it must be admitted by the keenest "pig-sticker" that there was some excuse for my committing such an atrocity, for what business had a mere jungle pig to dispute our right to a salt-water bath? "The world was wide enough for him and us too," as Sterne said to the fly that he rescued from drowning; but the buzz of a fly and the rip-up of a pig are very different things, and I question if Master Lawrence, in our situation, would have carried his sentimentality so far as to spare the pig. Any how, we made the best of it, and ate piggy.

CHAPTER XVI.

Wild Tribes of Khunds and Sours—Information procured from them—Khund Paiks at Araug—Meriahs—Thugs—Remains of Victims discovered near Pooree—Conviction of the Thugs—Letter of a Convict to his Wife—Customs of the Thugs—Confessions of a Thug—The Thugs never shed Blood—Their Way of doing Business—Only one Instance known of their attacking an European.

A SHORT time after my trip to Sumbhulpore, I wished to ascertain something more about the wild and savage tribes of Khunds and Sours living amongst the hills and jungles of Khoordah, and also on the northern and western boundaries of the district. Accordingly, I crossed the Chilka Lake, and proceeded to Banpore, a large village containing two thousand inhabitants, situated about six miles from the lake. Here I pitched my tents. A few miles to the west of Banpore, and just within the boundaries of the Bengal Presidency, there is a district called Burra Mall. It is about six miles in extent, and peopled by some hundred and fifty Khund families. In ordinary times these Burra Mall Khunds are tolerably quiet, as there is a strict watch kept over them by a chief called a Bissooee. The Bissooee is not a Khund, but an Ooriah of the Maentee caste, and is responsible for the good behaviour of the people. This man paid me a visit, and I requested him to bring some of his protégés to my camp. Accordingly, about a score of them came, bearing little presents of honey, for which, by the way, I paid in rupees several hundred per cent.

of its value. Some of these men were almost black, and others comparatively fair. They were all of middle stature, and tolerably well-made about the body, but their legs were small, and with very little calf. The feet and hands were remarkably small. My visitors had villanously low foreheads and widely expanded nostrils, altogether greatly resembling the Mughs of Burmah. It has been conjectured, and with ample reason, that these people are descendants of the aborigines who many ages ago were driven by a stronger race from the fertile plains and valleys to the more remote hills and jungles, whence they sometimes issue and plunder the inhabitants of the country that formerly belonged to them.

From these people, and others of the same race from Arang, &c., I procured the following information. The Sours, Pauns and Khunds, are all of the same race and speak the same language. Besides the Bissooee, they have another chief called a Naigue, who settles their disputes, as in all other Indian communities. The office is hereditary. The eldest son commonly succeeds. If there is no male offspring, a consultation of the people is held, when a successor is appointed. They contribute nothing towards his support, but merely pay obedience to his orders. Every village has its Naigue. The Bissooee is allowed to levy a tax for his own benefit of two annas per annum on every plough, and the Khunds themselves allow him a small portion of the produce of their labour. For instance, each man generally produces about fifty pounds' weight of castor-oil seeds and as much mustard. The Bissooee takes four pounds of each. Besides oil seeds, the Khunds grow cotton, kullae (a sort of pulse), and a few brinjals *(solanum melongena)*. The cotton they have manufactured in Banpore into cloth for their own use. They are addicted to smoking and drunkenness. They eat a root resembling a yam, called "toonga," two others called respectively "cherinja" and "kurba," and a fruit named "karoona," which I take to be, from the description, averrhoa carambola. In the more remote jungles there is a tree called "surrup," which they say bears fruit after a growth of eight years, and then dies. They eat the fruit and pith of this tree; the sap is made into an intoxicating drink like toddy. They are seldom sober when they can procure it. I am totally at a loss to know to what species this tree belongs, as I have never had an opportunity of seeing it. The Khunds have few diseases, no cholera or syphilis, though in the more remote jungles the tribes are said to suffer greatly from the latter disease. Fevers and small-pox occasionally commit great ravages amongst them. Rice-water is their only medicine, and rice is in their estimation the greatest luxury in the world, except toddy! They procure rice and salt from Banpore in exchange for their honey, wax and oil-seeds, &c. They have no fixed cultivated lands, but clear patches in the jungle in favourable situations. These lands are tilled for two years, after which they lie fallow. The jungle soon springs up, and in a few years is again cut down and burnt. The ashes serve as manure. They possess a few cows, bullocks and goats. There are seldom more than two or three houses together. The average population is not more than two and a half to each house. If they are ill or unfortunate in any way, they make offerings to "Ram Deo." He is represented by a misshapen stone stuck against a tree. A priest of course officiates, and to him they bring their offerings of toddy, fowls or a kid. A little of the toddy is poured over the stone idol, and the remainder drank by the priest and devotee together. The animal is slain, and some blood sprinkled on the stone. The flesh is eaten by the priest and his dupe. The latter then goes home, while the priest proceeds to sleep upon the question of the devotee, the pleasure of the god being signified in a dream. The response, whether favourable or otherwise, is of course so worded as to bring about its fulfilment. After the pleasure of the god has been declared, another offering is made.

In their marriage ceremonies, the parents of the parties to be united accompany them to the stone Maha Deb, where they make an offering similar to the foregoing. The priest ties a string round the right wrist of both bride and bridegroom, then joining their hands the ceremony is concluded. Some bury their dead, and others burn them. They have some vague idea of rewards and punishment in a future state, and believe that good men will transmigrate into a good caste, others into cows, monkeys, &c. Very bad men will die at once, and never live again. Their ideas of good and evil are, however, very indefinite. Thus they say that it is not good to kill a man (albeit they have not much scruple about that), but it is good to steal.

At Arang, eight miles north of Banpore, there are about one hundred Khund Paiks, who are a degree more civilized than the others. These people, in consideration of the performance of almost nominal police duties in their neighbourhood, are allowed five beegas (about two acres) of land each. They are not, however, to be entirely depended upon; for either the hope of plunder or their innate love of a row is a sufficient inducement for them to desert their post. Thus, in 1836, these people joined several hundred Khunds from the more remote hills, and attacked Banpore, which they plundered and partly burnt. However, the policy must be admitted to be good which gives these Khunds small portions of land with some ostensible duties to perform; inasmuch as it keeps those who would otherwise be dacoits, tolerably quiet, and accustoms them to the authority of the law,—a great step towards the better management of these tribes generally.

My amiable Khunds professed total ignorance of Meriah sacrifices. However, the practice of human sacrifices to the earth god at certain seasons was pretty general amongst the barbarous people, by whatever name designated, living on the more remote hills to the west and north of Banpore, partly in the Madras Presidency, and partly in that of Bengal. Officers were appointed by the respective Governments to suppress these horrid rites. The first officer appointed to this duty by the Bengal Government was the late Captain George Hicks, from whom I obtained some interesting particulars.

The intended victims are, when young, stolen from the natives of the plains. Can this be a traditionary revenge for their having been expelled from the plains? It looks something like it. The captives are well treated for some years, and kept in ignorance of the fate awaiting them. When required for sacrifice, the victim is bound, with the back of his head in contact with a stout bamboo stuck in the ground. By gentle percussions of the bamboo above the victim's head, insensibility is gradually induced, when at a given signal the people rush in, and literally cut him to pieces. Each person hastens with a piece of the still quivering flesh and buries it in his patch of cultivated land; without this they say that the huldee (turmeric) would lose its colour, and the land its fertility. Captain Hicks was successful in rescuing several children who were in training for sacrifice. I saw some of them in Cuttack, where they were placed under the care of the Baptist missionaries, the Government allowing a certain sum for their support.

Not long before my visit to Banpore, a tribe of Thugs, called "Golahs," was discovered in the Pooree district and the adjoining tributary states of Runpore and Nyaghur. Some of these Thugs resided in the village of Dandmukunpore, close to the main road between Pooree and Cuttack. I once pitched my tents near this village for a couple of days, little suspecting what interesting neighbours I had. They had been settled there for some generations, and had intermarried with others of the tribe in Runpore, following the ostensible occupation of cultivators of the soil, with which they secretly combined the trade of murder and plunder, and that too, however strange it may seem, with a religious feeling. Suspicion was first excited against them in 1836, when Mr. Wilkinson, the then collector and magistrate, received information of a party having proceeded on an expedition. On their return they were apprehended, and a quantity of suspicious property being found upon them, they were kept in confinement several months, while the various articles were described and proclaimed; but no claimants coming forward (it would have been a wonder if they did) the Golahs were released, and the suspected property given up to them. A few years after this, several persons having disappeared in a mysterious manner between Pooree and Ganjam, the magistrate (the late Mr. J. K. Ewart) of Pooree caused strict search to be made for them, and the remains of several of the missing parties were found. Mr. Ewart, who personally superintended the search, remarked that the two front teeth in each jaw had been knocked out. This fact was communicated to Captain Vallancey, the assistant-general for the suppression of

Thuggee, who, aided by the indefatigable exertions of Mr. Ewart, succeeded in capturing forty-two Thugs, residents of the Pooree district or Runpore. These men were convicted on the clearest evidence of having been concerned in the murder of twenty-three persons, whose remains were found buried in the sands of the sea-shore between Pooree and Ganjam. I saw a lot of these wretches in custody, among whom was a respectable-looking, grey-headed old man, that no one would suspect of having earned a living by tugging at the life-strings of his fellow-creatures. Some of the convicts were hung in chains, and the remainder imprisoned for life. Their families, amounting to one hundred and twenty-seven individuals, were placed under the surveillance of the police. A letter which one of the convicts addressed to his wife was intercepted. The writer desired his wife to "look upon him as one dead, that he could never hope to recover his liberty, unless the Pindarees should get the upper hand, and there was no chance of that," &c., and concluded by requesting that she would send him some information about her domestic affairs. The letter was forwarded by the magistrate to its destination. Poor wretch! one could not help compassionating his forlorn situation after reading such a letter, proving that he had a soft place in his heart, albeit he had played with life and death.

The Munsurreas (killers of men), says Mr. Ewart, "have a slang language. Before going on an expedition, they assemble at the house of their Moquddum, where they are all shaved. A room is carefully swept, and there, after cooking food in a new earthen pot, and sacrificing a he-goat to the goddess (Kalee), they remain all night, and start at dawn.

"If one party has been unsuccessful and meets another which has obtained spoil, they receive a portion from them. But if the successful gang should arrive at home without meeting the others, they retain the whole. In the division of the spoil, the Moquddum always receive two shares, and each member of the gang one share. Each gang goes out twice a-year, marauding for about one or two months. One of the party calls himself the bundaree (servant), another, gowalla (cow-herd or bearer), and the rest pass as brahmins.

"It is the custom of the Arcottee Thugs only to knock out the teeth of the first victim they find after being out a long time on an unsuccessful expedition, whereas it is the custom of the two gangs who style themselves "Jungbegaree" and "Jungatee," to knock out the two front upper and lower teeth of every victim before burying the body. These gangs are from the neighbourhood of Poonah and Satarra, and generally travel as Jogees and Byraghees, resting at Byraghee, Muths or similar places."

To any one who has not read the "Confessions of a Thug," by Captain Meadows Taylor, the following confessions made before Captain Vallancey by one of the gang living in the Pooree district may prove interesting. I give the words as they occur in the official record, omitting only the unpronounceable names of the parties, and a few unimportant particulars:

"Deposition of Pooredah, son of Bulboodah, Golah caste 25 years of age, resident of Nundapore, Khoordah Talook, taken before Captain G. Vallancey, Assistant-General Superintendent, 2nd December, 1839:

"My name is Pooredah, my father's name Bulboodah; mine and my father's occupation was that of cultivators, and we are in the habit of murdering the travellers we meet with on the roads for their property. I have followed this work (Thuggee) since I was fifteen or sixteen years of age. I have been on three expeditions in this direction, the last one was in this year, when the following left our homes [I omit the names of eleven Thugs, one of whom was deponent's brother]. We went first to Balnussy (near the northern extremity of the Chilka Lake); here we took boat, and came down within four miles of Manickpatam, and landed. We walked to Manickpatam and slept there one night. The next morning we started for Ruttamutee; before we reached it, we fell in with two travellers, cloth-weavers, returning from Cuttack to Berhampore. We twelve (Thugs) and the two travellers took boat and crossed to the opposite side of the river. On landing we went onwards to Sumachul Dharha, half a mile from which place I, assisted by two others, strangled one traveller, while three other Thugs murdered his companion. We obtained from them thirty rupees in ready money, three gold ornaments, a brass lotah, and some old cotton cloths. The bodies were taken a short distance in the direction of the sea and buried in the sand. We slept that night at Sumachul Dharha, and next morning started for Nubba. When we had gone about half the distance, we met three travellers with some dried fish in two bhangies. We joined the travellers and went with them about four miles to an old well. It was then about mid-day; and there we strangled them. The three bodies were taken a short distance towards the sea and lightly buried in the sand. We obtained from them twenty rupees ready money, one brass cup, two rupees' worth of Cuttack pice, and five pieces of old cloth. From thence we went immediately to a village about two miles from Nubba, and remained there all night. Four of the party during the night went to the place where we had secreted the bodies, and digging a deep hole in the sand, buried them and returned. The next day we went off to the village of Bahmundea and slept there. The next day to Beilparah, and put up in the Dhurmsalla in consequence of rain falling. The next morning six of the party, including myself, left and went to the tank near the village of Humah; just then two travellers of the Ooriah caste, going to Rhumba, came up. We accompanied them towards Rhumba about three miles, to a small tank; there we stopped, and I remained in the road with the clothes of the party, while the others and the travellers went to the tank to wash themselves, and while doing

VIEW OF THE TEMPLE OF JE[illegible]GERNATH, FROM THE SOUTH

so the travellers were strangled. The bodies were hid in the water. It was then about six o'clock in the morning. We obtained fifty rupees in ready money, two gold ornaments, one lotah, one brass plate, two small looking-glasses in brass covers, two necklaces of toolsee seeds, two silver bracelets, five gold beads, two brass chunam boxes, one iron serotah or soopari nippers, one red cloth bag, one black cloth bag, one coarse silk cloth, two cotton cloths, six pieces of red dyed cloth, and one sheet. We returned immediately to Humah, and put up there. We sent two of the party to Beilparha to bring provisions. They returned, accompanied by the other party of six. We all remained there; the property was shewn to all and divided amongst the party. At night I and three others went to the Pagoda in the village and slept there. The remaining eight persons went to the tank where the bodies were and securely buried them, and returned from thence about midnight. The next morning, passing by Ganjam, we went to Chutterpore and slept there. The next morning we all proceeded to Naidepell; we remained there some time and cooked our rice. At three o'clock we left that village for Berhampore. After we had travelled about four miles, we overtook two travellers proceeding in the same direction; we accompanied them about a mile and a half, when they were strangled. We immediately carried the bodies into the jungle. Afterwards, four of the party and I went on to Berhampore and slept there; the other seven remained to bury the bodies. The next day, when we five reached the village of Kondah, the other party of seven joined us. We obtained by this murder one brass lotah, a string of white stone beads, one piece of figured silk saree, and one small carpet. A box in which the travellers had their property was thrown away into the jungle. The same day we went on to the village of Golunta; here six of the party remained; the other six went to the village of Bhulleaghur, about half a mile off, and slept there. The next day, the six who remained at Golunta joined us at Bhulleaghur, and told us that they had killed a traveller while at Golunta, and had obtained from him half a rupee's worth of pice, a blanket and a brass cup. From thence we left together and went to

Kunchelligoondum. There we cooked our rice, and about three or four o'clock we left that place, and had scarcely proceeded a mile when a party of six Ooriah travellers overtook us, and sat down with us where we were sitting. After a little while, one of our party left us with the travellers, and proceeded in front with them; we followed, and when they had reached the village of Ambrogaum, we joined them, and we all sat down, when it was decided that we should all pass the night there on the road. About seven o'clock the six travellers were murdered. The bodies were immediately taken into the jungle on the left side of the road about half a mile, and buried. Afterwards, we went directly to the tank at Hurreepore and slept there. We obtained by this murder one gold mohur, ten or twelve rupees, three blankets, four silk cloths, two yellow and two white, ten or twelve other cloths, one thick silk cloth, and one brass stamp, formed like a pair of feet. From Hurreepore we went in parties of two or three. One of these parties met a traveller of the goldsmith caste going from Hurreepore. They accompanied him for about half a mile and then murdered him. They obtained one rupee and twenty pice, one brass cup and one goldsmith's iron wire-drawer. Afterwards, I and three others took the body to the right side of the road and buried it. I can point out the place. Afterwards, we went to the village of Muckergolah, and remained there all night. The next day we went by Palassee to Rugonathpore; from thence we returned the following day, proceeding to Nundegaum, Pulassee, Hurreepore, and Kunchelligoondum, where we were apprehended by the Sircar's (government) people."

On being asked if he ever went on expeditions in any other direction besides the south, the deponent answered, "Yes, we go in other directions besides the south. In this year, about six months since, I went out in the west direction, by Bidwarpoonee, Kontaloo and Sontpore; and we are in the habit of going in the direction of Cuttack and Bengal."

"Mild and gentle Hindoos!" From the foregoing deposition it appears that in the course of a fortnight these twelve Thugs strangled seventeen men, and that their plunder consisted of about one hundred and thirty-two rupees in money, sundry gold and silver ornaments, with some blankets and cloths—the whole perhaps not worth more than fifty or sixty rupees, so that the value of each man's share would not be more than sixteen rupees, or thirty-two shillings. One party of Thugs, after murdering three travellers between Nursingpatam and Manickpatam, about twelve miles from Pooree, were dragging away the last body, when a woman came up and inquired what they were about. To prevent discovery, she was instantly strangled, and buried in the sands with the others. I have some other Thug confessions, but they are all of the same miserable and revolting character as those already given. "The Confessions of a Thug," by Captain Meadows Taylor, is, however, one of the most painfully interesting books I have ever read. It is the romance of Thuggee, and true withal—adding another to the many instances of "truth being stranger than fiction."

The Thugs never shed blood, but invariably despatch their victims by strangling. A single Thug rarely attacks a single man; for fear of accidents, they generally contrive to have assistance at hand. Thus, in Pooredah's gang of a dozen men, when it was decided that they should murder the six Ooriah travellers, two Thugs were attached to each traveller; and this is the way they transact their horrid business. Seated by the side or in rear of the unsuspecting travellers, these remorseless ministers of death take up their position, not at once, but apparently in an undesigning way, so as to lull suspicion. All being in readiness, at a signal previously decided on being given by the chief, such as his asking for tobacco, or any apparently indifferent question or word, the fatal knotted cloths are instantly thrown over the necks of the victims, who are at once powerless in the grasp of the Thugs. Not a cry escapes, and in a very short space of time six breathless bodies are lying dead on the ground. Then come the hurried dragging away and burial of the bodies in the jungle or their hasty interment in the sands, as may be most convenient, and the temporary dispersion of the gang to meet a day or two after at a given rendezvous.

Only one instance, that I am aware of, is known of the Thugs attacking Europeans. The victim was an officer who had been very actively engaged in pursuit of some parties of Thugs. I forget his name, but his remains lie in the grave-yard at Etawah, where, some three years before the mutinies, I saw a monument which had been erected to his memory.

CHAPTER XVII.

Village of Tanghee—Chilka Lake—Gradual Formation of Land—Scenery—Myriads of Aquatic Birds—Fish—Oysters—Commander-in-Chief and his Staff at the Oyster-beds—Agréments of a Residence near the Lake—Method of paying the Salt Manufacturers—Hot Spring at Utteer—Medicinal and other Uses of the Water—Skull Temple—Village Schools—Subjects taught—Method of paying the Schoolmaster—School-room—A Private Tutor—Comparison between the Situation of a Native and English Teacher—Remarkable Custom in signing any Documents—Novel Mode of Fishing in the Koosbuddra River—Silk Weavers—Plant Mulberry Garden—Aversion of the Natives to undertake the Cultivation of Silk.

AFTER leaving Banpore, I proceeded by the new road to Tanghee, a large village containing three hundred houses built in irregular streets. The houses appear very neat; most of them are coloured red and sprinkled with chunam (lime) in various figures, which give them a cleanly appearance externally. As in most of the houses in Khoordah, the entrance is devoted to the cows; beyond that is a square court, with perhaps a toolsee plant *(ocymum sanctum)* in the centre. On three sides of the court are the dwellings of the family. The houses are built of wattle and dab (wicker-work and mud), and, judging from their appearance, together with the attention paid to the simple adornment of the walls, the people must be in easy circumstances. The same remark may apply generally to the people of Khoordah. In the middle of the street is piled up the manure from the cow-sheds, which is carefully preserved for fuel or for agricultural purposes.

Tanghee is situated about three miles from the Chilka Lake, and backed by a range of hills covered to their summits with jungle, the haunts of tigers and bears, &c. The climate of this neighbourhood proved fatal to several of the officers who were employed there in the insurrection of 1817-18. From Tanghee I proceeded to Baleenussy, where I "took boat," as the Thug Pooredah said in his deposition; my object, however, being to take soundings of the northern extremity of the Chilka Lake. In places where the depth was three feet in 1820, I only found half that depth in 1840, at the same time of the year; so that it is evident the lake is rapidly filling up. I found land under cultivation four hundred yards distant from the lake, where I was assured by the natives that forty years ago the waters of the lake flowed. Between this new land and the lake is a low swampy belt of mud and weeds about two hundred yards in breadth. Long coarse grass, growing on a bed of fetid blue mud, extends far into the waters of the lake. The gradual formation of land may here be easily traced. A small river empties itself into the lake at this spot; the detritus brought down by the stream accumulating amongst the coarse grass, together with decomposed vegetable matter, in course of time becomes to a certain extent consolidated; the waters of the river in their overflow in the rains leave a fresh deposit of detritus from the hills, which gradually elevates the new-formed land above the level of the lake.

The Chilka Lake is stated by native histories to have been formed by an irruption of the sea about the commencement of the third century A.D.; and there is little doubt that it then extended to the foot of the hills on the west and north. At present the lake covers a superficies of two hundred and ninety-six square miles. Its form is very irregular; the greatest diameters being from north-east to south-west fifty-two miles, and from north-west to south-east sixteen miles. The greatest depth I found to be nine feet, and that in the south-west extremity, which literally swarms with polypi. Porpoises may often be seen disporting themselves on the surface of the water. The scenery is here very beautiful, diversified with hills, wood and water; while in the lake itself are several small islands more or less covered with wood and jungle. One island, on a former visit with Martel, we named "Juan Fernandez," from the circumstance of finding goats upon it. We landed and saw several snakes, a few goats and fowls, which were offerings made to the Thakoorannee (Kalee) by the natives. Only the males are left on the island.

These islands are composed of gneiss and coarse granite, with a coating of earth on the more fertile parts. The eastern shore of the lake is low and swampy, and it is here that the "karkutch," or solar evaporation salt, is chiefly produced, affording support to thousands of poor people. On the south, the lake is separated from the sea by a belt of sand, varying from a few hundred yards to nearly a mile in width. It is along this belt of sand that the road leads from Pooree to Ganjam, a nice place for the Thugs when *feeling a fellow.* Of "a fellow feeling," which Byron says "makes us wondrous kind," they have none of it. In nearly the narrowest part of this belt of sand is a well of remarkably pure water, considering its situation. This well is called "Meeta Kooa" (sweet well), and gives the name of Meetakooa to the adjacent village. The salt waters of the lake flow up to the very margin of the well on one side, and on the other the sea is about a pistol-shot distant. There are other wells in the immediate neighbourhood whose waters are slightly brackish.

The rocky islands and sand-banks in the lake are frequented by myriads of aquatic birds. I procured fine specimens of the flamingo, pelican, wild goose, teal, and several varieties of ducks, &c. The waters of the lake contain fish of various kinds and in considerable quantities. The chandnee and mullet are particularly esteemed. A bed of oysters has been formed near Manickpatam; and it was our custom to have a banghy load of oysters, prawns and crabs, brought thence to Pooree every day in the hot weather. A few years before I was stationed at Pooree, the then Commander-in-Chief (if I mistake not, the venerable Field-Marshal, Lord Combermere) and his staff visited the lake; and I was told that they had made such an onslaught on the oysters that the bed was nearly destroyed, and was when I arrived but just recovering. Be that as it may, there was an abundance for "all hands" in my time. There are few other places in this part of India where fresh oysters are procurable, so no doubt his Excellency and staff enjoyed themselves. In fact, independently of the oyster-bed, there are few more enjoyable places in India to any one fond of shooting, fishing, or a gallop after antelopes, and at the same time an admirer of beautiful scenery. Add to these, a refreshing sea-breeze in the hottest weather. I know few better places *out* of India where a man might desire to live, provided he had some agreeable society and good pay. I had no reason to complain of the latter, but as for society, I was alone; and Adam, I suppose, found even Paradise dull in such circumstances, as it was said not to be good for man to be alone. I know that I was tired of my own company for such a long time together. Some French author, whose name I forget, says that "solitude is a very nice thing indeed, if you have some one to talk to," or words to that effect; and I perfectly agree with Monsieur. Once or twice a year I was obliged by my ex-officio duties to visit the Chilka Lake, for the purpose of making advances to the molunghees (salt manufacturers); and as the Government of the East-India Company has been unjustly blamed for alleged ill-treatment of these people, I will give some account of the means taken to obviate any oppression on the part of the native officials. It was my duty to see every molungee receive a certain number of rupees, according to the quantity of salt to be manufactured by him. I never omitted seeing him count the money; after which I gave him a note signed by myself, with the figures in the Ooriah and English characters of the amount paid. This note was in due season presented to me again after delivering the salt agreed to be manufactured by him. It might be a little more or a little less than the quantity specified, but the difference of excess or deficiency was adjusted, and I saw him receive and count in my presence the amount due on his account, when I asked him if it was correct; so that it was impossible for the man to be defrauded, unless I myself were a rogue. So far from the natives being *compelled* to manufacture salt, it was a source of competition which they eagerly sought.

About forty miles north-west of Pooree is the hot spring of Utteer, to which my friend Colville and I paid a visit on the 8th of December. We saw the steam ascending in the cold morning air for a considerable distance from the spring. It forms a small pool in the middle of the Paddy fields, which are cultivated to its very margin. On a near approach we were immediately sensible of the presence of sulphuretted hydrogen. We saw the water bubbling up in several places, and to our astonishment numerous small fish swimming about in the hot water. While we were looking on these last, several of them darted suddenly into the bubbling spring, and instantly floated on the surface quite dead. I took some of them out of the water, and was informed by a friend learned in such matters that they were a new species. The temperature of the water near the side of the spring, where the fish were swimming about, was 128°. At the same time the water in a tank a quarter of a mile off was found to be 64°, while that of the air was 56° fahrenheit.

The spring is an intermitting one, and the temperature of the water varies accordingly. Sometimes two or three springs may be observed slowly bubbling together, when suddenly some six or eight more are added to the number. These act briskly for a minute or two, and then subside, again to be renewed after a short interval. In the evening, we found the springs nearly dormant, and the water merely tepid. When in full action, the odour of sulphuretted hydrogen is very powerful, and a silver spoon immersed in the spring was speedily blackened. The water is then so hot as not to admit of the hand being held in it for more than a second. We tried to boil some eggs, but must confess that they were very much underdone; however, we flattered ourselves that they were much more wholesome in that state.

Here I must relate a most shocking instance of depravity, which can only be accounted for by some mental aberration. One of our party (I refrain from giving his name) said that the name of the village Utteer, near to which the spring is situated, was evidently derived from the English words "hot here." Poor fellow! it is to be hoped that his friends will continue to look after him.

The waters of the spring are used by the natives as

an aperient, and also as an external application for diseases of the skin. Indeed, they seem to use them for the cure of almost every complaint. They are said to be useful to women who "wish to be," &c. With what effect the reader may judge when I describe the process. The barren women, at the annual festival of Hut Keysur, the presiding deity, whose temple is a quarter of a mile off, assemble together at the spring, and each throws a betel-nut into the bubbling water. If successful in recovering the nuts, their desires will be gratified; but if they fail, there remains no hope for them until the next year. Two thousand grains of the water submitted to evaporation yielded a little more than three grains of saline matter, consisting chiefly of chlorite of soda, with a little carbonate of lime.

About three miles north of Utteer is a remarkable building called the "Moond-o-Deol" (Skull Temple). It is a round tower, with pigeon-hole-like recesses on the outside. The tower is about fifteen feet high, and is said to have been built by Rajah Dirb Sinh Deo, about 1770 A.D., to contain the heads of sundry subjects of the Bankee Rajah, who were captured and slain by the former. The natives say that there were originally one hundred and twenty holes, but *eighty* would be nearer the mark. One of the Shahs of Persia (Shah Mahomed, I think), built a much larger tower for a similar purpose; so it appears to be a way they have in the East, which is unquestionably a very nice country for those who like it. In my opinion, it is all bosh that the poets sing about the clime of the sun, the lime-trees and citron groves, &c. Only let them try it, with their Lalla Rookhs, Zuleikas and Gulnares to boot, and ere long they would wish for civilized society again, and exclaim, with Alexander Selkirk—

"Society, friendship and love,
Divinely bestowed upon man,
Oh had I the wings of a dove,
How soon would I taste you again!"

In the course of my peregrinations, it was my custom to visit the village schools. Almost every village contains one or more; but education is, nevertheless, by no means general. Few schools contain more than from twelve to eighteen boys. Girls, as a rule, are never taught to read or write. A number of parents who wish to educate their children, club together, build a school-house, and appoint a master. Sir William Curtis's three R's, namely, "reading, *riteing* and *rithmetic*," are all that is taught. The office of a schoolmaster is coupled with that of an astrologer, and it is his business to predict a favourable hour for any undertaking of importance. I will give an extract from my journal, shewing the style of thing generally met with. "Mendisal contains about three hundred and fifty inhabitants. There are fifteen houses inhabited by Paiks, twelve by Brahmins and thirty-three by other castes. The houses are built of wattle, plastered over with mud inside and out, save near the roof at the gable end, where a space is left open for the escape of smoke. The floor is raised two or three feet above the general surface of the ground, and is washed over with cow-dung and mud. This may be thought very dirty, but it looks quite clean and comfortable when dry. The houses are all detached. In the village school I found eleven boys, from five to ten years of age, scribbling on the floor, and vociferating furiously all the time. They were the children of the fishermen, cow-herd, brahmin and blacksmith castes. There were no Paiks amongst them; these being fonder of shikar (hunting) than learning, rarely send their children to school. The boys are taught arithmetic, reading and writing in the Ooriah language, and remain at school about five years. The teacher is paid two annas (about threepence) a month for each boy the first year, four annas a month for the second year, and eight annas a month for the third, fourth and fifth years. Besides this, the schoolmaster receives from each boy alternately one pound and a half of rice, four ounces of dhal (a species of vetch or pulse), and a little salt daily; and at the end of the year the parents, amongst them, give him four yards of cotton cloth for clothes, six yards for a sheet, and a handkerchief; so that the schoolmaster may be considered sufficiently well off with ten or a dozen boys. The school-room is eighteen feet long by ten in breadth. The floor, on which the boys write with pieces of earthy talc found in the neighbourhood, is formed of iron-stone clay, and is very hard. When the boys have made some progress, they are taught to write on paper with a reed pen, and on palm-leaves with an iron style. Narain Putnaick, the surburekar of the village, keeps a *private tutor* for his son, and pays him only two rupees a month, no food or other extras." Yet this man could calculate an eclipse of the sun or moon, and had only the wages of a cooly or day-labourer. Fancy that, O ye teachers of the youth of England! After all, it is not worse than the remuneration offered to a tutor in civilized England, which is often below that of a footman; so perhaps the native teachers' situation is the preferable one, as he has no appearance to keep up, and earns sufficient to support his family. True, he is not so enlightened as an English teacher, but he is contented in his situation, and doubtless considers himself a very clever fellow when consulting the stars. His wife wears no crinoline or other fandangles; but is content with the same kind of simple and graceful dress worn by her great-grandmothers two thousand years ago, when our ancestors painted their hides and clad themselves with the skins of wild beasts. "Mais nous avons changé tout cela," certainly, and may affect in our fancied superiority to look down with pity akin to contempt on the ignorance and simplicity of the native; but somebody says, and he was no fool, "Where ignorance is bliss, 'tis folly to be wise." So, after all, I am inclined to think that a native teacher, with his three R's, has a better berth of it than an English one who teaches everything, and many other things besides, with no better prospect in life than eating the bitter bread of dependence, coupled too often with the "proud man's contumely," or, worse still, that of a proud woman. "I would rather be a kitten, and cry mew, than one of these same learned, ill-paid teachers," especially if I had the run of the dairy!

A remarkable custom exists in this district of a person, instead of signing his name, making a rude drawing of his caste on any document he may be called upon to attest, and this is done where the party is fully capable of writing his name. Thus the Maentee (or writer caste) makes a drawing of an iron style or pen; the cultivator, of a plough or harrow; the fisherman, of a fish; the boatman, of an anchor; the carpenter, of a hammer or mallet; the blacksmith, of a hammer or file; the mason, of a trowel; the potter, of his wheel; the tailor, of his scissors. Paiks make a drawing of a spear; Rajpoots, of a sort of dagger or a bow. Priests sign the name of Rama, or affix one of the emblems of Vishnu, &c., according to their sect. Married women make a drawing of some of their ornaments; widows, of the spindle of a spinning-wheel, or frequently the emblem of their late husband's trade, &c.

When crossing the Koosbuddra river, I observed a

novel mode of catching fish. A man advanced into the stream up to his waist, having in his hand a sort of fishing-rod, made of several pieces of light cane screwed to each other, and gradually tapering towards one end, which was armed with a barbed iron spike. This rod was allowed to rest on the water, and where many fish were observed near the surface, feeding on flies or other matters, it was rapidly advanced in that direction, and by a sudden dart the man transfixed a fish; frequently, however, he missed his aim, or rather the fish were too nimble for him.

In my travels about the district, I found three villages in which there were some silk-weavers. The wild or tesser silk of the jungle is mixed with good silk procured from Calcutta at the rate of seven rupees a seer, equal to seven shillings a pound. I thought it would be a capital thing for this poor and populous country to introduce the manufacture of good silk. Accordingly, I selected an eligible site on the banks of the Bargoby river, about six miles from Pooree, and planted between one and two acres of land with cuttings of mulberry plants procured from Cuttack and elsewhere. These cuttings soon took root and flourished most luxuriantly. Silk-worms were then procured, and in course of time I had a considerable quantity of silk. I then sent for some of the silk-weavers, and shewed them how the worms, &c., were managed. The silk was pronounced to be good. I then asked if they would undertake to produce some for themselves; if so, to give them a good start, I would for the first two years undertake to find silk-worms and cultivate mulberry plants for them gratis, and the silk should be their own. "No!" they replied; "their fathers had never done such a thing." "Well, but if *you* will do it, I will not only do what I have said, but purchase the silk from you, if you like, at the price you pay in Calcutta; only take it in hand, and you must succeed." No! I was met with the same reply about their fathers. I was disgusted. They seemed suspicious of my wishing to *do* them in some way or other. So, after expending some four hundred rupees on the experiment, I was compelled to give it up, as I had no desire to carry it on myself.

CHAPTER XVIII.

Strong Gales on change of the Monsoon—Wrecks—Visit a Wreck—Supposed to be the "Acasta"—Visit the Chilka Lake to inspect the Damage caused by the Gale—Terrific Gale while residing with Mr. and Mrs. Edwards—Roof of the House blown off—Perplexing Situation—Arrival of a Vessel in Distress—Determination to cross the Surf—Difficulties—A Damper to my Feelings—Roll over in the Surf—Relief of Shipwrecked Seamen—Loss of an English Ship and Death of the Captain—Arrival of the Crew in Pooree—Another Waif from the Sea—Terrific Gale in 1842—How I passed the Night—Escape of my Friend Shoreham—Several Wrecks on Shore—Pilgrim Hospital blown down and several People killed—Apathy of the Natives—Two Arabs washed Ashore—My Pet Deer blown away—My Garden buried in Sand—Portico of my House blown down in a Gale—Erection and Fall of another Portico—Escape of the Workmen—Tailor killed by one of the falling Bricks—Whale cast Ashore.

On the change of the Monsoon in October, the coast of Pooree is sometimes visited with very heavy gales, accompanied with a perfect deluge of rain. I have known six inches of rain to fall in the course of a single day and night.

Many wrecks occurred on the coast during the period of my residence at Pooree. On one occasion, upwards of twenty native craft, salt sloops, and vessels from the Maldive Islands, were totally lost on this coast, and an English ship with an European crew foundered in the night opposite my house, and every soul perished. In the morning after this disaster, we could distinguish something floating on the surface of the water, just beyond the surf. It was impossible to launch a boat, on account of the very heavy surf rolling in on the shore. We were all day anxiously peering through our telescopes, to try and make out what it was. Next day, both the wind and sea moderated, and I went off in the Government Masoolah boat. I found the top hamper of a wreck floating about, but fast to the masts under water. The spars and sails appeared to be nearly new. We could not see the vessel to which they belonged. An empty trunk and some broken cabin chairs were washed ashore, and the bodies of several seamen were found some miles up the coast. The fate of these people and the wreck haunted me day and night, and I determined to find out something about them. Day after day I went off to the wreck, endeavouring to peer down into the depth of the sea. Sometimes we could distinctly see the vessel, when a sudden lift of the waves again obscured the view. After many days, I found the sea quite smooth, and went out in company with an English traveller who was staying with me. On reaching the wreck, we could distinctly see the vessel laying with her head to the south-east, or thereby, as the sailors say. The main hatchway was open. Having provided ourselves with a sounding line, we lowered it with a stone attached to the end, and were thus poking about, when suddenly we saw some large light-coloured object rising from the deep. We held our breath in awe and expectation—at least, I did—thinking I know not what. Slowly it rose, and presented to our view, only a cabin door.

By the way, a cabin door (supposed to be from the wreck of the Protector), with a lady's reticule attached to the handle, was once cast on shore at Pooree; and also some cases of pickles, capers, preserves, and hogsheads of ale, undoubtedly from the wreck of the Protector, as they were marked. A sale was held for the benefit of the underwriters, and I saw natives buying bottles of preserves, &c., and emptying the contents on the sands, the bottles being all that they prized. My servant bought a twelve-dozen case of capers on my account for two or three rupees, and a lot of tart fruits and a cask of ale for a similar sum. The Protector was wrecked at the Sandheads, above a hundred miles from Pooree, and upwards of one hundred people were lost in her.

To return to my story. We brought the cabin-door and some of the top hamper of the wreck on shore. The magistrate reported to the proper authorities that the masts were in a dangerous situation for vessels passing near the coast, and a steamer was sent from Calcutta to remove them, and this is all we know for certain about the ill-fated ship and her crew. That the vessel was the Acasta there can be little doubt, as a well-found ship of that name left Nellore, laden with salt for Calcutta, about ten days before the gale came on, and would probably be off the coast of Pooree at the time. We supposed that, finding herself on a lee-shore in the night, as a last resource she dropped her anchors ; the sea swept her deck, carried away the main hatch, and the vessel being laden with salt, she would go down like a lump of lead, and this would account for no cargo being cast ashore. The Acasta was never heard of again after leaving Nellore.

Being ex-officio assistant to the salt agent, I went down to the Chilka Lake to inspect the damage done to the salt aurungs, where a whole village with its inhabitants were reported to have been washed away by the rising of the waters in the lake; and such was truly the case, for on my landing on a sandy beach, and walking a short distance, I inquired where were the ruins of the village. "Your lordship is standing upon it," was the reply. So complete was the destruction, that nothing remained to shew that a small village had been there not many days before.

On another occasion when one of these terrific gales occurred, I was residing with my friends Mr. and Mrs. Edwards, both, alas! no more. There were two visitors in the house; one of them a very tall Madras officer, the other an ensign from the same Presidency. The gale commenced in the afternoon, and rapidly increased. After dinner, Mrs. Edwards became alarmed and retired to her room, whither her husband soon followed, leaving myself, the jolly ensign, and Captain —— at table. The walls of the dining-room were twenty-two feet high, and instead of the usual ceiling of native cotton cloth stretched over the rooms of a bungalow, there was luckily a stout ceiling of painted boards. By and by, something fell heavily on the boards overhead. The tall Captain, concluding the roof was coming down, jumped up and ran to a doorway, where he prudently took up his position, and in trying to make himself as thin as he could, so as to expose the least possible surface to the falling roof, he appeared longer than ever. Spar and I looked at each other and then at the long Captain, and burst out laughing. Presently, the rain began to penetrate through the boards, so I called for an umbrella, and was thinking that the worst was over, when suddenly there was a tremendous crash of beams and rafters, &c., falling overhead. This was too much. So Spar and I, following the long Captain's example, sprang up like a couple of lamplighters, and made a rapid retreat to the nearest doorway.

Somehow we did not see anything particular to laugh at *now*, but thought the affair wore rather a serious look. The room was soon flooded, and it was apparent that the thatched roof was off the bungalow. An alarm spread that the cook-room was on fire. On trying to get out, we could not open the door. We tried another and another with like result, and here we were in a pretty fix. Through a hole in the roof we could see the sparks flying past from the cook-room; and if our thatched roof, which had fallen so as to close the doors, were to catch fire, we should very soon have been roasted alive. The night was dark as Erebus, the gale at its height, and no help to be had. There were at least twenty doors opening outwards, and after trying all, we descended a few steps and found a way of exit through one of the bathing-rooms. Our minds thus placed at ease regarding our safety, so far as the fire was concerned, we got the plate-chest and some other valuables ready for removal if necessary, and asked, "What next?" On the lee side of the house three of the rooms were tolerably dry, having a tiled roof under the thatch. So I proposed to go to bed, as we could do nothing more. Three charpoys were found for the long Captain, Spar, and myself; and we all lay down in our accoutrements. Presently, Mrs. Edwards, who was dreadfully alarmed, sent her servant to request that I would come into their room, and there I found her babe sleeping quietly amidst all the clatter and howlings of the tempest. In truth, it was a pretty sight; and I thought of him who said, "Suffer the little children to come unto me, for of such is the kingdom of Heaven." Wrapped in my boat-cloak, I lay down on the floor and was soon fast asleep. At daylight, up and set about getting some hot water for tea. No fire was to be had then, so I heated some water in my handy little Etna, and served out some tea; then away to visit the other houses, to see how our neighbours had fared. Some of them I found in sorry plight. One bungalow had been blown completely down, and two ladies who were in it managed to make their escape, completely drenched of course, to a brick building not far off. The gale continued, with some remission, all the next day and the following one; when, in the evening, we perceived a vessel approaching the shore, apparently in distress. We could not make out what she was, or how manned, as it was dusk when she anchored. We thought that she had lost her masts, and was what the sailors call "jury-rigged," which was all we landsmen knew about it. The Government Masoolah boat was ordered off, but the boatmen declared that they could not get out. All our talk at dinner was about the poor creatures in distress on the other side of the surf, and I announced my intention of going off, if possible, at daybreak. Accordingly, the boat's crew were directed to be in readiness, and at peep of day, after commending myself to the protection of the Almighty, and placing my will handy for Edwards in case I did not come back, I was prepared for whatever might betide. Edwards offered to accompany me, but I would not allow it, as he, I said, had a wife and child to care for, wherêas I stood alone, and one person was quite enough to do what I proposed doing, and that was, to make the boat's crew do their duty, and cross the surf for the purpose of relieving those in distress. So taking off my watch, I handed it to Edwards to send to my mother, if the "worst came to the worst."

I have crossed the surf at Madras, and believe it to be much higher than that at Pooree, but the rollers are more regular at Madras, whereas at Pooree they are more broken. Every third roller, which perhaps takes its rise half a mile or more from the shore, is generally considerably higher than the two preceding, which we can often cross, comparatively speaking, easily enough; and are probably congratulating ourselves that the difficulty is over, when a tremendous wave, rising like a wall before us, threatens to overwhelm the boat, and bearing us back with irresistible force leaves us pretty near where we had started from, and again we have to commence the struggle. After being driven back perhaps twenty times, we at last manage to get into the open sea. Although, at most times, crossing the surf is apparently a formidable undertaking to any one not accustomed to it, yet in tolerably fine weather, with an experienced crew in a Masoolah boat, there is neither difficulty nor danger; but after a gale a considerable swell remains, and accidents sometimes occur; thus, an officer whom I knew, Major P——, A.A.G., of the Bengal army, was drowned in the surf at Madras by the capsizing of a Masoolah boat; and as I have a greater alacrity for sinking than swimming, I had some apprehension that such might be my fate; however, as my errand was one of mercy, I deliberately stared the grim tyrant Death in the face.

The sky was overcast; the sea looked like muddy water, and an angry surf, crested with dirty foam, was rolling in and breaking furiously on the shore. The boatmen did not like the prospect, and declared that it was impossible to go out; but as the saheb was going with them, they could not avoid making the attempt. Again and again were we driven back. The surf rose like a wall close to the boat, and many times it appeared that we must inevitably be swamped. I was standing nearly up to my knees in water in the middle of the boat, and shouting "Tano, tano!" (pull, pull!), with all my might whenever I saw any of the boatmen cease rowing or looking behind them at the surf, as it came roaring towards us. Our only chance was to keep the boat's head steadily towards the approaching wave; for if we broached to, it was all up with us, or rather with poor little me, for the natives swim like ducks. Well, to "make a long story short," after pulling an hour and a half we managed to cross the surf, and rowed towards the vessel I had come to board. My heart was full of compassion for the distressed people, and I felt infinite gratification in thinking that we had come to their relief. We approached, but did not see any anxious faces looking out for us, which I thought very strange, as they must have seen us battling with the surf. However, I concluded that their apparent indifference arose from the exceedingly distressed state they were in. When within hail, a dark face looked over the stern. "Kya hooa?" (What's the matter?), I shouted. "Ag munkta" (We want fire), was the reply. Oh what a damper to my excited feelings, and how very small I felt, after such a fit of heroics, on thinking that I had risked my life with no other result than to hear that a Bengalee wanted a fire! After all, the matter was of great importance to them. They had been knocking about in the gale, their decks swept clear by the sea, and some of the crew washed overboard and drowned. The vessel was manned entirely by natives. They had plenty of rice, but no means of cooking it. After some palaver, the commander of the craft got into my boat, with the view of procuring some supplies in the town, and getting off again when the sea went down. The return across the surf was easy enough; but the boatmen, I suppose by way of paying me off for compelling them to go out, allowed the boat to broach to in the last surf, and I of course rolled into the water, with no further damage than a good ducking, which did no harm, seeing that I was wet enough before; so I laughed at the fellows and thanked them, and, moreover, told them to come to my house for some buckshisk for taking me across the surf. A few rupees made us all right again.

The relief of shipwrecked seamen was at times a considerable tax on the few European residents at Pooree. At one time we had to support for many days the whole crew of an English ship, commanded by a Captain Latimer. The vessel was totally lost some twelve miles down the coast; the captain and (I think) a boy drowned. The death of the captain occurred in what the sailors would call a *lubberly* manner, if a landsman had done such a thing. Not being able to swim, he secured a bag of rupees round his neck (so the mate told us), and clung to a spar in the hope of being cast ashore; but he was washed off the spar by the surf, and of course went down head foremost with the weight of rupees round his neck. The rest of the crew escaped somehow or other, and marched into Pooree just as I was on the point of starting to see after them. We put them into an empty bungalow, with plenty of straw to lie upon, and collected all our spare clothing for them, as they had saved nothing from the wreck but the clothes in which they stood. We each of us took it in turns to kill a fat sheep, and find bread, grog and tobacco, &c., for them every day. Jack was in clover. After many days, when some of the men who had been injured were recovered and able to travel, we raised a purse amongst us, and forwarded them to Cuttack, en route for Calcutta. The Cuttackites of course treated the honest fellows liberally. When parting with us, they said that if ever they were wrecked again, they hoped it would be on the coast of Pooree.

Another waif from a wreck was a French gentleman, Monsieur Castelnau, who passed a week or ten days with me. He could not speak a word of English, nor I much

French; however, with the assistance of a dictionary and my billiard-table, we managed to get on very well together. In the evening, we usually dined with Hambledon, whose wife could converse with Monsieur C. in French.

The most terrific storm I ever witnessed was (I think) in 1842, when all the out-offices of every description attached to my house were blown down. The house, with exception of the billiard-room, was puckha, that is, built of brick and mortar. I had my horse brought into the billiard-room; and all the servants, with their wives and little ones, amounting, I suppose, to some forty or fifty souls, brought into the house. I nailed up the venetian doors, and made all as snug as possible. By and by, the end of the billiard-room gave way, when I ordered the horse to be brought into one of the bedrooms. O what a night that was! The stench from all these people, and the horse, and a dozen goats, shut up in a rather small house, was something overpowering; but there was no help for it: yes, there was; for I smoked cigars and sat up nearly all night reading "Sandford and Merton," a book I had not read since I was a child. Towards morning the gale moderated, and I ordered out my horse to ride along shore and into the town, to see what damage had been done. On opening the doors, I met my friend Shoreham, whose house had been blown down, and who managed to escape to a small puckha building, where he passed the night on or under a door-mat completely drenched. He lost nearly all his property, but particularly lamented his "Anwary Sohaily," which he was reading when his house began to shake. On the shore, I found three or four native craft, high and dry; some of the crews had escaped, and were seated on the sands as composedly as if nothing had happened, although some of their fellows, they said, had been drowned. What a scene of desolation in the town! Most of the houses unroofed, and many were destroyed. Trees torn up by the roots. The Pilgrim Hospital was blown down and several patients killed; but the strangest sight of all was to witness the utter apathy of some natives as they sat on the ruins of their houses, smoking hubble-bubbles, as if all was pleasant and serene around. Dickens might have taken his original of Mark Tapley from a native of Orissa. Two Arabs were washed ashore on pieces of wreck. They were the Nakoda and Tindal of a large Arab vessel; and out of sixty souls on board, were the only persons saved. The Tindal, who was first found, told a dark story about some slaves that were on board, which story he afterwards retracted when he found that his commander (the Nakoda) was saved. The latter was a fine portly man, and wore a large turquois ring on one of his fingers. He informed us that his ship had been at the Sand-heads for some days, waiting for a pilot. When the gale came on, they were compelled to put to sea again, and the vessel foundered off Pooree.

I had twelve or fourteen pet deer and antelopes in two large enclosures near my house. The fence was blown down, and the animals blown away; at least, I never saw them again, though I heard of one of the deer being in a native garden some miles off. A garden which I had made on the sands, and partly enclosed with a mud wall, at great labour and expense, was buried some three or four feet with drift sand. I set lots of coolies to work and soon exhumed it again. This garden I had formed in a time of famine, when all poor people who were willing to work, were invited to bring only once a day a basket-full of earth, or, if they could not carry a basket, even a handful, for which each person received a meal of cooked rice. To prevent any bother about loss of caste in eating my rice, I engaged a Brahmin to cook it. In the famine I have alluded to, a poor little orphan boy, about ten years of age, attracted my attention in the streets of Pooree. He was entirely dependent on the charity of strangers. I placed him in charge of one of my gardeners, and engaged a "private tutor" to teach him the "three R's" in my house, for the magnificent sum of two rupees a month. In a year or two the little chap got tired of this, played truant, and cut away to a fair at Bhovaneswar. After a week's absence he was brought back. He was too old for the Baptist Mission School in Cuttack, and when about leaving Pooree I was puzzled to know what to do with him. A big brother turned up when the youngster had found a friend. So I established them together in a shop for the sale of tobacco, ghee, dhal, &c.; paid the rent in advance for two or three years, in addition to plenishing the shop, that they might have a good start; and proud they were when I stopped at the shop and bought a bazar cigar, which I could not smoke. I requested the Rev. Dr. Sutton would kindly look after the lads whenever he visited Pooree. How they got on I never heard.

In the last gale which occurred at Pooree in my time, the thatched portico of my house was blown down. To prevent any accident of the kind in future, I determined to build it "puckha," that is to say, on columns of masonry, with a flat roof of the same. From the ground to the top of the portico the height was about eighteen feet. The work was nearly completed. Three or four men, on some scaffolding, were employed in giving the finishing touches underneath, and several more were on the top of the building, when I ascended to look at the work, which appeared all right; so I came down again and walked under the portico towards the stables, which had also been blown down. I had not left the portico a dozen yards behind, when down it came with a thundering crash, with all the people under and upon it. On hearing the noise I turned round, and could scarcely believe the evidence of my senses when I saw the ruin. I shall never forget the feeling of horror that came over me, when suddenly the thought flashed across my mind that the poor work-people must be killed or grievously wounded. With the assistance of others, I commenced pulling away furiously at bricks and rafters to release the men who were buried underneath. Strange to say, those who had been employed on the top were very little injured, and joined us in extricating the others, whom, with a feeling of deep thankfulness on my part, we also found not much the worse for the accident, save one boy whose right arm was much bruised. My attention was now directed to a poor tailor (a servant of my *Pooree Caloro's)*, who had been sitting at work in the veranda about eight feet from the portico. The poor man had been struck on the head by a falling brick, and was killed on the spot. I could not believe it at first, as he appeared so far out of harm's way; but, alas! it was too true, for he never spoke again. It appeared that some of the columns which supported the flat roof were built of bad bricks, hence the catastrophe.

After one of these terrific gales, a whale, nearly fifty feet long, was washed ashore quite dead. How he came by his death, deponent saith not; but there he was, "dead as herrings that are red;" and I had a walk on his huge carcase. In the course of a fortnight, the jackals, pariah-dogs and vultures, had devoured every part of the monster that was devourable.

So frequent were heavy gales about the change of the Monsoon in October, that I declared I would never be at sea in the Bay of Bengal at that season; and yet I was once very nearly caught when returning from Australia in the ship Bussorah, merchant, in 1847; but this is anticipating. I have to go to Mauritius first.

CHAPTER XIX.

Embark for Mauritius—Tempestuous Passage—Cottage near La Grande Rivière—Garrison Ball—Bay de Tombeau—Collecting Corals—Paul and Virginia's Tomb a Myth—Meet with a quondam Sepoy of 47th Native Infantry—Remarks on the Mutiny of that Regiment.

In July, 184—, I was advised to proceed to sea for the benefit of my health. Accordingly, I embarked with my friend Temple in a vessel bound to Mauritius. I had wished to go to Egypt and thence to Palestine; but owing to some irregularity on the part of a Madras official, who having obtained leave to Egypt crossed over to Malta, which was beyond the longitude allowed by the East-India Company to their officers, leave to Egypt was withdrawn, to my very great regret, as I had always looked forward to visiting those countries at some time or other; and now, when I thought I was on the point of gratifying my most earnest wishes, having made every arrangement for the journey, to have the cup of fruition, as it were, dashed from my lips, was indeed most mortifying, and I did not care where I went; so in the middle of the south-west Monsoon we found ourselves beating down the Bay of Bengal, amidst an almost constant succession of squalls. However, we made a very quick passage, considering the time of the year. My friend Temple, from the time we left the Sand-heads, had been confined to his cot with fever, and on our arrival was so weak that he was lowered over the ship's side in it. I had previously been on shore, and hired a ready-furnished house, called Erin Cottage, situated on the left bank of La Grande Rivière. This cottage was the property of the Rev. Langrishe Banks, who was about proceeding to the Seychelle Islands on a visitation tour, I believe. When I returned on board, we saw him sailing out of the harbour, while we were preparing to lower Temple into a boat, which was to take us direct to La Grande Rivière. The Custom-house officials, on my representation, waived the landing of our baggage at Port Louis, and politely allowed it to be transported at once to the residence I had engaged.

Mr. Banks had left his servants, carriage and horse for our use; so we stepped at once into a house furnished at all points, and ordered tea. Two days after we landed on this beautiful island, Temple was able to toddle into the garden, and in the course of a week could walk about pretty well. We could not eat the tough Madagascar beef supplied by our butcher, so I used to drive into Port Louis to market. Fowls were extremely dear, according to our Indian notions. In Calcutta, we could have got a dozen for two rupees, whereas here they were two rupees each. The floors of our cottage were waxed and polished in the way I remember them in Paris not quite a hundred and fifty years ago. At peep of day I was generally out and away over the country for eight or ten miles; then a cold bath in water fresh from La Grande Rivière; and at breakfast had the most delicious honey in the world. It is brought from the island of Bourbon, and acquires its exquisite flavour, I was told, from the bees feeding on the fragrant blossoms of the coffee-plant.

Soon after our arrival in Mauritius, we were invited to a garrison ball. I am no dancer, but wishing to see how they managed such affairs in this semi-French colony, I went. The room was of considerable length, and the ladies (chiefly French, I was told) were arranged in rows or tiers on either side, and at one end of the room. At the other end was the seat reserved for the Governor, Sir Lionel Smith. The gentlemen were huddled together in the middle of the room—rather a trying situation for a modest outsider to stand the fire of so many bright eyes, right and left. The Governor was so long in making his appearance that at last dancing commenced without him. In the middle of the first quadrille a whisper passed round, "The Governor, the Governor;" and presently Sir Lionel appeared, when the band struck up, God save the King; and his Excellency, breaking the line of dancers, walked up the centre of the room to his seat. As I was a stranger to almost everybody in the room, I found it rather slow work, and soon took my departure.

Everybody in my young days, though I suppose the case is different in this *fast* age, had read St. Pierre's beautiful tale of "Paul and Virginia." I had faith in the story, and one day hired a boat to take me and Captain W. to the Bay de Tombeau, and also to procure some corals. The day was as *lovely*, as a lady would say, as ever shone on earth or sea, not a breath of air to ruffle the surface of the water; so we could peer into the depths of the ocean; and when the rowers rested, it was wonderful to see the forests of coral of every shade of blue and crimson at a considerable depth beneath the boat. Numerous small fish were swimming amongst the coral branches. Beautiful as the scene was, the following well-known lines *would* intrude themselves on my memory:

"The sun from his vertical height
Illumin'd the depths of the sea,
And the fishes beginning to sweat,
Cried *dash* it, how hot it'll be!"

Why is it that a sense of the ludicrous *will* occur just where it ought not to do? I have not time to settle the question now. Having brought a diver with us, I pointed out any particular specimen of coral I required, when overboard he went and brought it up. I thought that the colours would remain, and was much disappointed to find that when the coral insect died the beautiful colours faded away, leaving only a dirty brown; but this I did not find out immediately. Having collected as much coral as I wanted, we landed, intending to proceed to the tomb of Paul and Virginia; but our romantic feelings received a rude shock from a matter-of-fact French gentleman at whose house we stopped for luncheon, and who informed us that Paul and Virginia were not buried there. I wished that he had kept this to himself, for one does not like to have these illusions torn so ruthlessly away. Nevertheless, I shall always consider my cruise to the Bay de Tombeau one of the most enjoyable days I ever spent.

In one of my early morning walks, I met with a quondam Sepoy of the 47th regiment Bengal Native Infantry. The man gave the military salute, or I should not have known him. I stopped, and had some conversation with him. The poor fellow was pining after his own country. I attempted to console him by praising the fine air and water of the island, and shall not readily forget his pathetic tone and look as he replied, "Aye, Sahib, but it is not the air and water of my country." Poor fellow! his sentence was a life-long banishment, leaving no hope on this side the grave. After all, there were some extenuating circumstances in the mutiny in which this man was concerned. It occurred at Barrackpore two or three years before I entered the service. The story is too long to relate here; but as I was doing duty with the regiment, after the number had been restored to the Army List, from which it had been erased, I may remark, *en passant,* that although the almost total destruction of the regiment was perhaps necessary in a military point of view, yet it was an "untoward event," as it might have been prevented, if a certain report had not been overlooked or mislaid, until the mischief was irreparable.

A few days before I left Mauritius a military execution took place. A soldier for some heinous crime was sentenced to be shot. I *could* not go, as many did, to witness the spectacle. In fact, I never could bear to see a human being, or even any animal, put to death in "cold blood." Though it has been my duty to attend at some executions, I always averted my glance at the fatal moment. I am not an advocate, however, for the abolition of death punishment; but think that the old law is as good now as ever, "Whoso sheddeth man's blood, by man shall his blood be shed."

CHAPTER XX.

Embark in the Ship C—— for Calcutta—Party on Board—Made Sail—Small-pox on Board—Death—Sacrifice of a Sheep to the Goddess of Small-pox—Raft—Dastardly Behaviour of the Captain—Leave the Ship—Monsieur Gr——l——r—Author lousy—Return to Pooree.

AFTER five weeks' sojourn at Mauritius, I took leave of Temple, and embarked on board the ship C——, then lying in Port Louis to leeward of the small-pox hospital, in which I understood there were many cases of the disease. Our crew consisted of between forty and fifty Lascars, besides the captain, mates, and a Chinese carpenter, &c. The night before we sailed, the captain gave a ball and supper on board to a party of ladies and gentlemen from the town. Amongst the party was Captain —— of the ship F——shire. He had been rather more than half-seas over at dinner, and went to roost in a queer place to steady himself. There was a bath-room attached to my stern cabin. When I went on board in the evening, the key of the cabin could not be found. I could partially open the door of the bath-room, but there was some resisting substance on the other side which prevented admission; so the lock of the cabin-door was forced, when I immediately proceeded to ascertain what caused the obstruction in the bath-room, and there found the redoubted captain of the "F——shire" in "full fig," stowed away on the deck and snoring loudly. The bath-room was a long and narrow one, just wide enough to accommodate his rather stout body; so I suppose he fancied himself in his bunk, and could not fetch way. By and by he joined the throng on deck, and I went to bed, but not to sleep, by reason of the racket overhead, which was kept up "till daylight in the morning." Owing to one delay or another we did not sail until towards evening. About a week or ten days after our departure, the small-pox appeared amongst the crew, to the great consternation of the captain. The ship being in ballast, a spacious sick-bay was rigged out on the main-deck, and the invalid was placed below, with a messmate to attend upon him; all communication with the rest of the crew being strictly forbidden. This was something like shutting the stable-door after the horse was stolen; for two or three days after, another case occurred, and then another and another; until we had at one time eighteen men down together in the sick-bay, leaving barely enough to work the ship in the event of bad weather. It is impossible to describe the state of consternation the captain and crew were in. The mates behaved nobly. There being no medical officer attached to the ship, the second mate, a plucky little fellow, was the only man, besides one of the passengers, who every day voluntarily went below to do what was possible for the sick men, and truly that was little enough; still it was some comfort to the sick, as well as to those yet in health, to find that they were not altogether uncared for. The captain, who, by the way, was only *half* an Englishman, was nearly frantic with terror, and seldom came out of his cabin, but had his meals sent in to him. Soon the grim king of terrors made his appearance; and early one morning a corpse, wrapped in a mat, was launched overboard, without any ceremony, and floated slowly astern, as I watched it from the stern-ports of my cabin, for we made but little way owing to a succession of light airs and calms. The Chinese carpenter, with the captain's sanction, after some ridiculous ceremonies, drew a line from the mainmast to the door of the dastard's cabin, and there drove a nail into the deck. This was to prevent the small-pox going any further. Vain hope! The next day the captain's own servant was attacked with the disease, and placed in the sick-bay. A fat sheep was given to the crew to sacrifice to the goddess of small-pox. The poor animal was dragged several times round the decks, and various ceremonies performed before it was slaughtered at the gangway. A small raft had previously been constructed of bamboos, and little bits of rag, corresponding to the number of the crew, I believe, stuck on sticks secured to the raft. The blood of the sheep was plentifully sprinkled over these, and then the raft was launched overboard; the crew wisely reserving the carcase of the sheep for dinner. The weather was nearly calm, and the horrible raft remained a long time in sight. The crew firmly believed that they had at last propitiated the goddess. The next day two more bodies were thrown overboard. The captain came to my cabin crying like a baby, but received small comfort from me. I could not disguise my contempt for the miserable wretch, and told him plainly that he ought to be ashamed of himself. I exhorted him to go on deck and set a proper example to his crew, who were utterly prostrated by terror; but I might as well have talked to the winds, so entirely was he the slave of his own selfish fears. At one time he talked of landing his sick on some part of the Madras coast; in that case I told him that I should consider it my duty to report the circumstance to Government. Then he would go to the Andaman Islands, and land them there. I protested against this as being most cruel, &c., and declared that I should expose him when we arrived in Calcutta. So we held on our course, and after a long voyage, owing to light winds, we arrived safely at the Sand-heads. Fortunately we had light winds and not a single gale the whole voyage; had we met with any bad weather, I believe we should have lost the ship, if not our own lives, owing to the apathetic state the crew were in. To make a long story short, from the time the first death occurred until the pilot came on board, we had thrown twelve bodies into the sea, and there were nearly twice as many sick on the main-deck when I left the ship. What became of them I never knew, as I jumped into one of the first boats that came alongside, and after rowing all night arrived safely in Calcutta early on the following morning; very happy to make my escape from what, at one time, I considered a doomed ship. I never sat eyes upon her again, and was only sorry to leave the mates and my fellow-passenger Monsieur Gr—l—r on board. How I should like to hear you, mon cher G——, sing once more "O Richard, O mon Roi," and "Marlbrook," as you used to do in the evening, when sitting on the poop before our troubles commenced!

On second thoughts, I have erased the name of the ship, as I do not wish to injure her commander, although he merits little forbearance from me, as, independent of what I have related, he treated us very scurvily in other respects. I paid liberally enough for my passage, giving him exactly what he asked, which was more than was usually paid in a "country ship," which the C—— was. However, I had a private store of comestibles of my own, which I shared with Monsieur G——; otherwise we should indeed have been badly off, for the biscuits placed on the cuddy table were disgustingly full of weavils, and the fresh provisions were very scanty; insomuch that we looked wistfully after the fat sheep sacrificed to the goddess of small-pox. Rice and pepper-water—I forget what it was called in Madrassee—formed the staple of our breakfasts. In going amongst the crew I became—shall I confess it?—out with it!—well, then, *lousy* is the shameful and detestable word. Before I left the ship I threw overboard the clothes I had worn, and had a thorough purification as soon as I arrived in Calcutta. A week after I landed I was at Pooree, after an absence of only six months; but from the events crowded into them, the period, on looking back, appeared at least thrice as long.

CHAPTER XXI.

Description of the Town of Pooree—Amusing Anecdote of a Law-suit about a Cow—Description of Houses in Pooree—Streets—Character of the People—Polygamy—Women seen in the Streets—Ornaments—Venetian Coins—Dress—Amusements—Musical Instruments—Customs—Suttees were never common in Pooree—Marriage Ceremonies—Ceremonies preceding and following the Birth of a Child—Funeral Ceremonies—Periods of Mourning—Shradha, or Offering of Food to deceased Persons—The Turpun or Offering of Water—The Brahmins—Their Vocation.

On my first arrival at Pooree I was in such a hurry to visit more distant, if not more interesting, scenes, that I have hitherto said nothing about the town and its inhabitants. As I have now more leisure, I may as well give some account of both.

The town of Pooree, or Juggurnath Pooree, i.e. the city of Juggurnath, or Lord of the World, is situated on a gentle elevation, apparently not more than fifteen or twenty feet above the level of the sea, from which it is separated by low ranges of sand-hills about a mile in width. On the opposite side, the ground slopes down towards the Kunchee river.

The town contains thirty-six thousand inhabitants, and six thousand six hundred and twenty houses; one-fourth of which is built of stone, and the rest of mud, or wattle and mud, with thatched roofs. Some curiously-situated temples, surrounded by a walled court, upwards of twenty feet below the neighbouring street, may be seen. The natives have a tradition that the site of these temples was the original level of the town, which is very probable, as the sands may now be observed to accumulate against the windward side of the houses in this part; insomuch that any one wishing to build a house in rear of the outermost now standing, would, unless the sand were removed, have the floor on a level with the roofs of other houses. In the course of time, it is easy to conceive that in this manner the original level of the town would be lost.

The town is built in a very irregular manner. Some of the streets are so narrow as scarcely to admit the passage of a hackery. In these streets the houses are built of mud, with floors generally elevated several feet above the level of the ground. In the wider streets the houses are chiefly built of stone, or wattle and mud plastered over with lime. Almost every house of this description has an elevated terrace before it, from three to six or more feet in width. Sometimes the terraces are faced with stone neatly cut. Some are roofed over, thus forming a sort of veranda to the house; and here the inhabitants may frequently be seen asleep, or playing at cards, pucheesee, &c.

Under the terrace and open to the street, is usually a small chamber or sewer, for the reception of all sorts of rubbish. A flight of from six to twelve or more steps rises from the street to the house; and it is amusing to see the cows ascending and descending, with the same regularity as the natives themselves, to and from a small chamber or cow-house immediately within the doorway. This recalls to mind a singular case which came before my friend Shoreham for decision. Two men laid claim to a certain cow which had been stolen or strayed away some time before. The men were both residents of Pooree, and equally respectable; each swore that the cow belonged to him, and moreover brought witnesses to prove his claim. Here was a dead lock—enough, one would think, to puzzle Themis herself if she had been sitting on the bench. At last an astute individual suggested that the cow should be turned loose. The magistrate ordered this to be done, and directed some persons should follow her. The cow naturally made her way to the house to which she had been accustomed, walked up the steps, and turning into the cow-house, thus decided the case.

The houses are usually built in the form of a square, with a court-yard in the centre. In some of the better kinds of houses, a low pillared veranda runs round the court. Three sides of the square are formed by the houses or rooms of the different members of the family, there being frequently two or three families (relations) in the same square. On the fourth side is a doorway common to all the inmates, and immediately within that is the cow-house; these animals being as well lodged as the natives themselves. In the centre of the square may be seen the sacred toolsee plant, or a patch of garden. Trained up and lying on the roofs of the houses are often to be seen the cucurbita pepo, and other plants of that kind; the fruits of which are eaten by the natives. In rear of the house is a small garden. Very few of the houses are more than one story in height. The front walls are frequently painted with grotesque figures of men wrestling with each other, or engaging in mortal combat with tigers and lions, nautches, and some rude representations of the customs of Europeans; for instance, an European officer in full-dress uniform may be seen seated on a chair with numerous attendants before him, one of whom is holding a goblet, while another is pouring into it some liquid for the great man to drink. In another street may be seen a painting of an European medical officer, also in full-dress uniform, visiting a sick man, the latter a native. The doctor is in the act of feeling the pulse of the invalid, who from his skeleton figure, all the ribs being visible, appears to be in a most deplorable state. The perspective of these figures is out of all proportion, but the design is nevertheless ingenious.

The main street, down which the cars of Juggurnath and his brother and sister are dragged, would, as far as width alone is concerned, be deemed handsome anywhere; and certainly one more picturesque is not to be met with. It is a mile and a half in length, slightly curved so that a person cannot see both extremities at once. The great temple of Juggurnath, with the beautiful column of Hanuman standing before the Gate of Lions, terminates the western end of the street; while three other streets converging near this spot, form a sort of square, where a bazaar is daily held; and here may be seen at all hours of the day and greater part of the night, particularly during the chief festivals, a crowd of persons, of perhaps every tribe in India, habited in their respective costumes. Leaving the Gate of Lions, and proceeding towards the Goondicha Noor (commonly called by Europeans Juggurnath's country-house), the street gradually widens; near the temple it is occupied by temporary sheds or shops for the sale of sweetmeats, images, cloth, rice, &c. These sheds are annually taken down to admit of the passage of the cars in the Ruth Jattra festival. On either side the street, for a distance of half a mile, are a few houses and various religious establishments built of stone. The window frames and cornices are generally very neatly carved in wood or stone, and on some are the usual obscene figures to be met with about the temples of this country. Half-way down the street is the Serai. Lower down, the line of buildings is broken by gardens and trees. One mile from the temple is situated the Government Dispensary, formerly the Pilgrim Hospital; and from this to the country-house, the street, except during the hot weather, is partially covered with green turf, while on either side it is bordered with gardens, trees, and a few houses interspersed. The gates and white tops of the Goondicha Noor temples, shining amongst a mass of foliage, terminate the view.

The Ooriahs have been described as "extremely effeminate," and their figures slight and delicate. Compared with natives of the northern parts of India, they are so; but they are certainly a more manly and athletic race than the Bengalees. It is by no means uncommon to see fine muscular-looking men in this district, particularly near the sea-coast, who generally possess mild and pleasing features; but a more ungainly and ugly race than the lower class of women does not exist in India. The natives of the plain country in this district are a quiet, inoffensive and easily managed race; indolent, ignorant and improvident; possessing, however, a considerable share of cunning and duplicity in their dispositions. They are exceedingly averse to change. With reference to their intellectual dulness as compared with other natives of India, Mr. Stirling says that the Ooriahs may be termed the "Bœotians of India." Like all ignorant people, they are very superstitious, being firm believers in ghosts, witchcraft, and all kinds of diablerie. On the occurrence of the eclipse of the sun or moon, they believe that it is caused by a demon devouring the orb, and invoke the gods to drive him away; the people themselves assisting by beating kunchas (a kind of cymbal), tomtoms, &c.; in short, making a *diabolical* noise. Everything in a house becomes impure on the occurrence of an eclipse. The people bathe at the commencement, and again at the termination. All earthen vessels in the house are destroyed. Poor people, however, who cannot afford such wholesale destruction, clean the earthen vessels the previous evening, and plaster a piece of ground near the house with cow-dung, upon which they place their culinary utensils, putting into each a little of the sacred toolsee plant, which prevents their contracting any impurity during the eclipse. When it is over, the floors of the houses and cooking places are purified by plastering them with cow-dung, and the people proceed to the temple to return thanks, by making offerings of course, for their release. During the eclipse they must not eat or drink, or perform any of the offices of nature; if they do, they will be smitten with an incurable disease. Those who can afford it distribute alms to the poor.

Morality is at a very low ebb amongst the natives of the town of Pooree, which is not to be wondered at, considering the prominence everywhere given to the obscene character of their religion. A stranger would be infinitely disgusted with the lewd and dissipated expression of countenance observable amongst many of the priests of Juggurnath. It is not uncommon for a husband, from mercenary motives, to connive at the dishonour of his wife. Polygamy is of course allowed, and practised by those who can afford to keep a plurality of wives.

None but the lower class of women are ever seen abroad, save at the festivals. The better classes are then closely muffled up, so that only an eye or the naked feet can be seen. The ancles are generally encircled with massive bangles of silver or other metal. Several rings are worn in the ears, round the fingers and toes, and a large gold ring hangs pendant from the nose. Bangles of gold or silver are worn round the wrists; and about the neck, a necklace of silver or golden ornaments; the latter frequently composed of old Venetian coins of a very pure quality. On some of these coins I have seen figures of the Virgin and Child, with "Venetia" and "Paul Regnier Dux" in Roman letters. Some have other devices. None have been observed of an earlier date than the 15th century. The arms of the lower class of women are absolutely loaded with large brass bangles, many pounds in weight. Some wear bangles of coloured glass, &c. Children are also frequently decorated with silver bangles round the wrists and ancles, a silver chain round the waist, and a gold coin or two suspended by a thread round the neck; in other respects perfectly naked, until they are five or six years of age.

There is little difference in the dress of the sexes—a cloth passed round the loins and between the legs, and another over the head and shoulders, constitutes the dress of the bulk of the people.

The amusements of the people consist chiefly in playing at cards (both English and native), pucheesee, flying kites, fighting bul-buls (the Indian nightingale), wrestling and nautches. In almost every street in Pooree there is an akhra, a house built by subscription amongst the inhabitants; and here a few of them assemble in the evening to drink sidhee, eat ganjah, wrestle, dance and sing, &c. In fact, they may be considered as very *fast* men; for of course the females of their respective families are not admitted, but only nautch girls.

The musical instruments, or, as they might be more fitly called (with two or three exceptions), *discordant* instruments, consist of brass cymbals of different sizes, horns, conch-shells, a sort of tambourine, and double flageolet, a fife, and fifteen different kinds of drums; one, called "burra kato," is six feet long, and is suspended lengthwise on a pole between two men, who beat the drum at their respective ends. These instruments are chiefly used at marriages and other festivals. In their more private amusements the natives use the well-known setar or a tanpoora, which instruments bear some resemblance to a guitar. Occasionally they use a fiddle, a madullee (an instrument made of reeds), and a sarunjee, a kind of violin with four strings made of skin, and below them seven fine metal strings. A somewhat similar instrument appears to be used in Norway, for, in a note to the translation of Miss Bremer's novel, entitled, "Strife and Peace," we read that "the under-strings of the hardanger fela are four metal strings tuned to accord with the upper catgut strings. It is by means of these, and the peculiar form of the instrument itself, that this violin gives out peculiar deep and melancholy tones." Such are not exactly the tones drawn by the Ooriahs from the rudely-shaped sarunjee, but it is easy to imagine that it might be made an instrument of great power and beauty. The tones of the setar and fife are tolerably sweet, and some of the airs simple and pretty; but it must be confessed that the natives generally have little music in their souls, *noise* appearing to be the chief desideratum in their festivities.

Previous to lighting a lamp in the evening, it is customary to light a wick dipped in oil, placing it in a recess or on the ground on the outside of the house, as an offering to Juggurnath.

Suttees were never so common in Pooree as in other parts of India, the widows of many castes being permitted to marry again. A younger brother may even marry his elder brother's widow, but the elder brother cannot marry the younger's widow. Such marriages are not common, but are nevertheless considered lawful. The widow more frequently marries another man; in which case a sort of marriage ceremony called "Neeka" is performed by a Brahmin, at an expense of six or seven rupees. The marriage ceremonies of children are attended with much greater expense; so it is easy to see why the "Neeka" should be preferred by many people. Boys and girls are betrothed when they are about eleven and five years of age respectively; a boy of the former age being usually betrothed to a girl five or six years his junior; and the marriage takes place when the Brahmin predicts a fortunate season. The age of puberty commences in the female about the eleventh year, and the parties then live together. Marriages are never contracted between blood relations. Married women wear a saree, or cloth with a red or blue border, and a variety of ornaments; they have also a red spot (seendur), made with vermilion, between the eyebrows. The widow of a Brahmin, Maentee or Buniah, cannot marry again, but must, if she is poor, remain in the house of her deceased husband's nearest relative, who, if he has the means, is bound to support her; should he be too poor, she may beg from people of the same caste, or become a servant. She wears no ornaments or saree cloth, but a plain white one instead. Two days in each month she abstains from all food. Should she become unchaste while living in her relative's house, she not only loses caste herself, but also involves her relative's family. The latter, however, can recover caste by expending certain sums of money amongst the Brahmins; but the woman becomes an outcast, without any further claims on her relatives.

The marriage ceremonies vary according to the caste of the parties. The following is a description of the ceremonies practised by some of the Sudra castes, who form the great bulk of the people.

When the respective parents of a boy and girl wish to

betroth them, they each send for a naek (astrologer) to whom they deliver the papers relating to the horoscopes of the children which were taken at the time of birth. If, after comparing the horoscopes together, the naeks declare that the proposed marriage will have a fortunate issue, then the father of the boy sends some mahapursad (holy food), cloth and ornaments to the girl; and before some respectable people of the caste, the parents declare their wish for an union between the children. If the year is thought by the naeks to be a lucky one, then the marriage-day is fixed upon at once; but if it is declared to be unfavourable, the marriage is postponed sometimes for three or four years, and in the interval presents of sweetmeats, clothes, &c., are occasionally sent by the boy's father to the girl, and by the girl's father to the boy.

On the day previous to the marriage, the neighbouring women of the caste are called in by the respective parents, They proceed separately to offer pawn, betel-nut and turmeric to Mungola Devi, an image of the good Devi (a form of Parvati), which may frequently be observed under a tree in the neighbourhood of a village. A priest, after worshiping the image, takes some flowers which had been suspended round its neck, and places them in the hands of the mother of the boy or girl. The women then proceed to the koomar (potter), where, while he is shaping an earthen vessel, they worship the potter's wheel. In the town of Pooree, some worship the chuckha, or wheel (one of the emblems of Vishnu) on the top of the temple, instead of the potter's wheel. From the koomar, each party takes seven small earthen vessels, called "ghurrees," which have been prepared some days previously by being dried only in the sun. The parties then receive water from seven neighbouring families of the caste, and return to the houses of the betrothed, where the women rub the bodies of the boy and girl with turmeric and water, and touch their heads seven times with pawn-leaves and betel-nuts. On the next day, the women bathe the bodies of the betrothed with the water received on the previous day from the neighbours, and afterwards with sandal-wood water. The people of the caste being assembled, the parents call upon them to declare their approval of the marriage; and if they all agree that it is suitable in point of caste, then betel-nuts are distributed to each man according to his rank. Neither the boy nor girl partakes of any food until the ceremonies are concluded, which is not before night. At noon, however, the fathers of the children invite their respective friends to a feast; after which the boy's father invites his friends to accompany him and his son to the house of the girl. On the lad's head is placed a crown made of sola and flowers. He is then put into a nalkee (a sort of palanquin), and, preceded by wreaths of sola and flowers, borne aloft on a pole, the seven ghurrees received from the potter and now filled with fried paddy, musals (torches) and music, is escorted to the house, when he is for the first time introduced to his intended wife; and while a priest and naek are pronouncing certain muntras, the boy and girl throw their respective ghurrees of paddy into the same fire; after which the priest joins their hands, and the ceremony is concluded. The bride and bridegroom remain together in the same room with the female friends of the family, who are making merry the whole night. On the next day the children are escorted to the bridegroom's house, where the bride remains seven days; the women nightly making arotees before them by burning wicks dipped in ghee. During the day the poor children are amused with games of chance with cowries. On the eighth day the bride's father conveys her to his own house, where she remains until arrived at the age of puberty; intelligence of which event is sent to the boy's friends, who call in a naek to decide whether its occurrence at this time forbodes good or evil to the lad. The naek, after consulting the horoscope, gives his opinion; and if it is favourable, the bridegroom's father sends on the following month a present of sweetmeats to the bride's house, and a message announcing his intention of sending for his son's wife on a certain day. At the time appointed, the friends of the bridegroom proceed to the bride's house, and convey her in a palanquin to her future home, where on her arrival a priest, muttering certain muntras, burns some ghee before them, and a feast concludes the ceremony. The expense of these ceremonies from first to last is generally from thirty to one hundred rupees, and a man must be poor indeed who does not exceed the former sum. Amongst the very lowest castes the cost is from eight to ten rupees. Many people impoverish themselves for years by their thoughtless extravagance on these occasions.

The ceremonies preceding and following the birth of a child are as follows. In the fifth month of pregnancy, a priest is called in, by those who can afford it, to perform certain religious ceremonies. On the birth of the child, a naek is employed to take its horoscope; and on the fifth day, some poor people, who cannot afford to employ a priest, use the following ceremony. Some straw and bur-leaves *(ficus Indica)* being prepared, the maternal uncle, or other near relative of the mother, proceeds to twist the straw into a rope, sticking here and there some bur-leaves, and chewing at the same time a mixture of rice and kullae; after which the rope is hung up as a charm in the birth-chamber for twenty-one days, and the parent of the child distributes sweetmeats to his friends. On the sixth day the chamber is cleaned and smoothed with cow-dung, the fire extinguished, and not re-lighted until the following morning, when it is not suffered to expire again until the end of the month. The mother and child are bathed; a rude representation of a tree is formed of mud on the wall of the chamber, and cowrie-shells stuck all over the boughs and roots. Some seen-durs are marked on these by the women of the caste, and sandal-wood water is sprinkled over all. A piece of yel-low-coloured cloth is then suspended before the tree, and a Brahmin, or the neighbouring women, according to the circumstances of the party, worship it as Sustee Devi. Sweet cakes are then distributed to the friends of the family. At night, a palm-leaf, a pen and ink, are placed in the room for the use of Beedahta, the Ruler of the world, or Destiny, who, it is supposed, writes in the night the child's fate, whether for good or evil, first on its forehead and then on the palm-leaf. The mother must not sleep, but sit with the child in her lap the whole night. On the twenty-first day the mother and child are bathed and new clothes put on them. The naek then names the child. On the expiration of a month the mother becomes pure. In some castes she is pronounced pure after twenty-one days, and in others the naek is not called in to name the child until it is six months old. The cost of these ceremonies, for those above the lowest castes, is from ten to twenty-five rupees. Rich people of course fool away as much as they like.

In the funeral ceremonies, when a person is thought to be dying, some mahapursad is put into his mouth, or water in which mahapursad has been steeped until it becomes sour, is poured down his throat. When he expires, the family members of his caste are collected together as soon as possible to carry the corpse to the moosanee, a place where the dead are burned. A sweeper, a barber, and a dhobee (washerman), accompany the funeral party. The sweeper is by no means allowed to touch the body of the defunct, as in that case the surviving members of his family would lose caste; he is merely employed to carry wood for the funeral pile. The body is conveyed on a charpoy to the moosanee, and is there placed on the ground, while the members of the caste prepare the pile, and the barber pares the nail on the little finger of the right hand. In some castes all the nails are pared and the head shaved. The body is then anointed with oil and turmeric, and afterwards washed. A new dhotee (cloth for the loins) is put on; after which the corpse is carried three times round the pile, and then placed upon it. The face is left exposed, while the rest of the body is covered with wood. The nearest relative of the deceased then proceeds to give fire (a sacred duty) to the corpse, by touching its mouth with a lighted brand or bundle of straw, with which he afterwards lights the pile; the people of the caste then set fire to it on the other side. When the body is consumed, the funeral party proceed to purify themselves from the pollution incurred in touching a corpse, by having their nails pared by the barber, and by bathing and changing their clothes. The impure clothes are washed previous to being returned by the dhobee, who accompanies the funeral party for this purpose, as well as to receive the clothes taken off the corpse, which are divided between himself and the barber. On the following day, the people of the caste again go the moosanee, and extinguish the embers of the pile by pouring water on them. The place is then plastered over with mud or sand, and a rude representation of the human figure made thereon. Into various parts of this figure are stuck nine small wooden pegs, with a saffron-coloured piece of cloth on each. Some sugared water, curdled milk and khoee (fried paddy), are then separately placed in small earthen vessels near the head of the figure; after which, the party returns home.

When a wife dies before her husband, it is considered a fortunate event. Cowries and khoee are thrown behind the corpse while it is being carried to the moosanee, accompanied with the beating of tom-toms, &c. When a woman dies during pregnancy, the Cæsarean operation is performed, and the fœtus is consumed on a separate pile. Children dying under two years of age are buried with no particular ceremonies. The cost of the funeral ceremonies, for those above the very lowest castes, is from two rupees and a half to five rupees. Very few, except the rich, expend more than the latter sum, but reserve all their funds for the Shradha.

When a death occurs in any family, the whole household are impure for a greater or less time, according to circumstances. Amongst some of the Sudra castes, a son is impure for ten days after the death of his father or mother. For the death of an unmarried daughter, her father, mother and brother, are impure for a period of ten days; but if married, then only five days. For the death of a son, whether married or not, the parents are impure ten days. In some castes the season of mourning extends to a month. A Brahmin is impure for a period of from three to ten days, for the death of any of the above relations. During that time he can perform no religious ceremonies. A son, after the death of his father, allows his hair, beard and nails, to remain uncut. He wears no ornaments and few clothes, never changing the latter day or night. He eats once a day, and that only of mahapursad, or plantains, and arooah rice cooked by himself in a fresh place and in a new earthen vessel every day. He must not sleep in the customary bed, but on the floor. Each day a handful or two of rice, mixed with milk, is by means of a priest offered to the manes of the dead. This rice is never eaten; but the priest, accompanied by the mourner, proceeds to a tank or river, into which, after pronouncing certain muntras, the oblation is thrown. If absolutely necessary, by reason of sickness or other imperative cause, the whole of the ten days' ceremonies are concluded at once. On the expiration of the period of mourning, the mustaches are shaved off, and then allowed to grow as before. The head and beard are shaved as usual, and the body is anointed with oil. On the following day, the Shradha, an offering of food to the deceased, is performed. This ceremony is attended with considerable expense in the distribution of alms and feasting the Brahmins. The very lowest cost is four rupees, but generally from twenty-five to thirty rupees are expended. Rich people spend many lacs of rupees on such occasions. Once a year (in Aussin or Kartick) the Turpun, or offering of water to the manes of ancestors, is performed. The ceremony continues fifteen days. On the last day, a Shradha is given, and by some again at the Dewali, a festival not generally observed at Pooree. The very poor people cannot perform all these ceremonies, though they usually have some trifling observances. Thus, in the performance of the Turpun, a little water held in the hand is offered to the manes of their ancestors, while repeating their names, with appropriate invocations.

The people themselves do not seem to attach any particular meaning to any of the foregoing ceremonies; for, on inquiry, I was always told that it was the "dustoor" or *custom* of the caste. Whatever the *priests* think, they, like the Egyptians of old, keep to themselves, and doubtless with equal loss to the world, whatever that may be. No affair of even the least importance can be transacted without the Brahmin priests. From the first entrance of a child into the world to the funeral pile, he is surrounded by the ministrations of these pretenders to sanctity, who hold his mind in subjection.

To feed the Brahmins on various occasions, is esteemed a particularly meritorious act. A man sometimes makes oath that he will feed a certain number of Brahmins for eight or ten years. This oath is particularly sacred, and is administered by a Brahmin, of course, after the following manner. A copper vessel, called a kosah, used in religious ceremonies, is filled with water from the Ganges, if procurable; if not, any other water will do. Toolsee-leaves and a suparee or horeera-nut *(terminalia chebula)*, are put therein. Into the vessel thus filled, the devotee's hand is inserted, while he recites certain muntras after the priest. If the former should die before the completion of his vow, his nearest relative must carry it out, otherwise he will become impure. Cunning rogues these "twice-born" men! they contrive to lose nothing, whatever others may do. The interposition of any of the gods, save Mahadev, the Ban-ling (a type of Siva), and the devotee's own sectarial deity, must be sought through a Brahmin priest, to whom the petitioner relates his wishes, whether the birth of a son, preservation from danger, &c. He then places in the hand of the priest, either a suparee or horeera-nut; the latter is preferred, if procurable. This act is called "Sunkulpo," signifying an engagement for a religious purpose, whereby the priest engages on his part faithfully to perform the intercession required by the devotee. After reciting certain muntras, the priest exclaims, "Hear, O Kalee" (or whoever the deity invoked may be), "this man" (mentioning his name) "has sent for me, and, placing a 'sunkulpo' in my hand, requested me to intercede with you on his behalf," &c. The reward of the priest is in proportion to the means of the petitioner and the length or importance of his request. The priest's part of the performance is acted either in the temple or in the house of his employer, according to the wish of the latter. If there is no image of the god whose favour it is proposed to beseech in the house, then the priest consecrates a picture of the idol and worships it; or if it is the wish of his employer, he proceeds to make an image by placing in a brass or earthenware vessel containing water the bough of a mango-tree, on which a cocoa-nut is suspended. These are marked with seendurs of sandal-wood, and sandal-wood water is sprinkled over all; after which they are pronounced pure. An image of any deity may be made in this way. After the ceremony and worship is concluded, these materials are thrown into a river or tank. Sometimes a salagram is the object worshiped, in which case the priest either worships one belonging to his employer or brings one with him, and after the ceremony takes it away again.

A person having either a salagram, an idol, or a consecrated picture of an idol in his house, must daily pay the expense of its worship by a priest; and if unable to continue doing so, he must deliver it to the priest, and engage at any future time, should he be able, to defray the expenses of its daily worship. A man cannot stick up the rude images, so often met with under trees, without assigning lands for their support, or making other arrangements for the payment of the daily ministrations of a Brahmin.

CHAPTER XXII.

Ride through the Town of Pooree—Pilgrims measuring their Length on the Ground—People seldom throw themselves under the Wheels of Juggurnath's Car—Fine Tanks—People killed by Alligators—We offer a Reward for the Capture of a particular Alligator—An Alligator brought to us—Trick—Indian Conjurors—Head of an old Man brought to the Billiard-room—Jugglers' Tricks—Snake-charmers—Method of taming a Snake—Thieves of India can steal a Sheet from beneath a Sleeping Person—The Manner of it—Apathy of the Natives—Drowned Lad—Natives attend affectionately on a dying Cow.

In the morning and evening, I usually walked or rode on an elephant into the town of Pooree, and occasionally witnessed very strange sights. Pilgrims may sometimes be seen measuring their length on the ground around the enclosure of the temple of Juggurnath. Some of these men have perchance come a distance of more than a thousand miles. I once met with one from the north-western provinces who had been engaged two years in measuring his length towards Pooree. When I saw him, he had about two miles more to go to complete his task. The temple was in view to animate him, and I stopped some time to watch his progress. The way of it was this. The man stretched himself at full length on the ground, and made a mark thereon, as far as he could reach with his fingers; he then got up, placed his toes in the mark, prostrated himself as before, extended his arms, and made another mark, and so lengthened out his way.

It is erroneously supposed that people often throw

themselves under the wheels of Juggurnath's car when in progress. Only one instance of this occurred during the many years I was at Pooree. I happened to be riding down the main street when the cars were in rapid motion, and word was brought to me that a man had been run over. I proceeded immediately to the spot, and there, extended across the track which the wheels of the car had made, was the dead body of a poor, miserably diseased wretch, who had evidently, from the position in which I saw him, deliberately thrown himself under the wheels, which had passed over the middle of his body. His arms were extended, and in his momentary agony he had torn up the earth with his hands. This, I believe, was a case of suicide.

In and near the city of Pooree there are some remarkably fine tanks, with flights of steps all round leading down to the water, on the surface of which numerous alligators may often be seen floating. Sometimes, though rarely, these animals seize the bathers. I remember but two instances, both of which occurred about the same time. One, an old woman, who was killed; and the other, a man, who was seized by the leg, but managed to escape. Subsequently, however, he died from the injuries he had received. The natives alleged that it was one particular alligator that had a taste for human flesh. So Hambledon and I offered a reward for his capture. Next day, an alligator about eight feet in length was brought to us. We paid the promised reward, and offered a similar one for another. The captive alligator, which was bound with strong cords, was dragged away to be killed, as they said. The following day, a second was brought. We paid for him, too; and promised a further donation for another. Accordingly, a third was brought, marvellously like the others. We suspected some trickery was at work; but the natives, who dearly love lying, stoutly protested that it was another beast. Now, as one alligator, if of the same size, is as like another as two peas, we could not be certain that such was not the case, so paid the money. However, I determined to put a mark on the animal, and accordingly pierced his mail with a Mahratta spear, after which we saw no more of our friend.

Everybody has heard of the Indian conjurors and snake-charmers. One evening, a fine old man, said to be above a hundred years of age, performed some very clever tricks for our amusement. Amongst others, he caused a small mango-tree to grow and produce fruit. The scene of the performance was my billiard-room. A few days after, while H. and myself were playing at billiards, a human head was brought by the police to one of the windows of the room. I at once recognized the gory head to be that of the old conjuror. He had been murdered near the temple, and his head was found on the sands, but his body was never discovered.

Another juggler I saw place a lad on the bare ground and cover him with a large wicker basket, after which he carried on a conversation in the most natural manner, the boy's treble tones issuing from beneath the basket. The man's voice became louder; and apparently in a great rage he seized a sword, and plunged it through the basket, whence the shriek and dying tones of the boy issued. The whole was so well simulated, that I confess it was with a feeling of relief I saw the basket raised, and no body beneath it.

In the third chapter of Genesis, we read that "the serpent was more subtile than any beast of the field," and truly it appears to be endowed with almost human intelligence. The command snake-charmers obtain over these reptiles, and the tricks they teach them, are very wonderful. I have often witnessed the charmers at work, clearing, as they pretend, a garden or other place of snakes, when, if there are no wild ones, they secretly drop some of their tame reptiles, and go piping about until these come forth from their hiding-places, the men of course declaring that they are wild ones. I have seen half-a-dozen snakes issue one after another from behind a box in my room, where I was perfectly certain that there were none before the charmer was admitted. It was difficult to detect the deception, although M. and myself watched the man's proceedings very carefully. If our eyes wandered from him for an instant, the trick was done. We offered the man a rupee or two to explain how it was, which, after some hesitation, he did. The snake was concealed about his person, and at certain signals glided behind a box or came therefrom, the man playing on a sort of pipe all the time.

In the course of my ride one evening, I saw a man taming, as he said, a cobra di capello. I offered him a rupee to kill it, but from a superstitious feeling he declined doing so. I stopped to watch his proceedings. In his hand he held a globular earthenware vessel, which he waved to and fro before the snake. Now and then the snake would make a dart at the man, but knocked its jaws against the earthen vessel. After some time the reptile got tired of this sport, and refused to come to the scratch again. The man then tried it with his bare knee, which he swayed before the snake, but the latter had had enough, and declined the encounter. The charmer said it would never bite again, and placed it in a neighbouring hedge, though I still offered him a rupee to kill it. But these are ordinary tricks to others I have heard of, but never witnessed; such as men sitting in the air; others being buried alive for a month, and then exhumed apparently dead, but resuscitated. A late writer in the "Dial" newspaper (George Thompson) has given a very graphic description of the latter, at which a friend of mine, the late General B., was present, and who described the scene to me.

The thieves of India are amongst the most expert in the world. They will even steal a sheet from underneath a sleeping person. The way of it is this. Suppose the sleeper is reclining on one side. The thief proceeds to fold up the sheet very carefully until close to the body of the sleeper, when he gently rouses him by tickling his ear (say) with a feather. Half-awake, the sleeper very naturally turns over, and away goes the thief with the sheet.

The apathy of the natives is astounding. I once saw a young lad, about fifteen years of age, taken out of the river at Pooree, quite dead. Some of his relatives were present, and did not appear to think much about it, until a big brother took the corpse up in his arms to carry it away. The face of the dead lad then fell against his own. At first he appeared surprised, and then, looking affectionately at the face of his poor brother, burst into tears. "One touch of nature makes the whole world kin;" and I am not ashamed to confess that on witnessing this pitiful sight, my own eyes filled with tears.

I have seen several natives in affectionate attendance on a dying cow, and I have seen them pass a fellow-creature dying alone by the road-side without notice, but bowing down and reverently kissing the feet of a Brahmin. It is curious that, though the natives venerate a cow or a bull, they have no such feeling for a cow's brother when he becomes a bullock, but belabour him most unmercifully. I have mentioned elsewhere how cruelly the natives twist the tails of the poor animals.

CHAPTER XXIII.

Fall from my Horse—A Knock on the Head a pleasant Death—Go to Calcutta—Rent a House near the Martiniere—Total Deafness—Mysterious Death of a Sailor-boy—Calcutta Bazaars—Jemmy Jumps—Jemmy Jumps' Opinion of Rasselas—Intelligence of the Battle of Moodkee.

ONE evening in June, 184—, I was cantering down the main street of Pooree, in company with some friends, when my horse fell and rolled over me, dislocating one of my fingers, and causing many severe contusions, besides some degree of concussion of the brain. Notwithstanding all this, I did not feel the slightest pain, but mounted again, and rode home in company with my friends. I wished to continue our ride, but they insisted upon my going home, as they could perceive that I was more severely hurt than I was aware of. I only experienced a most delightful sensation, as if I were floating on the clouds; so I conclude that a knock on the head must be rather an easy death. Enough of this. Suffice it to say that I was very ill for some weeks afterwards, and to this day feel the effects of that fall. I was totally deaf for a long time, and was advised to proceed to England; but, instead of doing so, I obtained leave to visit Australia on medical certificate.

I remained upwards of two months in Calcutta, waiting for the sailing of a ship. During this time I rented a small house (I should think it a large one in England) in Moira Street, the back of which overlooked the playground of the Martiniere school. It was a source of amusement, though rather a melancholy one to me, to watch the boys at play within a few yards of my house, running, jumping, and I suppose shouting, as I could see them gesticulating, with their mouth wide open, but no sound reached me. It was like the phantasmagoria of a dream. In conversation I was obliged to use the most powerful trumpets, and thus was not cut off altogether from association with my fellows; and I had some kind friends in Calcutta who patiently bore with my infirmity. In the evening, I occasionally walked along the Strand road after all the gay world had departed. One evening, an incident occurred which made a very strong impression upon me. Everybody acquainted with the boatmen of the Hoogly river is aware that amongst them are many dacoits (robbers or pirates, as the case may be), who think no more of taking the life of a man than that of a puppy-dog. Some gentlemen crossing from the opposite side of the river, passed a dinghee (small boat) in which was an European lad about eighteen years of age. He was dressed like a sailor, and had a bundle in his hand. When the gentlemen landed, they heard a dispute between the lad and his boatmen respecting the amount of fare demanded by them; but as this is an hourly occurrence at a crowded ghât, the gentlemen thought nothing of it, and shortly after were about getting into their carriage, when they were startled by hearing a piercing shriek, followed by a plunge in the river; after which all was still. The gentlemen descended the ghât to the river-side to ascertain the cause of the noise they had heard. There were a great many boats about the landing-place, but the boatmen pretended to be asleep, and on being aroused declared that they knew nothing about it; and the river kept the secret of the poor lad's fate, for he was never seen again. Neither was it positively discovered who he was. Perchance a mother, with that "hope deferred which maketh the heart sick," is still expecting the return of her long-lost son. He was doubtless murdered by the boatmen and thrown into the river, from which a body seldom rises by reason of the strong under-current. My friend Captain H., the Superintendent of Police, declared that he would find out the murderers; but the cunning of the natives was too much for his sagacity, great as that was.

I occasionally amused myself by visiting the bazaars, which to a stranger are exceedingly amusing places; at least I always found them so. The instant a palanquin is seen entering the bazaar, the occupant is besieged by a number of natives, most of whom speak a little English, as thus: "What master want? I everything got. Master want silkee stocking? I got. Silkee handkerchief? I got. Master come to my shop?"—and so on. In former days, I used to find the clamour of these people almost deafening, as half-a-dozen of them were vociferating on either side of my palkee; but it was not so now, and I literally turned a deaf ear to the noise, as I was not obliged to use my trumpet unless I wished—some comfort in that. I used to get out of my palanquin at the first shop on the left hand side of the old China Bazaar, look round; then into the next, look at whatever was exposed for sale; then into another, and so on; down that side of the bazaar, a distance, I suppose, of half a mile or more, and return up the other side after a visit to the "Burra Bazaar," where almost everything, "from a needle to an anchor," can be procured. If the anchor is not in the bazaar, it is not far off. There are all sorts of hardware, broadcloths, costly silks and shawls, &c.; and in queer, out-of-the-way places, some dirty precipitous stairs lead to small chambers where precious stones can be purchased. These latter are not exposed for sale, but brought from some dark recess when inquired for. Then there is the new China Bazaar, a superior sort of place, where ladies used to go shopping some thirty years ago; but owing to the numerous European shops which have been opened of late years, this bazaar is comparatively deserted, and had the last time I saw it quite a ruinous and desolate appearance. In former days it used to present quite a gay scene, with numerous carriages standing at the doors of the principal shops; but now, one might say, "There's something ails the place, methinks 'tis cursed;" for scarcely a single respectable-looking carriage is to be seen, and comparatively few visitors of any kind. In former days, there was one native shopkeeper in the new China Bazaar, named Bindawbun Pall, who dealt in "*everything*, and many other things besides." He was generally known amongst Europeans by the sobriquet of "Jemmy Jumps," of which he was rather proud. Jemmy used to attend the Calcutta races, on which occasions his nether extremities were cased in top-boots. He was a fat, jolly-looking, intelligent man. His shop was a very extensive one, consisting of two or three large upper rooms, where all kinds of things were exposed for sale in extensive glass-cases. At one end of the entrance room, up-stairs, were a few chairs, a not over-clean couch, and a small table. Here have I often sat for hours together, talking of things in general and politics in particular, with Jemmy Jumps, who spoke English pretty well. The late Bishop of Madras, when Archdeacon of Calcutta, endeavoured to make a convert of Jemmy, and on one occasion rather indiscreetly told him that he would go to hell. "Who told you I should go to hell?" asked Jemmy. This was a poser. I sometimes found Jemmy reading Johnson's Rasselas. When he had finished the book, I said, "Well, Jemmy, what do you think of Rasselas?" To which Jemmy replied, "Rasselas—he just like all men; he everything got, but he not appee;" and added, "It's a funn*ee* world." Alas, poor Jemmy! he died not long after of cholera, and I missed him much on my return to Calcutta, as, besides my liking for the man, he was my factotum in the way of procuring supplies, &c. Thus passed the time away.

A few days before I embarked for Australia, news arrived of the indecisive battle of Moodkee, where my friend T. fell. He was treacherously slain, as I learnt long after, by a Seikh to whom he had given quarter. Intelligence of the battle was current in the bazaar two or three days before the arrival of the Government despatches. Indeed, the natives, to whom it would appear that the birds of the air convey a whisper, generally hear of such events long before the constituted authorities. It is said that the wealthy bankers procure the earliest intelligence; and it may be so. To meet with a check, particularly as both the Governor-General and Commander-in-Chief were present in the fight, was something new to a British army in India; and when days elapsed before any further news from the army arrived, many people began to look with a gloomy aspect at the state of affairs, as if "the beginning of the end" had already commenced. However, I had faith in our "kismet" and indomitable British pluck, so had no doubt that all would come right at last; and in this faith I left Calcutta before intelligence arrived of any decisive action having been fought.

CHAPTER XXIV.

Embark for Sydney—Shipwreck and remarkable Escape of my Friend M. C. —Arrive in Port Jackson—Names of my Indian Servants—English Groom —Situation of my House—Visits from my Friend Mac———Wanderings in the Bush—Numerous Snakes—Tiger Mosquitoes—Fleas and Flies—Drive into Sydney—My Garden—Hot Wind—Accept an Invitation to accompany a Party of Ladies and Gentlemen down the Harbour.

I EMBARKED in the ship Theresa early in January, 1846, bound for Sydney. I scarcely remember anything of the voyage, save that we sighted the island of Amsterdam, which brought to my recollection the circumstance of an unfortunate friend of mine being wrecked thereon some years previously when proceeding to some part of Australia; and as his escape was very remarkable, I will give a brief account of it. The captain of the ship had his wife and family on board, and amongst the passengers was my friend M. C., as well as some other officers with their wives and several children. One Saturday night, they had, as is customary in most ships, been toasting sweethearts and wives with old friends at home, beside talking about the land they expected to see in the morning. The party retired for the night; and M. C. had not gone to bed, when the mate came to his cabin, and in joking, as he thought, said that land was in sight. M. C. went on the poop with the mate, and saw something like a very dark cloud looming to leeward, when presently the ship struck—a huge wave rolled over them. M. C., who had grasped the stanchions in front of the poop, was torn away with them in his hands. He let go, strove to swim, and was carried by a wave high up on the rocks, and there he remained, thinking that he was the only person saved. When daylight appeared, the ship was not to be seen; but an European convict and the mate, together with several lascars and M. C.'s servant, came from the places where they had found refuge during the night. Most forlorn was their situation, on an almost barren rock in the middle of the ocean. A considerable quantity of rice, and, nearly as important, singular as it may seem to relate, a large silver tea-pot, was washed on shore, with some other articles. They contrived to light a fire, and boiled some rice in the tea-pot, which was their sole cooking utensil while they remained on the rock. Most melancholy it was to see the dead bodies of their shipmates washed on shore, and the survivors had no means of burying them in the scanty soil of the island. M. C.'s khidmutgar had his leg broken by being dashed against the rocks. After many days, starvation staring them in the face if they remained where they were, they crossed to the other side of the island in hopes of falling in with some whaling ships, in which they were successful, and were conveyed to Mauritius, and thence to Calcutta, where I had the pleasure of meeting M. C., and drinking tea poured from the silver tea-pot which had stood them in such good stead; M. C.'s broken-legged khidmutgar being in attendance at table. Most remarkable was my friend's escape; had it not been for the mate's trying to "take a rise" out of him, he would have been below when the ship struck, and in all human probability drowned with the others, for none of those who were below had time to reach the deck before they were overwhelmed with the waves.

To return from this digression. We pursued our uneventful voyage. Before leaving Calcutta I had purchased a large chart, and two works on the law of storms, which I understood theoretically, but now intended studying the subject practically. However, we had little more than a cap-full of wind during the voyage, which terminated by our dropping anchor in Port Jackson on the 17th of March. I had brought two Indian servants with me, a father and son; the latter was a handsome-looking lad, named "Hafiz Oolah," which was soon turned by the English into "Happy Fellow," as they could make nothing of his own name; while his father's name of Ram Jan was transmogrified into "Rum John."

I had letters of introduction to two or three gentlemen in Sydney and its neighbourhood, one of whom had spent many years in India. I rented a small cottage a short distance from his house. My establishment consisted of an English groom and my two Indian servants. Having nothing to do, I took it into my head to instruct the groom in reading and writing, of which he only knew the rudiments. He was no genius, for after some months' tuition and daily spelling the two words *yes* and *yet*, he could not spell them correctly at last. "Now, Charles," I would say in the morning, "after breakfast I shall ask you to spell *yes* and *yet;* mind you know how to do it." "Very well, Sir." After breakfast in comes Charles, rather redolent of the stable. "Well, Charles, how do you spell *yet?*" whereupon Charles would boggle and hum, looking the while inexpressibly bewildered, and at last say, "I can't spell that word, Sir." Verily, Charles was no brighter a youth than he who could not count the little pig amongst a lot of others because he frisked about so much. After the lesson, I generally walked or rode about the bush for two or three hours.

Within a couple of miles to the rear of my house, there

rolled the great Pacific Ocean, while to the right was the harbour, and in front the city of Sydney, three miles distant. In the evening, my friend Mac—— usually walked over to my cottage, when we used to spin very long yarns about "our country," as we called India. I soon knew almost every track in the bush within two or three miles of my cottage, and tried in vain to lose myself, so that I might have something to break the monotony of my daily rides in trying to find myself again. I did once nearly succeed, and speculated about passing a night in the bush, but, unluckily, I found myself again ere it became quite dark, and I had no excuse for "camping out," which I should rather have liked by way of a change, were it not for the numerous snakes about the neighbourhood. During the first month of my residence at Waverley (the name of my place), I saw more snakes than I had done during the many years I had been in India. Then, again, there were huge mosquitoes, "tiger mosquitoes," I called them, such as I have seen in the Sunderbunds of Bengal, stout, speckled fellows, that without any preliminary coquetting and humming, after the manner of the light-brown coloured and slim mosquito, pounce upon their prey, say the back of your left hand, and commence work at once with their blood-suckers; when, feeling the smart, down goes your right paw, and causes a disgusting little splash of blood and smashed mosquito bones on the back of your hand, and so on. The insidious attacks of the slim mosquito are more tormenting, as it flits lightly to and fro; now skimming across your forehead, anon lighting gently on your hand, or humming in your ear. After many ineffectual slaps on your hand or face, as the case may be, your lose your temper, and hit out savagely, to your own increasing annoyance; until at length, by a lucky hit, you extinguish him; or he perhaps sails away to wait for quieter times, and you think that you have got rid of him, but he is watching you all the while from the roof or corner of the room; and when you have comfortably settled yourself in your arm-chair, and perchance are in the middle of the most interesting article of the last Review, from which it would take a forty-mosquito power to divert your attention, softly the slim moskee sweeps down again, and lightly settles on your forehead, bald-pate, or other exposed place, and contrives to sup quietly after all the trouble you have given him, poor thing!—you find out, when too late, the mischief he has done by the mark and tingling sensation he has left behind. Or suppose that you have finished the article you were reading before the mosquito has quite finished *his* interesting occupation, then, little moskee, look out sharp, or it is all up with you—quick! the hand of fate is uplifted—away! no—it descends, and never more will you re-visit the jungle's pleasant glades or the cool recesses of the marsh, for your bones are dashed to pieces on the hand of him whom you tormented so long; while he triumphantly exclaims, with a feeling of gratified revenge, "There, I have done for you at last, you pestilent little devil!" There are some people so dried up and mummified by long residence in the colony, that the mosquito instinctively seems to be aware there is nothing to be got out of them, and passes on accordingly to the nearest new-comer or "new chum," as a recent arrival in the colony is elegantly termed in Sydney.

In addition to mosquitoes, there are fleas and flies in myriads. Every week my rooms were flooded with boiling water to destroy the fleas. To keep out the flies and mosquitoes I invented some wire doors, so that

I might have the place a little to myself. I used to say at Pooree, that every grain of sand was a white ant, whereas in Australia I said that every grain of sand was a flea, so numerous were these pestilent little insects in some places. Such are some of the agrémens of bush life in Australia.

Once a week I usually drove into Sydney to procure books from the Australian library—which, by the way, is a very valuable collection—or went to the bank for rhino. I amused myself by making a garden, which was just beginning to bloom, when a hot wind from the west withered nearly all my plants in the course of a few hours. I was disgusted, and gave up gardening. This hot wind, which continued between two and three days, was something like the simoom I have read of, the thermometer rising in the shade to 110°, when suddenly the wind chopped round to the southward, blowing directly from the icebergs, and we were shivering with cold. I was elected an honorary member of the Australian Club, but never once availed myself of the privilege, as I had a great objection to mix with strangers on account of my deafness, albeit I found the people very hospitably inclined.

Thus passed away an uneventful year of my life. I now made inquiries for a passage to New Zealand and Tahiti, purposing to return to India viâ China, when an event occurred which altered the complexion of my life. One evening my good neighbour Mac—— brought a note from a friend in Sydney, inviting me to accompany a party of ladies and gentlemen down the harbour on the following morning. I could not answer the note then, but said I would drive into town early in the morning, and make my excuses in person; which I did. Nothing,

I felt assured, would induce me to accept the invitation; but my friend expressed so much disappointment, and, in short, said so much about it, that I very reluctantly suffered my good-nature to prevail, and I went. The end of it was, that some months after I was ——. But here I must pause for breath, the pace is too quick; besides, I ought to commence with a new chapter.

CHAPTER XXV.

Take a House in Town—Love, honour and obey—Married—Embark for Calcutta—Narrow escape of Shipwreck—Death of my Horse—Enter Torres Strait—Dirty-looking Savages—King of the Cannibal Islands—Booby Island—Copang—Dutch Sloop of War—Dutch Officers—Inhabitants of Copang—German Missionary—"Happy Fellow" drunk—Punishment of "Happy Fellow"—Leave Copang—Supply a Ship with Water—Approach Sand-heads in threatening Weather—Arrive in Calcutta.

WELL, now, reader—why should I call you *dear*, when I know nothing about you?—fill up the intervening months in any way you like, for I don't mean to say, if I could, how I passed them. I gave up my cottage at Waverley, and took a house in town. My hearing was so much improved that I distinctly heard, without a trumpet, the momentous words, "love, honour and obey," pronounced in my favour in Christ church, Sydney, and I was married; and instead of returning to India viâ the South-Sea Islands and China, I engaged a passage direct to Calcutta in the ship "Bussorah Merchant," which vessel was freighted with nearly one hundred horses, and amongst them my saddle and carriage horses, as passengers. Instead of going the usual route into Torres Straits by way of the narrow and intricate channel called the "inner passage," our captain determined on trying the more open and outer one, which had lately been surveyed. We left Sydney on the 4th of August with a fair wind, and went rolling along most uncomfortably for several days, when at dusk on the evening of the 12th, there was suddenly a tremendous hubbub on deck, occasioned by the look-out man shouting, "Breakers ahead!" Then came hasty words of command, the hurried tread of men, banging of ropes on the deck, pulling, hauling and bawling, followed shortly after by the leaning over of the ship, as she hugged the wind as closely as possible to claw off the reef. I was so accustomed to these noises in a merchant ship that I did not think anything about them; in fact, I did not even go on deck. Soon after, the doctor came to our cabin-door, and said that we had had a very narrow escape of shipwreck, for the reef was so near, when they put the ship about, that he could have chucked a biscuit upon it. I thought this was exaggeration, so ascended the poop to judge for myself; and, sure enough, I could through the gloom distinctly see the breakers within a short distance of the ship. Had she struck the reef, no earthly power could have saved us. The wind was blowing pretty fresh, with a chopping sea. As this reef was not laid down in our chart, the captain was apprehensive that there might be others, and was afraid to proceed in the dark; so we "lay to" all night, rolling about fearfully. My saddle-horse, "Bob Dawson," was so disgusted with the motion, I suppose, that he declined proceeding any further in the ship, and, dying in the night, was thrown overboard in the morning, and his bones added to those of hundreds of other gallant horses that have been lost in sundry wrecks on the barrier reef. Alas, poor Bob! the companion of many solitary hours; I felt as if I had lost a friend when I saw his lifeless carcase hauled up and cast into the sea. On the following day we sailed through a wide opening in the barrier reef into Torres Strait, to our very great relief, for there we had a smooth sea. At night we anchored, as it is not considered safe to proceed after sunset, nor before the sun has attained a considerable elevation above the horizon in the morning, by reason of the numerous reefs below the surface of the water. A man is always on the look-out from the mast-head while the ship is under way, as from that height he can distinguish a sunken reef a considerable distance off.

We saw some dirty-looking savages on the Australian shore, waving palm branches with one hand, while they scratched themselves with the other. By the first motion they were inviting us to land, and the last was equally significant of something to be avoided. We did not accept their friendly invitation, but glided gently on our way. The water was smooth as a mill-pond; the only annoyance we experienced was from the stench caused by the horses. Poor brutes! they must have felt as much relief as we did on getting into smooth water.

One Sunday morning, while we were at anchor, we saw a couple of large canoes full of men from the Guinea coast pulling rapidly towards us, with the king of the Cannibal Islands on board, as we jokingly said. However, not knowing whether their intentions were peaceful or otherwise, our four guns, which had been stowed away below, were hastily fished up and placed in position. The canoes approached within two or three hundred yards of our ship, and then bore away, without apparently taking any notice of us, though no doubt the crews kept a sharp look-out from the corners of their eyes. The steersman of the nearest canoe had a long feather stuck upright in his hair, and was a magnificent-looking savage, at least six feet or more in height. He stood like a statue on a platform at the stern of the boat, without once turning his head to look after us. Anybody would have thought, from the apparently careless behaviour of these natives, that ships were as plenty as blackberries, instead of being rather scarce objects in Torres Straits; but I suppose the true reason of their feigned indifference was, that they thought our ship was too big for them, and that they saw our guns through the open ports, for these savages have been known to attack vessels in distress. We kept a sharp look-out at night, in case they should favour us with a visit; but we saw no more of them. We touched at Booby Island, where we landed; and found in a cave near the landing-place sundry provisions and water in casks, left there by the Government of New South Wales for the use of shipwrecked sailors. We added to the store some clothes, &c.; and in a snug little place found the "Post-office," as it is called, where were sundry letters and cards, but none addressed to ourselves or the port to which we were bound; so we deposited them in the place where we found them, and added our own cards and letters, addressed to friends in Sydney, to the number. Our captain deposited an official letter to the officer commanding the surveying expedition, giving the latitude and longitude of the reef where we were so nearly wrecked before entering Torres Straits. Booby Island is a small rocky islet, partially clothed with coarse grass and a few straggling dwarf shrubs. We clambered all over it in the course of a few minutes. The depôt of provisions has been the means of saving many lives, and it is customary for every ship touching at the island to add to the store.

In due time we dropped anchor at Copang, a Dutch settlement in the island of Timor. We put into this place to procure water for the horses. The town is a rather large straggling place, with many Chinese inhabitants. Including the Governor, there were only seven European residents, and about twice as many dirty-looking Timor Sepoys formed the army. A Dutch sloop of war, as clean as a new pin, was lying in the harbour, within a few hundred yards of our ship. The officers looked every whit as smart and gentlemanly as those of the British navy, which excited the surprise of some wiseacres on board the Bussorah Merchant, whose ideas of Dutchmen were evidently associated with huge meerschaums and baggy inexpressibles, or haply with the silly words of Sir Henry Bishop's beautiful glee:

"Mynheer Vandunk, though he never was drunk,
Sipp'd his brandy and water gaily;
And he quench'd his thirst with two quarts of the first
To a pint of the latter daily," &c.

A pretty stiff allowance, certainly!—but the words are a libel on Mynheer. For my part, I think the Dutch a fine set of fellows. It is little more than two hundred years since they ran a race of glory with us for the dominion of the seas, and the famous Admiral Van Tromp sailed up the English Channel with a broom at the masthead of his ship; but the English bull-dog prevailed at last. All honour to the unsuccessful brave! I viewed this tidy little Dutch war-sloop with great interest, it being the first vessel of the kind I had ever seen.

Amongst the European inhabitants of Copang were a German missionary and his wife. They had been seventeen years resident at Rotten Island and Copang. Seeing strangers strolling about the town, the Reverend —— very courteously invited us to his house, where we had a long and very interesting conversation, flavoured, by the way, with some of the best tea I ever tasted. The day before we left the island, the good padre came on board to take leave of us. We invited him into our cabin, in which was a pianoforte; and at his request my wife played and sang until the tears rolled down his face while she was singing, "By the sad Sea-waves." Sad indeed was his lot by the sea-waves! He had a son and daughter growing up in that secluded place, their only associates being the natives of the island; and it was for his children's sake that the poor man lamented his isolated situation. It was with sincere sorrow that we parted. We sent his wife a present of some needles and thread—articles of which they were in great need. Think of this, O ye housewives of England! who will scarce stoop to pick up such an every-day occurrence as a stray pin or needle; and here was a lady in actual want of what ye so little regard. Poor people! the love of God was in their hearts, and that was their support, as they said, in their trying situation. Verily, they will have their reward from Him whose kingdom is not of this world.

The day before we left Copang, my servant, "Happy Fellow," went on shore, and was brought on board in the evening quite drunk and very obstreperous. The young rascal knocked his father down. The poor man came weeping to me, and complained of his son's conduct. I told him that he ought to rope's-end the young rebel when he became sober, but he was afraid to do it. So in the morning I accompanied "Rum John" to the forecastle, and held "Happy Fellow" while his worthy progenitor flogged him. I hope you will agree with me, reader, that I did right.

Having completed our watering, we sailed. Nothing particular occurred during the rest of the voyage, save that we fell in with a vessel short of water, and supplied her with a cask or two of the precious fluid. The smell of it was as bad as that from a cesspool. People, however, in actual want are not very dainty, and our friends were very glad to get what they required, with or without *per-*

fume. The disgusting smell, I was told, would disappear on the water being exposed to the air for a day or two. Since iron tanks have been so generally introduced, it is not often that we meet with bad water in a well-found ship in these days; but thirty years ago the case was different, and I have drank water so offensive that I was obliged to hold my nose while swallowing the dose.

I have said, in another place, that owing to the frequency of severe gales at Pooree on the change of the monsoon in October, I had determined never to be at sea in the Bay of Bengal at that season; but "the best-laid schemes of mice and men gang wrang," for now we were approaching the pilot station within a day or two of the time when a gale might be expected. The weather looked very threatening, and I thought that we were in for it, after all my calculations. The vessel we had supplied with water kept company with us, but we, being first, luckily received the only pilot available for duty, and soon after we made fast to a steam-tug, and arrived safely in Calcutta on the 18th of October; whereas our unfortunate companion was obliged to put to sea again, and did not arrive in Calcutta until we had been a fortnight on shore. After all, the gale was not a very severe one.

CHAPTER XXVI.

Amusements—Lord Hardinge—Sir Henry Lawrence—Leave Calcutta for Dacca—Arrive in Dacca—Manufactures of Dacca—Trade—Catholic Bishop—Death of my Friend Donell—His Body conveyed by Colonel Hungerford in his Boat to Calcutta—Frequent Changes of Society in India—Two old Officers meet and quarrel—Manufacture of Ice in Dacca—Mango Tiffin—Situation of our House—Cantonments of Dacca—Regiment becomes sickly.

We remained between two and three months in Calcutta, enjoying (?) a succession of balls, concerts and dinner-parties, until we were obliged to declare, "Hold, enough!" and decline going out more than three times a-week. Shortly before we left, the Governor-General (Lord Hardinge) arrived from the Upper Provinces, and I saw the hero of Albuera, for the first time, at a very large party. The portraits I had seen of him gave me the idea of his being rather a portly personage, whereas I was surprised to find him a little, unassuming man. He stood for some time reclining against a cheffionier near the wall; and immediately in front of him was another notability, standing with his back to the little man, and talking to another gentleman very energetically. I was induced to ask who they were, and was surprised to find that the little man was no less a person than the Governor-General, and the one with his back turned towards him was Sir Henry Lawrence. Poor fellow! a few years later and all India mourned his death in the siege of Lucknow.

Cards were issued for a grand gathering at Government

House to meet the Earl and Countess of Dalhousie, who were hourly expected; but our arrangements having been made for leaving Calcutta, we could not conveniently wait, and as the guns from Fort William thundered forth a royal salute on the morning of New-year's Day, we unmoored, and sailed away, viâ the Sundurbunds, for Dacca, at which place my regiment was stationed. After a pleasant but uneventful voyage of three months' duration we reached our destination.

Dacca, as all the world knows, was at one time famed for its cotton fabrics. So extremely fine was the manufacture, that I have heard of a lady's dress being drawn through a wedding-ring; but nothing nearly so fine is made now-a-days. Still the muslins are much prized; more, I am told, for their extreme softness than any other quality; for I have seen finer muslins from an English loom. Be that as it may, the cheapness of the English articles has driven the native fabrics almost entirely out of the market.

The trade of Dacca is not a tithe of what it was. Of all its once famous buildings there are few remains, and the town has a melancholy, poverty-stricken appearance. The native population is still said to be somewhere about three hundred thousand; and there are also some Portuguese, Armenians, Cashmerians and Greeks. Some of them associate with the English residents, amongst whom are several indigo planters and merchants. There is a convent containing a few nuns, who are happy to receive visits from the ladies of the station; and also a Roman Catholic bishop, Dr. O——e, a most accomplished and gentlemanly man, whom I had frequently the pleasure of meeting at my friend Donell's house. If ever his eyes should rest on these pages, he will be pleased to know that we still bear him and his worthy chaplain, Father

Thomas, in kindly remembrance, heretics though we must be in his eyes. I shall have occasion by and by to relate an instance of his truly Christian tolerance. On second thoughts, I may as well state it at once. My friend Donell, whom I had known at Midnapore and Pooree, died of cholera while we were in Dacca. He was a Protestant, and when ill of course received the sacrament from a Protestant clergyman. Dr. O——e called to inquire after his friend; and hearing that he was insensible and not expected to recover, requested that he might be permitted to see him once more, and also to pray by his bed-side, adding that his prayers could do no harm. The kind and feeling manner in which this was done, I shall not readily forget. At poor Donell's table we had the most friendly intercourse, although we were all Protestants except the bishop and his chaplain. Not long before his death, D. expressed a wish to his wife that his body should be sent to Europe and interred in his father's tomb. This was done.

The late Lieutenant-Colonel T. Hungerford, who subsequently distinguished himself so much in the mutinies, and who died in Australia from the effects of the fatigue and anxiety experienced at that time, conveyed poor Donell's remains to Calcutta in his pinnace. On my going on board to view the arrangements, I found that the case containing the coffin was placed alongside Colonel Hungerford's bed. I expressed surprise at this. H. replied, "Why not? I never did him any harm." H. sailed away with his melancholy freight, and we never met again. Such is too often the case in India: we meet, begin to know and esteem people, when suddenly the route comes, and we must away—east, west, north or south, as the case may be—perhaps never to meet again. In some instances it is as well that it should be so. I remember two officers who entered the service at the same time, and went out to India in the same ship, where they were very good friends. They parted, and did not meet again until nearly forty years after, when in the course of service they were both appointed to the —— Board in Calcutta, where they more than disagreed, for Government was called upon to settle the dispute between them. They never spoke to each other further than duty compelled them to do. I knew them both very well. Apart, they were most estimable persons; but together, they were like a couple of Kilkenny cats, ready to tear each other to pieces. Alas for poor human nature! Their squabbles are now over, for "ashes to ashes, and dust to dust," has long since been pronounced over their remains.

The manufacture of ice was going on when we arrived in Dacca. The process is after this manner. Hundreds of shallow and porous earthen pans, like saucers, are placed on layers of straw or twigs, and filled with water. The nights in December and January are generally sufficiently cold to produce a thin plate of ice in the shallow pans. This ice is carefully removed at sunrise, and placed in pits for use in the hot weather; and of all the boasted luxuries of the East, commend me to a glass of iced water, or, better still, soda-water, in that season, especially at night.

One of the strangest and most amusing feeding-parties I ever assisted at, as the French say, was a mango-tiffin at the house of a wealthy Cashmerian gentleman. There were some forty or fifty gentlemen seated at a long table, which was literally covered with mangoes of every kind. On side-tables there were more substantial viands for those who preferred them; but the old hands generally made a set at the fruit, and great was the demolition thereof. In the course of little more than half an hour but few mangoes remained untasted, and the table was covered with the fragments. For my part, I preferred a mutton-chop and bottle of sparkling Moselle with my friend Lovain (I'm sure you remember *that*, my dear L.!). I never could bring myself to eat mangoes otherwise than with a knife and spoon; but your orthodox mango connoisseur tucks up his sleeves, and bites and sups and slobbers at the fruit, while the thick yellow juice streams down his jaws and fingers. The fruit is delicious, but the manner of eating it is something hoggish, mais chacun a son gout.

We occupied a pleasantly situated house in a large garden on the left bank of the river. The coffee-shrub grew luxuriantly, and its blossoms loaded the air with the most delicious perfume.

The cantonments of Dacca are about two miles from the banks of the river, and situated in about the most unhealthy place that could possibly be found, there being extensive swamps and low jungle close to the lines. Not a regiment is cantoned there for more than a year without losing many men from fever. We escaped very well until towards the end of our term, and were congratulating ourselves that we had been singularly fortunate in escaping without any particular loss, when the enemy was upon us; and nearly all the officers and men were prostrated with fever, &c. All the station-guards were reduced one-half, and at one time there was no relief for them. The adjutant, on going to the parade-ground one evening, found only one man present and fit for duty, and this out of some eight or nine hundred men.

CHAPTER XXVII.

Ordered to the Punjab—Embark in Boats—Arrive at Monghyr—Major M. swimming on Shore with Captain A. in his Arms—Arrive at Benares—Number of Deaths—Leave Benares—Second Day's March—Description of Tents—Noises in Camp at Night—How we marched—Arrive at Allahabad—Ordered to halt—Preparations for passing the Hot Weather—Ordered to Etawah—Harassing March—Regimental Band—Heat in Tents—Thermantidote—Arrive at Etawah—Rest—New Residence—How Time flies—Sport about Etawah—Presents of Game.

THE regiment about this time was under orders to proceed towards the Punjab, to form part of the army of reserve under Sir Dudley Hill. The officers were in despair at the prospect of losing this chance of distinguishing themselves. There was no help for it. The regiment was embarked in boats, and directed to proceed by water to Monghyr, and eventually to Benares. Death dogged our track the whole voyage. We halted for a couple of days at Monghyr, where we found two officers who a few months before the regiment left Dacca had been transferred to the invalid establishment. These officers proceeded in the same boat to Monghyr, within a day's journey of which place their boat foundered in a gale of wind, and they had a narrow escape of being drowned. When we arrived at Monghyr, Major M. came on board our boat to pay us a visit. I knew him very well, but he had never seen my wife, although we had been in the same station many months. However, the Major, who was a most amusing *romancer*, accosted her as an old friend, and gave an account of the wreck of their boat; "when," as he said, "I seized Captain A., who could not swim, and swam ashore with him in my arms. I thought at one time I should have been obliged to let him go, as his breath smelt so strong of onions!" I heard afterwards that the Major himself could not swim a yard.

After a tedious and disastrous voyage, we arrived in the course of a couple of months at Benares, losing by death upwards of ninety men. The regiment was completely disorganized, and we halted for a week or ten days, when a medical committee sent many of the sick to their homes, more were directed to proceed by water to Allahabad, and the remainder who were able to walk marched to that place.

The day after our departure from Benares, the weather, which had presented a threatening appearance for some days, turned to rain, and truly comfortless was our situation. In fine, cool weather, marching is pleasant enough; but in wet weather it is most detestable. We had two sets of tents—a large one sixteen feet square, with a double roof, a veranda six feet high and four feet wide all round. The best description is to imagine a small tent inside a larger one, which in fact it is. The inner or little tent is sixteen feet square, and the larger or outer one is twenty-four feet square. One tent-pole serves for both. The double roof and walls are to prevent the sun's shining on the inside tent, which is thus many degrees cooler than it otherwise would be. In this tent we spent the day. We had a smaller tent for sleeping in—a tent for the servants and another for the cook. Soon after sunset we moved into our small tent, when the large one was immediately struck, packed on camels or carts, and started off to the next days' halting-place, so as to be ready for our reception in the morning. We retired early to rest, but were soon roused by the sounds of creaking cart-wheels (for the natives never grease them), growling camels, trumpeting elephants and knocking of tent-pegs, &c., caused by the striking and packing of sepoy tents and baggage, &c. In an hour or two this business was finished, and there was a little quiet in the camp. The troops marched some three or four hours before sunrise, so as to arrive at the next encamping ground before the heat became oppressive. We remained behind for an hour or two longer, when we arose, drank a cup of tea or coffee, jumped into our carriage and followed at our leisure, after all the hubbub and dust caused by the marching of several hundred men had subsided. We arrived in camp soon after the regiment, and found our large tent pitched and breakfast ready. This was our usual way of marching; but, as I have said, on the second day of our departure from Benares, the weather turned to rain. The large tent became so saturated with water, and consequently heavy, that it was with difficulty dragged to the next encamping ground, and quite impossible to pitch it. So on our arrival, instead of finding everything comfortable, there was no place of shelter for us. However, the cook's tent was shortly erected, and into this we all huddled, servants included, to seek shelter from the rain, which continued to fall pitilessly. Everybody in camp seemed wet and miserable. The next day was a little better, and we managed to get the large tent pitched and dried by lighting fires inside. In due time we arrived at Allahabad, where the regiment was ordered to halt, as the military authorities had found out that our sickly force was not likely to be of much service in Sir Dudley Hill's army of reserve. We remained at Allahabad between three and four months, and were making preparations to spend the hot weather there, when orders arrived for us to march immediately to Etawah. Accordingly, in the middle of April, we were off, and after a most harassing march in the hot winds arrived at Cawnpore, from which place one wing of the regiment was to proceed to Mynpoorie, while the other, with the head-quarters, moved towards Etawah. When the two wings separated, the band of course went with the head-quarters; and it was truly ridiculous to hear a solitary squeaking fife strike up its treble tones as we commenced our march. The fifer was the only member of the band off the sick-list.

The heat in tents without tatties or thermantidotes was terrific; the thermometer standing in the day-time, in some of the officers' tents, at 117°. We fared very well, as we had brought a thermantidote with us from Allahabad, by which means we were able to keep our tent at a temperature of from 80° to 83°. A thermantidote is something like a winnowing machine. The open sides are covered with tatties of kus-kus grass, over which water is frequently thrown. By the action of a wheel and fans, the air is drawn through the tatties, cooled in the process, and expelled from the end of the thermantidote, as in a winnowing machine. This end of the thermantidote is placed in a hole in the side of a tent, or in a hole through a door or window of a house, and, all the other doors being closed, the house is kept as cool as could well be desired, even in the hottest weather, provided the external air is not loaded with moisture, as in some parts of the lower provinces.

Towards the end of April we arrived at Etawah, where we relieved my old regiment, the 47th Native Infantry, which fifteen years previously I had left at Cuttack. Truly glad we were to rest under a roof, without the prospect of being half-stewed at night, or roused in the middle thereof by preparations for a march. Our thermantidote was speedily placed in position, and we proceeded to make ourselves as comfortable as possible by purchasing some articles of furniture, &c., left for sale by our predecessors.

A very short time sufficed to make the acquaintance of the usual residents, seeing that they were only three in number; to wit, two bachelor civilians and a married one, whose wife was absent at the time, but joined him soon after our arrival. In our wing of the regiment we mustered four ladies and about ten officers, so that our society was rather a limited one, but pleasant enough, as we all pulled together, and there were no squabbles amongst us.

In this station we remained upwards of four years. One day passed so much like another, that there were few incidents to mark the lapse of time. To many people this would have been extremely wearisome, but it was not so to us; and we still look back upon the time we spent in Etawah as by no means the least happy of our lives. "Slow coaches," methinks I hear the fast ones of the present day call us. Wait a few years, my frisky young compatriots, and you will yourselves long for such a peaceful haven, and haply find it not, though you strive ever so much! Meantime, your motto is, Dum vivimus vivamus; but it can't last long, and *then* what have you to fall back upon? Well, well, let us hope that you will, like a good ship, right when the gale is over and reach port safely at last.

The country about Etawah afforded very good sport for those who were fond of shooting. Partridges and pea-fowl were especially numerous, and here I first saw partridges roosting in a tree at night. On mentioning this, as I thought, very singular thing, to an old sportsman, he assured me that it was by no means uncommon; but, on the contrary, the usual habit of these birds in India. I certainly can vouch for the fact of witnessing every evening for some time a covey coming to roost in a tree within twenty yards of my house. The commanding officer of the regiment, Colonel Yasmar, besides being every inch a soldier and gentleman, was a first-rate sportsman, and very often we were indebted to him for a bountiful supply of game. On one occasion he sent an elephant to us literally covered with pea-fowl. The birds, in their gorgeous plumage, hung so thickly round the carcase of the immense beast, that nothing, save his legs, head and hind-quarters, was visible. I took what we required, sent some to the other officers, and, as requested by the Colonel, the remainder to the band-boys. A young pea-fowl is, I think, far better eating than a turkey; but the old birds are generally tough and insipid, and only fit for mulligatawnee. If you should ever peruse these pages, my dear Colonel, you will recognize the hand of one who still bears you in kind remembrance, albeit seas have for many years parted us. I heard from L——n of your narrow escape in the mutiny.

CHAPTER XXVIII.

Introduction of Foreign Words into our Language—Cheez, Bosh, Bustle—Mahometan Sects—My Convert—Dialogue between Mrs. Dorcas and Mrs. Carlisle—Receipt for Chutney—Curry-powder—Dust Storm—Hot Weather—Rains—Evening Drive—A Mess-party—Music and Musketry—Military Music—March of the British Grenadiers—Anecdote of the Duke of Wellington—Mess-dinner in my honour—Fate of the Regiment—Steps preparatory to retiring from the Service—Visionary Plans—Arcadia.

It is curious to trace the gradual introduction of foreign words into our language. In my time I can remember several eastern words which have become *acclimatized* in England,—two in particular, namely, "bosh" and "cheez." The former is, as everybody knows, a contemptuous expression signifying *nonsense.* Few who use the word "cheez" are aware of the exact meaning; it is simply the Hindoostanee word for "thing." In my young days we used to say that so and so was "just the thing," whereas now we often hear that it is just the cheez. Many persons doubtless think that it has some ridiculous allusion to a double-Gloucester cheese.

Does any one know the Hindoostanee word for the article of a lady's dress called a "bustle"? A story is told of that inevitable griff who was engaged to be married. After such an engagement it is usual for the lovers to drive out together, or to be *carted,* as it is humorously called, when all the world understands that the affair is settled. Our griff was in want of a cushion to place on the back of the buggy for the young lady to recline against, and not being *up* in the native language, he told the ayah (lady's-maid) to bring a peechee-ka-cheez, literally, a thing for behind. The ayah ran into the house, and soon re-appeared with the lady's bustle!

All the world knows that there are two sects of Mahometans, called respectively Soonees and Sheeahs, and that they hate each other just as bitterly as some so-called Christian sects. I once made a convert from one to the other of these Mahometan sects in a very ridiculous way. When an European mother is unable from any cause to nurse her own offspring, it is the custom in India to procure a native wet-nurse, who forfeits her caste, so the priests say, by performing such an office for the child of a feringhee (foreigner). However, there are ways of getting over this. In addition to the woman's wages, it is stipulated that she shall receive a present of thirty or forty rupees, to give a feast to the members of her caste after she has completed the service required of her. The lower class of Mahometans talk as much about their *caste* as the Hindoos themselves, though, properly speaking, they have no more *caste*, as such, than we have.

Our child's wet-nurse was a Soonee, but through some absurd mistake I had sent for a Sheeah priest, who read her into the wrong caste; in consequence of which her husband refused to have anything more to do with her. The woman complained to me, and as I had procured her husband some small office in the police, I sent for him; and hinting that the same power which had made his fortune could unmake it, I advised him to adopt his wife's new creed, as it could not be undone. He was very indignant at first, but I persisted, and after some time he thought it better to be a prosperous Sheeah than a half-starved Soonee. Are there not such in the English churches at this day? I trow, yes; for human nature is just the same whether under a dark or a white skin.

Not one hundred miles from Etawah, there dwelt a certain country-born lady who prided herself on being a bit of a doctor. A good cook she certainly was, and made excellent mango-sauce. Here is her receipt:—Green mangoes, ginger, garlic, raisins and fine sugar, 8 ounces of each; chillies, 4 ounces; salt, 6 ounces. Grind the whole separately on a curry-stone. Add 6 bottles of vinegar and half a bottle of lime-juice. Put all into a jar, and place it in the sun or near a fire for one month, then strain and bottle for use. N.B. Unripe apples will be found a good substitute for mangoes.

The above I know to be good, but have had no experience of the receipt mentioned in the following dialogue, which took place between my wife and the good lady whom I will call Mrs. Dorcas:

Mrs. Dorcas. I have given you several good receipts, but there is one which I forgot, and which I will send.

Mrs. Carlisle. Thank you; what is it for?

Mrs. Dorcas. A most excellent thing for babies when cutting their teeth.

Mrs. Carlisle. Oh! I should be so much obliged to you for the receipt. Pray what is it?

Mrs. Dorcas. It is slut's milk. If you use it you will have no further trouble with your baby's teeth.

Mrs. Carlisle. Thank you; but pray what is it?

Mrs. Dorcas. Slut's milk. One of the young officers will give you some. A teaspoonful will be sufficient. Rub a little on the child's gums, and it will remove all pain.

Mrs. Carlisle. Pardon me, but I don't understand what it is.

Mrs. Dorcas. Why don't you know what a slut is?

Mrs. Carlisle. No, really, I do not.

Mrs. Dorcas. Why, it's a female-dog!

While on the subject of receipts, I will give two of the best I know of their kind. Some horrid old cynic says that the way to a man's heart lies through his stomach. This may be the exceptional rule, but, as far as my experience goes, it is not the general one. At the same time, I must confess that no man ever quarrelled with any delicate little attentions rendered to his appetite by the placens uxor; but to say that a heart is to be gained by a good dinner is a libel on human-kind. A *beast* might be won in that way, but not a heart worth a withered nut. To be sure, love in a cottage without a butcher and baker is a sore stomach test; but I am not writing for such sentimental young folks; for if you can't pay the butcher, how could you expect to procure a bottle of

CHUTNEY?

4 pounds of brown sugar,
2 pounds of sultana raisins,
1 pound of salt,
½ a pound of mustard (powdered),
6 ounces of ginger (powdered),
7 ounces of garlic,
7 ounces of onions,
2 ounces of cayenne pepper,
40 large unripe apples,
6 quarts of vinegar.

Pare the apples and take out the cores. Stone the raisins, Boil these together with the garlic and onions in four quarts of vinegar. When they are quite soft, add the sugar and salt. Let it stand till cold, then add the other ingredients, mixed with the remaining two quarts of vinegar. Put the mess in a covered jar, and place it in the sun for a month, stirring it every day. As there is no sun in England, the jar had better be placed near a fire, so as to keep it lukewarm.—This chutney is declared by my English friends to be the best that they ever tasted. It will not certainly "create an appetite under the ribs of death," but it is a first-rate appetizer nevertheless. Try it, my dear madam, if you wish to please your dear lord or master, as the case may be, when he comes home wet, wayworn and weary, from the hunting-field after a bad day's sport, or haply from going to and fro about the city-world in quest of the wherewithal to deck your ladyship and infant prodigy in the newest and sweetest of fashions.

If perchance your dear lord or master as aforesaid prefers a curry—presto! here is the love-powder that will charm his stomach or heart, as the case may be, a great deal more than your singing to "enchant his ear" or "dancing like a fairy on the green" (as one of your songs says), at a time when the dear man is almost used up, and disgusted with things in general and the funds in particular. If he is not asleep after dinner, he will perhaps be in much better humour to listen to your singing if you have given him a nice curry. "O the brute!" the young ladies may exclaim; but it is not for you, young misses, that I am inditing these lines: albeit the time may, and probably will, come, my dear Miss Saucebox, especially if you are half as handsome as you think you are, when you will agree with me, that besides the delightful accomplishments of dancing and singing, there are some others necessary for every-day use. Then perhaps you will be glad to know how to *order* for the idol of your heart—I could not think of asking you to prepare with your own dainty fingers—my

CURRY POWDER.

2 pounds of coriander seeds,
2 ounces of ginger,
2 ounces of cayenne pepper,
½ an ounce of cardamom seeds,
3 ounces of black pepper,
2 ounces of cummin seeds,
1 ounce of cloves,
12 ounces of turmeric.

All to be powdered and mixed together, then bottled for use. A tablespoonful of this powder, a large onion and half an ounce of butter, are sufficient for a moderate-sized curry, say one fowl or a pound and a half of meat. It is a remarkable fact that I never saw a young unmarried lady eat curry. Oh, no, they never eat such messes! This affected refinement soon vanishes when they fall into the married ranks.

One fine sunny afternoon my sirdar-bearer reported that a tuffaun (storm) was rapidly approaching. We went to the door, and, looking through the venetians, saw a dark cloud, in appearance like unto some huge cliff, steadily and noiselessly sweeping along the earth. One object after another disappeared from view. Speedily our garden was engulfed; in an instant it was over and around our bungalow, and we were in Egyptian darkness. The impression was as if we had been struck with sudden blindness. To say that I had never *seen* any darkness like unto this would be a misnomer; it conveyed the idea of darkness that might be *felt*, and was probably similar to that described in the 10th chapter of Exodus: "And the Lord said unto Moses, Stretch out thine hand towards heaven, that there may be darkness over the land of Egypt, even darkness that may be felt." Telling my wife to remain where she was standing, I groped my way along the wall to my writing-table, where I always kept matches and a taper. On striking a light, the air seemed lurid and dense. On subsequent examination, every article of furniture, and even the clothes in drawers and closed boxes, were found covered with impalpable dust, which penetrated through every crevice. In the course of ten minutes the darkness passed away, and the sun shone as bright as it had done before the advent of this portentous cloud. On looking out to leeward we saw the rear of the cloud retreating noiselessly from us, even as it had advanced, but leaving a trail of dust behind. I had seen dust-storms before, but nothing like unto this, which I shall hold in life-long remembrance.

During what is called, *par excellence*, "the hot weather," i.e. from April until the middle of June, the heat out of doors is excessive, the thermometer rising to 110° or 116° in an open veranda, while in the house, with the aid of tatties and thermantidotes, it was cool enough. At sunset the hot wind ceased, when we usually took a drive for an hour or so before dinner.

If any of my readers have ever been in a glass-house, and stood near one of the open furnaces, they will have a pretty correct idea of the heat occasioned by the hot winds of Upper India, when blowing on the face, if unprotected by a veil. About the middle of June the rains commence. It is impossible to describe the refreshing effect of the first heavy fall of rain. All nature seems to breathe again. The parched and cracked earth, the drooping trees, the lowing herds, the feathered tribe, and man, all seem imbued with new life and to rejoice together; but if perchance, as is sometimes the case, the first shower of rain is not followed by another for some hours, the steaming heat and disagreeably earthy smell from the before parched ground is ten times more oppressive than the dry hot winds. When once the earth is fairly saturated with diurnal showers, the rainy season is by no means unpleasant, save towards its termination, when there is a recurrence of moist, suffocating weather for some days. From the middle or end of October until towards the end of March, I fearlessly assert that the climate of the North-western Provinces is one of the finest in the world. The boasted climate of Australia is not to be compared to it. In Etawah, for nearly five months together, save for a few days about Christmas, we had generally a clear blue sky with an agreeable temperature; and even a walk in the sunshine of December and January was especially agreeable. At sunrise ice was sometimes found, and the ground was frequently covered with hoar-frost. In the evening the sun sank in the horizon without a cloud to veil his glory. The clearness of the atmosphere was astonishing. The outlines of leaves on distant trees, and other objects, appeared sharply defined against the glowing sky. Not a breath of air stirred, and the smoke from village fires hung lazily about the roofs of the native huts. Everything breathed of peace, save the pariah curs which rushed out, barking furiously, as our buggy passed by. Driving slowly along one evening, I said to my wife, "Did you ever, either in England or elsewhere, see such glorious sunsets and such splendid weather as we have in these Upper Provinces in the cold weather? and is it not all bosh which we read about instant darkness following the setting sun? Why you see we have at least an hour's agreeable twilight?" "All very true, my dear; but had you not better drive a little faster? I heard the mess-bugle some time ago, and we shall be too late for dinner." "Allons donc; go along, Badger;" and with a slight shake of the reins the gallant Waler, as New South Wales horses are called, stepped out at a ten-knot pace, which soon brought our drive to an end, and in time for a chat round the fire before dinner was served.

After I became a benedict, as a general rule, I never dined at the mess; but on some particular occasions it was a duty to do so. Thus there was a farewell party to Colonel Yasmar, who was about returning to England, which of course I attended; and being the senior officer present, it fell to my lot to make a speech in honour of the Colonel, and sad bungling work I made of it, for it was the first time I had ever been called upon to make an oration. The most memorable event of the evening was a performance by the regimental band. Our band-master had composed a piece of music, which he called (I think) "the Etawah Sports," and dedicated to the Colonel, who, as I have said, was a great sportsman. After my speech and proposing the Colonel's health, the band struck up a rather lively measure, when suddenly a couple of shots were fired in quick succession by two sepoys who were stationed in the veranda of the mess-house. At first we did not know what to make of these alarming noises, as people ere now have been fired at on such occasions. The music and its strange accompaniment had been kept a close secret from all except the Colonel and Quarter-master. Presently another shot was heard; then another and another. All this time the band was playing sometimes a slow measure, at others a lively one. When we were given to understand that the firing of the muskets at intervals in the music was to represent our Colonel in his sports, the double reports representing right and left shots, it is impossible to describe the fits of laughter which burst forth. The piece was encored; and truly none was ever received with greater merriment. Now the music represented the Colonel walking gently up to his game; then bang, bang, went the muskets. The Colonel loaded to music, stepped out rather quickly, then slowly; bang again, and so on. Fancy all this set to music and musketry—never was such a wild conceit. However, it amused us greatly.

I am particularly fond of military music, and think the March of the "British Grenadiers" the most spirit-stirring of all martial strains. I well remember the day when I and two other officers were wending our weary way up the steep hill-side leading to Napoleon's tomb at St. Helena. We stopped to rest, and looking down on the troops below, when the band struck up the "British Grenadiers," away we went at a charging pace, which carried us a considerable way up the hill.

After the indecisive battle of Moodkee—which commencing late in the afternoon of the 18th of December, 1845, was maintained above an hour after "the sentinel stars set their watch in the sky"—our troops were anxiously expecting reinforcements. On their approach, the Governor-General (Sir Henry Hardinge) sent out his band to meet them, when they marched into camp to the animating strains of the "British Grenadiers." To some, perhaps, the last they were to hear; for the battle of Ferozeshuhur (or Ferozeshah, as it is sometimes called) was fought on the 21st and 22nd of December, and many braves fell not to rise again—amongst them my old friend H., who had his head carried off by a cannon-ball. I never hear the "British Grenadiers" played now without thinking of the troops marching into camp before the battle of Ferozeshuhur.

While we were at Etawah, intelligence arrived of the death of the Duke of Wellington, when, of course, an order was issued for the troops to put on mourning. Every one appeared to feel the great Duke's death as a personal loss. I only saw him once, and that in very peculiar circumstances. I happened to be in London in 1827, when a dinner was given at the Albion Tavern, Aldersgate Street, by the Court of Directors to some magnate (Lord William Bentinck, I think), prior to his departure for India. Amongst the guests was the great Duke. From my window I saw his carriage drive slowly up to the door of the Albion. The Duke, it may be remembered, was at that time exceedingly unpopular in England, and the mob greeted him with hooting and hissing. Some of the people actually thrust their hands through the open windows of the carriage close to the face of the Duke, who sat calm and bolt upright, not deigning the least notice of the insulting flourishing of hands before his face. When the carriage stopped, and the Duke alighted, he passed unconcernedly across the footpath into the tavern, when the mob, hitherto so insulting, apparently struck by the coolness and magnanimity of the man, immediately cheered him as lustily as they had previously hooted him. In truth, he was a man, "take him for all in all, we ne'er shall look upon his like again."

Preparatory to resigning the service, I had obtained leave to visit the Presidency; and when I left my old regiment a mess-dinner was given in my honour, and a very complimentary speech delivered by the commanding officer, Major R., to which it was of course expected that I should reply; but I felt tongue-tied, and could think of no words which could give utterance to my thoughts. No sooner did the Major sit down than the band struck up, I know not what; but suddenly the thought flashed across my mind that this was my opportunity, as the music of the band would conceal any halting and stumbling in my oration; so up I sprang, and under cover of the band I made a very eloquent speech indeed—only nobody could hear it! No matter; it did just as well; for when the band finished playing, I concluded by audibly wishing all happiness to the gallant 62nd, which of course elicited immense applause and prolonged rapping on the table. Thus terminated my connection with the regiment, from which I was very sorry to part. Two of the officers were killed in the mutinies when absent from the corps, the rest escaped; but the great bulk of the regiment was cut to pieces at Mooltan, being one of the very last to rise in rebellion.

On retiring from the service, with a view of settling in the Colonies, an officer was—and is now, for aught I know to the contrary—entitled to a free grant of land by the British Government. It was this which induced me to think of proceeding to Australia. Accordingly, a year before our intended departure, I commenced preparations by building castles in the air, at which I was always an adept. My friends in vain urged me to give up my wild-goose scheme, as *they* thought it; but then I argued that they could not see it from my stand-point, which was quite another thing. Two of my brother-officers shewed me letters from their respective brothers, both of whom had retired from the service. One of them was settled in New Zealand, and wrote most despondingly of his situation. The other, preparatory to settling in the colony, learnt carpentry in England, so as to be able to do anything in that line about his house. He then went out to look at the country, leaving his wife and family behind. After visiting the several colonies, he came to the conclusion that it was "no go;" and, like a sensible man (as I have since thought him), he relinquished the idea of squatting, and returned to England. My plan was different to this; I was—*obstinately*, as it turned out—determined to govern adverse circumstances, and if I had succeeded it would have been said that I had exhibited the most laudable *perseverance*. 'Tis *success* that makes all the difference, and puts a stopper on the ready and triumphant observation of your kind, good-natured people, "Aye, I told you so; but you *would* have your own way." Well, to go on with my story. Understanding that labour was very scarce in Australia, in consequence of everybody flocking to the gold fields, I commenced by planning a house, which I proposed building in some part of the colony, with the aid of some ten or a dozen carpenters, masons and coolies, who volunteered to accompany us. Having arranged the plan, I set carpenters to work making doors, door-posts, window-frames, chairs, tables, couches, &c., ready to put together on our arrival. We were to take tents to live in while the house was in course of erection on our own land. I procured an American plough, and innumerable other things which I imagined might be useful. When once I had taken possession of the land and erected my house, I argued that if other people could pay rent, and yet live on the produce of their farms, why should not I, who had no rent to pay, live on the produce of mine, and thus allow the pension I was entitled to after twenty-five years' service to accumulate for the benefit of my family. The thing was plain as a pike-staff; and a year before resigning the service I busied and amused myself by making the aforesaid preparations. Nay, so far did I carry what I thought my *prudence*, though I have had many a laugh since at my infatuation, that I actually timed our departure for Australia so as to arrive in time to sow our first crop of corn, and thus lose not a single harvest. Being, when a boy, used to a country life in England, I could fancy no life more delightful than that of a gentleman farmer. In short, I planned the prettiest little Arcadia in the world.

CHAPTER XXIX.

Journey to Agra—Dâk Bungalows—Eastern Habits unchangeable—Unleavened Bread of the Israelites—Corn-mill—Bed—Despatching a Fowl at the Dâk Bungalow—Horse Garree—Arrive at Dâk Bungalow in Agra—A Fairy brings a Dish of Ice for us—First Visit to the Taj—Visit the Taj by Moonlight—at Sunrise—A new Sensation—Gates of Somnath—Jeu d'Esprit on Marriage of Sir William Nott—Visit Cawnpore and meet with an old Friend.

PRIOR to leaving India for Arcadia, we determined to visit the far-famed Taj. Before commencing our journey, I will tell you, reader, supposing that you have never been in India, how to pronounce that word, which is spelt in such a variety of ways: try the English word *large*, then Targe, and you have it; for so Taj, as it is usually written, is pronounced. Now we will proceed. We left Etawah for Mynpoorie in our palanquins, and after travelling the greater part of the night arrived at the Mynpoorie dâk bungalow about sunrise. These bungalows, which are erected by Government for the accommodation of travellers, and situated at convenient distances on all the principal roads of India, are simply thatched cottages containing one or two sitting-rooms and a corresponding number of bed and bath rooms, with a cook-room near by. The furniture of the sitting-room usually consists of a ricketty table, a few old arm-chairs, and perhaps (but not always) a suspicious-looking nondescript couch. The furniture of the bed-room is equally spare in its way, and ditto the bathing-room. With regard to the table apparatus, a few dishes and plates of that immortal "willow pattern" which was thought something superfine in the days when George the Third was king, a few cups and saucers of divers patterns, two or three dubious-looking spoons, of what metal I know not, but *certainly* not silver, and a few old knives, with steel forks, comprise nearly all that is to be found in most of the dâk bungalows; but in others more frequented, near to a station, the furnishing is on a somewhat better scale. Five-and-twenty years ago, in rather an out-of-the-way bungalow between Balasore and Cuttack, a soup tureen containing water was brought for me to perform my morning ablutions; and I have heard a dark story of its having been applied to worse uses than that. This bungalow, at the time of my visit, did not possess a decent knife and fork, and I made the khidmutgar a present of mine for the benefit of future travellers. Of late years, all these things are better managed; but there is ample room for further improvement. The traveller provides his own tea and sugar, &c., the only provisions in general procurable being a few eggs, fowls, rice, a little milk, and some chupatties, which latter are simply unleavened cakes or bread, such as I suppose the Israelites to have made on their flight from Egypt. Eastern habits are proverbially unchangeable. The same kind of mill, alluded to by our Saviour in the 24th chapter of St. Matthew, "Two women shall be grinding at the mill," &c., is still to be seen in every village in India, and so is the bed. "Take up thy bed, and walk," said the Lord. A man may often be seen carrying his bed without any difficulty. The unsophisticated youth of England perhaps think, as I did when young, that it was part of the miracle for the man to walk away with a regular four-poster and all its appurtenances of mattress, feather-bed and bolster, &c., whereas the bed in question was most probably similar to a common Indian charpae, weighing perhaps ten or twelve pounds.

To return from this digression. Two or three servants are attached to each dâk bungalow, and it is their duty to attend upon travellers. As soon as it is ascertained that a traveller requires a fowl for his breakfast or dinner, one of the men makes a grab at an unsuspicious chicken, perchance pecking about the cook-room door—off with its head in a trice—and there it lies fluttering on the ground, and for a short time making vain efforts to run away. Query, did it feel? 'Tis said that Charlotte Corday blushed after her head was cut off! Meanwhile the executioner is lighting a fire to boil some water. I had *once* the curiosity to watch the whole process. As soon as the water was hot enough, the fowl was plunged therein for a few seconds, when the skin, together with the feathers, was stripped off in an instant. The denuded body was speedily opened, disembowelled, and placed on the embers, and in much less than an hour from the time it was pecking away with its brothers and sisters at the cook-room door, it was served up "all hot" as a regular grilled moorghee (fowl). A traveller must not be too fastidious, and after le premier pas one gets used to many things which would disgust the "gentlemen of England who sit at home at ease;" so I ate my moorghee, and was thankful.—The servants of the dâk bungalow are of course paid for what they supply; and, if they are attentive, it is customary to give them a present of a few annas in addition to the cost of the provisions. For the use of these bungalows the Government demand one rupee a day from each traveller, whether he stay one hour or twenty-four. In a country where there are no hotels out of the large stations, few persons would grudge such a trifle for the great accommodation afforded, notwithstanding the scanty furniture. There is a rule that no person shall occupy the apartments more than twenty-four hours, if another traveller should require them.

It is now time we were on the road; so leaving our palkees at Mynpoorie, we proceeded by horse garree dâk to Agra. These horse garrees are something like a large palkee without poles, and placed on springs and wheels, with a seat for the garreewan (driver) in front. They are drawn by one horse (and that too often a vicious one), which is changed every six or seven miles. When once started (and there is the difficulty), they do get over the ground famously.—Before starting on our journey, I had written to an agent to have a conveyance in waiting at the dâk bungalow in Agra to take us at once to the Taj. The journey, however, proved much more fatiguing than we had anticipated, and, together with the heat and dust encountered on the road, rendered us ill disposed to commence a further trip of some miles to the Taj that evening. We therefore directed the garreewan to bring his trap at daybreak next morning. We found the dâk bungalow quite full, so could not gain admittance at once; but having ascertained that a gentleman from the neighbourhood had been occupying one set of rooms for several weeks, I requested an interview with him, and explained that, although we had a right to all the accommodation, I did not wish to put him to greater inconvenience than was absolutely necessary, and that, provided he would give up the bed and bath rooms, he might retain the sitting-room. This treaty being satisfactorily concluded, we were, pending the clearance of the rooms, sitting in the garree, hot and tired, when a fairy, in the shape of an ugly, grey-bearded man, appeared at the carriage-door with a dish-full of ice. I am not a gourmand, but the refreshing coolness of that ice, and the unexpected kindness of our unknown friends, dwell in my grateful remembrance to this day. The donors we had never seen or heard of before. They were Captain and Mrs. L——n, en route to Calcutta, and occupying the other side of the bungalow, and who, having received a present of ice from the mess of a regiment stationed at Agra, most generously presented us with a large portion of it. Doubtless they had ascertained from the dâk bungalow servants who we were; and belonging to the old Company's honoured service was somewhat like a sign of freemasonry amongst us, and a sure passport to the good offices of almost every one.

Well, about the Taj. The first glimpse we caught of it was from a distance of three miles, when on a sudden turn of the road I exclaimed, "There's the Taj!" I felt sure that such it must be, as it was so beautiful, and at the same time so unlike anything I had ever seen before. On inquiry, the garreewan corroborated my surmise. Next morning we dressed by candle-light, and hastened to see the Taj at sunrise. Some months before our visit, one of my brother officers had been to the Taj. On his return, I asked him to give me some account of it. He replied that it was "indescribable," and far exceeded his expectations, as indeed it did mine, after all I had heard about it. One generally feels disappointed on visiting a place spoken of in such glowing terms; but it was not so with the Taj. In fact, the more we looked at it, the greater was our admiration. At first sight we were inclined, on a near view, to be captious about the shape of the dome; but on further inspection we were convinced that it was precisely what it ought to be.

The elevated white marble terrace on which the Taj stands is four hundred and eighty yards square. At each of the four corners is a beautiful minaret, also of white marble. These minarets are about two hundred feet in height. In the middle of the terrace is the Taj, which, as nearly as I could judge by pacing the distance several times, is two hundred and fifty-six yards in circumference. The whole building is of white marble, and its height from the base to the top of the dome is said to be two hundred and sixty-two feet. From these measurements it will be seen that this wondrous structure is of considerable size, yet such is the faultless harmony of its several parts, that the visitor is not at all prepared to find it so large. I know no better expression than "fairy-like" to convey an idea of its extremely light and elegant appearance. Viewing this pure white and fairy-like building from the grand gateway at the entrance to the gardens, and looking over the fountains, down the long avenue of cypress and other trees, at the extremity of which the Taj stands—I had almost said *floats*—amidst bright green foliage bathed in sunshine, with a clear blue sky above, the *tout ensemble* is unique and exceedingly beautiful, not to be matched by anything I have ever seen, save a gorgeous iceberg off Cape Horn; but of that more anon.

We had been told that we ought to see the Taj by moonlight, and had arranged our visit so as to be there at the time of full-moon, which occurred on the evening of our arrival, when we were too much fatigued to go. However, the next day we were there before sunset, and after walking about the gardens, we sat down on the steps of a minaret in the gloom of the evening, awaiting the rising of the moon, while visions of the past flitted dimly before us, as we called to mind some remarkable passages in the history of Noor Jehan (the Light of the World). Within a few yards of our seat reposed the remains of this beautiful woman, and also those of her uxorious spouse, Shah Jehan (King of the World), who erected this splendid pile to her memory. For the reception of his own remains, the emperor had commenced, on the opposite bank of the river Jumna, what was to have been a still more magnificent mausoleum, and connected with the Taj by a bridge across the river, when his grand projects were arrested by the successful rebellion of his son, the famous Aurungzebe, who, seating himself on the throne of the Moguls, abandoned the works commenced by his father Shah Jehan; whom he retained in confinement until the great democrat, Death, released him from captivity, eight years afterwards, when his remains were placed by the side of Noor Jehan, whose tomb is exactly in the centre of the Taj. A light is still kept burning all night before the tombs in the underground chamber, which can scarcely be called a vault. Seeing the lamps lit, we descended into "darkness visible," but were soon glad to emerge from the stifling atmosphere of the gloomy chamber of death into the fresh upper air, leaving the emperor and his begum "sleeping the sleep that will know no waking," until the great trumpet-day. Sic transit gloria mundi. Anon the moon rose above the groves of the garden, shedding a faint and ghastly light on the dome and minarets of the Taj. Gradually, as the orb ascended, its beams brightened, until the whole magic scene was flooded with light. We scarcely ventured to speak above a breath, when suddenly the charm was rudely broken by sounds of revelry from a noisy pic-nic party who had been dining in the gardens. What vile profanation of the precincts of a tomb—and such a tomb! We wandered away in disgust, when lo, in unison with the scene and our own thoughts, from the other side of the gardens the solemn strains of a hymn, sung by some of the mission converts, ascended to heaven on the calm evening air. We remained a long time after this, walking slowly about the wondrous building, with which and its associations we were enthralled as with a spell. When leaving the gardens, we nearly stumbled over some of the merry-making party, who were reclining on the ground in deep shade, and wished them—further.

At sunrise we were again at the Taj, and afterwards visited the Motee Musjid (Pearl Mosque) and the great Akbar's Tomb at Secundra, both very remarkable structures, and worthy of more notice than we could bestow upon them; for the Taj engaged so much of our attention, that we had scant time to spare for anything else during the three days we remained at Agra.

The Taj is said to have been erected at a cost of nearly two crores of rupees (about two millions sterling), an almost incredible sum; but when we consider the elaborate ornamentation externally as well as internally, and the lavish profusion of precious stones and gold, especially about the tombs and the beautiful screen surrounding them, one feels inclined to admit that there may be some truth in the statement. We were informed that one hundred and thirty-six pieces of cornelian and other stones were used in the formation of a single flower, so delicately is the shading effected, and there are thousands of such flowers. On the walls, both externally and internally, there are panels of marble richly sculptured with flowers, &c. in relievo, and as fresh as when they issued from the hands of the sculptor upwards of two centuries ago. Each panel is surrounded by an ornamental scroll of coloured stones. One cannot help wondering at the ingenuity of the artist on seeing the petals of flowers cut in white marble not much thicker than ordinary paper. In fact, marble appears to have been used by the natives as if it were almost a plastic substance.

The Taj has been so often and at the same time imperfectly described, that I will not attempt a further description of that which my brother officer said was "indescribable." The frontispiece to this volume may serve to convey some faint idea of this splendid and unique mausoleum.

To any one in want of a new sensation, I would recommend a visit to the Taj by moonlight, and if he did not experience the feeling *above* ground, I think it highly probable that he would find his feelings roused by a descent into the under-ground chamber containing the tombs, after the lamps are lit for the night. I do not mean to say that the sensation would be very pleasing, but it would certainly be a novel one, which is something in this fast age.

We had so little time to spare during our stay in Agra, that we did not even see the gates of Somnath, which were in the Fort, and concerning which the "great Duke" in the House of Lords said that Lord Ellenborough's address to the natives of India about the insult of eight centuries being avenged by the restoration of the gates, &c., was a "sort of song of triumph." We cared nought for these old gates, any more than for the idol temple to which they originally belonged, and from which they were taken by Shah Mahmood some time before William the Conqueror commenced working his sweet will in England. If the gates could have spoken, and spoken the truth, they might have told us something worth listening to: as it is, shut up, old gates! I have heard an officer who was with the retreating army tell of the trouble he had with these gates in the Cabul Pass. Pity they were not allowed to rot at Shah Mahmood's tomb in Ghuzni; for the conveyance and defence of them and the "big gun" (which, after all, was blown to pieces) cost the blood of some brave men.

The late General Sir William Nott, who by command of the Governor-general despoiled Shah Mahmood's tomb of these gates, was afterwards married to a Miss Dore, when the following *jeu d'esprit* appeared in "The Friend of India." I quote from memory, and may not give the exact words, but am right in the *point*.

"Strange as a decree of the Fates
In the brave old days of yore,
The gallant captor of the *Gates*
Is now captive to a *Door!*" (Dore?)

A more gallant and chivalrous officer never donned a soldier's uniform. I have mentioned elsewhere that at one time I had the honour to serve under his command.

On our return from Agra I had occasion to proceed to Cawnpore. Shortly after my arrival at my friend Spil's house, I was looking at some pictures, when S. said that they were painted by Mrs. Major E. "What! is John Edwards in Cawnpore?" I exclaimed. "Will you send immediately and let him know that I am here for a few hours only?" "He won't come," quoth old Spil, "as his wife is hourly expecting an addition to her family." "He will come through fire and water to see me," I replied. A note was despatched, and Major Edwards speedily followed the bearer of it. I told him what I had said to Spil about his not coming to see me. "You were right," he replied; "of course I would come if possible." We spent an hour in talking of days long past, and I slily asked him if he ever upset the chess-board now, a deed of which I had known him to be guilty in the olden time. We parted, and I never saw him again, as he with his family were amongst the victims massacred in Cawnpore by order of Nana Saheb in 1857. A more warm-hearted, honourable and upright man than J. E. never lived. I offer this brief but poor tribute to his memory.

CHAPTER XXX.

Return to Etawah and commence Preparations for leaving—Embark in Boats—My old Carpenter—Treatment of Indian Servants by Europeans—Arrive at Benares—Description of the City—Scenes on the Ghats—Religious Beggars—Exchange our Boats—Departure—Arrive at Chandernagore—Night Alarm.

I RETURNED to Etawah and commenced preparations to proceed to Calcutta. Having procured two large flat-bottomed boats, one for ourselves and the other for the baggage, besides a smaller one for the cook, we embarked on the 23rd of October, after taking leave of our kind friends Monkhouse; and commenced our voyage down the Jumna river at daybreak on the following morning, some of our old servants running along the bank to take a final leave of us. I particularly regretted parting with my old carpenter, who had been with me upwards of four years, during which time he had built for me a travelling-carriage on a plan of my own, a Bath chair, and a little four-wheeled pony-coach for the children, besides innumerable other things. I have some of his handiwork to this day, in the shape of an ingenious kind of writing-desk, with all sorts of contrivances. It is astonishing what these people can do with the few simple tools they possess. Only give them a pattern, and they will copy it faithfully. At any time, if my carpenter was at a loss for work, I would say, "Make a chair," or "Make a chest of drawers," &c., and it would be done, and done well too. Yet this man's wages were only eight rupees a month (equal to sixteen shillings), and out of this he found his own tools, such as they were, and everything needful for himself and family. He did not even live in a hut near the house, like most of my other servants. Poor old man! I see him now, with his long spindle-shanks, running along the bank of the river to keep us in view, after I had bade him farewell in the boat, until a projecting headland hid him from our sight. He was a faithful servant, and I not a bad master. A late writer on the manners and customs of India leads one to suppose that many of the European officers treat their servants with great cruelty. This does not correspond with my experience; and the general good conduct of the native servants to their masters during the mutinies is a sufficient answer to the calumny. It is not in the nature of an English gentleman to be cruel.

In the course of a fortnight we arrived at Allahabad, where the Jumna joins the mighty Ganges; and after a stay of two or three days we pursued our voyage to Benares, where we remained a week with our kind friend J. G. Garden, for the purpose of changing our boats for others, the boatmen being afraid of encountering the "strong water" of the lower provinces. I had thus an opportunity of seeing more of this famous city than I had hitherto done. Early one morning I walked quite through the city, and returned chiefly along the ghats. I met with nothing but civility from the natives, although I had only one servant with me; but the fat bulls, sacred to Siva, obstructed our progress greatly. I longed to give them an impetus with my walking-stick.

Benares is said to contain half a million of inhabitants, and is truly a wonderful place. The houses are in general built of masonry, several stories in height, and rising one above another on the slope of a rocky elevation on the left bank of the river. Long flights of steps lead down to the water, and it is amusing to watch the crowds ascending and descending throughout the day. Some come to obtain water for domestic purposes, others to bathe, and others again to pray. A Brahmin may be seen performing the "turpun," and holding water in his hand while he is muttering his muntras; and perchance, within a few feet of these people, a bloated and putrid corpse may be seen floating in the water, without exciting the least attention. The bathers continue bathing, the water-drinkers sip the muddy water, and those who pray continue praying, as if nothing more than a rose-leaf floated by. I could scarcely have believed this had I not seen it. Fancy what a commotion there would be amongst a crowd in London on seeing a naked and bloated corpse floating down the Thames!

On account of the sacred character of the place, many rich people resort to Benares to spend the evening of their days, as any one dying there is sure of salvation!

The city swarms with religious beggars of every denomination, covered with ashes of cow-dung. I have seen some who had held one of their hands closed until the nails pierced the palm and projected several inches beyond the back of the hand, the arm itself being held upwards until it became fixed at the shoulder-joint. There were also some still more disgusting distortions than even these, but which decency forbids me to describe.

The minarets of the mosque built by Aurungzebe overlook the city and a vast extent of country—at least I was told so by our host, for I confess that I had not the curiosity to ascend them. I cannot understand the feeling which prompts many people to ascend a height or descend into a coal-mine, for the mere purpose of saying that they have done it.

Having completed the exchange of our boats, we took leave of our kind host, and pursued our pleasant but uneventful voyage on the Ganges until we anchored in the stream off the French settlement of Chandernagore. This part of the river is a noted place for dacoits, and I had been cautioned to be on my guard; however, I thought nothing about it, and was fast asleep in the middle of the night, when my wife awoke me to say that she had heard a boat paddling about for some time, and was apprehensive that it was approaching with dacoits to attack us. Scarcely were the words out of her mouth when there arose a tremendous uproar—the boat came in violent collision with our budgerow. Our boatmen, who had been asleep on the roof of the cabin, jumped up and were stamping about just over our heads, shouting with all their might, "Mar, mar! maro, maro!—beat him! kill him, kill him!" I sprang up, and rushed out of the cabin to join in the melée. The night was rather dark, but not too much so for me to see at a glance almost what was the cause of the hubbub; so I re-entered the cabin to tell my wife not to be alarmed, as it was simply an accident which we should soon rectify. It appeared that a boat which had been anchored higher up the stream than ourselves snapped her cable, owing to the strong downward current of the river and tide combined. The boatmen tried to avoid striking us by taking to their oars, but the current was too strong for them, and their boat came with a bang against our budgerow. There was a chance of our being carried away with the shock and drifting against others lower down, when there would have been a pretty commotion. Luckily, our cable stood the strain; and as it was found impossible to thrust the intruding boat from us, they dropped another anchor, and we payed away our cable until we were well clear of them.

Before sunrise I went on shore to look at the town of Chandernagore, which I found a very neat and clean place. I thought that the Calcutta municipal authorities might learn a lesson from the French.

CHAPTER XXXI.

Arrive in Calcutta and leave for Sydney—A nice Captain—Knocking about off Mount Dromedary—Land in Sydney—Gold Fever—Disappointed Hopes—Conversation with a Gold-digger—Sydney Boys—Drunkenness—Want of Drainage—Description of Port Jackson—Natives.

THE next day we arrived at Calcutta. Our first inquiries were for ships bound for Van Dieman's Land or Sydney. There was only a small barque of two hundred and seventy tons burthen laid on for the latter place, and advertised to sail in the course of six weeks. There was no help for it; so we engaged a passage for ourselves and four native servants in the miserable little craft, which was commanded by a renegade Englishman. I call him a renegade, for on coming on board the first evening we embarked, he bawled out, "Haul down that damned English flag!" On my remarking that it was a good flag to sail under, he added that before many years were over, they (the Colonies) would be independent of England and have a flag of their own. The man was, I believe, a good seaman, and that is all I have to say in his favour. We had tolerably fine weather until we entered Bass's Straits, but the wretched little craft kicked about so much that our decks were seldom dry. When we were within a day's sail of Sydney, and congratulating ourselves on a speedy termination of the voyage, a strong breeze, accompanied with rain, sprang up from the northward, and there we were rolling and tumbling about for a week in sight of Mount Dromedary. Every morning at daybreak I looked out, and there was the detestable mountain. It seemed as if, Penelope-like, we undid at night the performance of the previous day. I never was in such a comfortless plight, and once—God forgive me! —impatiently exclaimed that I wished the ship would go down. Our servants required attending upon, as I was the only one of our party who was free from sea-sickness. If I sought for a little rest, my bed-place being on the stern lockers, it was from the motion of the little vessel alternately head up and feet down, or vice versâ, with an occasional roll on to the deck. At length, on the eighth day of our "sea sorrow," the wind changed, and the next day we entered Port Jackson. Once fairly within the Heads, as the entrance is called, the change from a tempestuous ocean to smooth water seemed almost magical.

I landed immediately to look out for quarters, and soon found that Sydney was no longer the Sydney we had left between six and seven years before. Then it was a quiet, respectable, steady-going place; whereas now all was bustle and excitement. Everybody's talk was of gold, gold-diggings and nuggets. There was a great display of the latter in many of the shop-windows. The people hurried along the streets as if they were afraid of losing a chance of picking up a nugget. In fact, I remarked to my old friend Mac——, that their very souls seemed ahungered and athirst after gold. I entered a shop to make some trifling purchase to the amount of half-a-crown. The shopkeeper seemed scarce to think it worth his while to attend to my insignificant demand, and when I tendered a sovereign in payment, he asked inquiringly, "Got no change?" "Not enough," I replied. "How much?" "Two shillings and twopence." "That'll do." So rather than trouble himself to go or send for silver, the man preferred losing fourpence out of half-a-crown. The hotel charges were somewhat fabulous. House-rent was enormously high. The very house I rented seven years before at seventy pounds a year, was now let at two hundred and fifty pounds a year. Provisions and wages had risen in proportion. Before I had been an hour on shore I began to think that I had come to the wrong place; and before a dozen more hours had elapsed, I saw Arcadia recede further and further from the view, until at last it disappeared altogether; and all the fine castles in the air I had been so elaborately building during the two previous years, tumbled down at once, and it was with a feeling of dismay I contemplated the ruins, thinking that I had better make my *escape* from the colony at once. However, I was persuaded to stay some time, and was told that things would settle down by and by. Bad advice for a man with a fixed income! Some speculators made large fortunes; others, again, were ruined. There were some lucky gold-diggers, but the unlucky ones far outnumbered them.

I was one day walking through the market, and entered into conversation with a stall-keeper about the all-absorbing subject—gold. I inquired if he had been to the diggings. He replied in the affirmative. "Then I suppose you drew a blank in the lottery?" "No," he said; "I had to work very hard, and at last did pretty well; and any man might do the same if he had only two things." "What are they?" I asked. "*Patience* and *perseverance;* if he has not these he had better stop at home." In taking leave of the honest fellow he offered me his hand, which I of course shook after the manner of the Sydneyites; for in Sydney everybody shakes hands with everybody. The people have a very Yankee-like way of interlarding their talk with such expressions as "You see," and "You know," pronounced in a drawling nasal twang. The boys born in the colony are the most wicked, wizened-looking little imps I ever saw. I never was in Yankeedom, but from all I have read and heard of the Yankees, the native-born Australians greatly resemble them—long, lanky, sallow-looking fellows, very partial to stimulants and tall talk. I never saw so many drunken people in any given time. Go into Sydney at any hour of the day, and one is sure to meet with drunkards, both male and female. The disgusting smells of the undrained streets may vie with those of Cologne. No city in the world could be more easily drained than Sydney, and for that very reason, I suppose, it is almost totally neglected. Were it not for the occasionally heavy rains which clean the streets, and the fresh sea-breezes, Sydney would perhaps rival Batavia in unhealthiness.

Everybody has heard of Port Jackson, the beautiful harbour of Sydney; and certes, after tossing about the misnamed *Pacific* Ocean, no haven can be more charming. We enter the harbour through an opening in the precipitous rock-bound coast called "the Heads," which are more than a mile apart. The north head is quite perpendicular, and appears as though it had been built by giant hands. The harbour is soon completely landlocked; and after a long voyage, the almost sudden change from the heaving billows of the ocean to the peaceful waters of the cove is inexpressibly delightful. The city of Sydney is advantageously placed some six or seven miles from "the Heads," and as we sail quietly along, on either hand are seen numerous inlets, with snug villas here and there, situated on gentle eminences sloping down to the water. The hills are of no great elevation, and are covered with bush and trees bearing foliage of the most sombre hue, the prevailing tint being a dull brownish green. From this cause and the similarity of outline amongst the hills, there is some degree of sameness in the scenery as viewed from the water, but from the land it is different. Standing in the Domain near Sir Richard Bourke's statue, or in the Botanical Gardens and some other choice spots, I know no scenery of the kind which can compare with it, the general character being softness and beauty. There is "the blue above and the blue below," numerous little coves running into the wooded hills, picturesquely situated villas, tiny pleasure-boats skimming along the water "like wild swans in their flight," and ships of every kind sailing up or down the harbour. Occasionally the poetical aspect of the scene is marred by the passing of a smoking, fussy, business-like little steamer splashing and skuttling through the bright waters, and all this in the immediate neighbourhood of a large and generally well-built town containing some seventy thousand inhabitants, and in a country scarcely known to civilized man less than eighty years ago, but where "wild in woods the noble (query, dirty?) savage ran." Often have I sat for hours on one of the benches in the Botanical Gardens contemplating the beautiful scene, and eke "chewing the cud of sweet and bitter fancy," until an inward monitor has warned me that I had better go home to dinner.

Annexed is a portrait of one of the noble savages, "the Chief of Botany," whom I have frequently seen in the streets of Sydney. Is he not a man and a brother? I certainly was not inclined to claim kinship with his sable majesty further than bestowing an occasional sixpence upon him. And there, madam, is a portrait of one of the "fair sex," a companion of the above gentleman. It is a faithful likeness—can you call her sister?

These sketches are from drawings by Charles Rodius.

NATIVES OF AUSTRALIA.

I can vouch for their correctness. Poor creatures! we have taken possession of their heritage, the land, with no better title than that of

> "The good old rule, the simple plan,
> That they should take who have the power,
> And they should keep who can."

It is a sad reflection that under the combined influence of the accursed "fire-water" and certain diseases introduced amongst them by Europeans, the native tribes on our borders are fast vanishing from the face of the earth. A reproachful voice seems to issue from the deserted and gloomy forest, O, Cain, where is thy brother?

CHAPTER XXXII.

Visit to Hobart Town—Pleasant Impressions of the Town, &c.—Return to Sydney and rent a Cottage in the Country—Description of the Cottage and Land—Thieves—Agréments of Bush Life—False Alarm of bush-rangers—Free and easy Life of Gentlemen in the Bush—Medical Treatment of a Tree covered with Smut—Grapes—Wine—Indigenous Fruits good for nothing—Flies and Mosquitoes—Extreme Heat—Bush Fires—Remove to Sydney—Move to Fairlight—European Servants—Novel Way of cleaning a Dog-cart—Servants Nine Years in one Place—Cutting Wood in the Bush—Decide on leaving the Colony—My Son saves the Servant-lad from Drowning—My Opinion of the Country—Climate.

When we left Calcutta it was with the intention of ultimately settling in Van Dieman's Land or "Tasmania," as it is now called, but friends in Sydney said so much about the expense of living there that I was rather staggered. However, a few months after our arrival in Sydney, I paid a visit to Hobart Town, and remained there a few weeks, making excursions into the adjacent country. I was quite charmed with the place, and thought Hobart Town one of the prettiest, most cleanly and respectable-looking towns I had ever seen. There was not so much bustle in the streets as there usually is in Sydney, but there was very little drunkenness observable. This may have been because most of the roughs were away to the Melbourne diggings. I was in the streets of Hobart Town for several hours every day, and for many days after my arrival did not see a single drunken person. I could not help remarking it to my friend as a very singular fact, so much had I been accustomed to see drunken people reeling about the streets of Sydney. If "boxing-day" had not occurred while I was in Hobart Town, I should probably have left the island without seeing a single case of drunkenness; but on that day I did see a few tipsy men. A vessel had arrived from Melbourne the day before with some lucky diggers. I was walking in the streets with a gentleman when a man on horseback rode close up to us. We drew back. "Don't be affeard," said he; "I've got more money than you have." "I dare say you have," replied my companion. "Yes, I have; good day," said the tipsy digger, as he rode off.

After all the inquiries I made, I found that the cost of living in Hobart Town differed very little from that of Sydney; at the same time the climate of the former place was decidedly superior to the other. I have often regretted that we did not carry out our original intention of settling in Tasmania; but—oh, never mind!—I returned to the island continent, and after a residence of six months in Sydney we rented a small cottage and twenty acres of bush-land about eight miles from the city. Our cottage consisted of four rooms on the ground-floor and two attics. We could only stand upright in the middle of the latter, and the lower rooms were so small that two of them might more appropriately be called closets, there being just room for a bed at one side. If the bed had been placed in the middle of the room we could not have walked round it. Our drawing-room—save the mark!—which was the largest room in the house, measured fourteen feet by twelve and a half. A staircase leading to the attics was in the fourth room. There being no hall or passage of any kind, we entered immediately from the open air into the drawing-room; the ceiling was so low that I could touch it with my hand when standing on the floor. The kitchen was detached;

i.e. a few paces from the cottage. For this splendid mansion we paid £100 per annum. The land was good for nothing. Three or four acres of it had been cleared, and we were told that anything would grow, as it was a virgin soil; but it proved a very tough old virgin. I planted about a quarter of an acre with potatoes, and gathered nearly half the weight of the seed. The next year, by a plentiful use of manure, we did much better. We kept a couple of cows, but were obliged to purchase food for them, as the land yielded nothing but fern and an extremely coarse kind of grass, just enough for the cattle to starve on. As large cabbages were selling at half-a-crown each in the market, I tried to grow some; but my plants came to nothing. In fact, the soil required no end of manure to make it worth anything. I tried melons next, and succeeded better, but the crops were stolen. I captured one of the thieves, a lad about twelve years of age, and felt very much inclined to give him a good thrashing; but as he seemed half-starved, I gave him a plateful of curry and rice, and sixpence to take him to some relations he said he had in Sydney. Very wrong all this towards the public perhaps, but I knew not what better to do with such a child.

Amongst the other *agréments* of our country residence were bush-fires, legions of insects, snakes, centipedes and house-breakers. The neighbourhood was for some time infested by the latter, until one of the robbers was shot by a gentleman whose house they had broken into. Almost every house except my own was robbed. Why I was spared I know not, unless it was that the thieves were afraid of the four black faces in our kitchen: if so, they little knew what arrant cowards these faces belonged to. In order to let the thieves know what they might expect, I was accustomed to fire a gun every evening.

One night I was quietly reading to my wife, when suddenly a great noise of screaming and shouting occurred near the kitchen, which, I have said, was some short distance from the house. I jumped up and hastened to join in the fray, thinking of course that the bushrangers were upon us at last. On opening the door, I met our English nurse. "What's the matter?" I inquired. "It's only me," she said. I crossed to the kitchen, but the door was held fast, and the servants were screaming within like so many bedlamites. I shouted out to them to open the door, and when they recognized my voice I was admitted, and a pretty set of fools they looked. It appeared that in the dusk of the evening one of them saw the nurse suddenly appear round the corner of the house, and was so frightened that he screamed—another took up the cry, and they rushed into the kitchen, where the other two joined in chorus, and all four pushed against the door with all their might to prevent any one from entering.

Gentlemen residing in the country lead a free and easy sort of life. I one day found a neighbour of mine, a man of good family and estate, loading a cart with sand in the bush, two miles from his house. My friend had a large vineyard and orchard. Some of his fruit trees were covered with smut. He had heard that a few grains of calomel was a good remedy, and pointed out one of the trees to which he had administered five grains of the powder. I thought he was joking; but no; he took me to the tree and shewed the slit in the bark where he had introduced the dose. I laughingly recommended a black draught after the calomel. Yet why laugh? The remedy may be a very potent one, after all. I never saw or tasted finer grapes in my life than this gentleman's vineyard produced, and the wine manufactured therefrom was excellent. In Paris I have drank worse claret at three francs a bottle than some of the colonial wines at less than half the price.

The vine flourishes extremely well in Australia, and if people would only pay more attention to the fermentation of their wines, the colony would in the course of a few years be able to supply the English market entirely with most excellent wine. Grapes are in such profusion in the vine-growing districts, that hundreds of tons are annually allowed to fall and rot on the ground, the produce far exceeding the demand.

The indigenous fruits of the country are not worth a button, whatever the colonists may say to the contrary. An English blackberry is far superior to any indigenous fruit in Australia.

Flies and mosquitoes were two of our greatest plagues in the bush. It was impossible to keep them out of the house. We suspended Chinese blinds to the doorways and windows; still the pestilent little tormentors would force their way in. It was with a smothering sensation that we slept under mosquito curtains in the hot weather; but of two evils it was the least. I have heard people in England complain of the heat when the thermometer stood at 76°. What would they do in a hot wind in Australia, where I have seen the thermometer rise to 112° in the shade? On the 29th of January, 1855, the thermometer at Burwood, about four miles from our house, rose to 145° in the sun and 114° in the shade. On the following day it rose to 144° in the sun and 116° in the shade. Happily these extremely hot winds do not continue more than two or three days, when they are suddenly succeeded by a cold blast from the icy south, and a fire is requisite for comfort. I have been twenty-five years in India, but never suffered so much from the heat there as I did during the last year of our residence in the bush. There had been a drought of long continuance. Day after day, for weeks together, the sun rose like a ball of fire. Not a cloud was visible, and the heavens seemed to glow like brass. The whole country was parched up, and people had to send a considerable distance for water. Bush fires were observed at night in various directions; they came nearer and nearer; and at length approached our house, which happily had a considerable space of cleared ground around it. The fire seemed to lick up the dry grass and run along the ground until it communicated with our fences, and all one miserable night people were employed in beating down the fire with branches of trees. Some of our neighbours' houses were burnt, with everything in them, the inhabitants escaping with little more than the clothes they stood in. This was enough to disgust us with bush life, and we considered it a notice to quit, which we did, and again took up our quarters in Sydney, where we rented a house containing seven small rooms and a kitchen for £150 a year. Besides this, we had to pay from twelve to fifteen shillings a week for water, as there was none "laid on" near our residence.

We soon got tired of town life, and again took a house in the country, where there was no danger of bush fires and plenty of water, both fresh and salt, the house being situated near one of the numerous coves of the harbour. We sent all our native servants back to Calcutta, and commenced housekeeping with four European female servants and a man. The united wages of these persons amounted to £120 a year. People complain of the servants in England, but in Australia they are very dear, and equally bad, to say the least. For instance, we engaged a married couple (Irish) without incumbrance,—

the man as groom and the woman as cook. They professed to be accomplished in their respective capacities. We took them without a character, as they had recently arrived in the colony. However, they said that they had lived nine years in one place in England; so we thought that they must be good servants. A day or two after their arrival, Pat remarked to me that our dog-cart was very dirty. "Well, then, you had better clean it, Pat." I walked away, thinking nothing more about it, and Pat set to work to clean the dog-cart. Now how, my patient reader, do you think he managed it? You would never guess if you tried till the skies fall; so I will tell you an original Irish way of cleaning a dog-cart. The man actually took off one of the wheels, cleaned it—and then could not put it on again. It was a Collings' patent axle, and I wondered how he managed to get the wheel off. Pat called his wife to help him, but both together could not replace it, and at last I was obliged to do it myself. The annoyance was, for once, well worth the amusement it caused us. Pat did not know how to groom a horse; so I was obliged to teach even that. On questioning him and his wife about the situation they had held so long in England, it came out that they had been nine years in a cotton-factory in Stockport! A nice place, certainly, to learn the arts of cookery and grooming horses. However, they were willing to learn, so we put up with their shortcomings, and they on their part were content to receive £50 a year and everything found for their *services.* What a paradise for servants!—but what sort of a place is it for masters and mistresses?

I rather pride myself on having been a "hewer of wood and drawer of water" in Australia; for during the last year of our residence at Fairlight I amused myself by cutting wood in the bush for the use of the house, and assisting Pat in filling his water-cart at some distance from home. Had I been *compelled* to do it, I might have thought it a great hardship; but I liked the work of knocking an axe about, at which I became pretty expert. It was with strangely mingled feelings of pity and triumph that I have seen many a tall tree fall under the strokes of my axe—pity, on thinking that the growth of years had fallen for ever, like a strong man cut off in his prime—and triumph, that it was my hand that had done it. Not bad work that for an old Indian of twenty-five years' service, and on the shady side of fifty! However, even that occupation began to pall at last; for one could not *always* be cutting wood; and I began to think that for an idle man we had come to the wrong place to settle down in for the remainder of our lives; so we commenced turning our thoughts homewards. Our decision, once made, was speedily carried into execution. Before quitting our country residence, I must relate an anecdote of our eldest boy Alfred, then little more than twelve years of age, when he could only swim a few yards. He and two other youngsters were, together with our servant lad "Ben," bathing in the creek near our house, when Ben, who could not swim, got into a hole and disappeared beneath the surface of the water. He soon rose again and sunk a second time. The third time he rose no more, but the boys saw bubbles of air rise to the surface; whereupon Alfred swam to the spot, fished up Ben, and managed somehow or other to get him to bank, when he himself was so much exhausted that he sank on the ground, exclaiming, "Thank God, he is saved!" Now I call that a plucky act for a boy of his age. The other two boys were too young to render any assistance. Ben was insensible when landed, and remained so for some minutes. I did not hear of all this until some days afterwards, as the boys thought I should put a stop to their bathing. Pity there are no cadetships available now-a-days for such gallant lads!

In taking leave of Australia, I trust for ever, I may as well state my opinion of this overrated country. It is undoubtedly a capital place for those who can handle a spade, or those who have four or five thousand pounds to invest in cattle or sheep-farming. A gentleman who had been some years at it assured me that in these times it was scarcely worth while beginning with less. As for clerks and others who have to earn a living by brain-work, there is scant room. Lawyers and doctors, it is true, sometimes do well; but the field is overstocked with them; and as for art, why the less said about it the better: not that there is no demand for works of art, but the field is a very narrow one. In short, Australia is essentially a country for muscles and sinews; yet almost every emigrant of this class whom I saw—and I was in the habit of conversing with all I met with—wished themselves back in the "old country." Notwithstanding this, they acted the part of the well-known fable of the fox and his tail, by inciting their relatives to "come out,"—unwittingly, perhaps, concealing the drawbacks, and dwelling only on the advantages, particularly in the low price of land, high wages, and no limit to the allowance of flesh-meat. Such is the staple of most of the letters I have seen. They say nothing of the scorching sun, of snakes in the bush, centipedes, ants, white and black, or the plagues of mosquitoes, flies and fleas. The annoyance from these pests is alone sufficient to detract considerably from the comforts of life in any country. I speak not to ye Sydney merchants, who are comfortable enough in your well-furnished houses in Wooloomooloo and elsewhere, but I speak of life in the bush.

A steady, hard-working man, if he does not take to drinking—the curse of the colony—is sure to do well ultimately; but it is up-hill work even for him.

Poor people in England, who have been accustomed to comparatively low wages and who seldom eat flesh-meat, when they hear of the high wages paid in the colony and the plentifulness of meat, and, above all, the low price of land, are apt to think that Australia must be a perfect paradise. They picture to themselves a nice field—say of ten acres—with trim hedge-rows to be had for twenty shillings an acre; but when they arrive in the colony the delusion is quickly dispelled. When they see the chosen land away in the bush, and perhaps covered with forest which must be cut down before the land is worth a penny, the prospect is most disheartening. However, a brave heart and strong arm will win through it at last, and ultimately may achieve a moderate independence; but this is not the lot of many; for numbers hasten to the gold-fields, dazzled by the flaming accounts in the newspapers of some lucky find, and the exhibition in the shop-windows of fine nuggets of gold. They see and hear of the prizes which fall but to few in the gold lottery, but of the very far more numerous blanks they hear nothing, and in their haste to be rich too often lose health, and perhaps life itself.

From the paucity of rivers and general scarcity of water, save in the more favoured regions, such, for instance, as the districts bordering on the Murray and Murrumbidgee rivers, &c., Australia can never become a thickly-populated country. Fearful droughts are not unfrequent, when thousands of cattle and sheep perish for want of water and food, all vegetation being parched up in such seasons.

With regard to the boasted climate of Australia, I think it extremely trying for Europeans, owing to the frequent and sudden changes—not that those terrific hot winds I have elsewhere spoken of blow very often, for I have only known four such during my residence in the colony; but the climate is altogether disagreeable. Even in the cold season the sun is far too hot to be pleasant, but in the summer-time the heat is perfectly sickening. In fact, I suffered more from the heat in Australia than I ever did in India. In the latter country we have means of mitigating the extreme heats of the hot season; but in Australia we must "grin and bear it" as best we may, for labour is far too scarce and expensive to be devoted to pulling punkahs or watering tatties, &c. &c. Finally, my advice to any one who can get a living in England is, to stay there and be thankful.

CHAPTER XXXIII.

Embark for England—Ship and Captain—A Gale at Sea—Icebergs—Narrow Escape of Wreck on a Berg—My Berg—Death of old George—Dead Lights—Fall of a Man from Mizen Topsail-yard—Fall in with the Ship Robert Lowe—Arrive in England—Conclusion.

After a residence of nearly six years in Australia, we embarked for Old England in a fine ship bearing the classical name of a nymph beloved by Apollo, and commanded by a gentleman whose name signified "first-rate man," and such he truly was, for I have rarely met his equal. His Christian cognomen was that of the second king of Israel. Esteeming the captain's modesty, I refrain from giving his name; but those who know the man will recognize him from what I have said. His temper never varied. Blow high, blow low, fair wind or foul, he used to say that he would not alter the weather if he could, but relied fully on Him who knew what was best; at the same time he studied the comfort of his crew and passengers to the utmost of his power. Our paths of life have diverged, but I shall ever bear him in grateful remembrance.

The last sun of January, 186—, saw us leaving the Heads of Port Jackson. A gale from the north-west sprang up shortly after, and we bowled along at a great rate before it. We passed to the southward of New Zealand, and had we been bound to Otago should perhaps have made the quickest passage on record; but on and onward still we flew, and soon lost sight of the island.

I like a gale of wind at sea, provided the wind is fair. Stand by! Hurrah!

> Spread wide, spread wide, the flowing sail!
> Blow on, ye breezes, blow;
> And speed our vessel o'er the waves,
> To England's happy isle!
>
> Home of the gallant and the free,
> Home of the exil'd brave,
> Home of the unforgotten dead,
> Again I come to thee!

And so on through half-a-dozen more stanzas which I will not inflict on the reader. We have a great deal more to go through before we arrive at our destination. We went as far south as 60° 30″, and were soon amongst the icebergs. Sometimes half-a-dozen or more were in sight at the same time, and this for many days together. There is something inexpressibly sublime in the appearance of these majestic masses in the vast solitude and waste of waters around. Nothing I had ever seen before so strongly brought home to my mind one's utter insignificance in the scale of creation. We read with a vague sort of wonder and admiration of the movements of the heavenly bodies, of the vast distance of the earth from the sun, and of the immense size of the latter; but *here* was something, though comparatively insignificant, yet tangible as it were, and giving one a real and visible sense of irresistible power, as these vast masses floated grandly in the water, slowly making their way towards the equator, until they are gradually resolved in the element from which they were formed in the eternal realms of frost by the fiat of Omnipotence.

I was never tired of watching the bergs. Some of them were like mountains of smoothly-quarried marble, all the irregularities having been washed away by the spray from the billows, which we could see dashing to a great height against the sides of the bergs. Others, again, were of various fantastic shapes. A squeeze between two of these large bergs would crush the Great Eastern ship as easily as we crush beneath our feet the smallest shell which lies on the sea-shore. One small berg which we passed within pistol-shot was the most beautiful object I ever beheld. The memory of it haunted my dreams and waking thoughts alike for many days after. It was a fragment from a very large berg on which we were near being wrecked—so near indeed that some of the ship's coppers were scraped off the side. My wife heard the mate in the middle of the night hurry to the captain's cabin, and beg him to come on deck immediately, and that the captain had instantly given orders to put the ship about; and then commenced the sounds which are so terrifying to an unaccustomed ear, when decision and prompt execution are urgently required. Trampling feet, with a *thudding* sort of tread, hurried along the decks. Heavy coils of rope were flung hastily down on the deck, and the sailors commenced pulling and hauling, with a "Heave ho!" as if for dear life. I remarked that it was no business of mine, and that I could not help it; so remained quietly where I was. By and by the hubbub subsided, and the kind captain came to our cabin-door to say that all was right again. At daylight I was on deck, and saw within a few miles of us an immense berg about two miles in length, with numerous fragments of ice floating in the adjacent sea. My berg, as I called it, was one of these. The part above water was about thrice the size of the ship, and when first seen was two or three miles ahead, so as we approached with a gentle breeze it was a long time in sight. There was nothing of the *terribly* sublime about it; but, on the contrary, heavenly beauty and purity. The outer surface was very irregular and of the purest white, crusted like filagree-work, with here and there caverns of the deepest sapphire blue fading into the palest azure. I said at the time that it seemed too pure for this world, and more like a fragment of the gates of heaven. Our ship, which, by the way, was a beauty of its kind, appeared a mean and dirty scrub of a thing alongside this splendid berg. The captain, who had been many times round Cape Horn, said that he had never seen any berg so beautiful as the one I have vainly attempted to describe. I gazed after we passed it until it disappeared from view. We sailed away, and at eight o'clock prayers were as usual offered up in the cabin, and a hymn sung by the sailors.

Doubtless Noah and his family, when shut up in the ark and alone on the face of the waters, sang to the praise and glory of God. There was something singularly impressive in the devotion and singing, simple as it was, of our old sea-dogs. Whatever the weather might be, so long as there was no immediate duty to perform on deck, the voice of morning and evening prayer and praise ascended from the cuddy of the good ship D——, the roaring of the wind and sea at times forming a rude accompaniment. A better-ordered ship than the D—— never floated, and a more steady and kindly set of seamen never reefed a sail than those who manned her. Many of them had been several voyages with the captain. One fine old sailor died very suddenly after we had been two months at sea, and his body, sewn in a hammock, was committed to the deep. The wind, which was blowing almost a gale, sang the requiem of poor old George as his body sank beneath the waves. There was a hush in the ship all the day after, for old George was a general favourite, and his shipmates appeared to speak with bated breath. The weather, too, was in keeping, being gloomy with rain and a foul wind. Altogether a chill, as the saying is, was cast over us all. Happily, "hope springs eternal in the human breast," or we should never be able to get through the business of life.

To a young sailor, what fearfully ominous words, when heard for the first time, are those of, "Carpenter, put in the dead lights!" Presently the carpenter or his mate knocks at your cabin-door, and says that he must put in your dead lights. "Good God! what is the matter?" a young lady exclaims. "Nothing, Miss, only the sea will come in at your port if I don't put in the dead light;" which, for the information of landsmen, I may compare to a good stout window-shutter, which, when closed, not only excludes the water, but light also, if there are no bull's-eyes (thick plates of glass) in the deck. "Is there any danger?" is the anxious inquiry. "No; it's only blowing a stiff breeze," is perhaps the reply. In such a breeze, not many days after we left poor old George in his ocean grave, our ship, with the yards braced sharp up, was slowly making way against a head sea, when the fall of a heavy body on the poop vibrated through the vessel. "What's that?" some of us exclaimed. Soon after a voice shouted down the companion hatch, "One of the men has fallen from the mizen topsail-yard and is killed!" O what a thrill of horror was that! We hastened on deck, and found the poor fellow supported in the arms of a messmate. After a little while he began to move and stare about, as if he were taking his last look of the world; but, wonderful to say, he was not much injured,—not a bone was broken, and the man was as well as ever in the course of a fortnight. The height from which he fell was about forty-five feet, and there was nothing whatever to break his fall.

Soon after crossing the line, which was my sixteenth and I trust the last time of doing so, we fell in with the Robert Lowe auxiliary screw-ship. We had spoken her before some degrees south of the equator, when she passed us under steam. We were therefore as much surprised to see her again as they were to see us. The captain and some of the passengers came on board our ship to compare notes, and then parted. She was going to the western islands for water, &c. We thus got the start of her again, and arrived first in England, from which I had been absent twenty-nine years. And now, reader, farewell!

In the foregoing pages I have carefully omitted all matters which might possibly wound the feelings of others. Had I not done so, I could perhaps have made the book more entertaining, for I have mingled in many strange scenes; but I have not written a line that, "dying, I would wish to blot."

APPENDIX.

The annual money donation for the support of Juggurnath was abolished by an order of Government dated the 12th of November, 1856; and in lieu thereof a grant of land, yielding 16,517 rupees per annum, was made over to the superintendent of the temple, Government stipulating to keep up a police force at a cost of 6804 rupees.

CPSIA information can be obtained
at www.ICGtesting.com
Printed in the USA
LVHW111958050422
715401LV00006B/264

9 783752 589665